NEW HAMPSHIRE
LITERATURE
A SAMPLER

NEW HAMPSHIRE
LITERATURE

⇒ A SAMPLER ⇐

EDITED BY ROBERT C. GILMORE

PUBLISHED FOR
THE UNIVERSITY OF NEW HAMPSHIRE BY
UNIVERSITY PRESS OF NEW ENGLAND
HANOVER AND LONDON, 1981

Copyright © 1981 by Trustees of University of New Hampshire

Excerpts from *Coniston, Mr. Crewe's Career,* and *The Dwelling Place of Light* reprinted by permission of the Julian Bach Literary Agency, Inc. Copyright © 1906, 1908, 1917 by Creighton Churchill.

"New Hampshire" and "The Census-Taker" from *The Poetry of Robert Frost* edited by Edward Connery Latham, Copyright 1916, 1923, 1930, 1939, © 1969 by Holt, Rinehart and Winston. Copyright 1944, 1951, © 1958 by Robert Frost. Copyright © 1967 by Lesley Frost Ballantine. Reprinted by permission of Holt, Rinehart and Winston, Publishers.

Excerpt from *Jeremy Hamlin* by Alice Brown reprinted by permission of Hawthorn Properties (Elsevier-Dutton Publishing Co., Inc.).

Excerpt from *Peyton Place,* Copyright © 1956 by Grace Metalious, reprinted by permission of Simon & Schuster, a Division of Gulf & Western Corporation.

"Ah, New Hampshire" by Noel Perrin and "The Buck in Trotevale's" by Thomas Williams are reprinted by permission of the authors.

"Names of Horses" by Donald Hill. Reprinted with permission; Copyright © 1977 The New Yorker Magazine, Inc.

"The Black Faced Sheep" from *Kicking the Leaves* by Donald Hall. Copyright © 1976 by Donald Hall. Reprinted by permission of Harper and Row Publishers, Inc.

"As Does New Hampshire," "A Recognition," "We Have Seen the Wind," "Plant Dreaming Deep," and "Death of the Maple" by May Sarton from *As Does New Hampshire,* 1967; reprinted by permission of William L. Bauhan, Publisher, Dublin, N.H. All, except "Death of the Maple," reprinted in *Collected Poems* by May Sarton, W. W. Norton Co., New York, 1972.

Library of Congress Catalogue Card Number 81-51608
International Standard Book Number 0-87451-210-7 (cloth)
0-87451-211-5 (paper)
Printed in the United States of America
Library of Congress Cataloging in Publication data will be found on the last printed page of this book.

To the memory of my mother and father

CONTENTS

ACKNOWLEDGMENTS   ix

MAP: LITERARY NEW HAMPSHIRE   x

INTRODUCTION   I

I   THE BEGINNINGS

SAMUEL PENHALLOW / *The History of the Wars of New England
with the Eastern Indians* 26

THE REVEREND JABEZ FITCH / *The Work of the Lord
in the Earthquake* 30

MATTHEW PATTEN / *A Farmer's Diary* 36

II   REVOLUTION AND STATEHOOD:
The Republic of Virtue

THE REVEREND JEREMY BELKNAP / *The History of
New Hampshire* 47

THE REVEREND ISRAEL EVANS / *A Discourse Delivered at Easton,
on the 17th of October, 1779* 75

GENERAL JOHN STARK / *Account of the Battle of Bennington* 79

HENRY SHERBURNE / *The Oriental Philanthropist; or,
The True Republican* 83

TABITHA GILMAN TENNEY / *Female Quixotism: Exhibited in
the Romantic Opinions and Extravagant Adventures of
Dorcasina Sheldon* 86

III   THE WHITE MOUNTAINS

LUCY HOWE CRAWFORD / *History of the White Mountains* 94

NATHANIEL HAWTHORNE / *Sketches from Memory* 105
The Ambitious Guest 111

THOMAS STARR KING / *The White Hills: Their Legends,
Landscape, and Poetry* 120

DR. BENJAMIN BALL / *Three Days on the White Mountains* 128

FRANKLIN LEAVITT / *The Willey Slide* 132
Through Crawford Notch by Rail 132

IV THE IDEALIZED COMMUNITY

SARAH BUELL HALE / *Northwood: A Tale of New England* 141

THOMAS BAILEY ALDRICH / *The Story of a Bad Boy* 155
An Old Town by the Sea 163 / *Unguarded Gates* 167

HENRY AUGUSTUS SHUTE / *The Real Diary of a Real Boy* 170

ALICE BROWN / *Joint Owners in Spain* 174

CELIA THAXTER / *Among the Isles of Shoals* 189 / *Land-
Locked* 194 / *Off Shore* 195 / *The Sandpiper* 196
The Spaniards' Graves 197

SAM WALTER FOSS / *Deserted Farms* 200 / *The Candidates at
the Fair* 200

EDNA DEAN PROCTOR / *New Hampshire* 204 / *Monadnock
in October* 208 / *The Hills Are Home* 209

DENMAN THOMPSON / *The Old Homestead* 212

THE GRANITE MONTHLY / *Obituary of Gilman Tuttle* 220
The Old Home Week Festal Day 221

V THE CHANGING ORDER:
Decline and Revolt

WILLIAM DEAN HOWELLS / *The Landlord at Lion's Head* 227

WINSTON CHURCHILL / *Coniston* 231 / *Mr. Crewe's
Career* 248 / *The Dwelling-Place of Light* 251

ROBERT FROST / *New Hampshire* 258 / *The Census-
Taker* 269

ALICE BROWN / *Jeremy Hamlin* 272

GRACE METALIOUS / *Peyton Place* 284

VI THE RETURN

THOMAS WILLIAMS / *The Buck in Trotevale's* 299

NOEL PERRIN / *Ah, New Hampshire* 322

DONALD HALL / *Names of Horses* 326 / *The Black Faced
Sheep* 327

MAY SARTON / *As Does New Hampshire* 331 / *A Recognition* 331 / *Death of the Maple* 333 / *We Have Seen the
Wind* 333 / *Plant Dreaming Deep* 334

APPENDIX: *Some Early New Hampshire Presses* 335

INDEX 337

ACKNOWLEDGMENTS

Many people have provided invaluable assistance in the editing of this anthology. I wish to thank my colleagues in the Department of History at the University of New Hampshire, Robert Mennel, Charles Clark, and the late William Greenleaf at whose suggestion this work was undertaken. Barbara White, Special Collections Librarian, Stephen Powell, former Special Collections Librarian, and Elizabeth Witham, Special Collections Assistant at the Dimond Library, University of New Hampshire, all provided enthusiastic support. Also of the Dimond Library, Diane Tebbetts, Assistant Librarian, John Bardwell, Director of Media Services, and Evelyn Pearson, of Media Services, have been helpful. Walter Wright, former Special Collections Librarian at Baker Library, Dartmouth College, provided useful information on the White Mountains. Dorothy Vaughan of Portsmouth supplied biographical information on Henry Sherburne. Jere Daniell, Professor of History, Dartmouth College, made significant contributions to the organization and content of the book. By their lively discussions the students at U.N.H. in my senior colloquium on New Hampshire literature during the 1980 spring and autumn terms helped to clarify my thinking on a number of pertinent subjects. My graduate assistant, Gary Waldron, undertook many laborious tasks and always managed to preserve his good nature. I wish to thank those who helped to prepare the manuscript: Deena Peschke, Jeanne Mitchell, Marjorie Andruskiewicz, Paul Farrell, Elaine Gilmore Purdy, and Linda and Alan Shelvey. Research on the anthology was supported in part by a grant from the Central University Research Fund, University of New Hampshire.

Durham, New Hampshire   R. C. G.
May 1981

Literary New Hampshire

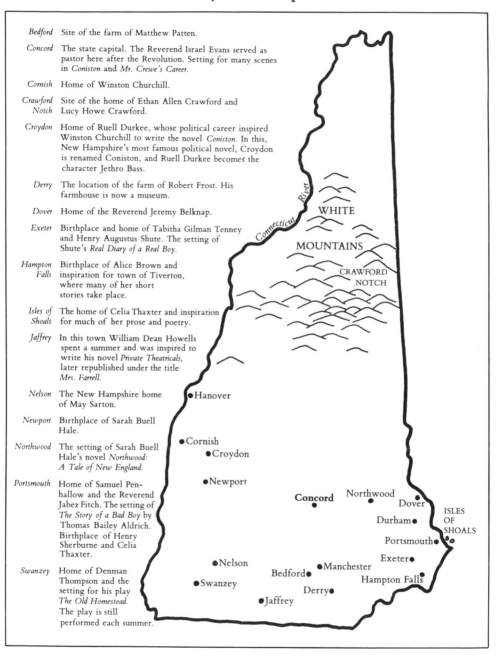

Bedford   Site of the farm of Matthew Patten.

Concord   The state capital. The Reverend Israel Evans served as pastor here after the Revolution. Setting for many scenes in *Coniston* and *Mr. Crewe's Career.*

Cornish   Home of Winston Churchill.

Crawford Notch   Site of the home of Ethan Allen Crawford and Lucy Howe Crawford.

Croydon   Home of Ruell Durkee, whose political career inspired Winston Churchill to write the novel *Coniston*. In this, New Hampshire's most famous political novel, Croydon is renamed Coniston, and Ruell Durkee becomes the character Jethro Bass.

Derry   The location of the farm of Robert Frost. His farmhouse is now a museum.

Dover   Home of the Reverend Jeremy Belknap.

Exeter   Birthplace and home of Tabitha Gilman Tenney and Henry Augustus Shute. The setting of Shute's *Real Diary of a Real Boy.*

Hampton Falls   Birthplace of Alice Brown and inspiration for town of Tiverton, where many of her short stories take place.

Isles of Shoals   The home of Celia Thaxter and inspiration for much of her prose and poetry.

Jaffrey   In this town William Dean Howells spent a summer and was inspired to write his novel *Private Theatricals,* later republished under the title *Mrs. Farrell.*

Nelson   The New Hampshire home of May Sarton.

Newport   Birthplace of Sarah Buell Hale.

Northwood   The setting of Sarah Buell Hale's novel *Northwood: A Tale of New England.*

Portsmouth   Home of Samuel Penhallow and the Reverend Jabez Fitch. The setting of *The Story of a Bad Boy* by Thomas Bailey Aldrich. Birthplace of Henry Sherburne and Celia Thaxter.

Swanzey   Home of Denman Thompson and the setting for his play *The Old Homestead.* The play is still performed each summer.

NEW HAMPSHIRE
LITERATURE
A SAMPLER

INTRODUCTION

Just specimens is all New Hampshire has,
One each of everything as in a show-case. . . .

With these two lines, Robert Frost sets forth a major theme in his poem "New Hampshire" and simultaneously reveals in his deceptively simple fashion, a great truth about his adopted state. For here indeed is a bit of everything. Though small in area, New Hampshire is a geographic mélange of the loftiest mountains in the Northeast, lakes, forests, farms, factory towns, broad and fertile river valleys, and even a stretch of seacoast overlooking offshore islands. Here, too, is a replication in miniature of almost every constituency found elsewhere in the region. New Hampshire perhaps more than any of the other five states, is a microcosm of New England.

An environment so varied may amount to an embarrassment of riches for any writer who attempts to convey a valid imaginative representation of the whole state and at the same time to approximate reality. This may explain why it is difficult for those who write about New Hampshire to fix upon and sustain unifying images, even in relation to the rest of northern New England. Maine and Vermont appear more homogeneous in character than the Granite State. Even so, occasionally it is possible to glimpse a common vision of this place and its people.

For the first century and a half New Hampshire authors portrayed the land as both treacherous and bountiful, a paradox of danger and promise. Early in the eighteenth century, when its literary history began, the colony was little more than a sparsely settled extension of Massachusetts. Forces often beyond the control of the inhabitants threatened their efforts to make a home in the wilderness. There were continual Indian raids, the aching labor involved in coaxing reluctant harvests from uncooperative soil, and, perhaps most of all, the effort required to comprehend the will of a deity who often appeared to be inscrutable or even whimsical. Engrossed with such challenges, the first settlers of New Hampshire would have understood the assertion of John Adams that founding generations have little time to indulge in the arts.

New Hampshire literature appeared, therefore, as a by-product of the necessary battle for survival. When in 1726 Portsmouth magistrate Samuel Penhallow set about recording the local raids and skirmishes that were but a small part of Queen Anne's War, his motive was not the conscious creation of a work of literary art but rather the desire to produce a narrative of the painful events that darkened the lives of his contemporaries and inspired their heroic response. Likewise, in his memorable sermon the Reverend Jabez Fitch did not aim to dazzle his Portsmouth congregation with the elegance of his theological prose, but to awaken their awareness to the great earthquake of 1727 as a warning from God that they had a choice between redemption and destruction. And when Bedford farmer Matthew Patten set down in his diary the number of acres he planted with buckwheat and the price of his grog at McGregor's tavern, he merely responded to the impulses of an orderly man of business. The thought that his diary would become a resource for later generations of social historians must never have entered his mind. Together the careers of these literary pioneers span much of the eighteenth century. The magistrate's narrative of war, like the minister's sermons on topics ranging from earthquake to the "throat distemper" epidemic and the farmer's agricultural commentary, gave literary expression to mundane as well as important events of their time. This was the epic phase in New Hampshire's history, and although no Vergil gave it poetic shape, Penhallow did "sing of arms and the hero," and Patten's diary shares the primary subject of its inspiration with the *Georgics*.

*   *   *

The years of revolution and the attainment of statehood brought a new vitality to New Hampshire literature, introduced a more professional approach to the craft, and broadened the range of subjects. In addition, there emerged a unifying theme in persistent reminders of the need to encourage and strengthen the quality of personal and civic virtue that the enlightened had recognized since Montesquieu's *Spirit of the Laws* as the foundation of true republics. The scattered and disparate contributions of colonial writers gradually gave way to works combining the concept of New Hampshire as one state within a larger nation and a positive vision of the future. The parochial view that had characterized the early literature was replaced by an awareness of horizons beyond the Merrimack and Connecticut valleys. The transformation of colonial subjects into republican citizens found expression in history, sermons, poetry, and novels.

The writings of the Reverend Jeremy Belknap, Henry Sherburne, and Tabitha Gilman Tenney are characteristic of this new, far-ranging, and professional spirit. Belknap's meticulously researched *History of New Hampshire*, appearing in three successive volumes in 1784, 1791, and 1792, was no simple wartime narrative in the style of Penhallow but a sophisticated, fully developed enterprise—seldom equaled in state histories. Broadly conceived as a chronological account of the administrations of New Hampshire's governors, the opus described the state in terms of natural as well as political history. The Dover cleric who once failed in an attempt to climb Mount Washington may never have seen the panoramic view that the summit affords, but his scholarship has given generations of readers a wider vision and deeper comprehension of his adopted state.

A dramatically different kind of insight into the preoccupations of the time came in a new literary medium when, eight years after the appearance of Belknap's final volume, Henry Sherburne of Portsmouth published New Hampshire's first novel in 1800. *The Oriental Philanthropist; or, The True Republican* is a fanciful allegory celebrating the triumphant revolution and the founding of America. Reflecting the contemporary fascination of Western literati with orientalism, Sherburne chose as his hero Nytan, a Chinese prince estranged from his royal father by duplicitous ministers and forced by his principles into rebellion. The mythical island of Ravenzar becomes a refuge for him and like-minded immigrants. Although fabulous riches lie beneath the soil, citizens are enjoined to labor and never to squander these resources in lives of luxurious idleness. In a blending of classical and romantic elements, Sherburne emphasized simultaneously a disciplined, austere devotion to the common weal and the eternal impulse to achieve individual freedom. The exoticism of his locale contrasts with the simplicity of the virtues he preaches. Perhaps to make the moral of his allegory explicit, Sherburne ended his novel with a poem in praise of the new federal city of Washington, founded the same year the book was published.

This didactic and patriotic tradition continued in an antiromantic novel entitled *Female Quixotism: Exhibited in the Romantic Opinions and Extravagant Adventures of Dorcasina Sheldon.* Writing in the style of Jane Austen, Tabitha Gilman Tenney of Exeter detailed the absurd misadventures of an addle-pated lady who, until age has withered her, remains convinced that it is her beauty and not her wealth that attracts suitors. Each succeeding affair becomes increasingly grotesque in direct proportion to her advancing years, and whatever pity the reader might feel for the unfortunate heroine is quickly dissipated by the author's incisive wit. At last Dorcasina realizes both the extent and origin of her folly. Since childhood her addiction to romantic novels of European origin has distorted her perception of life and encouraged false goals. She vows to repudiate these malign influences and to devote her remaining years to good works. Tenney's moral is clear: foreign culture undermines the virtue of good Americans. Had Dorcasina considered more the common good and less her own vanity, her life would have been happier and her community better served.

These early novels owe their form to those of the Old World.

Episodic, crammed with marvelous coincidence, and burdened with rambling narrative, they imitated their more polished English counterparts. In their substance, however, these novels, whose milieu marked the periphery of cultivated society, expressed a set of republican standards with the exuberance and innocent joy associated with a fresh beginning. The tone was in keeping with the spirit of the motto on the Great Seal of the infant nation: *Novus Ordo Seclorum*—"The New Order of the Ages."

* * *

During the eighty years between the British surrender at Yorktown and the attack on Fort Sumter, a new America came into being. The accomplishments of the revolutionary period generated the potential for further experimentation by New Hampshire authors with a variety of subjects and literary themes. Although its quantity had been small, the range of literary forms was broad during the late eighteenth and early nineteenth centuries. However, the promise was not realized. The predominant romantic mode proved to be an important but rather provincializing influence for many nineteenth-century New Hampshire writers. Nature, innocent childhood in idyllic surroundings, self-sacrifice and unrequited love, individuality sometimes carried to the point of eccentricity, and sentiment—all these motifs combined to idealize the community and its immediate environment.

Nature served as a theme in at least three roles. First, and to a tedious extent, it was an inspiration to poets, both professional and amateur. In an anthology published in 1883, *The Poets of New Hampshire*, editor Bela Chapin included many poems, characteristic of the time, that both anthropomorphized and sentimentalized New Hampshire lakes, mountains, and rivers. Typical was Benjamin Shillaber's ode to the Piscataqua.

> Thou art still young and fair, Piscataqua,
> Thy voice as sweet and tuneful to my ear
> As when, in early boyhood's holiday,
> It gave me fervent happiness to hear:
> My neighbor, playmate and companion dear.

In another aspect nature provided a congenial backdrop, especially in the genre of local color. Beginning with Sarah Buell Hale's *Northwood: A Tale of New England* early in the century and continuing through the short stories of Alice Brown published in the 1890s, the peaceful countryside provided an agreeable setting for village and farm homes. Most of these works contain loving descriptions of flowers and plants of all sorts, gardens and cultivated fields, seasonal changes, and friendly animals. Although nature on occasion may display its destructive power, as when Tom Bailey's boyhood friend Binny Wallace is swept out to sea by a storm in Thomas Bailey Aldrich's *Story of a Bad Boy*, it is usually the beneficent qualities that predominate.

Finally, in contrast to the descriptions of arcadian utopia, an attitude verging on veneration prevailed among those who wrote about the White Mountains.[1] The mood of these pieces is typically one of awe mixed with terror. The same God who enjoined his people to look to the hills as a source of strength could strike them down with landslides and sudden storms or cause them to lose their way in the wilderness. Danger was present in places of overwhelming natural beauty. At a time when adventure was disappearing from the lives of inhabitants of placid communities in the lowlands, it remained a daily companion for the dwellers of the hills. Tragedy acquired mythic proportions in the fate of the Willey family, swept to oblivion in a great avalanche, or young Nancy in pursuit of a faithless lover, lost and frozen to death beside the brook that bears her name. And somewhere in misty heights survived the brooding spirit of the Indian Chocorua—a place of "unearthly wonders," Nathaniel Hawthorne has observed, "inhabited by deities."

* * *

The theme that above all others provided nineteenth-century New Hampshire literature with coherence was that of the idealized community. This motif subsumed all other concepts—nature, eccentric individualism, and carefree childhood. It embodied as the ideal locale all those friendly villages where church steeples overlooked white houses of ancient vintage demurely placed behind picket fences, crowded with larkspur and lilac. The product of selective memory, at once nowhere and everywhere, it was a Currier and Ives print frozen forever in mid-nineteenth century. Fragments

---

1. Thomas Starr King's *The White Hills: Their Legends, Landscape, and Poetry* is one example.

of half-forgotten places appeared through a prism that distorted and rearranged in accordance with the liberties of poetic license. Such a lens helped convert, for example, the Portsmouth of Thomas Bailey Aldrich's childhood into the Rivermouth of *The Story of a Bad Boy*; much the same, perhaps, but still, not quite the same. This idealization of a rural, small-town past persisted long after the economic and social base of these communities had begun to disappear. Though not unique to New Hampshire, it characterized in varying degrees the work of novelists such as Aldrich, Sarah Buell Hale, Alice Brown, and Henry Augustus Shute, playwright Denman Thompson, and almost every contributor to the state's literary journal, the *Granite Monthly*. Although the setting could often be identified as an actual place, their local particularism symbolized merely one aspect of a generalized utopian setting enhanced by the patina of a glamorized past.

The literary appeal is obvious: such towns are not just a refuge from a threatening outside world of cities and strangers; they are in themselves a microcosm of society. "Knowable communities," Raymond Williams has called them, containing "valuing societies" rooted in tradition and concerned with the welfare of inhabitants.[2] These villages are places small enough to be comprehensible yet large enough to contain a variety of characters interesting both in themselves and as they interact with others. New Hampshire towns had achieved the dignity of age; they had had sufficient time to establish traditions governing the conduct of conformists and ignored by the impious. Although the class structure tended to be egalitarian, in these nostalgic recreations there might be a village squire, offset by a few colorful indigents. But most characters represented gradations of the middle class, with the exception of those odd types who defy categorization. "There must have been something in the air of that place that generated eccentricity," wrote Thomas Bailey Aldrich of Portsmouth, and he might have extended his observation to the entire Granite State.[3] Nineteenth-century authors always included the obligatory eccentric. "Conservatism and respectability have their values, certainly," wrote Al-

2. Raymond Williams, *The Country and the City* (New York: Oxford University Press, 1973), p. 165.
3. Thomas Bailey Aldrich, *An Old Town by the Sea* (Cambridge, Mass.: Riverside Press, 1893), p. 82.

drich, "but has not the unconventional its values also?"[4] Unquestionably, for it relieved the monotony of the village and helped account for unorthodox behavior in the literature.

In the main, however, it was not the unusual that writers chose to emphasize; rather, a sense of place, a feeling for tradition, loyalty to family, concern for neighbors, and an appreciation of the country contributed to a setting that reassured through its familiarity. Nor were those values confined to the village; they extended to surrounding farms and even touched dwellers in remote places such as Lucy Howe Crawford, chronicler and denizen of the White Mountains. The idealized community could be a state of mind as well as a specific locale, it infused the spirit of New Hampshire literature regardless of its place of origin. Thus, far removed from national crises—or so it seemed—life drowsed on in Alice Brown's Tiverton, Sarah Hale's Northwood, Henry Augustus Shute's Exeter, and on Celia Thaxter's Isles of Shoals. Each day bore a likeness to the preceding one. An endless succession of such days and years must surely be part of an eternal plan, for simple routine reinforced an atmosphere of rural nirvana while the turbulence and uncertainty of cities remained remote.[5] Celia Thaxter, describing life on the Isles of Shoals, wrote, "People forget the hurry and worry and fret of life after living there awhile, and to the imaginative mind, all things become dreamy as they were to the lotus eaters." In her short story "Number Five," Alice Brown evoked a similar carefree and placid ambience. "We who are Tiverton born," she wrote, "though false ambition may have ridden us to market, or the world's voice incited us to kindred clamoring, have a way of shutting our eyes, now and then, to present changes, and seeing things as they were once, as they are still, in a certain sleepy yet altogether individual corner of country life."

Brown, Aldrich, Shute, and others often drew upon the stable realm of childhood memories. The age of innocence, for them as for the nation, had tarnished on the battlefields of Gettysburg and Antietam, and a new America, laced by railroads, studded with factories, and populated by new immigrants, had become almost a

4. Ibid., p. 83.
5. This particular tradition had earlier included such works as Oliver Goldsmith's "The Deserted Village" and, in America, Timothy Dwight's *Greenfield Hill*.

foreign land. As they grew older the world of their youth not only receded but began literally to disappear. It may be axiomatic that the golden age is ever the preceding one, but for the generation that came to maturity and middle age in the wake of the Civil War, transformations in society and the physical environment hammered home the passing of an era. It was no accident that stories of blissful small-town childhood flourished in the latter decades of the nineteenth century, for many authors must have felt a sense of urgency to preserve their own record of a waning culture. The fact that the old ways lingered on in a few remote places, as Alice Brown indicated, lent poignancy as well as authenticity to these literary journeys into the past.

Boyish pranks and girlish dreams, however, contributed themes to only a portion of the rural-based New Hampshire literature. Alice Brown, among others, expressed also the pain of growing old, the loneliness of self-sacrifice, and the disillusionment of failing marriages and lost love. In "Told in the Poorhouse" Josh and Lyddy Marden live in the same house for years without ever speaking to each other, and in "At Sudleigh Fair" Elvin Drew faces a jail sentence after he sets fire to his house and barn so that he may collect the insurance. Life in the idealized community guaranteed no insulation from misfortune, but among its compensations it offered companionship, a feeling of belonging, and a purpose in living. People who had shared a common tradition for two centuries knew how to communicate without speech. At its best, this was the republic of virtue writ small, a place where duty and concern for the welfare of others could never be forgotten. When Elvin Drew departs for prison, Dilly, the wise old "witch" of Tiverton, says to Molly, who loves him, "Folks don't know why they're uplifted sometimes, when there ain't no cause, but *I* say its other folks' love. . . . See if we can't dream us a nice pleasant dream—all about green gardins, an' the folks we love walkin' in the midst of them." [6]

This idealized, sentimental concept of life in the rural community received its primary impetus at the popular level from the state's major literary magazine, the *Granite Monthly*. First appear-

6. Alice Brown, *Meadow Grass: Tales of New England Life* (Boston: Copeland and Day, 1895), p. 228.

ing in 1877, the publication continued until 1930, when it succumbed to the Great Depression. Unabashedly for amateur writers with professional aspirations, the magazine attracted no major literary talent.[7] Perhaps for this reason, the *Granite Monthly* is a touchstone of popular perceptions of New Hampshire, either as the writers actually perceived it or as they wished it were. The state emerges from these pages as an Anglo-Saxon, Protestant, small-town paradise. The emphasis is on the rural nature of life, but among the profiles of different towns featured in each issue are scattered references to the textile mills and shoe factories that were spreading through the region. The authors' observations in these cases were usually confined to the potential for village prosperity such industries promised and to the fact that these blessings owed their origin to the vision and energy of Yankee entrepreneurs.

Equally significant are the omissions from these selections. Typically the mills are viewed in terms of their economic contributions, almost never in terms of the activities inside them. The immigrants who tended the looms, lathes, and lasts remained anonymous; their lives as laborers and as fellow townspeople held no interest for writers with a different background and tradition. Two self-contained societies lived side by side—one mute, the other with a literary voice but ethnocentric in its perceptions of the community.

The sixty-two volumes of the *Granite Monthly* thus furnish a peculiarly subjective view of New Hampshire. In retrospect this fact is not surprising. Its contributors wrote about what they knew best and admired most, and their like-minded reading public expected nothing else. Literary realism, the perspective perhaps best suited to describing factory life, would have been distasteful to them, and that form did not exert its influence locally until well after the turn of the century. The contributors to the *Granite Monthly* and their better-known literary colleagues Sarah Buell Hale, Alice Brown, Henry Augustus Shute, Thomas Bailey Aldrich, playwright Denman Thompson, and poets Edna Dean Proctor and Sam Walter Foss all kept the old faith. Aldrich, more prescient than most, recognized in *An Old Town by the Sea* that

---

7. An exception is Frances Parkinson Keyes, and her contributions came before she had become well-known.

Portsmouth changed irrevocably the day the railroad arrived, but in general all continued to praise the splendors of the small-town past.[8]

Though on an unconscious level, perhaps the very level that compelled them to exploit nostalgic childhood memories, writers in New Hampshire must have been aware that the economic and social base of their world was moving from beneath them. The bulk of their work spanned the period between the Civil War and the First World War, a time of declining agriculture and industrial expansion. This larger movement entailed necessary changes in the concept of community. In New Hampshire this change expressed itself in the removal of economic and political power from seafaring Portsmouth to manufacturing Manchester, from a town whose elegance evoked the eighteenth century to one whose energy derived from the rise of industry. Power shifted from the old, commercial aristocracy to the new bourgeoisie. Leadership shifted from the council chamber and countinghouse to the board rooms of impersonal corporations. Even in Portsmouth the future soon made itself manifest. While fading Copleys peered from the gloom of wainscotted walls in Federal mansions, the graven face of Frank Jones, brewer and entrepreneur, stared out over the city from the facade of the Rockingham Hotel, a plush caravansary built with profits from his newly acquired fortune.

How long could the literary establishment remain blind to the fact that its image of New Hampshire had been reduced to a meretricious cliché?

*   *   *

Toward the end of the nineteenth century William Dean Howells, Ohio native and Boston Brahmin by adoption, author, and editor of the prestigious *Atlantic Monthly*, became a frequent summer visitor in New Hampshire. Eventually he published two novels with New Hampshire locales: *The Landlord at Lion's Head* and *Mrs. Farrell*.[9] The plots of both evolve through the interaction of urban summer visitors with the local Yankees. Howells's ambivalent attitude toward the latter reveals his concern for the future of

8. Henry Adams made a similar observation about Boston in his *Education of Henry Adams*.

9. *Mrs. Farrell* first appeared under the title *Private Theatricals* in serialized form.

a proud race increasingly enervated with each successive generation. Such objectivity perhaps came more readily to an outsider.

Mrs. Farrell is set in a town in decline:

. . . one of those country places which have yielded to changing conditions and have ceased to be the simple farming towns of a past generation. The people are still farmers, but most of them are no longer farmers
only. In summer, they give up the habitable rooms of their old square
wooden houses to boarders from the cities. . . . In this way they eke out
the living grudged them by their neglected acres and keep their houses in
a repair that contrasts with the decay of their farming. . . . Many houses
in the region stand empty, absently glaring on the passer with their old
windows, as if striving to recall the households long gone West, to whom
they once were homes.

The church of this old village had become a metaphor for the
whole community.

The old church has no other grace than they give it, as it stands staring
white on the border of the Village Green, and sends over the valleys and
uplands the wild, plangent summons of its Sabbath bell. . . . It could no
longer call many youths to worship, but mostly a thinned and faltering
congregation of old men and women responding to its menace, and
sparsely scattered themselves among the long rows of pews. The stalwart
boys and ambitious, eager girls had emigrated or married out of town, till
now the very graves beside the church received none but aged dead, and
the newest stones hardly remembered anyone under sixty.

Howells further emphasized this atmosphere of decline through
brutal contrasts between newly arrived Irish settlers and the Yankees. "He thrives where the son of the soil starved; and if the bitter
truth must be owned, he seems to deserve his better fortune. He
has enterprise and energy, and to the summer boarder, used to the
drive and strain of the city, the Yankee farmer often seems to have
none of these qualities." And in referring to the French Canadians,
Howells described them as "a race whose indomitable light-heart-
edness no rigor of climate has appalled, whereas our Anglo-Saxon
stock in many country neighborhoods of New England seems
weatherbeaten in mind as in face."

This emphasis on the exhaustion of the old families recurs in
The Landlord at Lion's Head, with significant modification in the
introduction of a new kind of individual, a harbinger of imminent

and great social change. Living on an impoverished farm beneath a mountain whose rock profile forms the head of a lion, the Durgin family have been afflicted by tuberculosis, and the orchard shelters the graves of their children. The living have given way to resignation, with the exception of the mother and her youngest son, Jeff. These two have escaped the disease, and their vitality contrasts with the debility of the surroundings. Mrs. Durgin is proud, hardworking, and shrewd—the best of the old Yankees. Jeff is also proud, industrious when motivated, and shrewd—but there the similarity ends. Unlike his mother he is amoral, the perfect exemplar of Howells's realism. He knows how to get what he wants. "Prosperity and adversity," Jeff remarks, "they've got nothing to do with conduct. If you're a strong man you get there, and if you're a weak man, all the righteousness in the universe won't help you." Just as Hawthorne caused the Great Stone Face to dominate the moral as well as physical landscape of Ernest's life, so Jeff, with his yellow hair and animal strength, grows to resemble the Lion's Head, which overlooks his home. His leonine qualities make young Durgin a survivor and a very successful one. A man of the future even with his flaws, he is a striking character of rude charm without hypocrisy. Does the future of the race depend upon such men? Howells seems to be saying that in the granite hills there may be a rebirth of elemental power.

The dubious morality of men like Jeff Durgin is but one symbol of the breakdown of the old order. In his novel *Coniston*, Winston Churchill introduced Durgin's political counterpart in Jethro Bass, a ruthless politician whose career was obviously based on that of Ruell Durkee, an uneducated but shrewd village boss who rose from the obscurity of Croydon (Coniston) to a central position of power in Concord. Beloved by a few and feared by many, Bass makes a mockery of the democratic process and helps to create a legislature so debased and subservient that a large railroad (actually the Boston and Maine Railroad) is able to turn the state into a fiefdom. Churchill's second New Hampshire novel, *Mr. Crewe's Career*, treats this intrusion of corporate power as another aspect of the drift from the "republic of virtue." The idealized community as a civic goal has receded into legend; the decorum of old-time town meetings and the noblesse oblige of village squires like the

decent Romillee of Sarah Hale's *Northwood* have become anach-
ronisms. The corrupt bargaining and demagoguery of vulgar appeals to voters described in *Coniston* and *Mr. Crewe's Career*
characterize the seamy side of mass, romantic democracy. Churchill's books underscored the decline from that austere, classical republicanism for which Belknap had stood.

More conscientious than most New Hamphsire writers of his
generation, Churchill strove to identify some logical consequence
to the events that threatened to obliterate the old values. Gradually, the optimism inspired by Theodore Roosevelt and the Progres-
sives drained away. By 1917, in a world far removed from the opu-
lence of his Cornish retreat, the mill towns along the Merrimack
River had started a decline that marked the end of a century of
growth. Here was a far more serious crisis than that posed by the
inconsistencies of New Hampshire politics—one worthy of a last,
great literary venture. *The Dwelling-Place of Light*, a confusing testament, was Churchill's last novel. Written during the First World
War, it was the only major New Hampshire novel of that period to
attack the problems stemming from industrialization.

The setting is a city closely resembling Manchester, but the
events echo the Lowell, Massachusetts textile strike of 1912. The
tone is ominous. A rural New England family, spent and reduced
to mediocrity, symbolizes the hopeless struggle of Yankees whose
values have become irrelevant. This is a world of satanic mills and
urban slums packed with immigrants whose ability to adjust and
prosper is a reproach to the old families lacking resilience and energy. A strike kindles violence from which neither management
nor labor emerges without having used cynical and inflammatory
tactics. The book's despondent and inconclusive ending emphasizes the frustration of those upper-class, Anglo-Saxon reformers
who had been galvanized by Roosevelt's leadership. The plutocrats
might be ruining the country, but labor organizers with foreign-
sounding names who quoted Marx and Sorel were not the sort of
people on whom a Winston Churchill could bestow his blessing as
the harbingers of a new and enlightened era.

The view that an end had come to a once-predominant pattern
of New Hampshire life was shared by Howells and Churchill with
the poet Robert Frost, who immediately caught the significance of
events in old, rural New England. Whether the Yankees dwelt in

town or on the farm, their lives demonstrated the disintegration of the old order of integrated institutions, visualized by its propagandists as the harmonious community. Everywhere around him was evidence of the cruel paradox of lives deteriorating amid scenes of great natural beauty. Everywhere spread the abandoned farms Howells had noted a quarter-century before, stone walls trailing off into the woods where once lay open pasture, church pews empty of sons and daughters gone West while small communities atrophied or disappeared. In his poem "New Hampshire," Frost explained the nomenclature of one such place, Still Corners:

> . . . so called not because
> The place is silent all day long, nor yet
> Because it boasts a whiskey still—because
> It set out once to be a city and still
> Is only Corners, cross-roads in a wood.

Many of Frost's poems describe the loneliness that affected so many, stranded in isolated farms far from sympathetic human society. "An Old Man's Winter Night" speaks of such aloneness.

> One aged man—one man—can't keep a house,
> A farm, a countryside, or if he can,
> It's thus he does it of a winter night.[10]

In his poem "The Census-Taker," the poet comes upon an empty house:

> The only dwelling in a waste cut over
> A hundred square miles round it in the mountains.

Even the irony of being a census taker in such an empty place is not enough to raise the poet's spirits.

> The melancholy of having to count souls
> Where they grow fewer and fewer every year
> Is extreme where they shrink to none at all.
> It must be I want life to go on living.

Despite decay, lost hopes, and loneliness, Frost found much in New Hampshire worth affirming. There is optimism in someone who wants "life to go on living." Frost respected tenacity and ad-

---

10. "An Old Man's Winter Night," *The Poetry of Robert Frost*, edited by Edward Connery Lathem (New York: Holt, Rinehart & Winston, 1969), p. 108.

herence to principle. In "The Black Cottage" a minister and the poet visit an abandoned house once occupied by a woman whose husband had died in the Civil War. Her sons now "live so far away—one is out west." She had carried on alone, indomitable in her belief in the old Apostles' Creed and the maxim that "all men are created free and equal."

> Strange how such innocence gets its own way.
> I shouldn't be surprised if in this world
> It were the force that would at last prevail.[11]

To Frost, it did not appear to matter so much that the culture of old, rural New Hampshire showed signs of stress; to him "the force that would at last prevail" resided in the tenacious few who refused to give up and desert the countryside. Unlike many writers of an earlier generation, he saw a more sinister side to rural life that had always to some degree been present. His keen eye took him beyond bending birches and snowy woods.

*   *   *

Before the First World War had ended, changes in attitudes toward the small town became even more obvious. Less and less was the community idealized as writers increasingly found fault with the old ways; what had once been described as cozy now became stifling, and neighborly concern took on the aspect of malicious prying. Simplicity began to appear as naiveté, and staunch beliefs as bigotry. Whereas friendly villages had once served as idyllic settings, authors began to describe them as traps from which the intelligent young must escape or suffer the consequences of intellectual and spiritual stagnation. In a country whose frontier had become history, where urbanization increased every year and industrialization brought new, complex social problems, writers sought contemporary themes that stressed realism with a perspective inherently unsympathetic to the nostalgic yearnings embodied in the positive features of small community life. In 1915, when Edgar Lee Masters published *Spoon River Anthology*, he launched what Carl Van Doren later termed "the revolt from the village." This attitude of rebellion continued in the work of Willa Cather and others and found classic expression in Sinclair Lewis's *Main Street*.

11. "The Black Cottage," ibid., p. 57.

In New Hampshire, the later work of Alice Brown provides an example of this rising skepticism. This flexibility reflects a long career that spanned two epochs, in the course of which the artist accommodated old beliefs to a new sense of disillusionment. Deeply affected by the First World War and changing life-styles of the 1920s, Brown realized that the world of Tiverton had vanished. In her book *Old Crow*, written just after the war, her doubts about the future recur again and again.

In 1934 Alice Brown's last novel, *Jeremy Hamlin*, appeared. By then she had moved far from the rather simple distinctions between good and evil that had characterized her early stories to the ambiguities of contemporary society. Hamlin, a brooding presence throughout the book, is an adopted child of unknown parentage. No one knows his origin; he possesses no heritage, and his destiny as village tycoon is not to build but to destroy. Like Howells's Jeff Durgin he is a primeval force, and he bequeaths a troubled legacy when his mills close and his workers find themselves unemployed. A demanding man, he has no interest in the welfare of these unfortunates. "I don't believe," his daughter remarks after his death, "he ever really saw his men. . . . He saw what he wanted done. He felt as a machine feels."

So much for the humanity that had dignified life in the old town of Tiverton where Alice Brown's literary journey began.

The revolt as a literary movement ended, but the spirit that animated it enlivened the popular novel *Peyton Place*. In the 1950s when other young authors were writing of Iwo Jima or the invasion of Normandy, Grace Metalious focused her realistic appraisal of life on a small New Hampshire community of the 1930s. This book, which sold more copies than any previous American novel, contained enough detail to imbue it with a sharp sense of locale. The characters derive from a social spectrum far more comprehensive than the majority of Metalious's New Hampshire predecessors had exploited. Mill workers, rural slum dwellers, and moral derelicts are mixed with the "proper" bourgeoisie. The hypocrisy of village life is revealed through the attempts of its people to conceal a guilty past. Having provided this setting, Metalious did not shrink from unpleasant subjects: she confronted the moral implications of abortion and illegitimacy, the loneliness of the sensitive in a philistine environment, and the isolation of the generations. Proximity in this confined milieu all too often encourages hatred and deceit instead of affection. The place name has entered the language as a symbol of all that is ugly in the small town.

* * *

The strains of disillusion that surfaced in the "revolt from the village" dissipated after the Second World War. Despite notable exceptions such as *Peyton Place*, most New Hampshire writers no longer condemned rural and small-town life. For the past three decades works with a New Hampshire locale by Thomas Williams, May Sarton, Donald Hall, and Noel Perrin, though not ignoring unattractive aspects of New England country culture, have emphasized a positive view. The result, in novels, short stories, essays, and poems, is an outlook more objective than the naive or cynical extremes of the idealized community or the "revolt from the village." Thomas Williams neither glorifies nor denigrates the town of Leah, the setting for several of his novels. It is a place "where crisp white houses were surrounded by grass so green it seemed to glow, even in the dusk, from within each blade."[12] There is obvious concern, even affection when, in *Town Burning*, the inhabitants gather to protect Leah from a forest fire that threatens to become a holocaust. But even as the conflagration approaches, John, the novel's leading character, in an unusually candid conversation with his father, speaks his mind about Leah. "Look," John said hesitantly, "you know how I've always felt about Leah. You have too—felt the same way, I mean. . . . We're both sort of misfits in Leah . . . only I can take off when it gets bad and you can't."

John wants something that Leah cannot offer—membership in a community without intrusion into his private domain. "I don't want to be king of the hill or anything like that, I just want to make them stop judging me all the time. I want to be a zero, an unknown quantity," he tells his father. "I never really feel persecuted unless I'm in this one particular little town. I swear I get along perfectly everywhere else. Why the hell should Leah do it to me?"

"You were born here," his father replies.

12. Thomas Williams, *The Hair of Harold Roux* (New York: Random House, 1974), p. 196.

Perhaps there are few Tivertons or Rivermouths anymore; Leah has its full complement of people who get drunk, act brutally, and care nothing for local tradition. Delilah, the witch of *Meadow-Grass: Tales of New England Life*, accepted with resigned tolerance by her fellow townsmen, lives a happy life. In *Town Burning*, eccentric Billy Muldrow suffers crude practical jokes; the cruelty of the town finally drives him to murder and self-destruction.

In a time when even "knowable communities" often fail to produce "valuing societies," the search for a congenial environment for creative endeavor becomes increasingly frantic. Is it possible to write literature that is rooted in a particular place when standardization wipes out everything unique and anonymity destroys all sense of community? Can tradition take hold when children never know the homes of their parents' childhood? Such questions may find answers in landscapes lacking regional definition; Manchester in the English Midlands may serve as well as Manchester on the Merrimack. The problems of the state are not contained within its borders as in Penhallow's time, for they are now the problems of the nation and of society everywhere. The steady encroachment of megalopolis through southern New Hampshire is visible evidence of changes more far-reaching than the growth of the mill towns more than a century ago.

At least for a time there remain, scattered throughout the Granite State, stretches of countryside and towns as yet relatively untouched and people determined to keep alive the independent spirit expressed in the state's motto, "Live Free or Die." To these places have come novelists, essayists, and poets such as May Sarton, Noel Perrin, and Donald Hall. Their response is affirmative; although they may feel discouraged by the contrariness they encounter, they regard it with understanding and affection. May Sarton, arriving in her midforties, wanted a place where she could satisfy her hunger for "all the natural world can give—a garden, woods, fields, brooks, birds; the hunger of the poet." Her search ended in the town of Nelson. Here for the next few years she lived, converting a dilapidated house into a home, a wilderness of weeds into a garden, and her ideas into books. The work she produced may have been in part a response to crises of midlife, but it was shaped also by her New Hampshire surroundings. Her appreciation of the climate, scenery, even the joy of the "great autumn light, . . . the glory of New England" breathes throughout each page of *Plant Dreaming Deep* and *Journal of a Solitude*.

But most important, it is the people—what endures of that "valuing society"—that has brought her and others like her to New Hampshire. In her novel *Kinds of Love* she writes of the town of Willard as "a place where people can still be judged for themselves, for what they truly are, not what they have been given by chance. . . . Willard is a place where people are still cherished." Here is that will to survive with integrity and grace—Frost's "force that would at last prevail." This is the home to which the writer gratefully returns.

> Here is a little province, poor and kind—
> Warmer than marble is the weathered wood.
> Dearer than holy Ganges, the wild brook;
> And sweeter than all Greece to this one mind
> A ragged pasture, open green, white steeple,
> And these whom I have come to call my people.

I

THE BEGINNINGS

THE EARLY literature of New Hampshire evolved directly from
the experiences of its inhabitants. Narrative in form and direct in
language, it was a literal and forceful presentation of the authors'
perceptions of significant aspects of daily existence. Portsmouth
magistrate Samuel Penhallow, for example, was motivated to write
his narrative of the Indian wars by the violent circumstances that
dominated the later years of his life. The hinterland of Portsmouth
underwent intermittent siege as frequent Indian raids created
anxieties and made life perilous. Queen Anne's War (1701–13),
another episode in the long series of colonial conflicts between England and France, brought terror to New Englanders. The Marquis de Vaudreuil, governor of New France, dispatched raiding
parties of Indians under French command that struck settlements
from Wells, Maine to Northampton, Massachusetts. Penhallow
saw it as his duty to commemorate these events.

The paradox of Penhallow's history is its incorporation, with
the grim account of Indian brutality, of a serene determinism de-

rived from the inhabitants' belief that, because they were further-
ing God's design, their ultimate victory was certain. Like Captain
Lovewell, who was "animated with an uncommon zeal of doing
what service he could," the people of New Hampshire persevered.
Even the Indians were not beyond redemption; Penhallow, unlike
Cotton Mather, did not see them simply as "unkenneled wolves."
The objectivity that made him a competent narrator also compelled him to recognize that the French maintained friendlier rela-
tionships with the native Americans than did the English. He revealed the reason in a comment by a wise Indian sachem, who,
when asked why his brethren gave preference to the French, replied, "They taught us how to pray." Penhallow observed that if
more people had followed the selfless example of the Reverend
John Eliot in his missionary work with the Indians, his own narrative would not have been one of continual bloodshed. However,
despite the amity prevailing between French and Indian, the narrator never doubted that the people of New Hampshire were God's
true servants.[1] He likened them to the Old Testament Israelites,
chastened by Jehovah on their journey to the Promised Land but
brought by His benevolence safely through the ordeal of fire and
sword.

After the restoration of peace, danger threatened elsewhere. On
the night of October 29, 1727, one year after the publication of
Penhallow's narrative, an earthquake more frightening than destructive shook southern New Hampshire. In Portsmouth's Congregational church, the Reverend Jabez Fitch responded quickly
with a memorable sermon. The Lord's purpose, he said, was not so
much to destroy as to admonish. Dwelling more on man's duty to
God than on human wickedness, he emphasized the role of Christianity in the home and in the state. "Let us worship God in our
houses," he said, and "let civil rulers, whom God has appointed to
be a terror to evil works, be careful to put the good and wholesome laws that are made into execution." Religion benignly inte-
grates family, government, and nature.

[1] "Not that I am insensible that many have stigmatized the English as chiefly culpable in
causing the first break between them [Indians] and us, by invading their properties and de-
frauding them in their dealings; but to censure the public for the sinister actions of a few
private persons is especially repugnant to reason and equity." From Penhallow's introduction to his *Narrative*.

Fitch had signed a petition to the General Court of Massachusetts requesting redress for those who had suffered in the witchcraft persecution. In his sermon, his enlightened attitude is evident in his assertion that the earthquake had natural causes, although he is quick to add that "these natural causes are under the Government of Divine Providence. . . . Though there may be a sober consideration of second causes, we should especially consider the First Cause."

The careers of the Reverend Jabez Fitch and of Samuel Penhallow span fifty years of New Hampshire history. Penhallow's narrative of war and Fitch's sermons on topics ranging from the earthquake to the need for a revival of piety gave literary expression to every important event of their time.

Lacking a formal education, Matthew Patten was a new man; a Scotch-Irishman of the Merrimack Valley, he exemplified the rising middle class. A transitional figure, his prosperity as a farmer and local magistrate was established during the final two decades of the colonial period, and his expanded career as state legislator and governor's councilor was launched by the American Revolution. For the greater part of his adult life he kept a diary in which he carefully accounted for each day's activities. To him, forests were for clearing because their shadows concealed no enemies, and the earth was to be tilled; should it tremble, that was but a temporary aberration. As a practical man of affairs, he never speculated in his journal on causation or the meaning of natural phenomena; to events both private and national he gave little space. The record he left reveals the range of eighteenth-century agricultural enterprise when the practitioner engages in more than subsistence farming. Caring for cattle and other livestock, sowing and reaping corn and rye, visiting Colonel Moor's mill, fishing at Namokeg Falls (where he caught an eleven-pound salmon), and journeying to Boston on business filled his days. Seasonal changes dictated the routine of his life, and his work as justice of the peace limited his interests to the immediate community.

The American Revolution wrenched Patten from his local sphere and raised him to state government. The diary, through its laconic style and sparse detail, continues to convey an appreciation of ordinary life in an extraordinary time. Patten offers no comment on the Boston Tea Party or the Battle of Bennington; his priorities stressed the labor of the farm even after 1775, when entries begin to note attendance at meetings of the Committee of Safety and of the new state legislature in Exeter. The diary suggests that the rhythm of Patten's life was established more by the weather, the soil, and the seasons than by events of great political significance.

Perhaps because the interests of Penhallow, Fitch, and Patten were not exclusively literary, their combined works provide insight into the quality of life in their time.

SAMUEL PENHALLOW

Samuel Penhallow (b. Cornwall, England, 1665; d. 1726) came to America intending to become a minister. He moved to Portsmouth, New Hampshire, married the daughter of John Cutt, president of the Province of New Hampshire, relinquished clerical ambitions, and entered provincial politics. He became speaker of the New Hampshire General Assembly in 1699 and then treasurer of the province. In 1714 he became a justice of the superior court, rising to chief justice in 1717. Throughout his political career he kept an account of the Indian wars. *The History of the Wars of New England with the Eastern Indians; or, A Narrative of Their Continued Perfidy and Cruelty from the 10th of August 1703 to the Peace Renewed the 13th of July 1713, and from the 25th of July 1722 to their Submission 15 December 1725: A Realistic Account* appeared in 1726, published by S. Gerrish and D. Henchman in Boston.

The following excerpt is an account of Captain Lovewell's heroism at the Battle of Pigwacket. These events inspired Nathaniel Hawthorne's short story "Roger Malvin's Burial."

FROM
Penhallow's Indian Wars

Capt. Lovewell being still animated with an uncommon zeal of doing what service he could, made another attempt on Pigwacket with forty-four men; who in his going built a small fort near Ossipee, to to have recourse unto in case of danger, as also for the relief of any that might be sick or wounded; and having one of his men at this time sick, he left the doctor with eight men more to guard him: with the rest of his company, he proceeded in quest of the enemy, who on May the 8th, about ten in the morning, forty miles from said fort, near Saco pond, he saw an Indian on a point of land: upon which they immediately put off their blankets and knapsacks, and made towards him; concluding that the enemy were ahead and not in the rear. Yet they were not without some apprehensions of their being discovered two days before, and that the appearing of one Indian in so bold a manner, was on purpose to ensnare them. Wherefore, the Captain calling his men together, proposed whether it was best to engage them or not; who boldly replied, "that as they came out on purpose to meet the enemy, they would rather trust providence with their lives and die for their country, than return without seeing them." Upon this, they proceeded and mortally wounded the Indian, who notwithstanding returned the fire, and wounded Captain Lovewell in the belly. Upon which Mr. Wyman fired and killed him. But their dismantling themselves at this juncture, proved an unhappy snare; for the enemy taking their baggage, knew their strength by the number of their packs, where they lay in ambush till they returned, and made the first shot; which our men answered with much bravery, and advancing within twice the length of their guns, slew nine. The encounter was smart and desperate, and the victory seemed to be in our favor, till Capt. Lovewell with several more were slain and wounded, to the number of twelve: upon which our men were forced to retreat unto a pond, between which and the enemy was a ridge of ground that proved a barrier unto us. The engagement continued ten hours, but although the shouts of the enemy were at first loud and terrible, yet after some time they became sensibly low and weak, and their appearance to lessen. Now whether it was through want of ammunition, or on the account of those that were slain and wounded, that the enemy retreated, certain it is, they first drew off and left the ground. And although many of our men were much enfeebled by reason of their wounds, yet none of the enemy pursued them in their return. Their number was uncertain, but by the advice which we afterwards received, they were seventy in the whole, whereof forty were said to be killed upon the spot, eighteen more died of their wounds, and that twelve only returned. An unhappy instance at this time fell out respecting one of our men, who when the fight began, was so dreadfully terrified, that he ran away unto the fort, telling those who were there, that Capt. Lovell was killed with most of his men; which put them into so great a consternation, that they all drew off, leaving a bag of bread and pork behind, in case any of their company might return and be in distress.

The whole that we lost in the engagement were fifteen, besides those that were wounded. Eleazar Davis of Concord, was the last that got in, who first came to Berwick and then to Portsmouth, where he was carefully provided for, and had a skillful surgeon to attend him. The report he gave me was, that after Capt. Lovewell was killed, and Lieut. Farwell and Mr. Robbins wounded, that Ensign Wyman took upon him the command of the shattered company, who behaved himself with great prudence and courage, by animating the men and telling them, "that the day would yet be their own, if their spirits did not flag"; which enlivened them anew, and caused them to fire so briskly, that several discharged between twenty and thirty times apiece. He further added, that Lieut. Farwell, with Mr. Frye their chaplain, Josiah Jones, and himself, who were all wounded, marched towards the fort; but Jones steered another way, and after a long fatigue and hardship, got safe into Saco. Mr. Frye three days after, through the extremity of his wounds, began to faint and languish, and died. He was a very worthy and promising young gentleman, the bud of whose youth was but just opening into a flower.

Mr. Jacob Fullam, who was an officer and an only son, distinguished himself with much bravery. One of the first that was killed was by his right hand; and when ready to encounter a second, it is said that he and his adversary fell at the very instant by each other's shot. Mr. Farwell held out in his return till the eleventh day; during which time he had nothing to eat but water and a few roots which he chewed; and by this time the wounds through his body were so mortified, that the worms made a thorough passage. The same day, this Davis caught a fish which he broiled, and was greatly refreshed therewith; but the Lieutenant was so much spent, that he could not taste a bit. Davis being now alone, in a melancholy desolate state, still made toward the fort, and next day came to it, where he found some pork and bread, by which he was enabled to return as before mentioned.

Just as I had finished this account, I saw the historical memoirs of the ingenious Mr. Symmes, wherein I find two things remarkable, which I had no account of before: one was of Lieut. Robbins, who being sensible of his dying state, desired one of the company to charge his gun and leave it with him, being persuaded that the Indians, by the morning, would come and scalp him, but was desirous of killing one more before he died. The other was of Solomon Kies, who being wounded in three places, lost so much blood as disabled him to stand any longer; but in the heat of the battle, calling to Mr. Wyman said, he was a dead man; however, said that if it was possible, he would endeavor to creep into some obscure hole, rather than be insulted by these bloody Indians: but by a strange providence, as he was creeping away, he saw a canoe in the pond, which he rolled himself into, and by a favorable wind (without any assistance of his own) was driven so many miles on, that he got safe unto the fort.

In 1 Sam. 31: 11, 12, 13, it is recorded to the immortal honor of the men of Jabesh Gilead, that when some of their renowned heroes fell by the hand of the Philistines, that they prepared a decent burial for their bodies.

THE REVEREND JABEZ FITCH

Jabez Fitch (b. Norwich, Connecticut, 1672; d. 1746), the son of a minister, graduated from Harvard in 1694 and remained there as a tutor until 1703. Ordained in that year, he served as pastor at Ipswich, Massachusetts, where he signed a petition to the general court asking for redress for those who had unjustly suffered in the witchcraft persecution. Despite the reluctance of his congregation to release him, he became pastor of the Portsmouth congregation in 1725. He became active in the community during a period of turbulence; Indian attacks, throat distemper, and, later, the Great Awakening, were among the topics of his sermons, many of which were published. He signed the treaty with the eastern Indians in 1726. The Reverend George Whitefield, one of the leaders of the Great Awakening, preached in his pulpit during the 1740s.

Among Fitch's better known sermons is his *Work of the Lord in the Earthquake to Be Duely Regarded by us: A Discourse Showing What Regard We Ought to Have to the Awful Work of Divine Providence in the Earthquake, Which Happened the Night after the 29th of October, 1727.* This sermon, of the type known as a jeremiad, warns the congregation that the earthquake is a sign from the Lord that they must repent. It was published in Boston in 1727. The following excerpt illustrates Fitch's means of inspiring awe in his congregation.

FROM

The Work of the Lord in the Earthquake

Psalms 25:5. "Because they regard not the works of the Lord in the operation of His hands, He shall destroy them, and not build them up." In these words we may observe (1) that we ought to have a due regard to the works of the Lord, and the operation of His Hands. This is implied in the Words. (2) Those that regard not the words of the Lord are highly Criminal. 'Tis alleged as a heavy charge against Sinners, "they regard not the words of the Lord, nor the operation of his hands." (3) Hence they are exposed to the destroying Judgements of God. For God threatens such, that He will "destroy them, and not build them up."

Now the Words of our text may fitly be applied to the awful and mighty Work of the Lord in the Earthquake, that was so surprizing to the whole Country, and I purpose (by Divine assistance) so to consider the Words, and shall accordingly show *first*, what regard we ought to have to the Work of the Lord in the Earthquake; secondly, how criminal those are that regard it not; thirdly, hence they expose themselves to the destroying Judgements of God.

I. I shall shew what regard the Work of the Lord in the Earthquake calls for from us. Now this intends our Serious Consideration of this Work of the Lord, and our suitable compliance with the design of God therein.

1. Our regarding the Work of the Lord in the Earthquake, intends our serious consideration of this work of the Lord. Isa. 5:12: 'Tis said, "They regard not the work of the Lord, neither consider the operation of his hands." To regard the Work of the Lord is to consider the operation of his hands. And we may take notice of several things in the Earthquake, that call for our Serious consideration.

a. We should consider the Earthquake as a work of the Lord, and as an operation of his hands. Tho' an Earthquake has natural causes, yet these natural causes are under the government of Divine Providence, and as Fire or Lightning and Hail and Snow and Vapour and Stormy Wind are said to fulfill God's Word (Psalms 148:8), like is to be said of an Earthquake. God doth whatsoever He pleases in Heaven, Earth and Sea, and all Deep Places, even in the deep places or Bowels of the Earth, whereby He Shaketh the Earth when and where He pleaseth (Job 9 : 5). He Shaketh the Earth out of her Place, and the Pillars thereof tremble. We ought to take notice of the Hand of the Lord, in the Shaking of the Earth; and tho' there may be a sober Consideration of Second Causes, we should especially consider the First Cause, who worketh all things after the counsel of his own Will. 'Tis said in Isa. 29 : 6, "Thou shalt be visited of the Lord of Hosts with thunder and with *Earthquake*, and the great noise, with storm and tempest, and the Flame of Devouring Fire." When any place is visited with an Earthquake, the visitation is from the Lord of Hosts. This is necessary to be considered in the first place.

2. We should consider the Earthquake as a token of the Divine displeasure at our Sins. God does not willingly grieve nor afflict the Children of Men, but when he is provoked, and as it were, constrained by the sins of men: how an Earthquake even without those woful consequents that have befallen some Places, is yet a grievous affliction, in regard of the Terror and Consternation attending it; as thousands in this land can experimentally witness; and God hereby testifies his high displeasure against the Sins of a People, causing the Earth to groan under the heavy Load of their Iniquities, and to tremble at the horrible Wickedness of its Inhabitants. Hence when the Prophet would express God's great displeasure against the wickedness of Men, He saith, "Shall not the land tremble for this?" (Amos 8.8) And 'tis said in Psalms 18 : 7, "Then the Earth shook and trembled, the foundations of the Hills moved and were shaken because He was wroth." The shaking and trembling of the Earth is a token of Divine Wrath. "At his Wrath the Earth shall tremble" (Jer. 10 : 10). And the trembling of the Earth will be a witness against us for our Stupidity if we do not tremble before the Lord of the whole Earth, when He testifies his displeasure against our sins in so awful a manner.

3. We should consider the Earthquake as an instance of the mighty power of God, wherein He has shew'd how easily He could destroy us. Job 9 : 4−5: "God is mighty in strength—which removeth the mountains, which overturneth them in his anger,

which shaketh the Earth out of her place, and the Pillars thereof tremble." God has sometimes removed mountains by Earthquakes and Subterraneous Fires; yea such is the Power of God, that he could shake the Earth from its Center, if he so pleased, and he can shake any part of it, in what degree and extent he pleases. Of what a large extent was the late Earthquake? What a vast quantity of Earth was terribly shaken at one and the same instant, which shews the mighty irresistible Power of God, and how easily he could destroy us. How can such poor Worms of the Earth as we are, stand before him, who is so "mighty in Strength as to shake the Earth out of its place, and cause the Pillars thereof to tremble"? In Job 26:11, "the Pillars of Heaven are said to tremble and be astonished at his reproof." By the Pillars of Heaven are meant high Mountains, which seem at a distance to touch the Sky, as Pillars do the top of a Structure. By Earthquakes these are made to tremble, as Servants before a frowning and rebuking master. "Who then can stand in his sight when he is angry? If the Mountains quake at him—who can stand before his indignation? And who can abide in the fierceness of his anger?" (Nah. 1:5–6) "At his Wrath the Earth shall tremble, and the nations shall not be able [to] abide his indignation" (Jer. 10:10).

*　*　*

I proceed, to take notice of some particular Dutys, that should be performed by us.

1. Let us remember the Sabbath Day to keep it holy. It is a common observation that the Religion of a People depends upon their due observation of the Sabbath, and that it flourishes or decays according as the Sabbath is sanctified or neglected. Now the great design of God's awakening Providence, in the Earthquake, is to revive Religion in the Land, and if we would comply with this design, we must be strict in Observing the Sabbath, by a due attendance in the Publick Worship of God, and a careful Performance of the Private Exercises of Religion in our Families: For the Lord's Day which is consecrated for the immediate Service of God, should be entirely spent in it.

2. Let us Worship God in our Houses, and walk within our Houses with a perfect Heart. God having wonderfully preserved our Houses, in the time of the Earthquake, which else might have

been shaken down on our Heads, and we buried in the Ruins of them, now justly expects that all of us who are Heads of Families should serve him in our Houses by daily Reading some Portion of the Sacred Scriptures, of Prayer and Praise to the God of all our mercies, with the greatest solemnity.

This Family Worship is our most Reasonable Service, and necessary to keep alive the Sense of God and Religion in our Families: And God expects that we should (as far as we are capable) encourage Virtue, and discountenance Vice in our Families; setting a bright Example of the one, and most cautiously avoiding the giving any Example of the other.

3. Let us Remember the Dying Love of our Redeemer, unto whom we are indebted for our Temporal Salvation, from the terrible Earthquake; and for the Hopes of Eternal Salvation. Had not our Blessed Saviour interposed, the Earth might have opened its Mouth and swallowed us up; we might have gone down alive into our Graves; and on him we have our sole dependence to save us from being swallowed up in the Fiery Gulph for ever. Shall we not then express our gratitude to him, by Remembering him, who is the only Rock of our Salvation in the way that he has instituted, namely, by coming to his Table?

Let those therefore that have hitherto neglected it, make haste and not delay, to be prepared to come to this Holy Ordinance; and let all that come to it, be careful to come in a worthy manner.

4. Let all that pretend to Christianity, shew themselves full of Humanity and Kindness towards all men, that so they may be instrumental to win others over to the Love of Religion. God justly expects that all Christians should now be quickened in their desires and endeavours that his Kingdom may come in the World; and when Christians are eminently kind and obliging in their carriage towards all men, it is of great force to draw others to love and embrace Christianity, and so to advance the Kingdom of Christ in the World.

5. Let Civil Rulers whom God has appointed to be a terror to Evil Works, be careful to put the good and wholesome Laws that are made in Execution against the open Prophanation of the Lord's Day, against Prophane Swearing and Cursing, against

Drunkeness, Uncleanness, and all Immorality. This will be a means to avert Publick Judgments. Phineas by executing justice on Zimri Cozbi, turned away God's Wrath from the children of Israel. When the open Wickedness of any Person is duly testified against, by those that bear the Sword of Justice, it prevents Publick Guilt from being imputed to a Land.

To conclude, has God threatened in our Text, that he will destroy those who regard not his Works, nor the Operation of His Hands; how then shall they escape who regard not so awful a Work of Divine Providence as that of the Earthquake? Now, "Shall not destruction from God be a Terror to us," as Job speaks, Chap. 31:23? And shall not the "Terror of the Lord" in the late Earthquake, and the Terror of his Threatenings against obstinate, irreclaimable Sinners, persuade us all, to break off our Sins by timely Repentance? And shall not his Wonderful Mercy in sparing us, and waiting to be gracious to us, induce us to an ingenuous Repentance and amendment of Life?

God of his Infinite Mercy grant that this may be the happy Effect of his awful, and yet merciful dispensations toward us.

FINIS

MATTHEW PATTEN

Matthew Patten (b. Ireland, May 19, 1719; d. August 27, 1795) emigrated in 1728 to America and settled in New Hampshire in 1738. He later purchased a farm and became a respected citizen, representing the towns of Bedford and Merrimack in the general court in 1776 and 1777. He served on the governor's council in 1778.

From 1754 to 1788 he kept a diary in which he described everyday events, particularly as they related to farming. This diary was published for the town of Bedford in 1903 by the Rumford Press in Concord, New Hampshire.

The following excerpt begins April 18, 1776.

FROM

Matthew Patten's Diary

[APRIL]

18th WAS THE COLONY FAST

20th I got a bushell of flaxseed from Lieut Samuell Vose & he said he owed me two shillings lawful and I gave him /5 and lawful and one the two he owed me made the price of the flaxseed and he could not make the change to give me the other shilling and I got my pumps from David Moor that he sowed the soles on he was from home and I did not pay him for his wife did not know how much it was and I got 6 pounds of flax from widow Little to be settled in my acct against the Estate.

22^d I sowed three or four quarts of peas and the afternoon I went to the Raising of Zechariah Chandler's house

23^d I took the proof of Thos Wallaces Will at my house and Reed six shillings Lawful from jos Wallace

24th I attended the Probate at Amherst and my part of the fees was the proof of the 3 Wills that I took at Goffestown and at home and granting Admr to john Gregg came to 27/ and the Register gave me a shilling more than my part and I paid my expences at Smiths And I bot a pair of plated knee buckles and 5 £ and 10 ounces of lead at Means for which I paid 6/ 1½ my Expences at Heldreths I did not pay

25th I went with jona Esqr to Col Goffes and he Recd the Probate Books and Files which Atherton had sent there to prevent their comeing into our hands as I suppose And I bot ½ a pound of shot from Mrs Rand for which I paid her /3⅓ Lawful money and I lent Esqr Blanchard 2/8 in cash and I paid our ferriage

26th I spent the day with my Cousin William Patten in the house

27th the forenoon helping to mend fence the afternoon I writ a Deed from Stephen Tuttle to William Rogers & I took the acknowledgement both unpaid and I took the acknowledgement of the Deed I writ last Tuesday from Zechariah Chandler to Hugh Campell Chandler paid the writing the Deed and Campbell could not make change to pay the acknowledgement

28th Mrs French gave me a fresh shad that her husband brot from the mouth of Concord river and Mr Cotton Preached in Bedford being the first we have had since last faull

29th I went to Col Moors Mill and I took 1½ bushell of Rie and 1½ bushell of Indian corn and got it Ground & I had the Toal and I went to McGaws and I got 7 £ of Shugar and a quart of Rum and a Glas of Rum into tody for which I paid 49/2 Bay old Tenor and I went with Widow Little to her house to see if Cairns would give up his Deed that she might take her thirds but he would not and I went to McGregores & I paid him six Dollars for six bushell of salt and I brot home three bushell of it and the other three I have to get

30th was some Rain last night and this morning we shelled 2 bushels of corn and I got some hoop poles and shaved some hoops to put into some barrels

MAY FIRST

was a very high wind at N: W: and exceeding cold and I went to McGregores and got the last three bushell of the salt that I paid him for day before yesterday and I went to Major Kelleys with the Rest of the Committee of this town for hiring preaching To treat with the Comtee for Goffestown about the two towns joining to to hire a minister to preach for both towns but there was but one of Goffstown comtee met us and we agreed to meet Tuesday come Sevenight at john Bells on the affair and I had a bowle of tody at Major Kelleys and they could not make change to pay for it

2d I got such a Cold yesterday that I was a good deal out of case and I put a New handle in one of our axes

3d I continued out of case and and Widow Smith of Goffestown and job Dow and john Clogston and signed a Bond on her admr on her Husbands Estate and I writ at Bonds and letters of Guardianship for her children

4th I went to Thos Boies and Samuell Kennedys to Get Hony for Alex McMurphy and I got a snuff bottle almost full at Samll Kennedys and some in another at Thos Boiess and they would not take any pay for it and john Smith breeches maker brot the breeches I took to him the 15th of last April he charged me a Dollar and I paid him the money

6th I went to Col Moors Mill and took 1½ bushell of Rie and 1½ bushell of Indian corn and got it Ground and I had the Toal it Rained considerable

7th Shed made a shoe of my iron and set it on my horses off fore foot and I went with my brors Sam[ll] to see Col: john Stark who came from New York yesterday my Expences was 2/10

8th I went to Col: Moors Mill and took 1½ bushell of Rie and 1½ bushell of Indian corn and got it Ground and I had the Toal it Rained considerable

9th William White Returned the Inventory of his fathers Estate and him and the apprizers were sworn in common form he paid 4/ and Widow Smith returned the Inventory of her husbands Estate and she and the apprizers were Sworn in common form she paid 4/ and she paid me 15/ for guardianship for 4 of her children and 5/ to get two deeds put on Record for her of her late husbands Estate the Deeds she is to send to me

11th we began to fellow the old field by my brors

12th we plowed at the field by my brors

13th the boys plowed in the field by my brors and I went to Col Goffes and took the points of the Compass on the side of a peice of land and Meadow that Major john Moor was geting from Col: Goffe and I writ a Deed of it and another Deed from the Col: to the Major of a lott in Derry and a peice on the River adjoining said lott where the Major lives I am to settle with the Major for my pay

15th I took a bond of Esqr Little and one of Lieut Sawyer as Guardians for john Smiths children of Goffestown and gave each of them a letter of Guardianship for which Widow smith paid me 15/ in may last and the afternoon I took home a Reed to Fugards that Susanna had weaveing a peice of Fustin in

16th I set out for Exeter to attend as one of the Comtee of Safty for the Colony and arived there that night

17th 18th 19th & 20th I attended on the Exeter on the affair and set out for home the afternoon of the 20th and came to Chester and lodged at Capt Underhills I left the Gown and near 26 yards of Fustin at Mr Barkers to cloathiers to be dyed and dressed My Expences was 13/ 4⅕ I bot 4/ worth of things viz 2 £ of tobacca a rub ball for my breeches and a Declaration for Independance

21st I came home and went to writing letters to Crown Point for on my journey down I got an account of my johns Death of the Small Pox at Canada and when I came home my wife had got a letter from Bob which gave us a particular account it informed us that he was sick of them at Chambike and that they moved him to

Saint johns where they tarried but one night when they moved him to Isle of Noix where he died on the 20th day of june the Reason of moveing him was the Retreat of the army which was very preceipitate and he must either be moved or be left behind whether the moveing him hurt him he does not inform us but it seems probable to me that it did He was shot through his left arm at Bunker Hill fight and now was lead after suffering much fategue to the place where he now lyes in defending the just Rights of America to whose end he came in the prime of life by means of that wicked Tyranical Brute (Nea worse than Brute) of Great Britan he was 24 years and 31 days old

22^d I writ at letters to send to the army in all I writ four one Col: Stark one to Major Moor one to Master Eagan and one to Bob

23^d I went to Robert McGregores to meet the Post and Tarried all day but he did not come and I got a pound of Coffie from Moly McNeill and I had a bowle of tody for which I paid her 2/2 four pence was in her hands before of it

24th I went to McGregores and waited for the post but he did not come and I got two pounds of Coffie from Moly McNeal and ½ a bowle of tody and did not pay her for want of change

25th I went set out to go to McGregores to meet the post and Met McGregores boy comeing for me on the post horse and I gave the post four letters for the carriag of which I paid him 4/ and he agreed to bring my johns things except the Gun and accoutraments toward his doing it I paid him 8/ and I had half a bowle of tody and 2 quarts of Oats for the post horse for Which and the two £ of coffee and ½ bowle of tody I had yesterday I paid 4/1 and Patrick Murfey paid me 3/ and Zechariah Chandler looked the bill and one of them handed the bill to me and I put it up in my book without looking at it

26th In the morning I found that the bill I took of Patrick Murfey yesterday was a 3 £ instead of a 3/ and I took after him to overtake him to Rectify the affair but he was Gone that I could not I went as far as Col: Moors and got back at 12 o Clock

27th I mowed three small cocks in the lower end of the meadow and the afternoon I turned and Raked some the boys mowed in the pasture and between and the meadow and a little before night I went to McGaws and bot 7 £ of Shugar at 5/6 and a Quart of Rum at ⅓ and ½ a bowle of Tody at /4 which I paid him

28th I heard Mr Webster preached in Bedford

29th we Shelled 4½ bushell of corn and I took 1½ bushell of Rie and 2 bushell of corn to Lieut Littles mill but could not get it ground

30th I went to Littles mill and got the meal of the grain I took there yesterday and I mowed in the afternoon in the meadow at home

31st I went to Amherst to the Probate and we did as much business as we took 16/ for and I had done as much at home as I took 15/ for of which the Register gave me 13/ and I paid him what I borrowed off him at Exeter being 52/ and I paid him 5/ that he had paid for me for my commission as a judge of Probt I tarried at Mr Hildreths over night

AUGUST FIRST

Col: Kelley according to orders from the Comtee of Safty published INDEPENDANCE in Amherst one of Amherst Companies under Capt John Bradford and Lindborough company under Capt Clark attended under arms the Whole was conducted with decence and Decorum and the people departed in peace and good order The prinsaple Gentlemen of the County attended but not any who have been suspected of being unfriendly to the country attended my Expences was 5/ I bot two scycles from Means for which I paid 5/ and I came home in the Evening and Doctr Nichols and I swore Col: Goffe jacob Abbot Robert MacGregore and Moses Little as justices for this county and john Hogg and Zechariah Chandler as Coroners AND I Paid Ensn Ames 7-16-0 in cash and 2-10-6 I paid Doctr Gillman for him was the whole of his wages for his attending the General Court in their last Sessions Except two pence which he gave me whose wages I drawed by his order

3[d] We began to Reap our Rie

5th we Reaped with what we did the 3[d] to make 20 Stooks and got it into the barn and Shed made a new Shoe for my horse of my iron and Set it and set another for me and we got Acct by a letter from Master Egan to my bror that Bob was gone to Fort George to the Hospital Sick

6th My bror borrowed ten Dollars for me and lent me four himself and we had sixteen dollars and 2/6 among us in the famely and

I set out for Fort George to see Bob and the 14th I arrived at Fort George and found that Bob had got Better and was Returned to Tyconderoga

16th I arrived at Tyconderoga and tarried at Col Starke and his other field officers untill the 22d in the morning which time I set off for fort George and Bob with me on Furlow We were two days comeing over Lake George and September first we arived home I was 27 days from home my Expenses was about 21 Dollars as I was going Samuel Pattersons wife lent me four Dollars of her own accord and I paid them to her as I came home While I was gone our folks hired Robt Giffen 2½ days or 3 days and jonathan Griffen one day and my Brothers Betty and Margaret helped to Reap from Tuesday noon till Saterday night when they finished they tell me that we have 25 Stooks of Rie in all this year and Deacon Moors john Reaped two days and a half for us

SEPTEMBER FIRST

I arrived home from the Army and Bob with me

2d Widow jean Barnets two sons helped me at the little meadow

3d I delivered to Mrs Newman the things her husband sent her from the Lake (viz) a pair of Silver shoe and knee buckles a peice of Ban leather and Eight Dollars in money and I gave Lieut McCalleys wife ten Dollars in cash that her husband sent to her by me and I went to Robert McGregores and got my Shoes mended and I directed him concerning the process agt Col Wm Stark and he would take nothing for the mending my shoes and I charged him nothing for what I did for him

4th Widow jean Barnets two sons helped us at the little meadow and I went to the afternoon and we brot home a load and Mr Caldwell sent Dina and their boys and helped to Rake a while the afternoon

5th we finished mowing Except what was among the bushes in the Governor lott and we brot home two jag

6th we finished Rakeing what we mowed we have 55 cocks beside a jag we brot home

7th my brors john went with their Team and brot a load of hay from the little meadow and we brot one ourselves and it Rained and we did not go a second time we had Mr Caldwells Cart

9ᵗʰ my brors john brot a load of hay from the meadow and we brot two ourselves and I went and met the funeral of Daniel McKinney who Died last Saterday

10ᵗʰ jamey brot home the last of the hay from the meadow We have had nineteen jag this year from the little meadow and I sent 4 bushel of Rie to Colonel Moors mill and he Ground two bushell of it and I had the Toal and we Cut some of the Stalks

11ᵗʰ 12ᵗʰ 13ᵗʰ & 14ᵗʰ we cut Stalks and worked at the hay in the meadow at home

16ᵗʰ I set out to Exeter to attend the General Court and sit in it 4 days my attendance and travil come to ³⁵/₈ my Expences was 17/4½ I bot things to the amount of 17/7²/₅ and I Recd my pay for my attending in the Comitee of Safty being 43/8

21ˢᵗ arrived home in the Evening from Exeter

23ᵈ I took the proof of Neal Taggarts will it was offered by Capt Robert Wallace and his Brother Thomas who are Excurs The Witnesses were james Wallace their brother and his son Robert Capt Wallace paid me 7/ for the Regtrs and my fees and the afternoon I lay abed with a bad Cold and the ague in my flesh

24ᵗʰ lay abed all day with the same disorder I got a little sweat in the evening and I got some easyer

A DAY BOOK CONTINUED FROM SEPTEMBER 25TH
1776

25ᵗʰ I went to Amherst to the Probate Court my part of the fees with my part of the fees of the takeing the proof of Neal Taggarts Will the 23d came to 26/4 the Register gave me 27/ my Expences was 2/ and I got ½ a gallon of Rum from Lieut Hildreth and 1/5 I owed him before came to 3/4 which I paid him and I came home in the night

26ᵗʰ I assisted Col: Moor in paying the men he mustered at McGregores that was Raised in his Regiment for New York I got home about four o Clock in the morning he paid my expences and I got a shilling for taking the acknowledgement of a Deed for Moses Wells

REVOLUTION AND STATEHOOD
The Republic of Virtue

BEFORE THE American Revolution had ended, the spirit of an awakened consciousness—a perception of the state as a political and geographic entity—appeared in New Hampshire. In the best tradition of the Enlightenment, a formal historical study could capture the past and use it as an inspiration for the future. New Hampshiremen knew that without the practical and orderly study of nature, their physical environment would remain a chaos of unrelated phenomena. The best response to these challenges came from the Reverend Jeremy Belknap of Dover. His three-volume history of New Hampshire is a compendium of both historical and scientific information.

The history is organized chronologically by the administrations of the governors of New Hampshire from its founding through the immediate postrevolutionary years. Belknap carried his analysis beyond mere factual description and probed issues in terms of political theory. More than immediate causes, he understood the long-range developments that had helped precipitate the revolution. "In those cases where dissatisfaction appeared," the Dover cleric asserted, "it was chiefly owing to the nature of a royal government in which the aristocratic feature was prominent and the democratic too depressed. The people of New Hampshire, though increasing in numbers, had not the privilege of an equal representation."

Unaffected by the diffidence that would affect subsequent, more specialized scholars, Belknap confidently discussed anthropology, geology, geography, demography, and political science. He wrote about heights of mountains, ranges in temperature, and customs of the Indians as well as intricacies of state and local government. Belknap's history, in the tradition of Thomas Jefferson's *Notes on Virginia*, is a proud assertion of the accomplishment of a determined people and the richness of their new environment. It concludes with a description of the kind of local setting the author considers to be the perfect basis for his ideal society. It is the sort of place that would have won the approval of Jefferson: honest and industrious husbandmen clustered in small towns, animated by republican principles and fraternal charity.

This theme of political and religious purity was echoed by Belknap's fellow cleric, the Reverend Israel Evans, in his *Thanksgiving Sermon*. Preaching to the veterans of General John Sullivan's expedition against the Indians of the Five Nations, Evans exhorted them to retain the steadfastness that had brought them victory over the Iroquois and their British allies. In what must be a very early statement of manifest destiny, he declared that their triumph would help to open the interior of the continent and make possible the new nation's expansion to the Pacific. Republicanism and Christianity would be the civilizing forces, but citizens must be wary of corruption; although Britain bore responsibility for America's past woes, new threats to domestic peace would arise from within. Selfishness and venality could be as deadly to the public weal as George III had been, and the only safeguard against future discord would be the virtue of individual citizens. The bravery of the soldier in battle bore witness to his public virtue. "The wise politician," said Evans, "must know that moral and political virtue are the bulwarks of a republic and that a republic without virtue is an absurdity in politics. . . . You soldiers possess the greatest share of public virtue—would to God your private virtues were as great and conspicuous."

This nationalistic spirit also found expression in the first novels published by New Hampshire authors. Henry Sherburne's *The Oriental Philanthropist; or, The True Republican* (1800) and Tabitha Gilman Tenney's *Female Quixotism: Exhibited in the Romantic Opinions and Extravagant Adventures of Dorcasina Sheldon* (1801) expressed similar themes. Sherburne's rambling plot is the stitching that holds together a series of homilies delivered by his hero, Prince Nytan, on the subject of good citizenship and the responsibilities inherent in living in a republic. His purpose is as much to teach and admonish as to entertain. The book bridges two ages, its classical theme emerging in a context of exotic romanticism.

Tabitha Gilman Tenney's humorous novel ridicules romantic notions of love but also contains a moral that gives the story a didactic function. Tenney reminds her readers that the duties of the virtuous citizen must take priority over vain, personal goals. Dorcasina's acceptance of this truth comes only in the book's final chapter—thus allowing the reader ample time to enjoy her many follies.

The most significant military contribution made by New Hampshire to the successful outcome of the American Revolution came at the Battle of Bennington in 1779. General John Stark, who commanded New Hampshire troops, described the victory in a letter to General Horatio Gates.

JEREMY BELKNAP

Jeremy Belknap (b. Boston, 1744; d. 1798) entered Harvard before he was fifteen and graduated in 1762. After teaching school in Milton, Massachusetts and in Portsmouth and Greenland, New Hampshire, he was ordained and called to the Congregational Church in Dover, New Hampshire in 1766. There he began the twenty years of research that resulted in his three-volume *History of New Hampshire*. In 1787 he returned to Boston as pastor of the Federal Street Church. Remaining in Boston for the rest of his life, he practiced the "cultural nationalism" he preached in his writings by helping to create, in 1794, the Massachusetts Historical Society.

The first volume of his *History of New Hampshire* was published in Philadelphia by Aithen in 1784, the second by Thomas and Andrews in Boston in 1791, and the third and final volume by Belknap and Young in Boston in 1792.

In the following selections, Belknap describes the people and government of New Hampshire and its part in the American Revolution. Included is the state's declaration of independence.

Rev. Jeremy Belknap, date unknown, frontispiece from Vol. 1 of his *History of New Hampshire*, published in Dover, N.H., 1831. Courtesy of Massachusetts Historical Society.

FROM

The History of New Hampshire

CHAPTER XV.

Political Character, Genius, Manners, Employments and Diversions of the People.

It is much less difficult and dangerous to describe the character of the dead than the living; but in so great a variety as the inhabitants of a whole State, there cannot but be some general traits which all must allow to be just; and which, however disagreeable, if applied particularly, yet will not be disrelished by any, when delivered only in general terms. It is not my wish to exaggerate either the virtues or defects of my countrymen; but as an American, I have a right to speak the truth, concerning them, if my language be within the limits of decency.

The genius and character of a community are in some measure influenced by their government and political connexions. Before the Revolution, the people of the different parts of New-Hampshire, had but little connexion with each other. They might have been divided into three classes. Those of the old towns, and the emigrants from them. Those on the southern border, most of whom were emigrants from Massachusetts; and those on Connecticut river, who came chiefly from Connecticut.

Of the first class the people might be subdivided into those who, having been trained in subjection to Crown Officers, were expectants of favours from government, and ready to promote the views of the aristocracy, and those who, from principle or habit, were in opposition to those views. A long and intimate connexion with Massachusetts, both in peace and war, kept alive a democratic principle; which, though it met with the frowns of men in office, yet when excited to action, could not be controlled by their authority. The people of the second class were naturally attached to Massachusetts, whence they originated, and where they were connected in trade. Some towns had suffered by the interference of grants made by both governments and by controversies concerning the line, which gave birth to law suits, carried on with great acrimony and expense for many years. Those of the third class brought with them an affection and respect for the colony whence they emigrated, and where the democratic principle had always prevailed. They entertained an inferior idea of the people in the maritime parts of the State; whilst these in return looked with an envious eye on those emigrants to whom were *sold* the lands which had been promised to be *given* to them as a reward for the exertions and sufferings of their parents and themselves in defending the country against its enemies.

Another source of disunion was the unequal representation of the people in the General Assembly. As late as the year 1773, of one hundred and forty-seven towns, forty-six only were represented, by thirty-four members; and several towns were classed, two or three together, for the choice of one. The towns of Nottingham and Concord, though full of people, and of above forty years standing had not once been admitted to the privilege of representation; and this was the case with many other towns; which, though not of so long settlement, yet contained more inhabitants than some others, which had always enjoyed the privilege. No uniform system of representation had been adopted. None could be established by law, because it was claimed by the Governor as part of the royal prerogative to call Representatives from new towns; and this prerogative was exercised without any regard to the rights, the petitions, or the sentiments of the people.

Before the year 1771 the Province was not divided into counties; but every cause from even the most remote parts was brought to Portsmouth, where the courts were held and the public offices were filled by a few men, most of whom were either members of the Council, or devoted to the interest of the Governor, or personally related to him. In the administration of justice, frequent complaints were made of partiality. Parties were sometimes heard out of court, and the practice of *watering the jury* was familiarly known to those persons who had much business in the Law. The dernier resort was to a court of appeals, consisting of the Governor and Council; of whom seven were a quorum and four a majority. Here the final sentence was often passed by the same persons who had been concerned in the former decisions; unless the cause were of such value as to admit of an appeal to the King in Council. During the administration of the last Governor, some of these sources of disaffection were removed; but others remained, for an experiment, whether a cure could be effected, by a change of government.

The Revolution which called the democratic power into action, has repressed the aristocratic spirit. The honors and emoluments of office are more generally diffused; the people enjoy more equal privileges, and, after long dissention, are better united. Government is a *science*, and requires education and information, as well as judgment and prudence. Indeed there are some who have struggled through all the disadvantages arising from the want of early education, and by force of native genius and industry, have acquired those qualifications which have enabled them to render eminent service to the community; and there are others who have been favoured with early education, and have improved their opportunity to good purpose. Notwithstanding which, the deficiency of persons qualified for the various departments in Government has been much regretted, and by none more than by those few, who know how public business ought to be conducted. This deficiency is daily decreasing; the means of knowledge are extending; prejudices are wearing away; and the political character of the people is manifestly improving.

But however late the inhabitants of New-Hampshire may be, in political improvement; yet they have long possessed other valuable qualities which have rendered them an important branch of the American union. Firmness of nerve, patience in fatigue, intrepidity in danger and alertness in action, are to be numbered among their native and essential characteristics.

Men who are concerned in travelling, hunting, cutting timber, making roads and other employments in the forest, are inured to hardships. They frequently lie out in the woods several days or weeks together in all seasons of the year. A hut, composed of poles and bark, suffices them for shelter; and on the open side of it, a large fire secures them from the severity of the weather. Wrapt in a blanket with their feet next the fire, they pass the longest and coldest nights, and awake vigorous for labour the succeeding day. Their food, when thus employed, is salted pork or beef, with potatoes and bread of Indian corn; and their best drink is water mixed with ginger; though many of them are fond of distilled spirits, which, however, are less noxious in such a situation than at home. Those who begin a new settlement, live at first in a style not less simple. They erect a square building of poles, notched at the ends to keep them fast together. The crevices are plaistered with clay or the stiffest earth which can be had, mixed with moss or straw. The roof is either bark or split boards. The chimney a pile of stones; within which a fire is made on the ground, and a hole is left in the roof for the smoke to pass out. Another hole is made in the side of the house for a window, which is occasionally closed with a wooden shutter. In winter, a constant fire is kept, by night as well as by day; and in summer it is necessary to have a continual smoke on account of the musquetos and other insects with which the woods abound. The same defence is used for the cattle; smokes of leaves and brush are made in the pastures where they feed by day, and in the pens where they are folded by night. Ovens are built at a small distance from the houses, of the best stones which can be found, cemented and plaistered with clay or stiff earth. Many of these first essays in housekeeping are to be met with in the new plantations, which serve to lodge whole families, till their industry can furnish them with materials, for a more regular and comfortable house; and till their land is so well cleared as that a proper situation for it can be chosen. By these methods of living, the people are familiarised to hardships; their children are early used to coarse food and hard lodging; and to be without shoes in all seasons of the year is scarcely accounted a want. By such hard fare, and the labour which accompanies it, many young men have raised up families, and in a few years have acquired property sufficient to render themselves independent freeholders; and they feel all the pride and importance which arises from a consciousness of having well earned their estates.

They have also been accustomed to hear their parents relate the dangers and hardships, the scenes of blood and desolation through which they and their ancestors have passed; and they have an ambition to emulate their hardy virtues. New-Hampshire may therefore be considered as a nursery of stern heroism; producing men of firmness and valor; who can traverse mountains and deserts, encounter hardships, and face an enemy without terror. Their martial spirit needs only opportunity to draw it into action; and when properly trained to regular military duty, and commanded by officers in whom they can place confidence, they form a militia fully equal to the defence of their country.

They are also very dextrous in the use of edge tools, and in applying mechanical powers to the elevation and removal of heavy bodies. In the management of cattle they are excelled by none. Most of their labor is performed by the help of oxen; horses are seldom employed in the team; but are used chiefly in the saddle, or in the winter season, in sleighs.

Land being easily obtained, and labour of every kind being familiar, there is great encouragement to population. A good husbandman, with the savings of a few years, can purchase new land enough to give his elder sons a settlement, and assist them in clearing a lot and building a hut; after which they soon learn to support themselves. The homestead is generally given to the youngest son, who provides for his parents, when age or infirmity incapacitates them for labour. An unmarried man of thirty years old is rarely to be found in our country towns. The women are grandmothers at forty, and it is not uncommon for a mother and daughter to have each a child at the breast, at the same time; nor for a father, son and grandson to be at work together in the same field. Thus population and cultivation proceed together, and a vigorous race of inhabitants grows up, on a soil, which labor vies with nature to render productive.

Those persons, who attend chiefly to husbandry, are the most thriving and substantial. Those who make the getting of lumber their principal business, generally work hard for little profit. This kind of employment interferes too much with husbandry. The best season for sawing logs is the spring, when the rivers are high; this is also the time for ploughing and planting. He who works in the saw-mill at that time, must buy his bread and clothing, and the hay for his cattle, with his lumber; and he generally anticipates the profit of his labor. Long credit is a disadvantage to him; and the too free indulgence of spiritous liquor, to which this class of people are much addicted, hurts their health, their morals and their interest. They are always in debt, and frequently at law. Their families are ill provided with necessaries, and their children are without education or morals. When a man makes husbandry his principal employment, and attends to lumber only at seasons of leisure; and can afford to keep it for a market, and be his own factor, then it becomes profitable. The profits of the other generally goes into the hands of the trader, who supplies him with necessaries at an advanced price, and keeps him in a state of dependance.

Where husbandry is the employment of the men, domestic manufactures are carried on by the women. They spin and weave their own flax and wool; and their families are clad in cloth of their own making. The people of Londonderry, and the towns which are made up of emigrants from it, attend largely to the manufacture of linen cloth and thread, and make great quantities for sale. These people are industrious, frugal and hospitable. The men are sanguine and robust. The women are of lively dispositions, and the native white and red complexion of Ireland is not lost in New-Hampshire. "The town is much indebted to them for its wealth and consequence."

The people of New-Hampshire, in general, are industrious, and allow themselves very little time for diversion. One who indulges himself in idleness and play, is stigmatised according to his demerit. At military musters, at Judicial Courts, at the raising of houses, at the launching of ships, and at the ordination of Ministers, which are seasons of public concourse, the young people amuse themselves with dancing. In some towns they have a practice, at Christmas, of shooting geese for wagers; and on many other occasions, the diversion of firing at marks is very common, and has an excellent effect in forming young men to a dexterous use of arms. The time of gathering the Indian corn is always a season of festivity. The ears are gathered and brought home by day; and in the evening a company of neighbours join in husking them, and conclude their labour with a supper and a dance. In the capital towns, they have regular assemblies for dancing; and sometimes theatrical entertainments have been given by the young gentlemen and ladies. In Portsmouth, there is as much elegance and politeness of manners, as in any of the capital towns of New-England. It is often visited by strangers, who always meet with a friendly and hospitable reception.

The free indulgence of spiritous liquors has been, and is now, one of the greatest faults of many of the people of New-Hampshire; especially in the neighbourhood of the river Pascataqua, and its branches, and wherever the business of getting lumber forms the principal employment of the people. If the reader is curious to form an estimate of the quantity of distilled spirits consumed in the State, he may satisfy himself, partly by inspecting the Table of importation; partly by inquiring the number of barrels of rum manufactured at the only distil house in the State; partly by considering the quantity transported by land from the different seaports of Massachusetts; and partly by knowing *"the allowance"* which is usually given to labouring people in the neighbourhood of the river Pascataqua; and which is obstinately persisted in, notwithstanding the remonstrances and endeavours of some worthy characters to abolish it.

In travelling up the country it affords pleasure to observe the various articles of produce and manufacture coming to market; but in travelling down the country, it is equally disgustful to meet the same teams returning, loaded with casks of rum, along with fish, salt, and other necessary articles.

Before the Revolution it was customary to give drams at funerals, and in some towns to repeat the baneful dose two or three times. During the war, a scarcity of materials gave opportunity to put a check on this pernicious practice. It is now less common in most places, and in some it is wholly disused.

Among husbandmen, cyder is their common drink. Malt liquor is not so frequent as its wholesomeness deserves; and as the facility with which barley and hops may be raised, seems to require. In some of the new towns a liquor is made of spruce twigs, boiled in maple sap, which is extremely pleasant. But after all, there are no persons more robust and healthy, than those, whose only or principal drink is the simple element, with which nature has universally and bountifully supplied this happy land.

CHAPTER XVI.
Constitution, Laws, Revenue, and Militia.

The form of government, established in 1784, is founded on these two grand principles, viz. 1. That "the people have the sole and exclusive right of governing themselves, as a free, sovereign and independent State; exercising and enjoying every power, jurisdiction and right pertaining thereto, which is not, or may not hereafter be by them expressly delegated to the United States of

America, in Congress assembled." And 2. That "the three essential powers of government, the legislative, executive and judicial, ought to be kept as separate from, and independent of, each other, as the nature of a free government will admit; or as is consistent with that chain of connexion which binds the whole fabric."

The rights of the people are particularly declared in thirty-eight articles prefixed to the form of government. The objects of this declaration are personal freedom, the security of property, and the peace and order of human society. . . .

CHAPTER XXV.

War with Britain. Change of government. Temporary constitution. Independence. Military exertions. Stark's expedition. Employment of troops during the war.

When the controversy with Britain shewed symptoms of hostility, and the design of the ministry and parliament to provoke us to arms became apparent, the people of New-Hampshire began seriously to meditate the defence of their country. It was uncertain in what manner the scene would open; for this and other reasons no regular plan of operations could be formed. By the old militia law, every male inhabitant, from sixteen years old to sixty, was obliged to be provided with a musket and bayonet, knapsack, cartridge-box, one pound of powder, twenty bullets and twelve flints. Every town was obliged to keep in readiness one barrel of powder, two hundred pounds of lead and three hundred flints, for every sixty men; besides a quantity of arms and ammunition for the supply of such as were not able to provide themselves with the necessary articles. Even those persons who were exempted from appearing at the common military trainings, were obliged to keep the same arms and ammunition. In a time of peace, these requisitions were neglected, and the people in general were not completely furnished, nor the towns supplied according to law. The care which the governor had taken to appoint officers of militia and review the regiments, for some years before, had awakened their attention to the duties of the parade; which were performed with renewed ardor, after the provincial convention had recommended the learning of military exercises and manoeuvres. Voluntary associations were formed for this purpose, and the most experienced persons

1775

were chosen to command on these occasions. To prevent false rumors and confusion, the committees of inspection in each town were also committees of correspondence, by whom all intelligence concerning the motions of the British, were to be communicated; and proper persons were retained to carry expresses when there should be occasion.

In this state of anxiety and expectation; when an early spring had invited the husbandman to the labor of the field; General Gage thought it proper to open the drama of war. The alarm was Apr. 19 immediately communicated from town to town through the whole country, and volunteers flocked from all parts; till a body of ten thousand men assembled in the neighborhood of Boston, completely invested it on the land side, and cut off all communication with the country.

On the first alarm, about twelve hundred men marched from the nearest parts of New-Hampshire, to join their brethren, who had assembled in arms about Boston. Of these, some returned; others formed themselves into two regiments, under the authority of the Massachusetts convention. As soon as the provincial congress of May 17 New-Hampshire met, they voted to raise two thousand men, to be formed into three regiments; those which were already there to be accounted as two, and another to be enlisted immediately. These men engaged to serve till the last day of December, unless sooner discharged. The command of these regiments was given to the Colonels John Stark, James Reed and Enoch Poor. The two former were present in the memorable battle on the heights of Charles- June 17 town, being posted on the left wing, behind a fence; from which they sorely galled the British as they advanced to the attack, and cut them down by whole ranks at once. In their retreat, they lost several men, and among others, the brave Major Andrew Mc-Clary, who was killed by a cannon shot after he had passed the isthmus of Charlestown. On the alarm occasioned by this battle, the third regiment collected and marched to the camp; and with June 20 the other New-Hampshire troops, was posted on the left wing of the army at Winter-Hill, under the immediate command of Brigadier-General Sullivan, who with the other general officers, received his appointment from congress.

It had been a common sentiment among the British troops, that the Americans would not dare to fight with them. This battle effectually convinced them of their mistake. They found that fighting with us was a serious thing; and the loss which they sustained in this battle, evidently had an influence on their subsequent operations.

Whilst the Scarborough frigate remained in the harbor of Pascataqua, frequent bickerings happened between her crew and the inhabitants. Captain Berkeley seized all inward bound vessels, and sent them to Boston. He also prevented the boats belonging to the river from going out to catch fish. This conduct was conformable to the orders which he had received to execute the restraining act. In return, his boats were not permitted to fetch provisions from the town; and one of them was fired upon in the night, by some of the guards stationed on the shore. A compromise, at length, was made between him and the committee of the town; open boats were permitted to pass, to catch fish for the inhabitants; and his boats were allowed to take fresh provisions for the use of the ship. This agreement subsisted but a short time, and finally all intercourse was cut off.

Aug. 24

After the departure of the ship, the people went in volunteer parties, under the direction of Major Ezekiel Worthen, whom the convention appointed engineer, and built forts on the points of two islands, which form a narrow channel, about a mile below the town of Portsmouth. One of these was called Fort Washington, and the other Fort Sullivan. The cannon which had been saved from the old fort and battery were mounted here, and the town was thought to be secure from being surprised by ships of war.

The tenth of September was the last day of exportation fixed by the general congress. Most of the vessels which sailed out of the harbor were seized by the British cruisers, and carried into Boston. One was retaken by a privateer of Beverly, and carried into Cape-Anne.

Oct. 18

In the following month, several British armed vessels were sent to burn the town of Falmouth; which was in part effected, by throwing carcases and sending a party on shore, under cover of their guns. It was suspected that they had the same design against Portsmouth. General Washington despatched Brigadier-General Sullivan from the camp at Cambridge, with orders to take the command of the militia and defend the harbor of Pascataqua. On this occasion, the works on the islands were strengthened; a boom, constructed with masts and chains, was thrown across the Narrows, which was several times broken by the rapidity of the current, until it was impossible to secure the passage by such means; an old ship was scuttled and sunk in the northern channel of the river; a company of rifle-men, from the camp, was posted on Great-Island; and fire-rafts were constructed to burn the enemy's shipping. These preparations served to keep up the spirits of the people; but many families, not thinking themselves safe in Portsmouth, removed into the country, and there remained till the next spring.

A spirit of violent resentment was excited against all who were suspected of a disposition inimical to the American cause. Some persons were taken up on suspicion and imprisoned; some fled to Nova-Scotia, or to England, or joined the British army in Boston. Others were restricted to certain limits and their motions continually watched. The passions of jealousy, hatred and revenge were freely indulged, and the tongue of slander was under no restraint. Wise and good men secretly lamented these excesses; but no effectual remedy could be administered. All commissions under the former authority being annulled, the courts of justice were shut, and the sword of magistracy was sheathed. The provincial convention directed the general affairs of the war; and town committees had a discretionary, but undefined power to preserve domestic peace. Habits of decency, family government, and the good examples of influential persons, contributed more to maintain order than any other authority. The value of these secret bonds of society was now more than ever conspicuous.

In the convention which met at Exeter, in May, and continued sitting with but little interruption till November, one hundred and two towns were represented, by one hundred and thirty-three members. Their first care was to establish post offices; to appoint a committee of supplies for the army, and a committee of safety. To this last committee, the general instruction was similar to that, given by the Romans, to their dictators, "to take under consideration, all matters in which the welfare of the province, in the security of their rights, is concerned; and to take the utmost care, that the public sustain no damage." Particular instructions were given to them, from time to time, as occasion required. They were considered as the supreme executive; and during the recess of the convention, their orders and recommendations had the same effect as the acts and resolves of that whole body.

By an order of the convention, the former secretary, Theodore Atkinson, Esquire, delivered up the province records, to a committee which was sent to receive them, and Ebenezer Thompson, Esquire, was appointed in his place. The records of deeds, and of the probate office, for the county of Rockingham, were also removed to Exeter, as a place of greater safety than Portsmouth. The former treasurer, George Jaffrey, Esquire, was applied to for the public money in his hands, which, to the amount of one thousand five hundred and sixteen pounds, four shillings and eight pence, he delivered; and Nicholas Gilman, Esquire, was appointed treasurer in his room.

During this year, three emissions of paper bills were made. The first, of ten thousand and fifty pounds; the second, of ten thousand pounds; and the third, of twenty thousand pounds. For the amount of those sums, the treasurer gave his obligation in small notes, which passed for a time, as current money, equal in value to silver and gold. But as emissions were multiplied, as the redemption of the bills was put off to distant periods, and the bills themselves were counterfeited, it was impossible for them long to hold their value.

Beside the three regiments which made part of the American army at Cambridge, a company of artillery was raised to do duty at the forts. A company of rangers was posted on Connecticut river; and two companies more were appointed, to be ready to march wherever the committee of safety should direct. The whole militia was divided into twelve regiments; the field officers were appointed by the convention, and the inferior officers were chosen by the companies. Out of the militia were inlisted four regiments of minute-men, so called, because they were to be ready at a minute's warning. They were constantly trained to military duty, and when called to service were allowed the same pay as the regiments in the continental army. In the succeeding winter, when the Connecticut forces had withdrawn from the camp, because their time of service was expired, sixteen companies of the New-Hampshire militia, of sixty-one men each, supplied their place, till the British troops evacuated Boston.

The convention having been appointed for six months only; before the expiration of that time, applied to the general congress for their advice, respecting some mode of government for the future. In answer to which, the congress recommended to them, "to call a full and free representation of the people; that these representatives, if they should think it necessary, might establish such a form of government, as, in their judgment, would best conduce to the happiness of the people, and most effectually tend to secure peace and good order in the province, during the continuance of the dispute between Great-Britain and the colonies." On receiving this advice, the convention took into their consideration the mode in which a full and free representation should be called; and finally agreed, that each elector should possess a real estate of twenty pounds value, and every candidate for election, one of three hundred pounds; that every town, consisting of one hundred families, should send one representative; and one more for every hundred families; and that those towns which contained a less number than one hundred should be classed. They had before ordered a survey to be made of the number of people in the several counties; and having obtained it, they determined, that the number of representatives to the next convention, should bear the following proportion to the number of people, viz.

Nov. 3

Nov. 14

Rockingham	37,850 people	38 representatives.
Strafford	12,713	13
Hillsborough	16,447	17
Cheshire	11,089	15
Grafton	4,101	6
In all,	82,200	89

These representatives were to be empowered, by their constituents, to assume government as recommended by the general congress, and to continue for one whole year from the time of such assumption. The wages of the members were to be paid by the several towns, and their travelling expenses out of the public treasury. Having formed this plan, and sent copies of it to the several towns, the convention dissolved.

Nov. 16

This convention was composed chiefly of men who knew nothing of the theory of government, and had never before been concerned in public business. In the short term of six months, they acquired so much knowledge by experience, as to be convinced, that it was improper for a legislative assembly to consist of one house only. As soon as the new convention came together, they drew up a temporary form of government; and, agreeably to the trust reposed in them by their constituents, having assumed the name and authority of the house of representatives, they proceeded to choose twelve persons, to be a distinct branch of the legislature, by the name of a council. Of these, five were chosen from the county of Rockingham, two from Strafford, two from Hillsborough, two from Cheshire and one from Grafton. These were empowered to elect their own president, and any seven of them were to be a quorum. It was ordained, that no act or resolve should be valid, unless passed by both branches of the legislature; that all money bills should originate in the house of representatives; that neither house should adjourn for more than two days, without the consent of the other; that a secretary, and all other public officers of the colony, and of each county, for the current year, all general and field officers of militia, and all officers of the marching regiments, should be appointed by the two houses; all subordinate militia officers by their respective companies; that the present assembly should subsist one year, and if the dispute with Britain should continue longer, and the general congress should give no directions to the contrary, that precepts should be issued annually to the several towns on or before the first day of November, for the choice of counsellors and representatives, to be returned by the third Wednesday in December.

In this hasty production, there were some material defects. One was the want of an executive branch of government. To remedy this, the two houses, during their session, performed executive as well as legislative duty; and at every adjournment appointed a committee of safety, to sit in the recess, with the same powers, as had been given in the preceding year, by the convention. The number of this committee varied from six to sixteen. The president of the council was also president of this executive committee. The person chosen to fill this chair was an old, tried, faithful servant of the public, the honorable Meshech Weare, Esquire, who was also appointed chief justice of the superior court. So great was the confidence of the people in this gentleman, that they scrupled not to

Dec. 21
1776
Jan. 5

invest him, at the same time, with the highest offices, legislative, executive, and judicial; in which he was continued by annual elections during the whole war.

This constitution was prefaced with several reasons for adopting government, viz. That the British parliament had, by many grievous and oppressive acts, deprived us of our native rights; to enforce obedience to which acts, the ministry of that kingdom had sent a powerful fleet and army into this county, and had wantonly and cruelly abused their power, in destroying our lives and property; that the sudden and abrupt departure of our late governor, had left us destitute of legislation; that no judicial courts were open to punish offenders; and that the continental congress had recommended the adoption of a form of government. Upon these grounds, the convention made a declaration in these words, "We conceive ourselves *reduced to the necessity* of establishing a form of government, to continue during the present unhappy and unnatural contest with Great-Britain; protesting and declaring, that we never sought to throw off our dependence on Great-Britain; but felt ourselves happy under her protection, whilst we could enjoy our constitutional rights and privileges; and that we shall rejoice, if such a reconciliation between us and our parent state can be effected, as shall be approved by the continental congress, in whose prudence and wisdom we confide."

Such was the language, and such were the sentiments of the people at that time; and had the British government, on the removal of their troops from Boston, treated with us, in answer to our last petition, upon the principle of reconciliation; and restored us to the state in which we were before the stamp-act was made, they might, even then, have preserved their connexion with us. But in the course of a few months, we not only found our petitions disregarded, and our professions of attachment to the parent state treated as hypocritical; but their hostile intentions became so apparent, and our situation was so singular, that there could be no hope of safety for us, without dissolving our connexion with them, and assuming that equal rank among the powers of the earth for which nature had destined us, and to which the voice of reason and providence loudly called us. Britain had engaged foreign mercenaries to assist in subjugating us; justice required that we should in our turn court foreign aid; but this could not be had, whilst we acknowledged ourselves subjects of the crown against whose power we were struggling. The exertions which we had made, and the blood which we had shed, were deemed too great a price for reconciliation to a power which still claimed the right "to bind us in all cases whatsoever," and which held out to us unconditional submission, as the only terms on which we were to expect even a pardon. Subjection to a prince who had thrown us out of his protection; who had ruined our commerce, destroyed our cities and spilled our blood; and who would not govern us at all, without the interposition of a legislative body, in whose election we had no voice, was an idea too absurd to be any longer entertained. These sentiments, being set in their just light by various publications and addresses, had such force as to produce a total change of the public opinion. Independence became the general voice of the same people, who but a few months before had petitioned for reconciliation. When this could not be had, but on terms disgraceful to the cause which we had undertaken to support, we were driven to that as our only refuge. The minds of the people at large in most of the colonies being thus influenced, they called upon their delegates in congress to execute the act which should sever us from foreign dominion, and put us into a situation to govern ourselves.*

* On the 11th of June, 1776, a committee was chosen by the assembly of New-Hampshire "to make a draught of a declaration of the general assembly for the INDEPENDENCE of the united colonies on Great Britain, to be transmitted to our delegates in congress." The proceedings of the assembly and the declaration are here introduced, copied from the records in the secretary's office.

DECLARATION OF INDEPENDENCE,
BY NEW-HAMPSHIRE IN 1776.
In the House of Representatives, June 11, 1776.

Voted, That Samuel Cutts, Timothy Walker and John Dudley, Esquires, be a committee of this house to join a committee of the honorable board, to make a draft of a declaration of this general assembly for INDEPENDENCE of the united colonies, on Great-Britain.

June 15, 1776.

The committee of both houses, appointed to prepare a draft setting forth the sentiments and opinion of the council and assembly of this colony relative to the united colonies setting up an independent state,

It ought ever to be remembered, that the declaration of our independence was made, at a point of time, when no royal governor
had even the shadow of authority in any of the colonies; and when

July 4

make report as on file—which report being read and considered, *Voted
unanimously,* That the report of said committee be received and accepted, and that the draft by them brought in be sent to our delegates at
the continental congress forthwith as the sense of the house.

The draft made by the committee of both houses, relating to indepen-
dency, and voted as the sense of this house, is as follows, viz.

Whereas it now appears an undoubted fact, that notwithstanding all
the dutiful petitions and decent remonstrances from the American colonies, and the utmost exertions of their best friends in England on their
behalf, the British ministry, arbitrary and vindictive, are yet determined
to reduce by fire and sword our bleeding country, to their absolute obedience; and for this purpose, in addition to their own forces, have engaged great numbers of foreign mercenaries, who may now be on their
passage here, accompanied by a formidable fleet to ravish and plunder
the sea-coast; from all which we may reasonably expect the most dismal
scenes of distress the ensuing year, unless we exert ourselves by every
means and precaution possible; and whereas we of this colony of New-
Hampshire have the example of several of the most respectable of our
sister colonies before us for entering upon that most important step of
disunion from Great-Britain, and declaring ourselves FREE and INDE-
PENDENT of the crown thereof, being impelled thereto by the most violent and injurious treatment; and it appearing absolutely necessary in this
most critical juncture of our public affairs, that the honorable the continental congress, who have this important object under immediate consideration, should be also informed of our resolutions thereon without loss
of time, we do hereby declare that it is the opinion of this assembly that
our delegates at the continental congress should be instructed, and they
are hereby instructed, to join with the other colonies in declaring the
thirteen united colonies a free and independent state—solemnly pledging
our faith and honor, that we will on our parts support the measure with
our lives and fortunes—and that in consequence thereof they, the continental congress, on whose wisdom, fidelity and integrity we rely, may enter into and form such alliances as they may judge most conducive to the
present safety and future advantage of these American colonies: *Provided,* the regulation of our own internal police be under the direction of
our own assembly.

Entered according to the original,

Attest,   NOAH EMERY, *Clr. D. Reps.*]

no British troops had any footing on this continent. The country was then absolutely our own. A formidable force was indeed collected on our coasts, ready to invade us; and in the face of that armament, this decisive step was taken. The declaration was received with joy by the American army then assembled at New-York. Within fourteen days, it was published by beat of drum in all

July 18

the shire towns of New-Hampshire. It relieved us from a state of embarrassment. We then knew the ground on which we stood, and from that time, every thing assumed a new appearance. The jargon of distinctions between the limits of authority on the one side, and of liberty on the other, was done away. The single question was, whether we should be conquered provinces, or free and independent states. On this question, every person was able to form his own judgment; and it was of such magnitude that no man could be at a loss to stake his life on its decision.

It is amusing to recollect, at this distance of time, that one effect of independence was an aversion to every thing which bore the name and marks of royalty. Sign boards on which were painted the king's arms, or the crown and sceptre, or the portraits of any branches of the royal family, were pulled down or defaced. Pictures and escutcheons of the same kind in private houses were inverted or concealed. The names of streets, which had been called after a king or queen were altered; and the half-pence, which bore the name of George III, were either refused in payment, or degraded to farthings. These last have not yet recovered their value.

The new assembly began their administration by establishing judicial courts, on the same system as before, excepting that the court of appeals, which had long been esteemed a grievance, was abolished, and all appeals to Great-Britain were prohibited. Appeals from the probate courts, which formerly came before the governor and council, were transferred to the superior court, whose judgment was now made final. Encouragement was given to fit out armed vessels, and a maritime court was established for the trial of captures by sea. A law was made to punish the counterfeiting of the paper bills of this and of the United States; and to make them "a tender for any money due by deed or simple contract." After the declaration of independence the style of *Colony* was changed for that of the STATE of New-Hampshire. A new law was enacted to regulate the militia. More paper bills were issued to pay the expenses of the war; and provision was made for drawing in some of the bills by taxes. Doubts had arisen, whether the former laws were in force; a special act was therefore passed, reviving and re-enacting all the laws which were in force, at the time when government was assumed; as far as they were not repugnant to the new form, or to the independence of the colonies, or not actually repealed.

The congress having ordered several frigates to be built in different places; one of thirty-two guns, called the Raleigh, was launched at Portsmouth, in sixty days from the time when her keel was laid; but for want of guns and ammunition, and other necessaries, it was a long time before she was completely fitted for the sea. The making of salt-petre was encouraged by a bounty; and many trials were made before it was produced in purity. Powder mills were erected, and the manufacture of gunpowder was, after some time, established; but notwithstanding all our exertions, foreign supplies were necessary.

For the service of this year, two thousand men were raised, and formed into three regiments, under the same commanders as in the former year. Three hundred men were posted at the forts in the harbor. Supplies of fire arms and ammunition were sent to the western parts of the state, and a regiment was raised in that quarter, under the command of Colonel Timothy Bedel, to be ready to march into Canada.

The three regiments went with the army under General Washington to New-York; and thence were ordered up the Hudson, and down the lakes into Canada, under the immediate command of Brigadier-General Sullivan. The design of this movement was to succor and reinforce the army, which had been sent, the preceding year, against Quebec; and which was now retreating before a superior force, which had arrived from Britain, as early as the navigation of the St. Lawrence was opened. Our troops having met the retreating army at the mouth of the Sorel, threw up some slight works round their camp. General Thomas, who had commanded the army after the fall of the brave Montgomery, was dead of the small-pox. Arnold was engaged in stripping the merchants of Montreal, under pretence of supplying the army; and Thompson was taken prisoner in an unsuccessful attack on the village of Trois Rivieres. The command therefore devolved on Sullivan, who, find-

May 21

ing a retreat necessary, conducted it with great prudence. At this time, the American troops, and in particular the regiments of New-Hampshire, had taken the infection of the small-pox. The sick were placed in batteaux, and with the cannon and stores, were drawn against the rapid current, by the strength of men on shore, or wading in the water; and so close was the pursuit of the enemy, that they could scarcely find time to kindle a fire to dress their victuals, or dry their clothes. At St. John's, the pursuit ceased. On the

July 1 arrival of our army at Ticonderoga, Sullivan, being superseded by Gates, returned to the main army at New-York. The troops in the northern department being reinforced by the militia of the neighboring states, fortified the posts of Ticonderoga and Mount Independence. Besides the small-pox, a dysentery and putrid fever raged among them; and it was computed, that of the New-Hampshire regiments, nearly one third part died this year by sickness.

When the danger of an attack on Ticonderoga for that season, was passed, the remaining part of the New-Hampshire troops marched, by the way of the Minisinks, into Pennsylvania. There they joined General Washington, and assisted in the glorious capture of the Hessians at Trenton, and afterward in the battle of Princeton. Though worn down with fatigue, and almost destitute of clothing, in that inclement season (December and January), they continued in the service six weeks after the term of their enlistment had expired; and two regiments of the militia which were sent to reinforce the army remained till March.

By this time, the inconvenience of maintaining an army, by annual enlistments and temporary levies, was severely felt, and gener-

1777 ally reprobated; and the congress, though slow in listening to remonstrances on this head, were obliged to adopt a more permanent establishment. In recruiting the army for the next year, the officers were appointed by congress, during the war; and the men enlisted either for that term, or for three years. The commanders of the three regiments of New-Hampshire, were the Colonels Joseph Cilley, Nathan Hale and Alexander Scammell. These regiments were supplied with new French arms; and their rendezvous was at Ticonderoga, under the immediate command of Brigadier-

July 6 General Poor. There they remained, till the approach of the British army under General Burgoyne, rendered it eligible to abandon that post. On the retreat, Colonel Hale's battalion was ordered to cover the rear of the invalids, by which means, he was seven miles behind the main body. The next morning, he was attacked, by an advanced party of the enemy at Hubberton. In this engagement, Major Titcomb of the New-Hampshire troops, was wounded. Colonel Hale, Captains Robertson, Carr, and Norris, Adjutant Elliot, and two other officers were taken prisoners, with about one hundred men. The main body of the army continued their retreat to Saratoga. On their way, they had a skirmish with the enemy at Fort Anne, in which Captain Weare, son of the president, was mortally wounded, and died at Albany.

Immediately after the evacuation of Ticonderoga, the committee of the New-Hampshire grants (who had now formed themselves into a new state) wrote in the most pressing terms, to the committee of safety at Exeter for assistance, and said that if none should be afforded to them, they should be obliged to retreat to the New-England states for safety. When the news of this affair reached New-Hampshire, the assembly had finished their spring session and returned home. A summons from the committee brought them together again; and in a short session of three days only, they took the most effectual and decisive steps for the defence of the country. They formed the whole militia of the state into two brigades; of the first, they gave the command to William Whipple, and of the second, to John Stark. They ordered one fourth part of Stark's brigade, and one fourth of three regiments of the other brigade, to march immediately under his command, "to stop the progress of the enemy on our western frontiers." They ordered the militia officers, to take away arms, from all persons, who scrupled or refused to assist, in defending the country; and appointed a day of fasting and prayer, which was observed with great solemnity.

The appointment of Stark, to this command, with the same pay as a brigadier in the continental service, was peculiarly grateful to the people, as well as to himself. In an arrangement of general officers, in the preceding year, Poor, a junior officer, had been promoted, whilst he was neglected. He had written on this subject to congress, and his letters were laid on the table. He therefore quitted the army, and retired to his own state. He was now by the unanimous voice of his fellow citizens, invested with a separate command, and received orders to "repair to Charlestown on Connecticut river; there to consult with a committee of New-Hamp-

July 8

July 17

shire grants, respecting his future operations and the supply of his men with provisions; to take the command of the militia and march into the grants to act in conjunction with the troops of that new state, or any other of the states, or of the United States, or separately, as it should appear expedient to him; for the protection of the people and the annoyance of the enemy."

In a few days, he proceeded to Charlestown, and as fast as his men arrived, he sent them forward, to join the forces of the new state, under Colonel Warner, who had taken post at Manchester, twenty miles northward of Bennington. Here, Stark joined him, and met with General Lincoln, who had been sent from Stillwater, by General Schuyler, commander of the northern department, to conduct the militia to the west side of Hudson's river. Stark informed him of his orders, and of the danger which the inhabitants of the grants apprehended from the enemy, and from their disaffected neighbors; that he had consulted with the committee, and that it was the determination of the people, in case he should join the continental army and leave them exposed, that they would retire to the east of Connecticut river; in which case New-Hampshire would be a frontier. He therefore determined to remain on the flank of the enemy, and to watch their motions. For this purpose, he collected his force at Bennington, and left Warner with his Aug. 9 regiment at Manchester. A report of this determination was transmitted to congress, and the orders on which it was founded were by them disapproved; but the propriety of it was evinced by the subsequent facts.

General Burgoyne, with the main body of the British army, lay at Fort Edward. Thence he detached Lieutenant Colonel Baum, with about fifteen hundred of his German troops, and one hundred Indians, to pervade the grants as far as Connecticut river, with a view to collect horses to mount the dragoons, and cattle, both for labor and provisions; and to return to the army with his booty. He was to persuade the people among whom he should pass, that his detachment was the advanced guard of the British army, which was marching to Boston. He was accompanied by Colonel Skeene, who was well acquainted with the country; and he was ordered to secure his camp by night.

The Indians who preceded this detachment, being discovered about twelve miles from Bennington; Stark detached Colonel

Gregg, with two hundred men, to stop their march. In the evening of the same day, he was informed that a body of regular troops, with a train of artillery, was in full march for Bennington. The next morning, he marched with his whole brigade, and some of the militia of the grants, to support Gregg, who found himself unable to withstand the superior number of the enemy. Having proceeded about four miles, he met Gregg retreating, and the main body of the enemy pursuing, within half a mile of his rear. When they discovered Stark's column, they halted in an advantageous position; and he drew up his men on an eminence in open view; but could not bring them to an engagement. He then marched back, about a mile, and encamped; leaving a few men to skirmish with them; who killed thirty of the enemy and two of the Indian chiefs. The next day was rainy. Stark kept his position, and sent out parties to harass the enemy. Many of the Indians took this opportunity to desert; because, as they said, "the woods were full of yankees."

On the following morning, Stark was joined by a company of militia from the grants, and another from the country of Berkshire, in Massachusetts. His whole force amounted to about sixteen hundred. He sent Colonel Nichols, with two hundred and fifty men, to the rear of the enemy's left wing; and Colonel Hendrick, with three hundred, to the rear of their right. He placed three hundred to oppose their front and draw their attention. Then sending Colonels Hubbard and Stickney, with two hundred to attack the right wing, and one hundred more to reinforce Nichols in the rear of their left, the attack began in that quarter precisely at three of the clock in the afternoon. It was immediately seconded by the other detachments; and at the same time, Stark himself advanced with the main body. The engagement lasted two hours; at the end of which he forced their breastworks, took two pieces of brass cannon and a number of prisoners; the rest retreated.

Just at this instant, he received intelligence that another body of the enemy was within two miles of him. This was a reinforcement for which Baum had sent, when he first knew the force which he was to oppose. It was commanded by Colonel Breyman. Happily Warner's regiment from Manchester came up with them and stopped them. Stark rallied his men and renewed the action; it was

Aug. 14

Aug. 15

Aug. 16

warm and desperate; he used, with success, the cannon which he had taken; and at sunset obliged the enemy to retreat. He pursued them till night, and then halted, to prevent his own men from killing each other, in the dark. He took from the enemy two other pieces of cannon, with all their baggage, wagons and horses. Two hundred and twenty-six men were found dead on the field. Their commander, Baum, was taken and died of his wounds; beside whom, thirty-three officers, and above seven hundred privates, were made prisoners. Of Stark's brigade, four officers and ten privates were killed and forty-two were wounded.

In the account of this battle, which Stark sent to the committee of New-Hampshire, he said, "Our people behaved with the greatest spirit and bravery imaginable. Had every man been an Alexander, or a Charles of Sweden, they could not have behaved better." He was sensible of the advantage of keeping on the flank of the enemy's main body; and therefore sent for one thousand men to replace those whose time had expired; but intimated to the committee that he himself should return with the brigade. They cordially thanked him for "the very essential service which he had done to the country," but earnestly pressed him to continue in the command; and sent him a reinforcement, "assuring the men that they were to serve under General Stark." This argument prevailed with the men to march, and with Stark to remain.

Aug. 18

The prisoners taken in this battle were sent to Boston. The trophies were divided between New-Hampshire and Massachusetts. But congress heard of this victory by accident. Having waited some time in expectation of letters, and none arriving; inquiry was made why Stark had not written to congress? He answered, that his correspondence with them was closed, as they had not attended to his last letters. They took the hint; and though they had but a few days before resolved, that the instructions which he had received were destructive of military subordination, and prejudicial to the common cause; yet they presented their thanks to him, and to the officers and troops under his command, and promoted him to the rank of a brigadier-general, in the army of the United States.

This victory gave a severe check to the hopes of the enemy, and raised the spirits of the people after long depression. It wholly changed the face of affairs in the northern department. Instead of disappointment and retreat, and the loss of men by hard labor and sickness; we now were convinced, not only that our militia could fight without being covered by intrenchments; but that they were able, even without artillery, to cope with regular troops in their intrenchments. The success thus gained was regarded as a good omen of farther advantages. "Let us get them into the woods," was the language of the whole country. Burgoyne was daily putting his army into a more hazardous situation; and we determined that no exertion should be wanting on our part to complete the ruin of his boasted enterprise. The northern army was reinforced by the militia of all the neighboring states. Brigadier Whipple marched with a great part of his brigade; besides which, volunteers in abundance from every part of New-Hampshire flew to the northern army now commanded by General Gates. Two desperate battles were fought, the one at Stillwater, and the other at Saratoga; in both of which, the troops of New Hampshire had a large share of the honor due to the American army. In the former action, two lieutenant-colonels, Adams and Colburn, and Lieutenant Thomas, were slain in the field; and several other brave officers were wounded, one of whom, Captain Bell, died in the hospital. In the latter, Lieutenant-Colonel Conner and Lieutenant McClary were killed, with a great number of their men; and Colonel Scammell was wounded. The consequence of these battles was the surrender of Burgoyne's army. This grand object being attained, the New-Hampshire regiments performed a march of forty miles, and forded the Mohawk river, below the falls, in the space of fourteen hours. The design of this rapid movement was to check the progress of a detachment, commanded by the British general, Clinton; who threatened Albany with the same destruction which he had spread in the country below; but on hearing the fate of Burgoyne, he returned quietly to New-York. The regiments then marched into Pennsylvania and passed the winter in huts at Valley-Forge. Besides those officers slain at the northward, we sustained a loss in the death of Major Edward Sherburne, aide de camp to General Sullivan, who was killed in a bold, but unsuccessful, action at Germantown.

After the capture of Burgoyne's army, all danger of invasion from Canada ceased; and the theatre of the war was removed to the southward. The troops of New-Hampshire, being formed into a distinct brigade, partook of all the services and sufferings, to which their brethren were exposed. In the battle of Monmouth, a part of them were closely engaged, under the conduct of Colonel

1778 Cilley and Lieutenant-Colonel Dearborn; and behaved with such bravery as to merit the particular approbation of their illustrious general. They continued with the main body, all that campaign, and were hutted, in the following winter, at Reading.

In the summer of 1778, when a French fleet appeared on our coast, to aid us in the contest with Britain; an invasion of Rhode-Island, then possessed by the British, was projected, and General Sullivan had the command. Detachments of militia and volunteers, from Massachusetts and New-Hampshire, formed a part of his troops. But a violent storm having prevented the co-operation of the French fleet and driven them to sea; the army, after a few skirmishes, was under the disagreeable necessity of quitting the island; and the retreat was conducted by Sullivan with the greatest caution and prudence.

When an expedition into the Indian country was determined on, General Sullivan was appointed to the command, and the New-

1779 Hampshire brigade made a part of his force. His route was up the river Susquehanna into the country of the Senecas; a tract imperfectly known, and into which no troops had ever penetrated. The order of his march was planned with great judgment, and executed with much regularity and perseverance. In several engagements with the savages, the troops of New-Hampshire behaved with their usual intrepidity. Captain Cloyes and Lieutenant McAulay were killed, and Major Titcomb was again badly wounded. The provisions of the army falling short, before the object of the expedition was completed, the troops generously agreed to subsist on such as could be found in the Indian country. After their return, they rejoined the main army, and passed a third winter in huts, at Newtown in Connecticut. In the latter end of this year, Sullivan resigned his command and retired.

In the following year, the New-Hampshire regiments did duty at

1780 the important post of West-Point, and afterward marched into New-Jersey, where General Poor died. Three regiments of militia were employed in the service of this year. The fourth winter was passed in a hutted cantonment, at a place called Soldier's Fortune, near Hudson's river. In the close of this year, the three regiments were reduced to two, which were commanded by the colonels, Scammell and George Reid.

The next year, a part of them remained in the state of New-York, and another part marched to Virginia, and were present at the capture of the second British army, under Earl Cornwallis. Here the brave and active Colonel Scammell was killed. In the winter, the first regiment, commanded by Lieutenant-Colonel Dearborn, was quartered at Saratoga, and the second on Mohawk river; in which places they were stationed, till the close of the following year; when the approach of peace relaxed the operations of war. In a few months, the negotiations were so far advanced, that a treaty was made; and the *same* royal lips, which from the throne had pronounced us "revolted subjects," now acknowledged us as "FREE AND INDEPENDENT STATES."

1781

THE REVEREND ISRAEL EVANS

The Reverend Israel Evans (b. Pennsylvania, 1747; d. March 9, 1807) graduated from Princeton, studied for the ministry, and after ordination became an army chaplain in 1776. Evans was assigned to the brigade of General Enoch Poor of New Hampshire.

In retaliation against Indian raids on the northern frontier, an expedition was mounted in 1779 against the Iroquois under command of General John Sullivan of Durham, New Hampshire. Evans accompanied this expedition as chaplain. To commemorate the American victory, Sullivan ordered Thanksgiving services to be held in Easton, Pennsylvania on the fifteenth and sixteenth of October 1779. This was the occasion for the sermon from which the following excerpt is taken. In it, Evans emphasizes the virtues necessary for citizens of a republic and stresses the future possibilities for a victorious America.

After the revolution Evans settled in Concord, New Hampshire and became pastor of the Congregational church there in 1780. He spent the rest of his life in Concord.

The following selection is from *A Discourse Delivered at Easton, on the 17th of October, 1779, to the Officers and Soldiers of the Western Army, after Their Return from an Expedition against the Five Nations of Hostile Indians*, which was originally printed by T. Bradford in Philadelphia in 1779. Listed as no. 16266 in the Charles Evans Index.

FROM

A Discourse Delivered at Easton, on the 17th of October, 1779

And here I find it much more easy to conceive of the many instances wherein this army has been girded with strength, to perform the hard duties of a campaign, than to give them a just and particular relation. However let me attempt this duty, that by recollecting the goodness and providential care of Heaven, our gratitude may be excited, and we may with the warmth and sincerity of our hearts offer that tribute of thanksgiving and praise, which is so justly due to our divine Benefactor and powerful Guardian, who has girded us with strength unto the battle, and made us superior to all the unavoidable toils, hardships, and dangers of a wilderness unknown and unexplored, unless by the wild beasts and the savages.

When the tyrant of Britain, not contented to expend his malignant wrath on our sea coasts, sent his emissaries to raise the savages of the wilderness to war, and to provoke them to break their faith with the United States of America; then our defenceless frontiers became the seat of savage fury, and hundreds of our countrymen bled, and hundreds of them suffered more than the tender ear can hear related, or the compassionate heart can endure. Then the expectations of our enemies were high and joyful, that half our country would fall by the hands of tories and savages, or be forced to flee from their habitations with scarcely a mouthful of bread to eat, or a garment to cover them. And indeed the prospect was full of horror to every compassionate friend of his country and mankind, and called, mercifully called, for the aid of an army, to save so large a part of the United States.

* * *

. . . But ah, my sons and citizens of the United States, whither fled that patriotic zeal which first warmed your disinterested breasts? Whither that public spirit, which made you willing to sacrifice not only your fortune but also your lives in defense of liberty? Whither is fled that happy union of sentiment in the great service of your country? And whither is fled that honorable love and practice of virtue, and that divine and generous religion, which cherishes the spirit of liberty and elevates it to an immortal height? She paused and wept, nor gained an answer: And then in a suppliant posture again renewed her address: I entreat you to re-kindle that public and generous zeal which first blazed forth in de-fence of that liberty which you have now too long slighted. I be-seech you to banish from your breasts that lust of gain, which is the baneful murderer of a generous and a public spirit. I entreat you to silence the demons of discord and animosity, and to banish them from the States of America, and let them find no place to set their feet, but in the assemblies of the enemies of this country. I conjure you by the spirit of heaven-born liberty, that you invite her to your bosom, and kindle your love for her to a never dying flame.

* * *

But whither have I been transported, from paying that particu-lar attention to you, my friends and fellow soldiers, which you are justly entitled to, especially on this day of public gratitude and praise? I return to you, who possess the greatest share of public virtue; would to God, your private virtues were as great and as conspicuous! I have taken notice of your honorable conduct, as far as my time and a discourse of this nature would admit, without descending too minutely into particulars. The design of this was, not only to remind you, that to overcome difficulties and dangers, is an evidence of fortitude and perseverance and is victory; and that we may be encouraged to encounter any future dangers and toils: For dangers and toils being now familiar to you, they cannot terrify you; knowing that you have been superior to them, you may well expect, that with like strength and assistance you shall again be conquerors.

* * *

The pleasure that we shall meet with, when we once more see the illustrious chief of the armies of the United States, and obtain his approbation, for he knows your worth, will make you forget all your past dangers and toils, and make you pant for an oppor-tunity to distinguish yourselves in his presence. And as it is more than probable that you will have the honor of serving in two expe-ditions in one campaign; let me entreat you, to maintain the char-acter of patient, obedient, persevering and brave soldiers. Think of the dignity, if it shall please God to succeed the united arms, of striking one capital blow, which shall astonish the world, and finish the American war. If I could think it necessary I should remind you, that as your reputation is higher than that of many others, you ought not to content yourselves with the same degree of merit and renown, but strive to maintain and perpetuate your present superiority and glory. May that Almighty Being, who has hitherto so carefully preserved you, still continue his goodness unto you, and keep you as in the hollow of His hand! And may such a sense of gratitude for past mercies, be impressed upon our hearts, that we may be constrained to forsake every sin, and fear nothing so much as to offend Him, and regard nothing so much as His divine approbation!

Before I close this discourse, suffer me to remind you of other happy consequences of your success. You have opened a passage into the wilderness, where the Gospel has never yet been received. That extensive region, which was never before traversed, except by wild beasts, and men as wild as they shall yet have the Gospel preached in it. Churches shall rise there, and flourish, when perhaps the truths of the Gospel shall be neglected on these eastern shores. For it cannot be supposed that so large a part of this continent shall forever continue the haunt of savages, and the dreary abodes of superstition and idolatry. As the Gospel, or Sun of Righteousness has only glanced on the shores of this western world, and it is predicted of it, that it shall be universally propogated, it will, probably like the Sun, travel to the western extremities of this continent. And when men from other nations, prompted by liberty and a love of the pure Gospel of truth, shall cross the ocean to this extensive empire, they will here find a safe asylum from persecution and tyranny. How honorable then must your employment appear, when considered in all these points of view. How happy to have been the instruments in the hand of God, for accomplishing so great a revolution, and extending the kingdom of His Son so far. Liberty and religion shall have their wide dominion from the Atlantic through the great continent to the western ocean. May you all, not only be the honorable instruments of promoting the kingdom of our Lord Jesus Christ, but may you more especially be the partakers of all the benefits and happiness, with which Christ will crown his faithful and dutiful subjects!

GENERAL JOHN STARK

John Stark (b. Londonderry, New Hampshire, 1728; d. 1822) was born eight years after his Scotch-Irish father emigrated from Ireland. He was a captain with Rogers' Rangers during the French and Indian War. Two years after leading the New Hampshire contingent in the Battle of Bunker Hill (1775), he resigned his commission because of his dissatisfaction with military politics. As commander of the New Hampshire militia he achieved an important victory at the Battle of Bennington (1777). He retired as a major-general of the Continental Army in 1783 and became a gentleman farmer in Londonderry.

The following letter to General Horatio Gates is Stark's account of the Battle of Bennington, New Hampshire's great hour of military glory in the American Revolution. The version below was published by McFarland and Jenks in Concord, New Hampshire in 1860.

Major General John Stark, 1876, from the city of Manchester Centennial Portrait by U. D. Tenney. Courtesy of Manchester Historical Association, Manchester, New Hampshire.

"An Account of the Battle of Bennington"

Bennington, August 23, 1777.

Dear General—Yours of the 19th was received with pleasure, and I should have answered it sooner, but I have been very unwell since. General Lincoln has written you upon the subject, with whom I most cordially concur in opinion.

I will now give you a short account of the action near this place. On the 13th of August, being informed that a party of Indians were at Cambridge, on their way to this place, I detached Lieutenant Colonel Gregg to stop their march, and, in the night, was informed that a large body of the enemy were advancing in their rear.

I rallied my brigade, sent orders to Colonel Warner, whose regiment lay at Manchester, and also expresses to the militia to come in with all speed to our assistance; which orders were all promptly obeyed. We then marched with our collected force in quest of the enemy, and, after proceeding five miles, we met Colonel Gregg in full retreat, the enemy being within a mile of him.

Our little army was immediately drawn up in order of battle; upon which the enemy halted, and commenced intrenching upon very advantageous ground. A party of skirmishers, sent out upon their front, had a good effect, and killed thirty of them, without loss on our side. The ground where I then was not being fit for a general action, we retired one mile, encamped, and called a council of war, where it was determined to send two detachments to the rear, while the remainder attacked in front. The 15th, proving rainy, afforded the enemy an opportunity to surround his camp with a log breast work, inform General Burgoyne of his situation, and request a reinforcement.

On the morning of the 16th, Colonel Symonds joined us, with a party of Berkshire militia. In pursuance of our plan, I detached Colonel Nichols, with two hundred men, to the left; and Colonel Herrick, with three hundred men, to the right, with orders to turn the enemy's flanks, and attack his rear. Colonels Hubbard and Stickney, with two hundred men, were posted upon his right, and one hundred men stationed in front, to attract their attention in that quarter.

About three o'clock P.M., Colonel Nichols began the attack, which was followed up by the remainder of my little army. I pushed up in front; and, in a few minutes, the action became general. It lasted about two hours, and was the hottest engagement I have ever witnessed, resembling a continual clap of thunder.

The enemy were at last compelled to abandon their field pieces and baggage, and surrender themselves prisoners of war. They were well inclosed by breast works, with artillery; but the superior courage and conduct of our people was too much for them.

In a few moments we were informed that a large reinforcement of the enemy were on their march, and within two miles of us. At this lucky moment, Col. Warner's regiment (one hundred and fifty men) came up fresh, who was directed to advance and commence the attack. I pushed up as many men as could be collected to his support, and the action continued obstinately on both sides until sunset, when the enemy gave way, and was pursued until dark. With one hour more of daylight, we should have captured the whole detachment.

We obtained four pieces of brass cannon, one thousand stand of arms, several Hessian swords, eight brass drums, and seven hundred and fifty prisoners. Two hundred and seven were killed on the spot; wounded unknown. The enemy effected his escape by marching all night, and we returned to camp.

Too much honor can not be awarded to our brave officers and soldiers, for their gallant behavior in advancing through fire and smoke, and mounting breast works supported by cannon. Had every man been an Alexander or Charles XII, they could not have behaved more gallantly. I can not particularize any officer, as they all behaved with the greatest spirit. Colonels Warner and Herrick, by their superior intelligence and experience, were of great service to me; and I desire they may be recommended to Congress.

As I promised, in my orders, that the soldiers should have all the plunder taken in the British camp, I pray you to inform me of the value of the cannon and other artillery stores.

I lost my horse in the action, and was glad to come off so

well. Our loss is inconsiderable—about thirty killed and forty wounded.

Very respectfully,
Yours, in the common cause,
JOHN STARK

Hon. Major General Gates

N. B. In this action, I think we have returned the enemy a proper compliment for their Hubbardston affair.

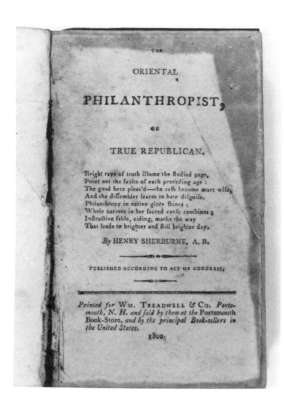

The title page of the original edition of *The Oriental Philanthropist, or True Republican* by Henry Sherburne, 1800. Courtesy of Dimond Library, University of New Hampshire.

HENRY SHERBURNE

Henry Sherburne was born in Portsmouth, New Hampshire in 1741, in the Old Sherburne House on Deer Street. He died in 1825. A member of the Portsmouth aristocracy, his father was chief justice of the court of common pleas and his mother a member of the Warner family. He graduated from Princeton in 1759. A merchant and revolutionary soldier, he served under General William Whipple at the Battle of Saratoga.

His novel, *The Oriental Philanthropist; or, The True Republican*, was the first written and published in New Hampshire. It was published by Treadwell in Portsmouth in 1800.

The first excerpt is typical of the lofty sentiments frequently contained in the exhortations of the novel's hero, Nytan. Here he is speaking to settlers recently arrived on the island of Ravenzar. The second selection is a tribute to the new city of Washington that concludes the book. The poem views the national destiny in terms of Christian millennialism.

FROM

The Oriental Philanthropist; or, The True Republican

. . . Whence (I shall add) whence arise the greatest distresses among mankind, but from the selfish contemptible tempers of the powerful and rich among you? When we can bravely deny ourselves to serve the indigent and reclaim the vicious; when we can give up our ardent pursuits of ambition and sensuality, and persevere, against all embarrassments, in promoting the good of every individual, however low and debased:—when we can thus nobly live to the creation, we shall wear, with real honor, the name of men, of a species gloriously formed, by omnipotence and love, for the true enjoyment of existence. But your ignoble ideas, your churlish disposition, your detestable pride and vanity, your vices, of every kind, place you below the brutal creation. Nay; the most noisome and loathsome of the inferior tribes of existence are far more excellent than you. If there be a spark of goodness buried among you, let it emerge from the darkness and ruin in which it hath been so long involved. Awake to real honour and glory! and become brilliant constellations in the unsullied galaxy of the virtuous sons and daughters of freedom and truth, whose splendors illuminate the world, and are as unfading as the day of Heaven! Experience the exalted pleasures of undissembled virtue and benevolence, and henceforward labor to do good, to render others happy. The generous labors of love, while they exalt and refine you for the high and grand enjoyments of immortals, will likewise add the greatest strength and glory to your national interests, and evince, in the most illustrious point of view, how dear they are to Heaven.

* * *

Rise Federal City—rise—in glory rise!
In wisdom cement thy firm basis lies.
Nor storms, nor ages shall thy strength impair;
Nations unborn thy splendors shall admire;
To thee shall flock, whilst Bards, inspir'd, proclaim
Thy patriot virtues, and immortal fame!
Heroes deceas'd the ruins of the grave survive,
In every clime, in every heart they live.

The just can never die—the just—the good—
Not death o'erwhelms, nor time's destroying flood.
Like Suns they shine with splendors ever bright,
Beyond the reach of malice, slander, spite,
Or gloomy frowns of an eternal night!
Blest sacred privilege of virtue's sons,
From earth remov'd, and greatly WASHINGTON'S!
But deaths and griefs soon shall forever cease,
And earth and Heaven be one inchangeless bliss!
A ray divine shows glory yet to come;
The living and the dead in one eternal home!
This Heaven's denizens and earth's incessant pray,
And hail the approach of God's illustrious day!

TABITHA GILMAN TENNEY

Tabitha Gilman Tenney was born in Exeter, N.H. in 1762 and died in 1837. The Gilman family was prominent in New Hampshire politics during the revolutionary period. She received a good education and married Samuel Tenney in 1788. While her husband served in the U.S. Congress from 1800 to 1807, Mrs. Tenney lived in Washington. In 1801 *Female Quixotism: Exhibited in the Romantic Opinions and Extravagant Adventures of Dorcasina Sheldon* was published in Boston by I. Thomas and E. T. Andrews. The book is a satire on popular, romantic literary modes. In the following excerpt, Dorcasina tells why she has fallen in love again.

Female Quixotism

CHAPTER II

"Well, Betty," said Dorcasina, as soon as she entered the chamber, "have you seen the wounded officer this morning? How is he? Better, I hope. And what did he say to the message I sent him?" "Yes, ma'am, I have seen him," replied Betty, "and he is a gentleman every inch of him; none of your proud upstarts, that think themselves too good to speak to a poor person. He was so gentle, and so kind, and so free! He sent his compliments to you, ma'am, and he asked me my name, and praised the coffee I carried him. He said he had fellen into such horsepitiable hands that he could not express his thanks." "But you have not told me how he is, this morning, Betty." "Why, ma'am, he said he was dry and feverish; but he hoped to recruit again after he had got over the fatigue of his journey." "How did he look and speak, when you mentioned my name?" "He look'd pale, and ask'd me who you was; and you may be sure, ma'am, I wasn't backward in giving you your due." "Well what then? What did he say then? Did not love and pleasure sparkle in his fine eyes?" "I didn't see any sparkles in his eyes, ma'am. I thought they look'd rather dull, owing to his weakness I spose; but he sent his compliments, and said he did not know how to thank you."

This conversation was carried on while Dorcasina was dressing, who asked Betty so many questions of the same nature, that she was quite at a loss for answers.

Capt. Barry slept the greater part of the day, in consequence of the opium he had taken the preceding night; and not discovering any inclination to be gotten up, the surgeon thought best not to have him disturbed. Dorcasina could not, with any degree of propriety, think of making him a visit that day, but she frequently, in the course of it, passed his chamber door, and would sometimes stop and listen to endeavour to catch the sound of his voice.

The next night our soldier slept well, and on the second morning was so much better as to be able, for a short time, to sit up. After dressing his wounds and finding them in a good way, the surgeon left him, promising to visit him again, as soon as he thought it necessary.

While the patient was sitting in an easy chair, Betty brought him Miss Dorcasina's compliments, with some nice preserves; "which," said Betty, "she prepared with her own hands, and hopes you will relish them. She moreover desires to know how you does today." "What an excellent young lady," said the captain. "Thank her, Betty, a thousand times for me; tell her I feel in a new world; and that the interest she takes in my welfare will greatly accelerate my recovery." Betty having reported to Dorcasina these gallant and grateful expressions of the captain she now insisted on preparing all his food herself; and charged Betty constantly to inform him of it. This attention produced new expressions of gratitude on the part of the captain, and new emotions of delight in the breast of Dorcasina. She even did not regret that they could not immediately see each other, as this way of carrying on a correspondence was infinitely pleasing to her, being in her opinion extremely delicate, tender and romantic. This intercourse was continued for two days longer, till they seemed mutually acquainted with, and felt a mutual desire of seeing each other. This desire was so strongly expressed by the captain, who was now able to sit up the greater part of the day, that Dorcasina determined no longer to withhold from him and herself the pleasure of a visit. Had she been going to be presented, for the first time, at the court of the greatest monarch in Europe, she would not have thought it a matter of more consequence. Nor was captain Barry without his emotions, occasioned by curiosity and gratitude.

The fashionable female dress at that time, was the little trig silk jacket and muslin skirt. Dorcasina was all the morning examining her clothes, and considering what colour would best become her. She first tried a white lustring jacket; then a purple satin; then a blue; and lastly a pink. But she finally rejected them all, concluding, as she was going to visit a sick chamber, that a plain white robe would be more proper than any of them. At length, about eleven o'clock, Betty being sent forward to announce her, with trembling steps and a palpitating heart, she approached the chamber of the invalid. He stood up out of respect, at her entrance; but the moment he beheld her, he sunk again involuntarily into his chair. A thin, plain woman, near fifty (as he thought her) was so different an object from the young and lovely female he was prepared to behold, that it was impossible for him to conceal his surprise at the disappointment. Dorcasina, on her part, notwithstanding her matronly age and appearance, being a woman of real delicacy, was, at this first interview, a good deal embarrassed. She blushed, and sitting down in a chair, with downcast eyes, and a confused air waited for the silence to be broken by the gentleman. Recovering at length, and ashamed of his want of politeness, the captain began by thanking her for her attention, since he had been in the house, and the honour she now did him by her visit. Dorcasina, who, notwithstanding her embarrassment, had noticed the first surprise of the captain, imputing it wholly to the force and splendor of her charms, now ventured to turn upon him her languishing eyes, and to reply, that she blessed the occasion which had thrown him in her way; that it was with pleasure she administered to the wants of a brave officer, suffering in the cause of his country, and that she hoped he had not wanted for any thing since he had been in the house. "No madam," said he, "thanks to the humanity of you and your father, I could not have been treated with more tenderness in the house of my parents." "You have parents living then, sir?" "I hope so, madam; they were both living three months ago." ".How must they be distressed at what you have suffered. They have been informed, I suppose, of your misfortune." "I fear they have, madam, and I was hurrying home to relieve their anxiety, when the breaking out of my wounds afresh brought me into this hospitable mansion." "Have you written to inform them of your present situation, or do you wish to write?" "I made it a point to write, madam, as soon as I was able to hold a pen, and my letter was dispatched by the post this morning." "It must afford them great satisfaction to receive a letter from you." "They are affectionate parents, and it will no doubt give them pleasure madam."

After this they conversed of the Indians, and the battle, of which she requested a particular account, especially of the part he had performed in it. During his narration, she cast upon him such languishing looks, and tender glances; her countenance so beamed with pleasure, while he was in safety; and her eyes so instantly overflowed, when he was wounded, that the poor man was almost too much embarrassed to proceed in the recital.

After an hour and a half passed in varied conversation, Dorcasina took her leave, giving him a thousand charges to be careful of his health, not to sit up too long, nor, by taking cold, expose himself to a relapse. The moment she was alone with Betty, she declared he was the most modest, the most charming, and the most interesting man she had ever seen. "And it has turned out just as I wished and expected; he is violently in love with me, Betty; that is sufficiently evident. My attentions gained his heart before he saw me, precisely the thing I intended and hoped. Did you not observe his delicate embarrassment on my entrance? the graceful manner of his sinking in his chair! his tender and languishing glances? I admire his modesty in not declaring his passion at once: It is a proof that his love is pure and unfeigned. A true lover is always diffident in the presence of the mistress of his affections."

THE WHITE MOUNTAINS

THE WHITE MOUNTAINS are a region apart—a "special state
within the state."[1] Isolated by geography and tradition, they have
been studied by natural scientists, mountaineers, guides, and historians. They have provided the subject matter of legend and the inspiration of novelists and poets as diverse as Nathaniel Hawthorne
and the unlettered balladeer Frank Leavitt. Even today they remain for many the almost impenetrable core of the state—tough,
awesome, and enigmatic, at once alluring and treacherous.

The writer who best conveys these attributes is Lucy Howe
Crawford. The Reverend Jeremy Belknap, with his educated in-
stincts for eighteenth-century natural history, cataloged the rele-
vant data on the White Mountains; but it remained for Lucy Howe
Crawford, wife of the pioneer Ethan Allen Crawford, to express
the attitudes that cannot be quantified. Her *History of the White
Mountains* is a mixture of statistical information, family biogra-

1. Elizabeth F. Morison and Elting E. Morison, *New Hampshire: A Bicentennial History*
(New York: W. W. Norton and Co., 1976), p. 4.

phy, stories, legends, and a biography of her husband. She both extols the grandeur and invigoration of the highlands and emphasizes the neighborliness of the mountain people. Not only does she blend the extremes of wild romanticism and cozy sentiment that distinguished her century; the self-sacrifice preached by republicans of the revolutionary age is also always evident. The *History* is a literary testimony to the virtues that provided excitement and satisfaction to the lives of pioneering individuals. The Crawfords, as Lucy saw them, lived during a kind of golden age when people recognized the difference between the worthwhile and the spurious. The family and their neighbors were specially blessed in sharing an experience that involved the creation of a new life in a splendid setting.

Ethan is the hero of the book. A giant, "well adapted to mountain life," he possessed both the strength and humanity required to carry home a wounded bear cub to nurse and make into a pet. Eminent men sought his company as guide on their wilderness jaunts and all admired him, for "no man was more ready and willing to administer to the distressed and suffering." He is a memorable figure—the archetype of the beloved patriarch.

The History of the White Mountains gains added significance as a medium for transforming legend into the substance of literature. Part of the Crawford family's distinction derived from their early ventures in running a hotel and in the quality of their guests. Among their visitors was Nathaniel Hawthorne, an avid listener to regional tales exchanged at the hospitable fireside of the Crawford Notch House. Stories of the Old Man of the Mountain, of the Willey family, who perished in a great landslide, and of a fabulous gem embedded in a cliff far in the mountain fastness inspired the imagination of the Concord recluse. This raw material he transformed into a triad of subtly allegorical short stories: the mythic Indian jewel became "The Great Carbuncle"; the tragic Willey family, the kindly hosts of "The Ambitious Guest"; and similarities between the noble Ernest of "The Great Stone Face" and Ethan Allen Crawford must have been apparent to those who loved that mountain wilderness and the family who made it their home.

The White Mountains have always held attraction for seekers of adventure. Mountain climbers and hikers without guides as experienced as Crawford often suffered the consequences of false confidence. The region abounds with stories of those who lost their way. Perhaps the most dramatic is that of Dr. Benjamin Ball. Overtaken by an early autumn snowstorm, Ball endured a harrowing three days until, suffering from frostbite so severe he could scarcely walk, he was found by a rescue party. The physician's literary ability and capacity for survival are demonstrated in his vivid account of the ordeal.

Thomas Starr King, a contemporary of Dr. Ball's, shared his enthusiasm for the mountains. Recognizing the peculiar quality of the region, King assembled a collection of legends, poems, and essays describing the landscape. In its variety and range of information King's volume is a useful supplement to that of Lucy Howe Crawford.

Poets, novelists, and essayists almost without exception have regarded the White Mountains as an exotic phenomenon—something to be experienced under special circumstances and to be appreciated as a wonder that existed outside everyday routine. To Lucy Howe Crawford, however, the mountains were her home, and she remains one of the few who wrote from an intimate perspective. This insider's advantage she shared with Frank Leavitt, a most unusual chronicler. An employee of the Crawford family's and a popular guide, Leavitt absorbed a kind of folk wisdom that he felt compelled to impart in poetry (some might call it doggerel) that commemorated ordinary events, recording random information and facts that seemed important to him. What might appear to be trivial actually is a storehouse of miscellaneous information, much of which would have been forgotten had it not been for the efforts—however misguided in poetic terms—of Frank Leavitt.

LUCY HOWE CRAWFORD

Lucy Howe Crawford (b. Vermont, 1793; d. 1869) was the wife of the noted mountaineer Ethan Allen Crawford. Their family was among the first to settle in the White Mountains and owned and operated the first hotel in the region, Crawford Notch House. There they entertained many famous visitors, including Nathaniel Hawthorne and Daniel Webster.

The History of the White Mountains was published by Hoyt, Fogg and Donham of Portland, Maine in 1883. The following excerpt, told in the first person by her husband, describes the great storm of 1826 and the loss of the Willey family. This incident was the basis for Nathaniel Hawthorne's "The Ambitious Guest."

The History of the White Mountains

The storm of 1826.
The great slide from the mountains.
The destruction of the Willey family.
Mr. Crawford's loss.

Singular as it may appear, not a person has ever been known to take cold in camping upon the summit, previous to the erection of the Tip-Top houses. Mr. Crawford, frequently, during his stay at the mountains, received letters from various invalids saying their health was much improved by their visits. Even at the present day, seldom can a person retire to rest upon the beds in the summit house without finding a damp blanket to get into; yet one always feels refreshed in the morning without any symptoms of having taken a cold.

Now we were in trouble again, there being a complaint for want of a shed and more stable room. The winter of 1826 was at hand with a great deal to do. After having done other necessary business, I went to hauling boards and shingles from the same short distance of twelve miles, only up through the Notch. My father had put him up a new saw-mill, and I could get boards from there now better than from anywhere else, but it was some trouble to draw them up the Notch hills. Some perhaps think this a heavy job, but when a thing is undertaken in good earnest, it is soon over; so with this job. In the spring I hired men and went to work and soon had timber prepared for a stable sixty feet by forty, and a shed to stand between the old stable and the new one, fifty feet by forty, which accommodated both stables, and the whole length of these buildings was nearly one hundred and fifty feet, in a straight line, facing the road. The outside of these buildings was nearly finished when a stop was put to all business in consequence of the great rain, which you will soon find recorded.

In June [1826], as my father with a number of men was at work repairing the turnpike road through the Notch, there came on a heavy rain, and they were obliged to leave their work and retire to the house, then occupied by the worthy Willey family, and it rained very hard. While there they saw on the west side of the road a small movement of rocks and earth coming down the hill, and it took all before it. They saw, likewise, whole trees coming down, standing upright, for ten rods together, before they would tip over—the whole still moving slowly on, making its way until it had crossed the road and then on a level surface some distance before it stopped. This grand and awful sight frightened the timid family very much, and Mrs. Willey proposed to have the horses harnessed and go to my father's, but the old gentleman told her not to be alarmed, as he said they were much safer there than they would be in the road; for, said he, there may be other difficulties in the way, like the one just described, or the swollen waters may have carried away some of the bridges and they could not be crossed; and after some reasoning with her in this way she was pacified and remained safely. The next day, as the storm had abated, they set about removing the burden from the road, which required much trouble and labor. This seemed to be a warning and it appeared so to them. Mr. Willey had looked round and about the mountains and tried to find out a safer place than the one they then occupied; and, having satisfied himself, as he thought, placed a good tight cart-body in such a manner as would secure them from the weather in case a similar thing should occur, as visitors had advised them to leave the place as they were anxious for their safety; and he, it appeared, was fearful, or he would not have made this effort. But there is an overruling God who knows all things and causes all things to happen for the best, although we short-sighted mortals cannot comprehend them. Had they taken the advice of St. Paul and all abode in the ship, they might have been saved; but this was not to be their case—they were suffered to perish.

August 26th, there came a party from the West to ascend the mountain, but as the wind had been blowing from the south for several days, I advised them not to go that afternoon, but they said their time was limited and they must proceed. Everything necessary for the expedition being put in readiness, we all, like so many good soldiers, with our staves in our hands, set forward at six o'clock and arrived at the camp at ten o'clock; and I with my knife and flint struck fire, which caught in a piece of dry punk which I carried for that purpose, and from that I could make a large fire. This was the only way we had in those days of obtaining fire. [The old-fashioned steel or jack-knife and flint were necessary appendages in those days in performing camp duty.] After my performing the duties of a cook and house maid, we sat down in the humble situation of Indians, not having the convenience of chairs, and told stories till the time for rest. The wind still continued to blow from the south. In the morning, about four o'clock, it commenced raining, which prevented their hopes of ascending the mountain that day, and not having provisions for another day, and they being unwilling now to give it up when they had got so near, a meeting was called and it was unanimously agreed that I should go home and get new supplies and then return to them again. I obeyed their commands, shouldered my empty pack, took my leave of them and returned; but, as the rain was falling so fast, and the mud collected about my feet, my progress was slow and wearisome. I at length got home, and being tired and my brother Thomas being there, I desired him to take my place, which he cheerfully consented to do, and in a short time he was laden and set forward; and when arriving at the camp, the party was holding a council as to what was to be done, for the rain had fallen so fast and steadily that it had entirely extinguished the fire. They consulted Thomas upon the matter to know if they had time to get in. He told them that to remain there would be very unpleasant, as they must suffer with the wet and cold, not considering danger, but if they would go as fast as they could, they might reach the house. Each taking a little refreshment in his hands, and having the precaution to take the axe with them, set off in full speed, and when they came to a swollen stream which they could not ford, Thomas would, with his axe, fell a tree for a bridge, and then they would walk over. They got along tolerably well until they came to a large branch, which came from the Notch. This was full and raging, and they had some difficulty to find a tree that would reach to the opposite bank, but at length succeeded in finding one, and they all got safely over, and those who could not walk, crawled along, holding on by the limbs; and when they came to the main stream, the water had risen and come into the road for several rods, and when they crossed the bridge it trembled under their feet. They all arrived in safety about eight o'clock in the evening, when they

were welcomed by two large fires to dry themselves. Here they
took off their wet garments, and those that had not a change of
their own put on mine and went to bed, while we sat up to dry
theirs. At eleven o'clock we had a clearing up shower, and it
seemed as though the windows of heaven were opened and the
rain came down almost in streams. It did not, however, last long
before it all cleared away and became a perfect calm. The next
morning we were awakened by our little boy coming into the room
and saying, "Father, the earth is nearly covered with water, and the
hogs are swimming for life." I arose immediately and went to their
rescue. I waded into the water and pulled away the fence, and they
swam to land. What a sight! The sun rose clear; not a cloud nor a
vapor was to be seen; all was still and silent excepting the rushing
sound of the water as it poured down the hills leaping over huge
precipices and centering in one vast ocean in the valley beneath.
The whole interval was covered with water a distance of over two
hundred acres of land, to be seen when standing on the little hill
which has been named and called Giant's Grave, just back of the
stable, where the house used to stand that was burnt. After standing here a short time, I saw the fog arise in different places on the
water, and it formed a beautiful sight. The bridge, which had so
lately been crossed, had come down and taken with it ninety feet
of shed which was attached to the barn that escaped the fire in
1818. Fourteen sheep that were under it were drowned, and those
which escaped looked as though they had been washed in a mud
puddle. The water came within eighteen inches of the door in the
house and a strong current was running between the house and
stable. It came up under the shed and underneath the new stable
and carried away timber and wood, passed by the west corner of
the house, and moved a wagon which stood in its course.

Now the safety of my father and of the Willey family occupied
our minds, but there was no way to find out their situation. At or
near the middle of the day (Tuesday), there came a traveler on foot
who was desirous of going down the Notch that night, as he said
his business was urgent and he must, if possible, go through. I told
him to be patient, as the water was then falling fast, and as soon as
it should fall and I could swim a horse, I would carry him over the
river. Owing to the narrowness of the intervals between the mountains here, when it begins to fall it soon drains away, and at four

o'clock I mounted a large strong horse, took the traveler on be-hind, swam the river, and landed him safely on the other side and returned. He made the best of his way down to the Notch house and arrived there just before dark. He found the house deserted by every living creature excepting the faithful dog, and he was unwill-ing at first to admit the stranger. He at length became friendly and acquainted. On going to the barn he found it had been touched by an avalanche and fallen in. The two horses that were in it were both killed, and the oxen confined under the broken timber tied in their stalls. These he set at liberty after finding an axe and cutting away the timber; they were lame but soon got over it. What must have been the feelings of this lonely traveler while occupying this deserted house, finding doors opened and bed and clothes as though they had been left in a hurry, Bible open and lying on the table as if it had lately been read? He went round the house and prepared for himself a supper and partook of it alone except the company of the dog, who seemed hungry like himself; then quietly lay down in one of these open deserted beds and consoled himself by thinking the family had made their escape and gone down to my father's. Early the next morning he proceeded on his way and he had some difficulty in getting across some places, as the earth and water were mixed together and made a complete quagmire. He succeeded in getting to Father's, but could obtain no informa-tion of the unfortunate family, and he therefore concluded that they must all have been buried beneath the slide. He told this story as he went down through Bartlett and Conway, and the news soon spread.

On Wednesday the waters had subsided so much that we could ford the Amanoosuc river with a horse and wagon, and some of the time-limited party agreed to try the ground over again; so they, with the addition of another small party who came from the West on Tuesday, with Thomas for guide, again set out, while I, with a gentleman from Connecticut, went toward the Notch. After travel-ing a distance of two miles in a wagon, we were obliged to leave it and take to our feet. We now found the road in some places en-tirely demolished and, seemingly, on a level surface; a crossway which had been laid down for many years and firmly covered with dirt—that to the eye of human reason it would be impossible to move—taken up, and every log had been disturbed and laid in dif-

ferent directions. On going still a little further, we found a gulf in
the middle of the road, in some places ten feet deep and twenty
rods in length. The rest of the road my pen would fail should I
attempt to describe it; suffice it to say, I could hardly believe my
own eyes, the water having made such destruction. Now, when
within a short distance of the house, I found the cows with their
bags filled with milk, and from their appearance, they had not
been milked for some days. My heart sickened as I thought what
had happened to the inmates of the house. We went in and there
found no living person and the house in the situation just described. I was going down to my father's to seek them out, but the
gentleman with me would not let me go, for he said he could not
find his way back alone, and I must return with him. We set out
and arrived home at four o'clock in the afternoon.

I could not be satisfied about the absent family and again returned, and when I got back to the house found a number of the
neighbors had assembled, and no information concerning them
could be obtained. My feelings were such that I could not remain
there during the night, although a younger brother of mine, being
one of the company, almost laid violent hands upon me to compel
me to stay, fearing some accident might befall me, as I should have
to feel my way through the Notch on my hands and knees, for the
water had in the narrowest place in the Notch taken out the rocks
which had been beat in from the ledge above to make the road,
and carried them into the gulf below and made a hole or gulf
twenty feet deep, and it was difficult, if not dangerous, to get
through in the night, as all those who visited this scene of desolation will bear testimony to; but my mind was fixed and unchangeable, and I would not be prevailed on to stay. I started and groped
my way home in the dark, where I arrived at ten o'clock in the
evening. Here I found that the party from the mountain had arrived; as they had nowhere to stay, they were obliged to come in
that night. Now we began to relate our discoveries. They had
much difficulty in finding their way, as the water had made as bad
work with their path as it had done with the road, in proportion
to its length. The water had risen and carried away every particle
of the camp and all my furniture there. The party seemed thankful
that they, on Monday, had made their escape. What must have
been their fortune had they remained there? They must have

shared the same fate the Willey family did, or suffered a great deal with fear, wet, cold, and hunger, for it would have been impossible for them to have come in until Wednesday, and their provisions must have been all gone, if not lost, on Monday night. It seemed really a providential thing in their being saved. No part of the iron chest was ever found, or anything it contained, excepting a few pieces of blanket that were caught on bushes in different places down the river.

The next morning our friends, with gratitude, left us; and we had the same grateful feelings toward them, wishing each other good luck.

The same day (Thursday) before I had time to look about me and learn the situation of my farm and estimate the loss I had sustained, the friends of the Willey family had come up to the deserted house and sent for me. At first I said I could not go down, but being advised to, I went. When I got there, on seeing the friends of that well-beloved family, and having been acquainted with them for many years, my heart was full and my tongue refused utterance, and I could not for a considerable length of time speak to one of them, and could only express the regard I had for them in pressing their hands and giving full vent to my tears. This was the second time my eyes were wet with tears since grown to manhood. The other time was when my family was in that destitute situation. Diligent search being made for them, and no traces to be found until night, the attention of the people was attracted by the flies as they were passing and repassing underneath a large pile of floodwood. They now began to haul away the rubbish and at length found Mr. and Mrs. Willey, Mr. Allen, the hired man, and the youngest child not far distant from each other. These were taken up, broken and mangled, as must naturally be expected, and were placed in coffins. The next day they were interred on a piece of ground near the house, there to remain until winter. Saturday, the other hired man was found and interred, and on Sunday the eldest daughter was found, some way from where the others were, across the river; and it was said her countenance was fair and pleasant, not a bruise or a mark was discovered upon her. It was supposed she was drowned. She had only a handkerchief around her waist, supposed to have been put there for someone to lead her by. This girl was not far from twelve years of age. She had acquired a good education, considering her advantages, and she seemed more like a gentleman's daughter, of fashion and affluence, than the daughter of one who had located himself in the midst of the mountains. It is said the earliest flowers are the soonest plucked, and this seems to be the case with this young, interesting family; the rest of the children were not inferior to the eldest, considering their age. In this singular act of Providence, there were nine taken from time into eternity, four adult persons and five children. It should remind us, we who are living, to "be also ready, for in such an hour as ye think not, the Son of Man cometh." It was a providential thing, said Zara Cutler, Esq., who was present afterward, that the house itself was saved, so near came the overwhelming avalanche. The length of the slides are several miles down the side of the mountain. The other three children, one daughter and two sons, have never to this day been found; not even a bone has ever been picked up or discovered. It is supposed they must have been buried deep underneath an avalanche. What must have been the feelings of that family as they rushed from the house under the darkness of night, knowing not where to flee for safety from the mighty torrent of earth and water which was hurrying itself along down into the valley beneath?

Mr. and Mrs. Willey sustained good and respectable characters, and were in good standing among the Christians in Conway, where they belonged. They were remarkable for their charities and kindness toward others, and commanded the respect of travelers and all who knew them. Much more could be said in their favor, but it would be superfluous to add. Suffice it to remark that the whole intention of their lives was to live humbly, walk uprightly, deal justly with all, speak evil of none.

There came a large slide down back of the house in a direction to take the house with it, and when within ten or fifteen rods of the house it came against a solid ledge of rock and there stopped and separated, one on either side of the house, taking the stable on one side, and the family on the other, or they might have got to the rendezvous; but there is no certainty which of these divisions overtook them, as they were buried partly by the three slides which had come together eighty rods from the house; the two that separated back of the house here met, and a still larger one had come down in the place where Mr. Willey had hunted out a safe refuge.

When the slide was coming down and separating, it had great quantities of timber with it, turned over the large boulders and set them in motion down the mountain. One log, six feet long and two feet through, still kept its course and came within three feet of the house, but fortunately it was stopped by coming against a brick, where it rested; the ends of trees were torn up and looked similar to an old peeled birch broom. The whole valley, which was once covered with beautiful green grass, was now a complete quagmire, exhibiting nothing but ruins of the mountains, heaps of timber, large rocks, sand, and gravel. All was dismal and desolate. Even the faithful dog seemed to partake of the sympathy, and after trying to arouse by his moanings a neighboring family but without success, it is said, he soon disappeared from the spot and was never heard from after. For a monument, I wrote with a piece of red chalk on a planed board this inscription:

THE FAMILY FOUND HERE.

I nailed it to a dead tree which was standing near the place where they were found; but it has since been taken away by some of the occupants of the house and used for fuel.

But to return to my own affairs at home. Fences mostly gone, farm in some places covered so deeply with sand and gravel that it was ruined, and , on the interval, floodwood was piled in great and immense quantities in different places all over it. The bridge now lay in pieces all around the meadow, and the shed also; there was a large field of oats just ready to harvest, from which I think I would have had four or six hundred bushels, which was destroyed; also, some hay in the field. My actual loss at this time was more than one thousand dollars, and truly things looked rather unfavorable. After the fire, we had worked hard and economized closely to live and pay our former dues, in which we made slow progress. As it was necessary for the benefit of the public to buy so many things which we could not get along without, I could do but little toward taking up my old notes, but still I must persevere and keep doing while the day lasted, and I thought no man would be punished for being unfortunate. Therefore, taking these things into consideration, I would still continue to do the best I could and trust the event. My father suffered still more than myself. The best part of his farm was entirely destroyed. A new saw-mill, which he had just put up, and a great number of logs and boards were swept away together into the sand; fences on the interval were all gone; twenty-eight sheep were drowned, and considerable grain which was in the field was swept away. The water rose on the outside of the house twenty-two inches, and ran through the whole house on the lower floors and swept out the coals and ashes from the fireplace. They had lighted candles, which were placed in the windows, and my mother took down a pole which she used as a clothes pole and stood at a window near the corner of the house when the current ran swift, and would push away the timber and other stuff that came down against the house to keep it from collecting in a great body, as she thought it might jam up and sweep away the house, for the water was rising fast. And while thus engaged, she was distressed by the cries of the poor bleating and drowning sheep that would pass by in the flood and seemed to cry for help, but none could be afforded.

My father at this time was from home, and but few of the family were there, so they made the best they could of it. This came on so suddenly and unexpectedly that almost everything in the cellar was ruined, and a part of the wall fell in.

This loss of my father's property, which he had accumulated only by the sweat of his brow, was so great that he will never be likely to regain it. Many suffered more or less who lived on this wild and uncultivated stream, as far as Saco.

We had now a difficulty which seemed almost insurmountable. The road in many places was entirely gone; the bridges, the whole length of the turnpike excepting two, a distance of seventeen miles, gone; the directors came and looked at it and found it would take a large sum to repair it. The good people of Portland, however, to encourage us, raised fifteen hundred dollars to help us with; it was put into the hands of Nathan Kinsman, Esq., to see it well laid out. The directors voted to raise an assessment on the shares, to make up the balance; and that, with some other assistance, was divided into jobs and let out, and we all went to work; and, as it was said, the sun shone so short a time in this Notch, that the hardy New Hampshire boys made up their hours by moonlight.

NATHANIEL HAWTHORNE

Nathaniel Hawthorne (b. Salem, Massachusetts, 1804; d. 1864) was the son of a sea captain and the direct descendant of the "hanging judge" of the Salem witchcraft trials. After attending Bowdoin College (where Franklin Pierce and Henry W. Longfellow were classmates) he held a variety of jobs, including that of treasurer of the Brook Farm commune, until he established himself as a writer of short stories and novels. Having written a campaign biography for his friend Franklin Pierce, he was rewarded with a consulship in Liverpool during Pierce's presidency (1853–57). The author of such classics as *The Scarlet Letter* and *The House of the Seven Gables*, he is recognized as one of the outstanding creators of American literature.

Long an admirer of the New Hampshire countryside, Hawthorne spent many vacations in the White Mountains.

Mosses from an Old Manse, containing "Sketches from Memory," was published in Boston by Ticknor and Fields in 1864; *Tales of the White Hills*, including "The Ambitious Guest," was published in Boston by Houghton Mifflin in 1899. "The Ambitious Guest" was first published in *Twice-Told Tales* in Boston by Ticknor, Reed and Fields in 1851. Houghton Mifflin Company republished *The Great Stone Face and Other Tales of the White Mountains* in 1935.

Nathaniel Hawthorne, 1840, from an oil portrait by Charles Osgood. Courtesy of the Essex Institute, Salem, Massachusetts.

Sketches from Memory

THE NOTCH OF THE WHITE MOUNTAINS

It was now the middle of September. We had come since sunrise from Bartlett, passing up through the valley of the Saco, which extends between mountainous walls, sometimes with a steep ascent, but often as level as a church aisle. All that day and two preceding ones we had been loitering towards the heart of the White Mountains—those old crystal hills, whose mysterious brilliancy had gleamed upon our distant wanderings before we thought of visiting them. Height after height had risen and towered one above another till the clouds began to hang below the peaks. Down their slopes were the red pathways of the slides, those avalanches of earth, stones and trees, which descend into the hollows, leaving vestiges of their track hardly to be effaced by the vegetation of ages. We had mountains behind us and mountains on each side, and a group of mightier ones ahead. Still our road went up along the Saco, right towards the centre of that group, as if to climb above the clouds in its passage to the farther region.

In old times the settlers used to be astounded by the inroads of the northern Indians coming down upon them from this mountain rampart through some defile known only to themselves. It is, indeed, a wondrous path. A demon, it might be fancied, or one of the Titans, was travelling up the valley, elbowing the heights carelessly aside as he passed, till at length a great mountain took its stand directly across his intended road. He tarries not for such an obstacle, but, rending it asunder a thousand feet from peak to base, discloses its treasures of hidden minerals, its sunless waters, all the secrets of the mountain's inmost heart, with a mighty fracture of rugged precipices on each side. This is the Notch of the White Hills. Shame on me that I have attempted to describe it by so mean an image—feeling, as I do, that it is one of those symbolic scenes which lead the mind to the sentiment, though not to the conception, of Omnipotence.

* * *

We had now reached a narrow passage, which showed almost the appearance of having been cut by human strength and artifice in the solid rock. There was a wall of granite on each side, high and precipitous, especially on our right, and so smooth that a few evergreens could hardly find foothold enough to grow there. This is the entrance, or, in the direction we were going, the extremity, of the romantic defile of the Notch. Before emerging from it, the rattling of wheels approached behind us, and a stage-coach rumbled out of the mountain, with seats on top and trunks behind, and a smart driver, in a drab greatcoat, touching the wheel horses with the whipstock and reining in the leaders. To my mind there was a sort of poetry in such an incident, hardly inferior to what would have accompanied the painted array of an Indian war party gliding forth from the same wild chasm. All the passengers, except a very fat lady on the back seat, had alighted. One was a mineralogist, a scientific, green-spectacled figure in black, bearing a heavy hammer, with which he did great damage to the precipices, and put the fragments in his pocket. Another was a well-dressed young man, who carried an opera glass set in gold, and seemed to be making a quotation from some of Byron's rhapsodies on mountain scenery. There was also a trader, returning from Portland to the upper part of Vermont; and a fair young girl, with a very faint bloom like one of those pale and delicate flowers which sometimes occur among alpine cliffs.

They disappeared, and we followed them, passing through a deep pine forest, which for some miles allowed us to see nothing but its own dismal shade. Towards nightfall we reached a level amphitheatre, surrounded by a great rampart of hills, which shut out the sunshine long before it left the external world. It was here that we obtained our first view, except at a distance, of the principal group of mountains. They are majestic, and even awful, when contemplated in a proper mood, yet, by their breadth of base and the long ridges which support them, give the idea of immense bulk rather than of towering height. Mount Washington, indeed, looked near to heaven: he was white with snow a mile downward, and had caught the only cloud that was sailing through the atmosphere to veil his head. Let us forget the other names of American statesmen that have been stamped upon these hills, but still call the loftiest WASHINGTON. Mountains are Earth's undecaying monuments. They must stand while she endures, and never should be consecrated to the mere great men of their own age and country, but to the mighty ones alone, whose glory is universal, and whom all time will render illustrious.

The air, not often sultry in this elevated region, nearly two thousand feet above the sea, was now sharp and cold, like that of a clear November evening in the lowlands. By morning, probably, there would be a frost, if not a snowfall, on the grass and rye, and an icy surface over the standing water. I was glad to perceive a prospect of comfortable quarters in a house which we were approaching, and of pleasant company in the guests who were assembled at the door.

OUR EVENING PARTY AMONG THE MOUNTAINS

We stood in front of a good substantial farmhouse, of old date in that wild country. A sign over the door denoted it to be the White Mountain Post Office—an establishment which distributes letters and newspapers to perhaps a score of persons, comprising the population of two or three townships among the hills. The broad and weighty antlers of a deer, "a stag of ten," were fastened at the corner of the house; a fox's bushy tail was nailed beneath them; and a huge black paw lay on the ground, newly severed and still bleeding—the trophy of a bear hunt. Among several persons collected about the doorsteps, the most remarkable was a sturdy mountaineer, of six feet two and corresponding bulk, with a heavy set of features, such as might be moulded on his own blacksmith's anvil, but yet indicative of mother wit and rough humor. As we appeared, he uplifted a tin trumpet, four or five feet long, and blew a tremendous blast, either in honor of our arrival or to awaken an echo from the opposite hill.

Ethan Crawford's guests were of such a motley description as to form quite a picturesque group, seldom seen together except at some place like this, at once the pleasure house of fashionable tourists and the homely inn of country travellers. Among the company at the door were the mineralogist and the owner of the gold opera glass whom we had encountered in the Notch; two Georgian gentlemen, who had chilled their southern blood that morning on the top of Mount Washington; a physician and his wife from Conway; a trader of Burlington, and an old squire of the Green Mountains; and two young married couples, all the way from Massachusetts, on the matrimonial jaunt. Besides these strangers, the rugged county of Coos, in which we were, was represented by half a dozen wood-cutters, who had slain a bear in the forest and smitten off his paw.

I had joined the party, and had a moment's leisure to examine them before the echo of Ethan's blast returned from the hill. Not one, but many echoes had caught up the harsh and tuneless sound, untwisted its complicated threads, and found a thousand aerial harmonies in one stern trumpet tone. It was a distinct yet distant and dreamlike symphony of melodious instruments, as if an airy band had been hidden on the hill-side and made faint music at the summons. No subsequent trial produced so clear, delicate, and spiritual a concert as the first. A field-piece was then discharged from the top of a neighboring hill, and gave birth to one long reverberation, which ran round the circle of mountains in an unbroken chain of sound and rolled away without a separate echo. After these experiments, the cold atmosphere drove us all into the house, with the keenest appetites for supper.

It did one's heart good to see the great fires that were kindled in the parlor and bar-room, especially the latter, where the fireplace was built of rough stone, and might have contained the trunk of an old tree for a backlog. A man keeps a comfortable hearth when his own forest is at his very door. In the parlor, when the evening was fairly set in, we held our hands before our eyes to shield them from the ruddy glow, and began a pleasant variety of conversation. The mineralogist and the physician talked about the invigorating qualities of the mountain air, and its excellent effect on Ethan Crawford's father, an old man of seventy-five, with the unbroken frame of middle life. The two brides and the doctor's wife held a whispered discussion, which, by their frequent titterings and a blush or two, seemed to have reference to the trials or enjoyments of the matrimonial state. The bridegrooms sat together in a corner, rigidly silent, like Quakers whom the spirit moveth not, being still in the odd predicament of bashfulness towards their own young wives. The Green Mountain squire chose me for his companion, and described the difficulties he had met with half a century ago in travelling from the Connecticut River through the Notch to Conway, now a single day's journey, though it had cost him eighteen. The Georgians held the album between them, and favored us with the few specimens of its contents which they considered ridiculous enough to be worth hearing. One extract met with deserved applause. It was a "Sonnet to the Snow on Mount Washington," and had been contributed that very afternoon, bearing a signature of great distinction in magazines and annals. The lines were elegant and full of fancy, but too remote from familiar sentiment, and cold as their subject, resembling those curious specimens of crystallized vapor which I observed next day on the mountain top. The poet was understood to be the young gentleman of the gold opera glass, who heard our laudatory remarks with the composure of a veteran.

Such was our party, and such their ways of amusement. But on a winter evening another set of guests assembled at the hearth where these summer travellers were now sitting. I once had it in contemplation to spend a month hereabouts, in sleighing time, for the sake of studying the yeomen of New England, who then elbow each other through the Notch by hundreds, on their way to Portland. There could be no better school for such a place than Ethan Crawford's inn. Let the student go thither in December, sit down with the teamsters at their meals, share their evening merriment, and repose with them at night when every bed has its three occupants, and parlor, bar-room, and kitchen are strewn with slumberers around the fire. Then let him rise before daylight, button his great-coat, muffle up his ears, and stride with the departing caravan a mile or two, to see how sturdily they make head against the blast. A treasure of characteristic traits will repay all inconveniences, even should a frozen nose be of the number.

The conversation of our party soon became more animated and sincere, and we recounted some traditions of the Indians, who believed that the father and mother of their race were saved from a deluge by ascending the peak of Mount Washington. The children of that pair have been overwhelmed, and found no such refuge. In the mythology of the savage, these mountains were afterwards considered sacred and inaccessible, full of unearthly wonders, illuminated at lofty heights by the blaze of precious stones, and inhabited by deities, who sometimes shrouded themselves in the snow-storm and came down on the lower world. There are few legends more poetical than that of the "Great Carbuncle" of the White Mountains. The belief was communicated to the English settlers, and is hardly yet extinct, that a gem, of such immense size as to be seen shining miles away, hangs from a rock over a clear, deep lake, high up among the hills. They who had once beheld its splendor were inthralled with an unutterable yearning to possess it. But a spirit guarded that inestimable jewel, and bewildered the adventurer with a dark mist from the enchanted lake. Thus life was worn away in the vain search for an unearthly treasure, till at length the deluded one went up the mountain, still sanguine as in youth, but returned no more. On this theme methinks I could frame a tale with a deep moral.

The hearts of the pale-faces would not thrill to these superstitions of the red men, though we spoke of them in the centre of the haunted region. The habits and sentiments of that departed people were too distinct from those of their successors to find much real sympathy. It has often been a matter of regret to me that I was shut out from the most peculiar field of American fiction by an inability to see any romance, or poetry, or grandeur, or beauty in the Indian character, at least till such traits were pointed out by others. I do abhor an Indian story. Yet no writer can be more secure of a permanent place in our literature than the biographer of the Indian chiefs. His subject, as referring to tribes which have mostly vanished from the earth, gives him a right to be placed on a classic shelf, apart from the merits which will sustain him there.

I made inquiries whether, in his researches about these parts, our mineralogist had found the three "Silver Hills" which an Indian sachem sold to an Englishman nearly two hundred years ago, and the treasure of which the posterity of the purchaser have been looking for ever since. But the man of science had ransacked every hill along the Saco, and knew nothing of these prodigious piles of wealth. By this time, as usual with men on the eve of great adventure, we had prolonged our session deep into the night, considering how early we were to set out on our six miles' ride to the foot of Mount Washington. There was now a general breaking up. I scrutinized the faces of the two bridegrooms, and saw but little probability of their leaving the bosom of earthly bliss, in the first week of the honeymoon and at the frosty hour of three, to climb above the clouds; nor when I felt how sharp the wind was as it rushed through a broken pane and eddied between the chinks of my unplastered chamber, did I anticipate much alacrity on my own part, though we were to seek for the "Great Carbuncle."

The Ambitious Guest

One September night a family had gathered round their hearth, and piled it high with the driftwood of mountain streams, the dry cones of the pine, and the splintered ruins of great trees that had come crashing down the precipice. Up the chimney roared the fire, and brightened the room with its broad blaze. The faces of the father and mother had a sober gladness; the children laughed; the eldest daughter was the image of Happiness at seventeen; and the aged grandmother who sat knitting in the warmest place, was the image of Happiness grown old. They had found the "herb, heart's-ease," in the bleakest spot of all New England. This family were situated in the Notch of the White Hills, where the wind was sharp throughout the year, and pitilessly cold in the winter—giving their cottage all its fresh inclemency before it descended on the valley of the Saco. They dwelt in a cold spot and a dangerous one; for a mountain towered above their heads, so steep, that the stones would often rumble down its sides and startle them at midnight.

The daughter had just uttered some simple jest that filled them all with mirth, when the wind came through the Notch and seemed to pause before their cottage—rattling the door, with a sound of wailing and lamentation, before it passed into the valley. For a moment it saddened them, though there was nothing unusual in the tones. But the family were glad again when they perceived that the latch was lifted by some traveller, whose footsteps had been unheard amid the dreary blast which heralded his approach, and wailed as he was entering, and went moaning away from the door.

Though they dwelt in such a solitude, these people held daily converse with the world. The romantic pass of the Notch is a great artery, through which the life-blood of internal commerce is continually throbbing between Maine, on one side, and the Green Mountains and the shores of the St. Lawrence, on the other. The stage-coach always drew up before the door of the cottage. The wayfarer, with no companion but his staff, paused here to exchange a word, that the sense of loneliness might not utterly overcome him ere he could pass through the cleft of the mountain, or reach the first house in the valley. And here the teamster, on his way to Portland market, would put up for the night; and, if a bachelor, might sit an hour beyond the usual bedtime, and steal a kiss from the mountain maid at parting. It was one of those primitive taverns where the traveller pays only for food and lodging, but meets with a homely kindness beyond all price. When the footsteps were heard, therefore, between the outer door and the inner one, the whole family rose up, grandmother, children, and all, as if about to welcome some one who belonged to them, and whose fate was linked with theirs.

The door was opened by a young man. His face at first wore the melancholy expression, almost despondency, of one who travels a wild and bleak road, at nightfall and alone, but soon brightened up when he saw the kindly warmth of his reception. He felt his heart spring forward to meet them all, from the old woman, who wiped a chair with her apron, to the little child that held out its arms to him. One glance and smile placed the stranger on a footing of innocent familiarity with the eldest daughter.

"Ah, this fire is the right thing!" cried he; "especially when there is such a pleasant circle round it. I am quite benumbed; for the Notch is just like the pipe of a great pair of bellows; it has blown a terrible blast in my face all the way from Bartlett."

"Then you are going towards Vermont?" said the master of the house, as he helped to take a light knapsack off the young man's shoulders.

"Yes; to Burlington, and far enough beyond," replied he. "I meant to have been at Ethan Crawford's tonight; but a pedestrian lingers along such a road as this. It is no matter; for, when I saw this good fire, and all your cheerful faces, I felt as if you had kindled it on purpose for me, and were waiting my arrival. So I shall sit down among you, and make myself at home."

The frank-hearted stranger had just drawn his chair to the fire when something like a heavy footstep was heard without, rushing down the steep side of the mountain, as with long and rapid strides, and taking such a leap in passing the cottage as to strike the opposite precipice. The family held their breath, because they knew the sound, and their guest held his by instinct.

"The old mountain has thrown a stone at us, for fear we should forget him," said the landlord, recovering himself. "He sometimes nods his head and threatens to come down; but we are old neighbors, and agree together pretty well upon the whole. Besides we have a sure place of refuge hard by if he should be coming in good earnest."

Let us now suppose the stranger to have finished his supper of bear's meat; and, by his natural felicity of manner, to have placed himself on a footing of kindness with the whole family, so that they talked as freely together as if he belonged to their mountain brood. He was of a proud, yet gentle spirit—haughty and reserved among the rich and great; but ever ready to stoop his head to the lowly cottage door, and be like a brother or a son at the poor man's fireside. In the household of the Notch he found warmth and simplicity of feeling, the pervading intelligence of New England, and a poetry of native growth, which they had gathered when they little thought of it from the mountain peaks and chasms, and at the very threshold of their romantic and dangerous abode. He had travelled far and alone; his whole life, indeed, had been a solitary path; for, with the lofty caution of his nature, he had kept himself apart from those who might otherwise have been his companions. The family, too, though so kind and hospitable, had that consciousness of unity among themselves, and separation from the world at large, which, in every domestic circle, should still keep a holy place where no stranger may intrude. But this evening a prophetic sympathy impelled the refined and educated youth to pour out his heart before the simple mountaineers, and constrained them to answer him with the same free confidence. And thus it should have been. Is not the kindred of a common fate a closer tie than that of birth?

The secret of the young man's character was a high and abstracted ambition. He could have borne to live an undistinguished life, but not to be forgotten in the grave. Yearning desire had been transformed to hope; and hope, long cherished, had become like certainty, that, obscurely as he journeyed now, a glory was to beam on all his pathway—though not, perhaps, while he was treading it. But when posterity should gaze back into the gloom of what was now the present, they would trace the brightness of his footsteps, brightening as meaner glories faded, and confess that a gifted one had passed from his cradle to his tomb with none to recognize him.

"As yet," cried the stranger—his cheek glowing and his eye

flashing with enthusiasm—"as yet, I have done nothing. Were I to vanish from the earth tomorrow, none would know so much of me as you: that a nameless youth came up at nightfall from the valley of the Saco, and opened his heart to you in the evening, and passed through the Notch by sunrise, and was seen no more. Not a soul would ask, 'Who was he? Whither did the wanderer go?' But I cannot die till I have achieved my destiny. Then, let Death come! I shall have built my monument!"

There was a continual flow of natural emotion, gushing forth amid abstracted reverie, which enabled the family to understand this young man's sentiments, though so foreign from their own. With quick sensibility of the ludicrous, he blushed at the ardor into which he had been betrayed.

"You laugh at me," said he, taking the eldest daughter's hand, and laughing himself. "You think my ambition as nonsensical as if I were to freeze myself to death on the top of Mount Washington, only that people might spy at me from the country round about. And, truly, that would be a noble pedestal for a man's statue!"

"It is better to sit here by this fire," answered the girl, blushing, "and be comfortable and contented, though nobody thinks about us."

"I suppose," said her father, after a fit of musing, "there is something natural in what the young man says; and if my mind had been turned that way, I might have felt just the same. It is strange, wife, how his talk has set my head running on things that are pretty certain never to come to pass."

"Perhaps they may," observed the wife. "Is the man thinking what he will do when he is a widower?"

"No, no!" cried he, repelling the idea with reproachful kindness. "When I think of your death, Esther, I think of mine, too. But I was wishing we had a good farm in Bartlett, or Bethlehem, or Littleton, or some other township round the White Mountains; but not where they could tumble on our heads. I should want to stand well with my neighbors and be called Squire, and sent to General Court for a term or two; for a plain, honest man may do as much good there as a lawyer. And when I should be grown quite an old man, and you an old woman, so as not to be long apart, I might die happy enough in my bed, and leave you all crying around me. A slate gravestone would suit me as well as a marble one—with just my name and age, and a verse of a hymn, and something to let people know that I lived an honest man and died a Christian."

"There now!" exclaimed the stranger; "it is our nature to desire a monument, be it slate or marble, or a pillar of granite, or a glorious memory in the universal heart of man."

"We're in a strange way, tonight," said the wife, with tears in her eyes. "They say it's a sign of something, when folks' minds go a wandering so. Hark to the children!"

They listened accordingly. The younger children had been put to bed in another room, but with an open door between, so that they could be heard talking busily among themselves. One and all seemed to have caught the infection from the fireside circle, and were outvying each other in wild wishes, and childish projects of what they would do when they came to be men and women. At length a little boy, instead of addressing his brothers and sisters, called out to his mother.

"I'll tell you what I wish, mother," cried he. "I want you and father and grandma'm, and all of us, and the stranger too, to start right away, and go and take a drink out of the basin of the Flume!"

Nobody could help laughing at the child's notion of leaving a warm bed, and dragging them from a cheerful fire, to visit the basin of the Flume—a brook, which tumbles over the precipice, deep within the Notch. The boy had hardly spoken when a wagon rattled along the road, and stopped a moment before the door. It appeared to contain two or three men, who were cheering their hearts with the rough chorus of a song, which resounded, in broken notes, between the cliffs, while the singers hesitated whether to continue their journey or put up here for the night.'

"Father," said the girl, "they are calling you by name."

But the good man doubted whether they had really called him, and was unwilling to show himself too solicitous of gain by inviting people to patronize his house. He therefore did not hurry to the door; and the lash being soon applied, the travellers plunged into the Notch, still singing and laughing, though their music and mirth came back drearily from the heart of the mountain.

"There, mother!" cried the boy, again. "They'd have given us a ride to the Flume."

Again they laughed at the child's pertinacious fancy for a night ramble. But it happened that a light cloud passed over the daughter's spirit; she looked gravely into the fire, and drew a breath that was almost a sigh. It forced its way, in spite of a little struggle to repress it. Then, starting and blushing, she looked quickly round the circle, as if they had caught a glimpse into her bosom. The stranger asked what she had been thinking of.

"Nothing," answered she, with a downcast smile. "Only I felt lonesome just then."

"Oh, I have always had a gift of feeling what is in other people's hearts," said he, half seriously. "Shall I tell the secrets of yours? For I know what to think when a young girl shivers by a warm hearth, and complains of lonesomeness at her mother's side. Shall I put these feelings into words?"

"They would not be a girl's feelings any longer if they could be put into words," replied the mountain nymph, laughing, but avoiding his eye.

All this was said apart. Perhaps a germ of love was springing in their hearts, so pure that it might blossom in Paradise, since it could not be matured on earth; for women worship such gentle dignity as his; and the proud, contemplative, yet kindly soul is oftenest captivated by simplicity like hers. But while they spoke softly, and he was watching the happy sadness, the lightsome shadows, the shy yearnings of a maiden's nature, the wind through the Notch took a deeper and drearier sound. It seemed, as the fanciful stranger said, like the choral strain of the spirits of the blast, who in old Indian times had their dwelling among these mountains, and made their heights and recesses a sacred region. There was a wail along the road, as if a funeral were passing. To chase away the gloom, the family threw pine branches on their fire, till the dry leaves crackled and the flame arose, discovering once again a scene of peace and humble happiness. The light hovered about them fondly, and caressed them all. There were the little faces of the children, peeping from their bed apart, and here the father's frame of strength, the mother's subdued and careful mien, the high-browed youth, the budding girl, and the good old grandam, still knitting in the warmest place. The aged woman looked up from her task, and, with fingers ever busy, was the next to speak.

"Old folks have their notions," said she, "as well as young ones. You've been wishing and planning; and letting your heads run on one thing and another, till you've set my mind a wandering too.

Now what should an old woman wish for, when she can go but a step or two before she comes to her grave? Children, it will haunt me night and day till I tell you."

"What is it, mother?" cried the husband and wife at once.

Then the old woman, with an air of mystery which drew the circle closer round the fire, informed them that she had provided her grave-clothes some years before—a nice linen shroud, a cap with a muslin ruff, and everything of a finer sort than she had worn since her wedding day. But this evening an old superstition had strangely recurred to her. It used to be said, in her younger days, that if anything were amiss with a corpse, if only the ruff were not smooth, or the cap did not set right, the corpse in the coffin and beneath the clods would strive to put up its cold hands and arrange it. The bare thought made her nervous.

"Don't talk so, grandmother!" said the girl, shuddering.

"Now"—continued the old woman, with singular earnestness, yet smiling strangely at her own folly—"I want one of you, my children—when your mother is dressed and in the coffin—I want one of you to hold a looking-glass over my face. Who knows but I may take a glimpse at myself, and see whether all's right?"

"Old and young, we dream of graves and monuments," murmured the stranger youth. "I wonder how mariners feel when the ship is sinking, and they, unknown and undistinguished, are to be buried together in the ocean—that wide and nameless sepulchre?"

For a moment, the old woman's ghastly conception so engrossed the minds of her hearers that a sound abroad in the night, rising like the roar of a blast, had grown broad, deep, and terrible, before the fated group were conscious of it. The house and all within it trembled; the foundations of the earth seemed to be shaken, as if this awful sound were the peal of the last trump. Young and old exchanged one wild glance, and remained an instant, pale, affrighted, without utterance, or power to move. Then the same shriek burst simultaneously from all their lips.

"The Slide! The Slide!"

The simplest words must intimate, but not portray, the unutterable horror of the catastrophe. The victims rushed from their cottage, and sought refuge in what they deemed a safer spot—where, in contemplation of such an emergency, a sort of barrier had been reared. Alas! they had quitted their security, and fled right into the pathway of destruction. Down came the whole side of the mountain, in a cataract of ruin. Just before it reached the house, the stream broke into two branches—shivered not a window there, but overwhelmed the whole vicinity, blocked up the road, and annihilated everything in its dreadful course. Long ere the thunder of the great Slide had ceased to roar among the mountains, the mortal agony had been endured, and the victims were at peace. Their bodies were never found.

The next morning, the light smoke was seen stealing from the cottage chimney up the mountain side. Within, the fire was yet smouldering on the hearth, and the chairs in a circle round it, as if the inhabitants had but gone forth to view the devastation of the Slide, and would shortly return, to thank Heaven for their miraculous escape. All had left separate tokens, by which those who had known the family were made to shed a tear for each. Who has not heard their name? The story has been told far and wide, and will forever be a legend of these mountains. Poets have sung their fate.

There were circumstances which led some to suppose that a stranger had been received into the cottage on this awful night, and had shared the catastrophe of all its inmates. Others denied that there were sufficient grounds for such a conjecture. Woe for the high-souled youth, with his dream of Earthly Immortality! His name and person utterly unknown; his history, his way of life, his plans, a mystery never to be solved, his death and his existence equally a doubt! Whose was the agony of that death moment?

THOMAS STARR KING

Thomas Starr King (b. New York City, 1824; d. 1864) moved with his family to Portsmouth when he was four. When his father, a minister, died in 1835, Thomas had to leave school to help support his five younger brothers and sisters. In 1846 he took the pulpit in Charlestown, New Hampshire and began writing about the White Mountains. In 1850 he went to San Francisco to preach and to agitate for the abolition of slavery. His skills as a lecturer, according to some reports rivaled only by Emerson, made him a popular speaker.

The White Hills: Their Legends, Landscape, and Poetry was published in Boston by Crosby, Nichols in 1860. The excerpt that follows describes some of the exploits of the Crawford family.

The White Hills:
Their Legends, Landscape, and Poetry

The hardships of which we have been writing are forcibly suggested at the Giant's Grave. Abel Crawford lived in a log hut on that mound some months, alone. But in 1792, the Rosebrook family moved into it when it was buried in snow, so that the entrance to it could be found with difficulty. For six weeks neither the sun, nor the heat from the cabin, would make a drop of water fall from the eaves. During the whole winter they were dependent upon the game they could catch, and often, from fear that the father might return empty, the children would be sent down through the Notch twelve miles, to Abel Crawford's, to obtain something for sustenance. Good Mrs. Rosebrook often lay awake late in the night, waiting anxiously for the children's return through the snows and winds of the awful Notch, and when they arrived would "pour out her love in prayer and thankfulness to her heavenly Father, for preserving them, and that she was permitted to receive them again to her humble mansion."

Abel Crawford, in his old age, was never tired of telling stories of the hardships and adventures of the pioneers. He was well named the "veteran pilot" of the hills; for he was the first guide that introduced visitors to the grandeur of the scenery so easily reached now, and he saw the gradual process of civilization applied to the wilderness between Bethlehem and Upper Bartlett. When he was about twenty-five years old, he wandered through the region alone for months, dressed in tanned mooseskin, lord of the

> Cradle, hunting-ground, and bier
> Of wolf and otter, bear and deer.

He assisted in cutting the first footpath to the ridge, and at seventy-five, in the year 1840, he rode the first horse that climbed the cone of Mount Washington. During the last ten years of his life he was a noble object of interest to thousands of visitors from all parts of the United States, for whom the whole tour of the hills had been smoothed into a pastime and luxury. He died at eighty-five. He had been so long accustomed to greet travellers in the summer, that he longed to have his life spared till the visitors made their appearance in Bartlett, on their way to the Notch. He used to sit in the warm spring days, supported by his daughter, his snow-white hair falling to his shoulders, waiting for the first ripple of that large tide which he had seen increasing in volume for twenty years. Not long after the stages began to carry their summer freight by his door, he passed away. We have a very pleasant recollection of the venerable appearance of the patriarch in front of his house under Mount Crawford, in the year 1849, when we made our first visit to the White Hills. A large bear was chained to a pole near the house, and the stage load of people had gathered around, equally interested in seeing a specimen of the first settlers and of the aboriginal tenants of the wilderness. The old man handed the writer a biscuit, and said: "Give it to the beast, young man, and then tell when you go back to Boston, that a bear ate out of your hand up in these mountains." The difference between an experience in the mountain region, as our party were then enjoying it for a week, and his early acquaintance with its hardships and solitude, was the difference between feeding a fettered bear with a biscuit, and wrestling in a tight hug with a hungry one alone in the forest.

In 1803 the first rude public-house for straggling visitors to the White Mountains, was erected on the Giant's Grave itself. And in 1819 the first rough path was cut through the forest on the side of the Mount Washington range to the rocky ridge. Ethan Allen Crawford, who lived on the Giant's Grave, marked and cleared this path in connection with Abel Crawford, his father, who was living eight miles below the Notch. A few years after, Ethan spotted and trimmed a footpath on the side of Mount Washington itself, along essentially the same route by which carriages are driven now from the White Mountain House to the Cold Spring. And it ought not to be forgotten that it was by Ethan Crawford that the first protection for visitors was built under the cone of Mount Washington. It was a stone hut, furnished with a small stove, an iron chest, a roll of sheet lead, and a plentiful supply of soft moss and hemlock boughs for bedding. The lead was the cabin-register on which visitors left their names engraved by a piece of sharp iron. Every particle of this camp and all the furniture, was swept off on the night of the storm by which the Willey family were overwhelmed.

Noble Ethan Crawford! we must pause a few moments before the career of this stalwart Jötun of the mountains, in the story of whose fortunes the savageness and hardships of the wilderness and the heroic qualities they nurse are shown in one picture. He was born in 1792. His early childhood was passed in a log hut a few miles from the Notch; and in his manhood, after a fire in 1818 had burned the comfortable house on the Giant's Grave, he lived again in a log house with but one apartment and no windows. In 1819, he had built a rough house of a larger size, with a stone chimney, in which during the cold spells of winter, more than a cord of wood would be burned in twenty-four hours. He tells us that he never owned a hat, mittens, or shoes until he was thirteen years old; yet could harness and unharness horses in the biting winter weather with bare head, hands, and feet, "and not mind, or complain of the cold, as I was used to it." As to what is called comfort in the lowlands, he found that

> Naught the mountain yields thereof,
> But savage health and sinews tough.

He grew to be nearly seven feet in height, and rejoiced in a strength which he would show in lifting five hundred weight into a boat; in dragging a bear that he had muzzled to his house, that he might be tamed; or in carrying a buck home alive, upon his shoulders. What a flavor of wild mountain life, what vivid suggestions of the closest tug of man with nature,—of raw courage and muscle against frost and gale, granite and savageness, do we find in his adventures and exploits;—his leaping from a load of hay in the Notch when a furious gust made it topple, and catching it on his shoulder to prevent it from falling over a precipice; his breaking out the road, for miles, through the wild winter drifts; his carrying the mail on his back, after freshets, to the next settlement, when a horse could not cross the streams; his climbings of Mount Washington with a party of adventurers, laden like a pack-horse, without suffering more fatigue than ordinary men would feel after a level walk of ten miles; his returns from the summit bearing some exhausted member of a party on his back; his long, lonely tramps, on snow-shoes, after moose, and his successful shooting of a pair of the noble beasts, two miles back of the Notch, about dark, and sleeping through the cold night in their warm skins, undismayed by the wolf howls that serenaded him!

The tribe of bears in a circumference of twenty miles knew him well. Many a den he made desolate of its cubs by shaking them, like apples, from trees into which they would run to escape him; then tying his handkerchief around their mouths he would take them home under his arm to tame them. Many a wrestle did he have with full grown ones who would get their feet in his traps. Scarcely a week passed while he lived among the mountains which was not marked by some encounter with a bear.

With the wolves also, he carried on a war of years. So long as he kept sheep he could not frighten the wolves into cessation of hostilities. The marauders showed the skill of a surgeon in their rapine and slaughter. Ethan found, now and then, a sheepskin a few rods from his house with no mark upon it except a smooth slit from the throat to the fore legs, as though it had been cut with a knife. The legs had been taken off as far as the lowest joint; all the flesh had been eaten out clean, and only the head and backbone had been left attached to the pelt. When the feat was accomplished, the wolves would give him notice by a joint howl, which the Washington range would echo from their "bleak concave," so that all the woods seemed filled with packs of the fierce pirates. Once in a December night four wolves made a descent upon his sheep, which fled among the carriages near the house, for safety. Ethan went out in his nightdress and faced them in the bright moonlight. He had no weapon, and so they rose on their haunches to hear what he might have to say. He harangued them, to little purpose for some time, and at last "observed to them that they had better make off with themselves," with the intimation that an axe or gun would be soon forthcoming. They then turned about and marched away, "giving us some of their lonesome music." But Ethan found, the next morning, that they had enjoyed his hospitality, by digging up carcasses of bears back of the stable, and gnawing them close to the bone.

He thinned the sables from the region by his traps. The banks of the neighboring brooks he depopulated of otters. Yet he had an affection for all the creatures of the wilderness, and loved to have

young wolves, and tame bucks, and well-behaved bears, and do-
mesticated sable, around his premises; while the collecting of rare
alpine plants from the snowy edges of the ravines on the ridge,
where Nature had "put them according to their merits," was "a
beautiful employment, which I always engaged in with much pleasure." But his most remarkable adventures were his contests with
the wild-cats, the fiercest animals which the mountains harbored.
The hills that slope towards the Ammonoosuc were cleared by him
of these furious freebooters, that made great havoc with his geese
and sheep. His greatest exploit was his capture of one of these
creatures in a tree within the Notch, by a lasso made of birch
sticks, which he twisted on the spot. He slipped it over the wild-
cat's neck, and jerked the animal down ten feet. The noose broke.
He repaired it instantly, fastened it once more around the creature's head, pulled him down within reach, and after a severe battle, killed him. He seems to have possessed a magic fetter, like that
which the dark elves of the Scandinavian myths wove to bind
the wolf Fenrir, and which was plaited of six things into a cord
smooth and soft as a silken string: the beards of women, the noise
of a cat's footfall, the roots of stones, the sinews of bears, the spit-
tle of birds, and the breath of fish.

What extremes in Ethan's experience! He entertained many of
the wisest and most distinguished of the country under his rude
roof, and was gratefully remembered for his hospitality, and his
faithful service in guiding them to the great ridge. He would come
home from a bear-fight, to find in his house, perhaps, "a member
of Congress, Daniel Webster," who desired his assistance on foot
to the summit of Mount Washington. *There* was a couple whose
talk would have been worth hearing! Ethan says that they went up
"without meeting anything worthy of note, more than was common for me to find, *but to him things appeared interesting*. And
when we arrived there, he addressed himself in this way, saying:
'Mount Washington, I have come a long distance, and have toiled
hard to arrive at your summit, and now you give me a cold reception. I am extremely sorry, that I shall not have time enough to
view this grand prospect which lies before me, and nothing prevents but the uncomfortable atmosphere in which you reside.'"
How accurately Ethan reported the address, we cannot certify; but
as the rostrum was the grandest, and the audience the smallest,

which was ever honored with a formal speech by the great orator, the picture should not be lost. The snow from a sudden squall froze upon the pair as they descended the cone. The statesman was evidently interested in his guide, for Ethan says that "the next morning, after paying his bill, he made me a handsome present of twenty dollars."

And Ethan's life was perpetually set in remarkable contrasts. From struggles with wild-cats in the forests of Cherry Mountain, to the society of his patient, faithful, pious wife, was a distance as wide as can be indicated on the planet. Mount Washington looked down into his uncouth domicile, and saw there

Sparta's stoutness, Bethlehem's heart.

Lucy taught him how to meet calamity without despair and repining. When his house burned down, and left him with no property but one new cheese and the milk of the cows, his wife, though sick, was not despondent. When his debts, caused by this fire, pressed heavy, and he staggered under difficulties as he never did under the heaviest load in the forest, she assured him that Providence had some wise purpose in their trouble. When his crops were swept off, and his meadows filled with sand by freshets, Lucy's courage was not crushed. He knocked down a swaggering bully, once, on a muster-field in Lancaster, and was obliged to promise Lucy that he would never give way to an angry passion again. When death invaded their household, and his own powerful frame was so shaken by disease and pain, that a flash of lightning, as he said, seemed to run from his spine to the ends of his hair, his wife's religious patience and trust proved an undrainable cordial. And after he became weakened by sickness, if he staid out long after dark, Lucy would take a lantern and go into the woods to search for him. He was put into jail at last in Lancaster for debt. Lucy wrote a pleading letter to his chief creditor to release him, but without effect. This, says Ethan, "forced me, in the jail, to reflect on human nature, and it overcame me, so that I was obliged to call for the advice of physicians and a nurse." Other forms of adversity, too, beset him—opposition to his public-house when travellers became more plentiful, which destroyed his prospects of profit; the breaking of a bargain for the sale of his lands; foul defamation of his character to the post-office authorities in Washington, from whom he held an appointment. Broken in health, oppressed by pecuniary burdens, and with shattered spirits, he left the plateau at the base of Mount Washington for a more pleasant home in Vermont, accompanied by Lucy, whose faith did not allow her to murmur. But he experienced hard fortune there, too, and returned to die, within sight of the range, an old man, before he had reached the age of fifty-six years.

Since the breaking up of his home on the Giant's Grave, the mountains have heard no music which they have echoed so heartily as the windings of his horn, and the roar of the cannon which he used to load to the muzzle, that his guests might hear a park of artillery reply. Few men that have ever visited the mountains have done more faithful work or borne so much adversity and suffering. The cutting of his heel-cord with an axe, when he was chopping out the first path up Mount Washington, was a type of the result to himself of his years of toil in the wilderness; and his own quaint reflection on that wound, which inflicted lameness upon him for months, is the most appropriate inscription, after the simple words, "an honest man," that could be reared over his grave: "So it is that men suffer various ways in advancing civilization, and through God, mankind are indebted to the labors of men in many different spheres of life."

DR. BENJAMIN BALL

Dr. Benjamin Ball (b. Northborough, [now Northboro] Massachusetts, 1820; d. Chiriqui, Panama, 1859.) M.D. Harvard, 1844. An experienced mountaineer, Ball ascended peaks in Switzerland and Java before climbing Mount Washington. The following excerpt is from his account *Three Days on the White Mountains: Being the Perilous Adventure of Dr. Benjamin L. Ball on Mount Washington, During October 25, 26, and 27, 1855*, published in Boston by N. Noyes in 1856.

Three Days on the White Mountains

. . . As I looked upon the dreary spot, the thought came, *Can it be* that I must go through with another night? Had the idea of *this* occurred this morning should I not have felt at least a little discouraged? O that I might awake, and find it a dreadful dream!

I fixed down my umbrella in the same place, and endeavored to close it in more securely than before. But I could effect little with my swollen and almost useless hands, and with my benumbed limbs bending and twisting under me. And it is of no use to attempt building a fire, thought I, for the wind is violent, like that of the last night, and the snow again comes driving and whirling. Perhaps it is better that I cannot have it. I might receive in my present state more injury than benefit.

But this *intolerable thirst!* My throat and stomach feel as if they were scorched. I must get some drink before commencing upon this long night. I believe I can find my way to the place where I discovered water during the day; but the risk in the storm would be too great. I must be content without it. Darkness advances. I dread, yet I must seek, my shelter. In how short a time should I be powerless without it!

For drink I gathered large crusts of frozen snow, which I could only take with me among the low branches by placing them on the ground before me, and drawing myself up to them. In this way, upon my hands and knees, through the cold snow I crept into my humble abode. And humble I found it; and, if ever I had in my heart anything like vain pride, I am sure there was none now remaining.

I endeavored to soften my bed, which was an uneven place, hard, rough, inclined and crooked, and as if made up of a mixture of snow, sharp stones, stubs and knobs of roots, by breaking out the frozen ice and snow from the fir-tops which I had gathered and placing them under me. But the improvement was slight, and I felt them pressing into my flesh painfully. Then, as I curled myself up to acquire warmth, thoughts came to my mind: "Well,—I cannot say—this may be my last 'Ramble.' This cold is stupefying—I cannot get warm; and if I lose myself for five minutes it is perhaps

decided. But I may as well take a humorous view of it. How singular, that so immediately after the publishing of "Rambles in Eastern Asia," this last and shortest of all my rambles, and within my
own country, should be the *winding up!*—the thread caught and
broken on Mount Washington, almost in sight of my own home.
Terminated in such a manner, no one could know the circumstances. Different reports, if any, would be circulated. Some, perhaps, would have it that I was insane; others that I wished to com-
mit suicide; and the most charitable might allow that I was lost in
the fog. Of course there would be no one to say to the contrary of
any of them.

But the second night was passed much like the first. I could not
control the shaking which extended through my whole muscular
system, it being like that experienced when one's teeth chatter with
the cold. It stormed and snowed all night, and the snow drifted in
considerably, entering by the open front of my covering, though
not so as to reach much the upper part of my body. The wind came
in violent gusts, threatening to strip to atoms my only shelter.
Should this take place, then would come a greater trial than any
before.

To be prepared for such an emergency, I decided, in my own
mind, that, if it should happen, I would use all my strength to descend the Mountain in whatever direction I could move, although
it appeared next to impossible to do so in the night and in the
midst of the thick brush with its sharp and angular limbs; and
that, wherever exhaustion obliged me to stop, I would fasten my
handkerchief in the most conspicuous place, as a signal to any who
might pass within its sight; and, when it came to the worst, I
would take from my pocket-book a piece of paper, and write upon
it a brief account of my misfortune, for the satisfaction of my
friends.

I suffered much from the want of water, notwithstanding every
few minutes I took into my mouth a piece of the snow-crust,
which alleviated the distress only while I was swallowing it. But it
would not melt fast enough to quench my thirst. With my mouth
chilled by repeated mouthfuls of snow or ice, there was left insufficient warmth to melt but a little, and that at intervals. I was also
distressed for breath. My respiration was short, and my lungs
would apparently inflate to but about half their natural capacity;

and with the greatest effort that I could exert there was little improvement, the sensation being constant of desiring to take a full
breath. This state of the lungs I attributed to the contracting action
of cold on the chest.

I also continually experienced a severe pain in my left side, as if
a heavy weight was resting there, or as if great compression was
being made over the heart.

Occasionally, as on the night before, I examined my pulse. It
could not be felt with my benumbed fingers, but with the palm of
my hand I could make it out. It was accelerated, as I judged, to
about eighty, with nearly a third less than its natural force, somewhat laboring, and very intermittent. I did not fear but that I
should be alive the next day, if I did not fall asleep.

The thought occurred, what if I am obliged to stay out a night
after this, without food, drink, or sleep? After a short consideration, taking into account my present state, that which had passed,
and the chances to come, I concluded that, *terrible* as it might be, I
should be able to survive it; but whether I could then walk or not, I
could not decide. And I was glad I *could* think so, for I much preferred to have my hopes leading ahead of my actual powers, than
to have them following behind short of reality.

FRANKLIN LEAVITT

Franklin Leavitt (b. Coos County near Lancaster, New Hampshire, August 6, 1824; d. 1890) achieved fame as a guide in the White Mountains; for much of that time, he was employed by the Crawford family. Leavitt later wrote verse about the White Mountains and events that took place there.

Leavitt's *Poems of the White Mountains* was published privately by the author. His verse was republished in an article by David Tatham, "Franklin Leavitt's White Mountain Verse," in *Historical New Hampshire* 33 (Fall 1978). The following two poems are typical.

The Willey Slide

Eighteen hundred and twenty-six
  The Willey mountain down did slip.
It missed the house and hit the barn;
  If they'd all staid in they'd met no harm.

It being in the dark of night
  The Willey family took a fright,
And out of the house they all did run
  And on to them the mountains come.

It buried them all up so deep
  They did not find them for three weeks,
And three of them were never found
  They were buried there so deep in the ground.

Through Crawford Notch by Rail

The Portland & Ogdensburg Railroad line
  Starts through the notch of the White Mountains about nine,
And is the best railroad I ever did find.
  They have good conductors and engineers too,
When "all aboard" they'll put you through.

The White Mountain snowdrifts are very high,
  When the snow plow strikes them it makes them fly.
Sometimes they fly up in the air,
  Then all on board it will scare.
But I for such things don't stand aside
  Because I was the mountain guide.

THE IDEALIZED COMMUNITY

"I THOUGHT Rivermouth the prettiest place in the world, and I think so still," wrote Thomas Bailey Aldrich. "We who are Tiverton born," Alice Brown reminisced, ". . . have a way of shutting our eyes now and then to present changes, and seeing things as they were once. . . ." Aldrich's *Story of a Bad Boy* and Brown's *Meadow-Grass: Tales of New England Life* thus voice the idealization of the old community that is characteristic of much New Hampshire literature in the nineteenth century. The pattern had been set even earlier, when Jeremy Belknap wrote: "Were I to form a picture of a happy society it would be a town consisting of a due mixture of hills, valleys, and streams of water: the land all fenced and cultivated, . . . the inhabitants mostly husbandmen, their wives and daughters domestic manufacturers. . . ."

To this kind of setting New Hampshire authors returned again and again. Appreciation of natural beauty, nostalgia for an era fast slipping away, and a blending of nature and agricultural endeavor were the predominant themes used to create the unifying image of perfect, rural community. The first major work to use these elements was *Northwood: A Tale of New England*, written by Sarah Josepha Buell Hale and published in 1827.

A transitional work, *Northwood* was the first major novel with a New Hampshire setting, marking the beginnings of the later genre of local color, and one of the last of the patriotic, postrevolutionary stories that compulsively stressed American superiority. Northwood, New Hampshire, as described by Sarah Buell Hale, is idyllic. The loosely constructed social history is interspersed with chauvinistic opinions on current issues. An English visitor to Northwood provides the motivation for the lectures of a didactic patriarch, a rural philosopher-squire who serves as the author's mouthpiece. This framework also permits the predominantly dialectical organization of the chapters. Foremost among the issues discussed at the fireside of Squire Romilly is slavery. This fact adds to the book's significance; Sarah Buell Hale was the first to address the issue in fiction. Although she deplored the inhumanity of slavery, as a northern Democrat she feared the disruptions of emancipation. When the English visitor boasts that Britain is about to free her slaves in the West Indies, Squire Romilly replies, "Well, try the experiment. We may learn something from its workings, though I do not anticipate any favorable results to the cause of freedom and humanity from such a step."

As the nation approached Civil War, the book was republished with the subtitle *A Tale of North and South*; the plot had in fact included a few brief episodes in South Carolina.

This pioneering novel contains careful descriptions of the rituals of daily life, home decoration, and food. Weddings, funerals, and holidays are included. Hale's ideal is a kind of Spartan elegance that suits the environment. Although such affairs have traditionally been the domain of women, her women are colorless— they express few opinions as they go about their household duties. Sarah Buell Hale was primarily a feminist only when it came to her own career.

Although Portsmouth seemed a more sophisticated community than Northwood, in the pre–Civil War years both shared a nostalgic atmosphere of peace and civility. For Thomas Bailey Aldrich the old colonial capital possessed every prerequisite for the ideal hometown; his affection is manifested not only in his sketches, *An Old Town by the Sea*, but also in *The Story of a Bad Boy*.

The Granite State was never better portrayed as the perfect setting for a happy childhood. Everyone must wish for a son like Tom Bailey, friends like Captain Nutter, and Miss Abigail, a Pepper Whitcomb to share youthful escapades, and a town like Rivermouth to grow up in.

As we drove through the quiet old town, I thought Rivermouth the prettiest place in the world; and I think so still. The streets are long and wide, shaded by gigantic American elms, whose drooping branches, interlaced here and there, span the avenues with arches graceful enough to be the handiwork of fairies. Many of the houses have small flower gardens in front, gay in the season with China-asters, and are substantially built, with massive chimney stacks and protruding eaves. A beautiful river goes rippling by the town, and, after turning and twisting among a lot of tiny islands, empties itself into the sea.

This is Portsmouth as Aldrich remembered it. Here Tom, Pepper, and their friends burn the old stagecoach in their Fourth of July bonfire; here the boys build a fortress of snow one glorious winter, and here Tom first falls in love. More than a century after its publication, the book retains its charm. Later, Henry Augustus Shute attempted in *The Real Diary of a Real Boy* to write of his Exeter boyhood as Aldrich had of his. The results, though pleasant, lack the quality of the original.

Down the coast from Portsmouth is Hampton Falls, birthplace of Alice Brown and inspiration for Tiverton, site of many of her short stories. No retired mariners walked these streets; Tiverton people were the yeoman farmers who serve as characters in what is called "local color" fiction. This particular genre was by no means unique to New Hampshire; such authors as Mary E. Wilkins Freeman, Sarah Orne Jewett, and Thomas Nelson Page wrote of their own regions. The distinguishing characteristics of the form in New Hampshire are the modest satisfactions of country life, delight in simple pleasures, self-sacrifice, and strength in adversity. Adjustment to life in a scenic but difficult terrain produces characters who develop a flinty integrity and survive with quiet grace. They are the people about whom Alice Brown wrote so sympathetically. In stories from *Meadow-Grass: Tales of New England Life* such as

"Farmer Eli's Vacation," "At Sudleigh Fair," and "Joint Owners in Spain" she recreated credible regional communities through her use of dialect, her appreciation of atmosphere, and her understanding of rural people. Puritan values are softened by Victorian sentiment; the stories explore nature, community, love, and religion. Plots are simple with few ambiguities. Even the elderly ladies of "Joint Owners in Spain," confined to an old folks' home, form a sort of subcommunity in a town that has not forgotten them.

This same appreciation of and respect for nature and the integrity of individuals appeared also in poetry, particularly in the work of a woman whose life is forever associated with New Hampshire's offshore islands.

Celia Thaxter loved the sea. Forced for a brief time to live in an inland town, she thought herself an exile; the experience produced "Land-Locked."

> O happy river, could I follow Thee!
> O yearning heart, that never can be still!
> O wistful eyes, that watch the steadfast hill,
> Longing for level line of solemn sea!

Most of her years she lived on the Isles of Shoals, overlooking that "level line of solemn sea." On Appledore Island she tended her garden, wrote poetry, and maintained a delightful correspondence with her friends. She occasionally visited her native Portsmouth and at least once traveled to Europe. But it was to her "enchanted islands" with their "strange charm" that she turned as her true home and the source of her joy. "The natives," she wrote, "or persons who have been brought up here, find it almost as difficult to tear themselves away as do the Swiss to leave their mountains. . . . No other place is able to furnish the inhabitants of the Shoals with sufficient air for their capacious lungs; there is never scope enough elsewhere, there is no horizon; they must have sea-room."

Throughout her life Celia Thaxter harbored a passionate sense of place—of her relationship to a special environment. This and a kind of transcendental faith permeate her poetry. Perceiving divine immanence in all things, she always treated nature with reverence. "To the heart of nature," she wrote, "one must needs be drawn in such a life; and very soon I learned how richly she repays in deep refreshment the reverent love of her worshipper." Flowers, birds, sunrises, storms, and always the sea recur in poem after poem. Her affinity with all creation prevails in the concluding lines of "The Sandpiper."

> I do not fear for thee, though wroth
> The tempest rushes through the sky:
> For are we not God's children both,
> Thou, little sandpiper, and I?

Although poets of the quality of Whittier and Longfellow also wrote about New Hampshire, and Edna Dean Proctor, whose work is more eclectic than Thaxter's, was chosen to write the official New Hampshire Old Home Week poem, in her fashion Celia Thaxter comes closest to expressing the essential quality of life in at least one corner of this small state.

Finally, there is no better summary of the values inherent in the concept of the idealized community than in the volumes of the *Granite Monthly*, subtitled *A New Hampshire Magazine Devoted to History, Biography, Literature, and State Progress*. This publication appeared from 1877 until 1930. The prejudices of the editors were perhaps best reflected in a few sentences in an article entitled "Picturesque Peterborough," published in 1895. The author, Edward French, rhapsodized on how uncommonly fortunate his town was

in the character of its early settlers. They were not a mixture of all nationalities and languages and habits, as in our new settlements of the present time, but were of that sturdy, remarkable race of Scotch-Irish, who themselves emigrated from Ireland, or were the immediate descendents of the same. They were not of the lower order of European population but were of the middle class, men considerably educated, so that they were well qualified to understand the tyrannical and exacting course pursued by their government toward them, and to fully appreciate their civil and religious rights.

That "lower order" of Europeans received short shrift in the *Granite Monthly*. Each issue usually featured a different town, and in descriptions of the local industry authors never ceased extolling mill owners, company agents, and managers. These men were "bold," "aggressive," "sagacious," and "humane," great "benefactors of the town." Rarely is there any reference to the faceless masses who tended the factories' machinery. Boston money and immigrant labor may have built New Hampshire industry, but the hometown boys who founded and ran the first enterprises receive all the plaudits of the *Granite Monthly*. The only significant reference to laborers occurs in a description of an early period of Sommersworth's development by Edward O. Lord: "Those were palmy days. The operatives were mostly young men and women from the country villages who were glad of a chance to earn a little extra money." Apparently French Canadians and Irish had yet to appear in this Yankee paradise, and even after they had, the *Granite Monthly* seemed unaware of their presence. In an article on Suncook, written when French Canadians constituted the bulk of the population, they are not mentioned.

The quality of much of the literature is questionable. Sentimental tales like "The Story of a Deserted Farmhouse" and even more sentimental poetry predominate in the issues. A few sequential entries in the table of contents of volume 35, for 1905, are representative: four poems, "My Boyhood Home," "My Father's Old Well," "My Grandmother's Garden," and "My Old New Hampshire Home"; and a short story by Dr. Arthur F. Sumner, "My Strange Adventure in India." Later the magazine began the cannibalistic practice of republishing earlier material. Remarkable also is the number of highly romantic serialized stories with foreign settings by non–New Hampshire authors. The publication never seemed to encourage the growth of good, imaginative, local literature. New Hampshire's best literary figures are not among the magazine's contributors: there are no poems by Celia Thaxter, no short stories by Alice Brown, no novels by Winston Churchill. Still, without any pretensions to literary excellence or encouragement of worthwhile authors, the volumes do vividly recreate many aspects of contemporary New Hampshire life. Photographs appear on almost every page, likenesses of the state's leading citizens— hirsute men and stern-visaged women. Their dwelling places are displayed, turreted and mansard roofed, with deep verandas draped in woodbine. And always there is history: stories of Stark and Webster, the battles of Bennington and Bunker Hill, the exploits of Rogers' Rangers, legends of the White Mountains, and stories of the sea. In terms of late Victorian and early twentieth-century popular middle-class culture, the *Granite Monthly*'s sixty-two volumes preserve a panorama of New Hampshire life. The journal is a valuable resource for the social and literary historian; its handsome volumes convey the poignancy of a time now lost.

The idealized community in its varied forms served as a frame of reference for a large body of literature about New Hampshire during the middle and later decades of the nineteenth century. A combination of neoclassical concepts of civic service emphasizing the priorities of citizens' public and private duties, and romantic individualism allowing for complete self-realization, this community united two ostensibly disparate ideals. Writers blithely assumed that these qualities could coexist in harmony. Authors also endowed their characters with puritan virtues of thrift and devotion to hard work and simultaneously lacquered them with Victorian sentiment. Despite its obvious contradictions, the image of the idealized community left a significant legacy, shaping the view that subsequent generations held of the New Hampshire of that time.

SARAH BUELL HALE

Sarah Josepha Buell Hale (b. Newport, New Hampshire, 1788; d. 1879) was the daughter of a captain in the American Revolution. Like most educated women of her time, she depended on her family, including a brother who attended Dartmouth, for her exposure to literature. In 1813 she married a Newport lawyer, David Hale, who encouraged her to write articles for local newspapers. After he died suddenly in 1822, leaving her with five children to support, she decided to exploit her literary skills. Starting with poetry, she went on to write a novel, which in 1827 became a bestseller. As a result she was offered and accepted a position as editor of the *Ladies' Magazine*, a new periodical published in Boston, and later became editor of Godey's *Ladies' Book*. She worked as an editor for about fifty years. She advocated many changes in contemporary views of women, although she withheld support for the women's rights movement, believing in separate "spheres" for men and women.

Her novel, *Northwood: A Tale of New England*, was published by Bowles and Dearborn in 1827 in Boston.

The following excerpt describes the homecoming of the young hero, Sidney Romilly, to Northwood.

Northwood: A Tale of New England

CHAPTER VI.
Home as Found

All hail, ye tender feelings dear!
The smile of love, the friendly tear,
The sympathetic glow.

ROBERT BURNS

The house before which our travelers now stood was a two-story building in front, with a range of low buildings behind; the whole painted yellow, with white window sashes and green doors, and everything around looked snug and finished. The house stood about five rods from the highway; and this fact deserves to be recorded, as a genuine, old-school Yankee, living twenty-five years ago, seldom left so many feet before his habitation. Indeed, they usually appear to have grudged every inch of ground devoted merely to ornament; the mowing lot, cow pasture and corn-field being all the park and lawn and garden they desired.

A neat railing, formed of slips of pine boards, painted white, and inserted in cross pieces, which were supported by wooden posts, ran from the highway to the house, on each side, and stretched across the front, enclosing an oblong square, to which was given the name of the "front door yard." Around this square were set Lombardy poplars, an exotic, which was then cherished in New England, to the exclusion of far more beautiful indigenous trees, as foreign articles are considered more valuable in proportion to the distance from whence they must be imported. It appeared, however, that the Romillys had discovered their error, and were endeavoring to correct it. This was evinced by the young elms and maples planted between the poplars, evidently with the design to have them for the guard and ornament of the scene, whenever their size would permit their tall, straight neighbors to be displaced. A graveled walk led up to the front door steps, which were formed of hewn granite, and wrought to appear nearly as beautiful as marble, and much more enduring. Clumps of rose bushes and lilacs were set around the paling, and, intermingled with evergreen shrubs, guarded, on each side, the graveled walk; but the pride of the parterre was the mountain ash. Several of these beautiful native trees, throwing up their heads as though proud of the coral clusters, now looking so bright in the absence of flowers, were scattered over the ground. It was evident that the forming hand of taste had been busy in disposing all to the best advantage; and had it been the season of sweets, the senses and imagination of even the most refined might have found full gratification.

On the east side of the railing, a gate opened into the back yard; and there was a carriage-way to drive round to the kitchen door, beyond which the barns, sheds, corn house, and all the various offices of a thriving and industrious farmer's establishment, were scattered about, like a young colony rising around a family mansion.

The last gleams of the setting sun yet lingered on the distant mountains, the village lights were beginning to appear, and a strong gleam, as of the blaze from a fire, illuminated the windows of one of the front apartments in the house of Mr. Romilly.

"What if this worshipful father of yours should not acknowledge you?" said Frankford. "We seem to be thrown entirely on his mercy."

"He will, at least, entertain us for the night," replied Sidney, opening the gate and going forward, "as we have money sufficient to clear our score."

"Yes," replied the Englishman, "I have been told a Yankee will sell any civility for cash; and it is usually on that alone we must depend for favors in our intercourse with them."

The last remark was uttered in a low tone, and did not reach the ear of Sidney, who was just knocking at the door for admittance. A masculine voice was heard, bidding him "walk in"; and immediately obeying, they entered what in Europe is called the hall, here the front entry. It was about ten feet wide, and ran through the building, and at its termination was a door leading to the kitchen. A flight of stairs, painted to imitate marble, conducted to the chambers; and doors, opening on either side below, led to apartments called the parlor and "keeping room."

As they entered the hall, the door of this keeping room was

thrown open by a little girl, with her knitting work in her hand, who, in a soft tone, said, "Walk in here, if you please."

They followed her, and entered an apartment about eighteen feet by twenty, and eight feet in height, finished in the style of the country. The floor was painted yellow; the wainscoating, reaching to the windows, blue. Above this and overhead, it was plastered and whitewashed.

There were no paper hangings, nor tapestry, nor pictures; but some itinerant painter had exerted his skill, probably to the no small admiration of the wondering community, to ornament the room, by drawing around on the plaster wall a grove of green trees, all looking as uniform in appearance as Quakers at a meeting, or soldiers on a parade, excepting that here and there one would tower his head above his fellows like a commander.

Over the mantel-piece, the eagle spread his ample pinions, his head powdered with stars, his body streaked with white and red alternately, his crooked talons grasping an olive branch and a bundle of arrows; thus significantly declaring, that although he loved peace, he was prepared for war; and in his beak he held a scroll, inscribed with the talisman of American liberty and power— *E pluribus unum*.

A very long, wide sofa or couch (in truth, a large, old-fashioned *settle*, well stuffed and covered with chintz) was ranged on one side of the room. A deep writing desk, that seemed designed for an *official bureau*—so multitudinous were its drawers and compartments—was surmounted by a book-case, whose open door showed it nearly filled with well-worn volumes. A large cherry table, a small work table, a wooden clock, and about a dozen chairs, completed the furniture of the apartment.

There was no candle burning; perhaps the precise time to light it had not arrived; but a large wood fire sent forth a bright blaze from the hearth; and before it, in an arm chair, was seated a serious but happy-looking man. In one hand he held a newspaper, which he had probably been perusing; and with the other he was pressing to his bosom a rosy-cheeked girl of three or four years, who sat on his knee.

Rising at the approach of the strangers, he set down his child, and offered them his hand with a "how d'y do?"—and then bidding Mary set some chairs, he resumed his own, while his little daughter immediately regained her station on his knee.

Sidney at once recognized his father, and his heart beat violently.

"A fine evening for the season!" said Squire Romilly—as he was always called, contracting his real title. He was, in fact, "justice of the peace and quorum" for the county; therefore legally an "esquire"; and I shall so designate him, to avoid confusion, though I do hate titles.

"It is quite cold, I think," replied Frankford, moving his chair towards the fire.

"You have been riding, I suppose," returned the Squire, "and that makes you feel the cold more sensibly. I have been at work all day, and thought it very moderate."

While he spoke, he gave the fire a rousing stir, and threw on some wood that was standing in the corner of the fire-place. He then looked several times from one to the other, as if endeavoring to recollect them, and, bidding Mary draw a mug of cider, again addressed himself to entertain them.

"Do you find the roads pretty good the way you travel?"

"Not the best," replied Sidney, who determined to speak, though the effort was a painful one.

"There ought to be better regulations respecting the highways, I think," said the Squire. "Where every man is permitted to work out his own tax, the public are but little benefited. I was telling Deacon Jones the other day—he is our surveyor this year—that I would take half the money and hire workmen, who should repair the roads better than they are done by collecting the whole in the manner it is now managed."

"Then Deacon Jones is living yet?" said Sidney, glad to hear a familiar name.

"Yes, he is living," answered the Squire, surveying Sidney attentively; "are you acquainted with him?"

"I have seen him many times, but it is now some years since," replied Sidney.

"I expect he will call here this evening," observed the Squire.

"He would not probably recollect me now," answered the other, "yet I have been at his house often."

"Then you once lived in this neighborhood?"

"I have."

"And how long since?" said the Squire, whose curiosity seemed powerfully awakened.

"It is nearly thirteen years," replied Sidney, raising his hat from his head and turning his fine eyes full on his father's face.

The truth flashed on his mind.—"My son!" exclaimed he, starting from his seat.

"My father!" replied his son, and they were locked in each others' arms.

Just then Mary entered with her pitcher of cider; she caught the last words, and, setting down her pitcher, darted out of the room, and

"Sidney's come! Sidney's come!" resounded through the house in a moment. In the next, the room was filled. Mother, brothers and sisters crowded around the long absent but never forgotten Sidney.

Oh! it was a meeting of unalloyed joy—one of those sunlit points of existence, when the heart lives an age of rapture in a moment of time.

Mr. Frankford, who often described the scene thus far, always declared it would be in vain for him to attempt more. And I must follow his example, leaving it to the reader's imagination, and those who have the best hearts will best portray it.

When the first burst of affectionate exclamations and interrogatories was over, Sidney introduced Mr. Frankford, as an Englishman, and his particular friend, with whom he had traveled from the south, and made a tour to Saratoga Springs, and north as far as Montreal. At the latter place, Mr. Frankford had been confined nearly three months, with the typhus fever, from which he was now recovering, and Sidney wished them to consider him with particular attention.

Mr. Frankford had hitherto sat entirely unnoticed, though not unnoticing; for he there learned a lesson from the exhibition of natural feelings, which made him ever after disgusted with the heartlessness and frivolity of the fashionable world. And whenever he wished to dwell on a holy and touching picture of nature, he always recalled that scene to his remembrance.

He was not, however, suffered to be any longer a stranger or a spectator. The friend of Sidney was the friend of the family, and every one seemed anxious to render him attentions. Mr. Romilly immediately resigned his arm-chair, in which one of the little girls officiously placed a cushion; and having persuaded Frankford to seat himself in it, Mrs. Romilly brought from her closet a cordial of her own preparation, which she recommended as "the best thing in the world to prevent a cold after riding"; and bidding the girls hasten supper, she told him that before going to bed he must bathe his feet in warm water, and then a good night's rest would restore his spirits at once; adding, "you must, sir, endeavor to be at home and enjoy yourself, for I cannot bear to think any one is sad while I am so happy."

She was a goodly looking woman of five-and-forty, perhaps dressed as if she had been engaged in domestic affairs, but still neatly. She had on a black flannel gown, a silk handkerchief pinned carefully over her bosom, and a very white muslin cap, trimmed with black ribbon—her mother had been dead more than a year, but she still wore her mourning. Her apron she would doubtless have thrown off before entering the room, had she thought of anything save her son; for when she returned, after leaving the apartment to assist her daughters in their culinary preparations, it was laid aside.

The dress of the daughters, which their mother observed was "according to their work," it may perhaps be interesting to describe, and then, a century hence, when our country boasts its tens of millions of inhabitants, all ladies and gentlemen arrayed in satins and silk velvets, muslins and Mecklin laces, chains of gold and combs of pearl, this unpretending book may be a reference, describing faithfully the age when to be industrious was to be respectable, and to be neatly dressed, fashionable.

Both sisters, who were of the ages of seventeen and fifteen, were habited precisely alike, in dresses of American calico, in which deep blue was the prevailing color. The frocks were fitted closely to the form, fastened behind with blue buttons, and displaying the finely rounded symmetry of the shape to the greatest advantage. The frocks were cut high in front, concealing all the bosom but the white neck, which was uncovered and ornamented—when does a girl forget her ornaments?—with several strings of braided beads, to imitate a chain; and no eye that rested on those lovely necks would deem they needed richer adornments. The only difference in their costume was in the manner they dressed their hair. Sophia, the eldest and tallest, confined hers on the top of the head with a comb, and Lucy let hers flow in curls around the neck. Both fashions were graceful and becoming, as not a lock on either head seemed displaced; both were combed till the dark hair resembled fine glossy silk. Around their foreheads the curls clustered lovingly, and those who gazed on their sweet faces, glowing with health and happiness, where the soul seemed beaming forth its innocence and intelligence, and the smile of serenity playing on lips that had never spoken, save in accents of gladness and love, would feel no regret that they were uninitiated in the fashionable mysteries of the toilet.

Mr. Frankford often declared he never, before seeing them, felt the justness of Thompson's assertion, that

> . . . Loveliness
> Needs not the foreign aid of ornament,
> But is, when unadorned, adorned the most.

They were, indeed, beautiful girls—the Romillys were a comely race—and every fair reader who honors these pages with a perusal, and does not think them, at least, as handsome as herself, may be certain she possesses either a vain head or an envious heart.

The supper was now in active preparation. The large table was set forth, and covered with a cloth as white as snow. Lucy placed all in order, while Sophia assisted her mother to bring in the various dishes. No domestics appeared, and none seemed necessary. Love, warm hearted love, supplied the place of cold duty; and the labor of preparing the entertainment was, to Mrs. Romilly, a pleasure which she would not have relinquished to have been made an empress, so proud was she to show Sidney her cookery; and she tried to recollect the savory dishes he used to like, and had prepared them now in the same manner. At length all was pronounced ready, and after Squire Romilly had fervently besought a blessing, they took their seats.

The supper consisted of every luxury the season afforded. First came fried chicken, floating in gravy; then broiled ham, wheat bread, as white as snow, and butter so yellow and sweet, that it drew encomiums from the Englishman, till Mrs. Romilly colored with pleasure while she told him she made it herself. Two or three kinds of pies, all excellent, as many kinds of cake, with pickles and

preserves, and cranberry sauce—the last particularly for Sidney—
furnished forth the feast. The best of young hyson, with cream and
loaf sugar, was dispensed around by the fair hand of Sophia, who
presided over the department of the tea pot; her mother being fully
employed in helping her guests to the viands, and urging them to
eat and make out a supper, if they could.

Sidney's feelings were too much occupied to allow any great appetite for mere corporeal food. He wanted every moment to gaze
on the loved faces smiling around him, or listen to voices whose
soft tones, when calling him *son* or *brother*, made every fibre of his
heart thrill with rapture.

But Frankford was as hungry as fasting and fever could make
him. He was just in that stage of convalescence when the appetite
demands it arrearages with such imperious calls, that the whole
mind is absorbed in the desire of satisfying its cravings. He did
honor to every dish on the table; till Sidney, fearing he would in-
jure himself by eating to excess, was obliged to beg he would defer
finishing his meal till the next morning; "for you know, Mr. Frankford," added he, laughing, "the physician forbade your making a
full meal till you could walk a mile before taking it."

"If that be the case," said Squire Romilly, "I hope you will exert
yourself to-morrow. It is our Thanksgiving, and I should be loath
to have the dinner of any one at my table abridged. It will, indeed,
be a day of joy to us, and Sidney could not have come home at a
more welcome season."

While he spoke, he directed a glance towards Silas, whose
cheeks, fresh as they were, showed a heightened color, and his
black eyes were involuntarily cast down. Sidney observed it, and
asked his father if there was to be any peculiarity in the approaching festival.

"Do you," said he, "still have your plum-pudding and pumpkin-
pies, as in former times?"

"O yes," replied his father, "our dinner will be the same; but our
evening's entertainment will be different."

A wink from Mrs. Romilly, who evidently pitied the embarrassment of Silas, prevented further inquiries or explanations, and
they soon obeyed her example of rising from the table.

Mr. Frankford, who they feared would exert himself too much,
was now installed on the wide sofa (or *settle*), drawn up to the fire,

and all the pillows to be found in the house, as he thought, were gathered for him to nestle in. When he was fairly arranged, like a Turk on his divan, half sitting, half reclining, he addressed Squire Romilly, and inquired the cause of the Thanksgiving he had heard mentioned.

"Is it a festival of your church?" said he.

"No; it is a festival of the people, and appointed by the Governor of the State."

"But there is some reason for the custom—is there not?" inquired the Englishman.

"Certainly; our Yankees seldom do what they cannot justify by reasons of some sort," replied the Squire. "This custom of a public Thanksgiving is, however, said to have originated in a providential manner."

Mr. Frankford smiled rather incredulously.

The Squire saw the smile, but took no heed, while he went on.

"Soon after the settlement of Boston, the colony was reduced to a state of destitution, and nearly without food. In this strait the pious leaders of the pilgrim band appointed a solemn and general fast."

"If they had no food they must have fasted without that formality," said Frankford.

"True; but to convert the necessity into a voluntary and religious act of homage to the Supreme Ruler they worshiped and trusted, shows their sagacity as well as piety. The faith that could thus turn to God in the extremity of physical want, must have been of the most glowing kind, and such enthusiasm actually sustains nature. It is the hidden manna."

"I hope it strengthened them: pray, how long did the fast continue?"

"It never began."

"Indeed! Why not?"

"On the very morning of the appointed day, a vessel from London arrived laden with provisions, and so the fast was changed into a Thanksgiving."

"Well, that was wise; and so the festival has been continued to the present day?"

"Not with any purpose of celebrating that event," replied the Squire. "It is considered as an appropriate tribute of gratitude to

God to set apart one day of Thanksgiving in each year; and autumn is the time when the overflowing garners of America call for this expression of joyful gratitude."

"Is Thanksgiving Day universally observed in America?" inquired Mr. Frankford.

"Not yet; but I trust it will become so. We have too few holidays. Thanksgiving, like the Fourth of July, should be considered a national festival, and observed by all our people."

"I see no particular reason for such an observance," remarked Frankford.

"I do," returned the Squire. "We want it as the exponent of our Republican institutions, which are based on the acknowledgment that God is our Lord, and that, as a nation, we derive our privileges and blessings from Him. You will hear this doctrine set forth in the sermon to-morrow."

"I thought you had no national religion."

"No established religion, you mean. Our people do not need compulsion to support the gospel. But to return to our Thanksgiving festival. When it shall be observed, on the same day, throughout all the states and territories, it will be a grand spectacle of moral power and human happiness, such as the world has never yet witnessed."

Here Mrs. Romilly interrupted her husband, to ask, in a whisper, which was rather loud,—

"Was that basket of things carried to old Mrs. Long?"

"Certainly; I sent Sam with it."

"She will have a good Thanksgiving then; for Mrs. Jones has sent her a pair of chickens and a loaf of cake," said Lucy.

"Every one ought to have a good dinner to-morrow," said Sophia.

"Is the day one of good gifts as well as good dinners?" inquired Mr. Frankford.

"So far as food is concerned," replied the Squire. "Everybody in our State will be provided with the means of enjoying a good dinner to-morrow: paupers, prisoners, all, will be feasted."

Mr. Frankford now confessing he felt wearied, was persuaded to retire, Mrs. Romilly all the time lamenting he had not reached Northwood before his sickness, and repeatedly saying, "If you and Sidney had only come here instead of going on to Montreal, how much better it would have been! I would have nursed you, and we have the best doctor in the country. I don't believe you would have been half as sick here."

"Nor do I," replied he, gratefully smiling. "And to have been a witness and partaker of so much goodness and benevolence, would have made disease not only tolerable, but pleasant; the sympathy and interest I should have awakened in such a kind heart as yours, would have more than indemnified me for my sufferings."

Squire Romilly attended him to his chamber. It was directly over the sitting-room, and finished nearly in the same style. The ornament of the eagle, however, was wanting; but its place over the mantel-piece was supplied, and, in Frankford's estimation, its beauty excelled, by a "Family Record," painted and lettered by Sophia Romilly.

There was an excellent looking bed in the chamber, with white curtains and counterpane; a mahogany bureau, half a dozen handsome chairs, a mirror, and a dressing-table, covered with white muslin and ornamented with fringe and balls. Everything was arranged with perfect neatness, order and taste—yes, taste; nor let the fashionable belle flatter herself that she monopolizes the sentiment. The mind of a rural lass may be possessed of as just conceptions of the sublime and beautiful, and less trammeled by fashion; she consults nature in selecting the appropriate, which is sure to please all who have good sense, whatever may be their refinement or station.

A glowing fire on the hearth, and a large deeply-cushioned rocking-chair (Mrs. Romilly's own chair) drawn up before the fire, looked as if inviting the stranger; a foot-bath and plenty of warm water was near; on a small table was a pitcher of hot chamomile tea (a favorite specific with Mrs. Romilly in diseases of all kinds), and also a small bottle of cordial.

Squire Romilly set down the light, and was about leaving the chamber, when Mr. Frankford, laying his hand on the door, remarked there was no lock nor fastening.

"We don't make use of any," said the Squire. "I never in my life fastened a door or window; you will be perfectly safe, sir."

"Why, have you no rogues in this country?" asked Frankford.

"None here that will enter your dwelling in the night with felonious intentions," replied the other. "I suppose you might find some in the cities, but they are mostly imported ones," he added, smiling.

"And can you really retire to rest," reiterated Frankford, with a look of incredulity, "and sleep soundly and securely with your doors unbarred?"

"I tell you, sir," replied the Squire, "I have lived here twenty-five years, and never had a fastening on a door or window, and never was my sleep disturbed except when some neighbor was sick and needed assistance."

"And what makes your community so honestly disposed?" asked Frankford.

"The fear of God," returned the Squire, "and the pride of character infused by our education and cherished by our free institutions."

"But I should think there might be some strolling vagrants," said Frankford, "against whom it might be prudence to guard."

"We seldom think of a shield when we never hear of an enemy," answered the Squire. "However, if you feel insecure, I will tell Sidney—he will sleep in this chamber," pointing to the open door of a small bed-room adjoining—"I will tell Sidney to place his knife or some fastening over the door, before going to bed."

"I hope," said Sidney to his mother, after his father and the Englishman had withdrawn, "that Mr. Frankford will have a good bed. He complains bitterly of his lodgings since he came to America."

The matron drew herself up with a look of exultation.

"He will find no fault here, I'll warrant him," said she. "My beds are as soft as down; indeed, those two in the chamber where you and he will sleep, are nearly all down. I made them for the girls, though I keep them now for spare beds; and I told your father I could afford to give each of the girls a down bed when they were married, as I have always had such capital luck with my geese."

Sidney bestowed a kiss on the blushing cheeks of each of his fair sisters, telling his mother he thought it much easier to provide beds for such sweet girls, than find husbands worthy to share them.

The idea of matrimony, however, awakened a desire in Mrs. Romilly's mind to communicate the intelligence her significant looks had prevented her husband from relating while at supper.

With true feminine delicacy, she did not wish to have Sidney first apprised of it in the presence of Silas; nor did she feel willing a stranger should hear the remarks and interrogations which Sidney might make. These objections were now removed, as Silas had gone out and Mr. Frankford retired to bed; and so she ventured to say that "to-morrow evening Silas is to be married to Priscilla Jones; and," said she, "it is an excellent match for him. Deacon Jones is very rich, and has only three daughters; the other two have already married and moved away, and so your brother will go there to live and have the *homestead*."

Squire Romilly now returning to the room, they drew their chairs around the fire and entered into a confidential family conversation. And the *conversaziones* of Italy offer no entertainment like that which the Romillys enjoyed—the interchange of reciprocal and holy affection. A thousand mutual inquiries were made, and Sidney listened, delighted, to many an anecdote of his boyish acquaintance, or the history of many an improvement in his native village. The clock struck twelve before they thought the evening half spent, and then, after a most fervent prayer from the father-priest, so full of gratitude and joy that all were melted to tears of thankfulness, Sidney was suffered to retire and dream over the scene he had just enjoyed.

THOMAS BAILEY ALDRICH

Thomas Bailey Aldrich (b. Portsmouth, New Hampshire, 1836; d. 1907) was the son of a wandering businessman who died when Thomas was thirteen. His mother's family belonged to genteel society in Portsmouth. Though starting as a clerk (with a maternal uncle's business in New York City), by the age of twenty Aldrich had chosen the literary life. From 1855 to 1874 he worked as an editor, war correspondent, critic, poet, and novelist. Moving to Boston in 1865, he became involved in the city's literary circle, whose society he enjoyed even during a period of semi-retirement from 1874 until 1881, when he succeeded William Dean Howells as editor of the *Atlantic Monthly*. During his ten years there Aldrich, like his predecessor, was arbiter of literary taste as well as guardian of the genteel sensibility. After retiring from the *Atlantic* he spent the remaining seventeen years of his life traveling and writing, most often about his boyhood in Portsmouth.

Aldrich's best known book is his classic *The Story of a Bad Boy*, published in Boston by Fields and Osgood in 1870. *An Old Town by the Sea*, a series of essays about Portsmouth, was published by Houghton Mifflin Company in Boston and New York in 1893. Aldrich's poem "Unguarded Gates" is representative of the nativism that grew out of the idealization of community in New Hampshire literature. The poem appeared in *Unguarded Gates, and Other Poems*, Houghton Mifflin Company, Boston, 1895.

The following excerpt from *The Story of a Bad Boy* recounts Tom's Fourth of July escapade.

Thomas Bailey Aldrich, circa 1903, engraving from a photograph by J. E. Purdy for *The Writings of Thomas Bailey Aldrich*. Courtesy of Dimond Library, University of New Hampshire.

FROM

The Story of a Bad Boy

CHAPTER VII

One Memorable Night

Two months had elapsed since my arrival at Rivermouth, when the approach of an important celebration produced the greatest excitement among the juvenile population of the town.

There was very little hard study done in the Temple Grammar School the week preceding the Fourth of July. For my part, my heart and brain were so full of fire-crackers, Roman-candles, rockets, pin-wheels, squibs, and gunpowder in various seductive forms, that I wonder I did not explode under Mr. Grimshaw's very nose. I could not do a sum to save me; I could not tell, for love or money, whether Tallahassee was the capital of Tennessee or of Florida; the present and the pluperfect tenses were inextricably mixed in my memory, and I did not know a verb from an adjective when I met one. This was not alone my condition, but that of every boy in the school.

Mr. Grimshaw considerately made allowances for our temporary distraction, and sought to fix our interest on the lessons by connecting them directly or indirectly with the coming Event. The class in arithmetic, for instance, was requested to state how many boxes of fire-crackers, each box measuring sixteen inches square, could be stored in a room of such and such dimensions. He gave us the Declaration of Independence for a parsing exercise, and in geography confined his questions almost exclusively to localities rendered famous in the Revolutionary War. "What did the people of Boston do with the tea on board the English vessels?" asked our wily instructor.

"Threw it into the river!" shrieked the smaller boys, with an impetuosity that made Mr. Grimshaw smile in spite of himself. One luckless urchin said, "Chucked it," for which happy expression he was kept in at recess.

Notwithstanding these clever stratagems, there was not much solid work done by anybody. The trail of the serpent (an inexpensive but dangerous fire-toy) was over us all. We went round deformed by quantities of Chinese crackers artlessly concealed in our trousers-pockets; and if a boy whipped out his handkerchief without proper precaution, he was sure to let off two or three torpedoes.

Even Mr. Grimshaw was made a sort of accessory to the universal demoralization. In calling the school to order, he always rapped on the table with a heavy ruler. Under the green baize table-cloth, on the exact spot where he usually struck, a certain boy, whose name I withhold, placed a fat torpedo. The result was a loud explosion, which caused Mr. Grimshaw to look queer. Charley Marden was at the water-pail at the time, and directed general attention to himself by strangling for several seconds and then squirting a slender thread of water over the blackboard.

Mr. Grimshaw fixed his eyes reproachfully on Charley, but said nothing. The real culprit (it was not Charley Marden, but the boy whose name I withhold) instantly regretted his badness, and after school confessed the whole thing to Mr. Grimshaw, who heaped coals of fire upon the nameless boy's head by giving him five cents for the Fourth of July. If Mr. Grimshaw had caned this unknown youth, the punishment would not have been half so severe.

On the last day of June the Captain received a letter from my father, enclosing five dollars "for my son Tom," which enabled that young gentleman to make regal preparations for the celebration of our national independence. A portion of this money, two dollars, I hastened to invest in fireworks; the balance I put by for contingencies. In placing the fund in my possession, the Captain imposed one condition that dampened my ardor considerably—I was to buy no gunpowder. I might have all the snapping-crackers and torpedoes I wanted; but gunpowder was out of the question.

I thought this rather hard, for all my young friends were provided with pistols of various sizes. Pepper Whitcomb had a horse-pistol nearly as large as himself, and Jack Harris, though he, to be sure, was a big boy, was going to have a real old-fashioned flint-lock musket. However, I did not mean to let this drawback destroy my happiness. I had one charge of powder stowed away in the little brass pistol which I brought from New Orleans, and was bound to make a noise in the world once, if I never did again.

It was a custom observed from time immemorial for the town boys to have a bonfire on the Square on the midnight before the

Fourth. I did not ask the Captain's leave to attend this ceremony, for I had a general idea that he would not give it. If the Captain, I reasoned, does not forbid me, I break no orders by going. Now this was a specious line of argument, and the mishaps that befell me in consequence of adopting it were richly deserved.

On the evening of the third I retired to bed very early, in order to disarm suspicion. I did not sleep a wink, waiting for eleven o'clock to come round; and I thought it never would come round, as I lay counting from time to time the slow strokes of the ponderous bell in the steeple of the Old North Church. At last the laggard hour arrived. While the clock was striking I jumped out of bed and began dressing.

My grandfather and Miss Abigail were heavy sleepers, and I might have stolen down-stairs and out at the front door undetected; but such a commonplace proceeding did not suit my adventurous disposition. I fastened one end of a rope (it was a few yards cut from Kitty Collins's clothes-line) to the bedpost nearest the window, and cautiously climbed out on the wide pediment over the hall door. I had neglected to knot the rope; the result was, that, the moment I swung clear of the pediment, I descended like a flash of lightning, and warmed both my hands smartly. The rope, moreover, was four or five feet too short; so I got a fall that would have proved serious had I not tumbled into the middle of one of the big rose-bushes growing on either side of the steps.

I scrambled out of that without delay, and was congratulating myself on my good luck, when I saw by the light of the setting moon the form of a man leaning over the garden gate. It was one of the town watch, who had probably been observing my operations with curiosity. Seeing no chance of escape, I put a bold face on the matter and walked directly up to him.

"What on airth air you a-doin'?" asked the man, grasping the collar of my jacket.

"I live here, sir, if you please," I replied, "and am going to the bonfire. I didn't want to wake up the old folks, that's all."

The man cocked his eye at me in the most amiable manner, and released his hold.

"Boys is boys," he muttered. He did not attempt to stop me as I slipped through the gate.

Once beyond his clutches, I took to my heels and soon reached the Square, where I found forty or fifty fellows assembled, engaged in building a pyramid of tar-barrels. The palms of my hands still tingled so that I could not join in the sport. I stood in the doorway of the Nautilus Bank, watching the workers, among whom I recognized lots of my school-mates. They looked like a legion of imps, coming and going in the twilight, busy in raising some infernal edifice. What a Babel of voices it was, everybody directing everybody else, and everybody doing everything wrong!

When all was prepared, some one applied a match to the sombre pile. A fiery tongue thrust itself out here and there, then suddenly the whole fabric burst into flames, blazing and crackling beautifully. This was a signal for the boys to join hands and dance around the burning barrels, which they did, shouting like mad creatures. When the fire had burnt down a little, fresh staves were brought and heaped on the pyre. In the excitement of the moment I forgot my tingling palms, and found myself in the thick of the carousal.

Before we were half ready, our combustible material was expended, and a disheartening kind of darkness settled down upon us. The boys collected together here and there in knots, consulting as to what should be done. It yet lacked several hours of daybreak, and none of us were in the humor to return to bed. I approached one of the groups standing near the town-pump, and discovered in the uncertain light of the dying brands the figures of Jack Harris, Phil Adams, Harry Blake, and Pepper Whitcomb, their faces streaked with perspiration and tar, and their whole appearance suggestive of New Zealand chiefs.

"Hullo! here's Tom Bailey!" shouted Pepper Whitcomb; "he'll join in!"

Of course he would. The sting had gone out of my hands, and I was ripe for anything—none the less ripe for not knowing what was on the *tapis*. After whispering together for a moment, the boys motioned me to follow them.

We glided out from the crowd and silently wended our way through a neighboring alley, at the head of which stood a tumble-down old barn, owned by one Ezra Wingate. In former days this was the stable of the mail-coach that ran between Rivermouth and Boston. When the railroad superseded that primitive mode of travel, the lumbering vehicle was rolled into the barn, and there it stayed. The stage-driver, after prophesying the immediate downfall of the nation, died of grief and apoplexy, and the old coach followed in his wake as fast as it could by quietly dropping to pieces. The barn had the reputation of being haunted, and I think we all kept very close together when we found ourselves standing in the black shadow cast by the tall gable. Here, in a low voice, Jack Harris laid bare his plan, which was to burn the ancient stage-coach.

"The old trundle-cart isn't worth twenty-five cents," said Jack Harris, "and Ezra Wingate ought to thank us for getting the rubbish out of the way. But if any fellow here doesn't want to have a hand in it, let him cut and run, and keep a quiet tongue in his head ever after."

With this he pulled out the staples that held the rusty padlock, and the big barn door swung slowly open. The interior of the stable was pitch-dark, of course. As we made a movement to enter, a sudden scrambling, and the sound of heavy bodies leaping in all directions, caused us to start back in terror.

"Rats!" cried Phil Adams.

"Bats!" exclaimed Harry Blake.

"Cats!" suggested Jack Harris. "Who's afraid?"

Well, the truth is, we were all afraid; and if the pole of the stage had not been lying close to the threshold, I do not believe anything on earth would have induced us to cross it. We seized hold of the pole-straps and succeeded with great trouble in dragging the coach out. The two fore wheels had rusted to the axle-tree, and refused to revolve. It was the merest skeleton of a coach. The cushions had long since been removed, and the leather hangings, where they had not crumbled away, dangled in shreds from the worm-eaten frame. A load of ghosts and a span of phantom horses to drag them would have made the ghastly thing complete.

Luckily for our undertaking, the stable stood at the top of a very steep hill. With three boys to push behind, and two in front to steer, we started the old coach on its last trip with little or no difficulty. Our speed increased every moment, and, the fore wheels becoming unlocked as we arrived at the foot of the declivity, we charged upon the crowd like a regiment of cavalry, scattering the people right and left. Before reaching the bonfire, to which some one had added several bushels of shavings, Jack Harris and Phil Adams, who were steering, dropped on the ground, and allowed the vehicle to pass over them, which it did without injuring them; but the boys who were clinging for dear life to the trunk-rack behind fell over the prostrate steersmen, and there we all lay in a heap, two or three of us quite picturesque with the nose-bleed.

The coach, with an intuitive perception of what was expected of it, plunged into the centre of the kindling shavings, and stopped. The flames sprung up and clung to the rotten woodwork, which burned like tinder. At this moment a figure was seen leaping wildly from the inside of the blazing coach. The figure made three bounds towards us, and tripped over Harry Blake. It was Pepper Whitcomb, with his hair somewhat singed, and his eyebrows completely scorched off!

Pepper had slyly ensconced himself on the back seat before we started, intending to have a neat little ride down hill, and a laugh at us afterwards. But the laugh, as it happened, was on our side, or would have been, if half a dozen watchmen had not suddenly pounced down upon us, as we lay scrambling on the ground, weak with mirth over Pepper's misfortune. We were collared and marched off before we well know what had happened.

The abrupt transition from the noise and light of the Square to the silent, gloomy brick room in the rear of the Meat Market seemed like the work of enchantment. We stared at one another aghast.

"Well," remarked Jack Harris, with a sickly smile, "this *is* a go!"

"No go, I should say," whimpered Harry Blake, glancing at the bare brick walls and the heavy iron-plated door.

"Never say die," muttered Phil Adams dolefully.

The bridewell was a small low-studded chamber built up against the rear end of the Meat Market, and approached from the Square by a narrow passageway. A portion of the room was partitioned off into eight cells, each capable of holding two or three persons. The cells were full at the time, as we presently discovered by seeing several hideous faces leering out at us through the gratings of the doors.

A smoky oil-lamp in a lantern suspended from the ceiling threw a flickering light over the apartment, which contained no furniture excepting a couple of stout wooden benches. It was a dismal place by night, and only little less dismal by day, for the tall houses surrounding "the lock-up" prevented the faintest ray of sunshine from penetrating the ventilator over the door—a long narrow window opening inward and propped up by a piece of lath.

As we seated ourselves in a row on one of the benches, I imagine that our aspect was anything but cheerful. Adams and Harris looked very anxious, and Harry Blake, whose nose had just stopped bleeding, was mournfully carving his name, by sheer force of habit, on the prison bench. I do not think I ever saw a more "wrecked" expression on any human countenance than Pepper Whitcomb's presented. His look of natural astonishment at finding himself incarcerated in a jail was considerably heightened by his lack of eyebrows.

As for me, it was only by thinking how the late Baron Trenck would have conducted himself under similar circumstances that I was able to restrain my tears.

None of us were inclined to conversation. A deep silence, broken now and then by a startling snore from the cells, reigned throughout the chamber. By and by Pepper Whitcomb glanced nervously towards Phil Adams and said, "Phil, do you think they will—*hang us?*"

"Hang your grandmother!" returned Adams impatiently; "what I'm afraid of is that they'll keep us locked up until the Fourth is over."

"You ain't smart ef they do!" cried a voice from one of the cells. It was a deep bass voice that sent a chill through me.

"Who are you?" said Jack Harris, addressing the cells in general; for the echoing qualities of the room made it difficult to locate the voice.

"That don't matter," replied the speaker, putting his face close up to the gratings of No. 3, "but ef I was a youngster like you, free an' easy outside there, this spot wouldn't hold *me* long."

"That's so!" chimed several of the prisonbirds, wagging their heads behind the iron lattices.

"Hush!" whispered Jack Harris, rising from his seat and walking on tip-toe to the door of cell No. 3. "What would you do?"

"Do? Why, I'd pile them 'ere benches up agin that 'ere door, an' crawl out of that 'ere winder in no time. That's my adwice."

"And werry good adwice it is, Jim," said the occupant of No. 5 approvingly.

Jack Harris seemed to be of the same opinion, for he hastily placed the benches one on the top of another under the ventilator, and, climbing up on the highest bench, peeped out into the passageway.

"If any gent happens to have a ninepence about him," said the man in cell No. 3, "there's a sufferin' family here as could make use of it. Smallest favors gratefully received, an' no questions axed."

This appeal touched a new silver quarter of a dollar in my trousers-pocket; I fished out the coin from a mass of fireworks, and gave it to the prisoner. He appeared to be so good-natured a fellow that I ventured to ask what he had done to get into jail.

"Intirely innocent. I was clapped in here by a rascally nevew as wishes to enjoy my wealth afore I'm dead."

"Your name, sir?" I inquired, with a view of reporting the outrage to my grandfather and having the injured person reinstated in society.

"Git out, you insolent young reptyle!" shouted the man, in a passion.

I retreated precipitately, amid a roar of laughter from the other cells.

"Can't you keep still?" exclaimed Harris, withdrawing his head from the window.

A portly watchman usually sat on a stool outside the door day and night; but on this particular occasion, his services being required elsewhere, the bridewell had been left to guard itself.

"All clear," whispered Jack Harris, as he vanished through the aperture and dropped softly on the ground outside. We all followed him expeditiously—Pepper Whitcomb and myself getting stuck in the window for a moment in our frantic efforts not to be last.

"Now, boys, everybody for himself!"

FROM
An Old Town by the Sea

CHAPTER III
A Stroll about Town

As you leave the river front behind you, and pass "up town," the streets grow wider, and the architecture becomes more ambitious—streets fringed with beautiful old trees and lined with commodious private dwellings, mostly square white houses, with spacious halls running through the centre. Previous to the Revolution, white paint was seldom used on houses, and the diamond-shaped window pane was almost universal. Many of the residences stand back from the brick or flagstone sidewalk, and have pretty gardens at the side or in the rear, made bright with dahlias and sweet with cinnamon roses. If you chance to live in a town where the authorities cannot rest until they have destroyed every precious tree within their blighting reach, you will be especially charmed by the beauty of the streets of Portsmouth. In some parts of the town, when the chestnuts are in blossom, you would fancy yourself in a garden in fairyland. In spring, summer, and autumn the foliage is the glory of the fair town—her luxuriant green and golden tresses! Nothing could seem more like the work of enchantment than the spectacle which certain streets in Portsmouth present in midwinter after a heavy snowstorm. You may walk for miles under wonderful silvery arches formed by the overhanging and interlaced boughs of the trees, festooned with a drapery even more graceful and dazzling than springtime gives them. The numerous elms and maples which shade the principal thoroughfares are not the result of chance, but the ample reward of the loving care that is taken to preserve the trees. There is a society in Portsmouth devoted to arboriculture. It is not unusual there for persons to leave legacies to be expended in setting out shade and ornamental trees along some favorite walk. Richards Avenue, a long, unbuilt thoroughfare leading from Middle Street to the South Burying-Ground, perpetuates the name of a citizen who gave the labor of his own hands to the beautifying of that wind-swept and barren road to the cemetery. This fondness and care for trees seems to be a matter of heredity.

So far back as 1660 the selectmen instituted a fine of five shillings for the cutting of timber or any other wood from off the town common, excepting under special conditions.

In the business section of the town trees are few. The chief business streets are Congress and Market. Market Street is the stronghold of the dry-goods shops. There are seasons, I suppose, when these shops are crowded, but I have never happened to be in Portsmouth at the time. I seldom pass through the narrow cobble-paved streets without wondering where the customers are that must keep all these flourishing little establishments going. Congress Street—a more elegant thoroughfare than Market—is the Nevski Prospekt of Portsmouth. Among the prominent buildings is the Athenæum, containing a reading-room and library. From the high roof of this building the stroller will do well to take a glance at the surrounding country. He will naturally turn seaward for the more picturesque aspects. If the day is clear, he will see the famous Isles of Shoals, lying nine miles away—Appledore, Smutty-Nose, Star Island, White Island, etc.; there are nine of them in all. On Appledore is Laighton's Hotel, and near it the summer cottage of Celia Thaxter, the poet of the Isles. On the northern end of Star Island is the quaint town of Gosport, with a tiny stone church perched like a sea-gull on its highest rock. A mile southwest from Star Island lies White Island, on which is a lighthouse. Mrs. Thaxter calls this the most picturesque of the group. Perilous neighbors, O mariner! in any but the serenest weather, these wrinkled, scarred, and storm-smitten rocks, flanked by wicked sunken ledges that grow white at the lip with rage when the great winds blow!

How peaceful it all looks off there, on the smooth emerald sea! and how softly the waves seem to break on yonder point where the unfinished fort is! That is the ancient town of Newcastle, to reach which from Portsmouth you have to cross three bridges with the most enchanting scenery in New Hampshire lying on either hand. At Newcastle the poet Stedman has built for his summerings an enviable little stone château—a seashell into which I fancy the sirens creep to warm themselves during the winter months. So it is never without its singer.

Opposite Newcastle is Kittery Point, a romantic spot, where Sir William Pepperell, the first American baronet, once lived, and where his tomb now is, in his orchard across the road, a few hundred yards from the "goodly mansion" he built. The knight's tomb and the old Pepperell House, which has been somewhat curtailed of its fair proportions, are the objects of frequent pilgrimages to Kittery Point.

From this elevation (the roof of the Athenæum) the navy yard, the river with its bridges and islands, the clustered gables of Kittery and Newcastle, and the illimitable ocean beyond make a picture worth climbing four or five flights of stairs to gaze upon. Glancing down on the town nestled in the foliage, it seems like a town dropped by chance in the midst of a forest. Among the prominent objects which lift themselves above the tree tops are the belfries of the various churches, the white façade of the custom house, and the mansard and chimneys of the Rockingham, the principal hotel. The pilgrim will be surprised to find in Portsmouth one of the most completely appointed hotels in the United States. The antiquarian may lament the demolition of the old Bell Tavern, and think regretfully of the good cheer once furnished the wayfarer by Master Stavers at the sign of the Earl of Halifax, and by Master Stoodley at his inn on Daniel Street; but the ordinary traveler will thank his stars, and confess that his lines have fallen in pleasant places, when he finds himself among the frescoes of the Rockingham.

Obliquely opposite the doorstep of the Athenæum—we are supposed to be on terra firma again—stands the Old North Church, a substantial wooden building, handsomely set on what is called The Parade, a large open space formed by the junction of Congress, Market, Daniel, and Pleasant streets. Here in days innocent of water-works stood the town pump, which on more than one occasion served as whipping-post.

The churches of Portsmouth are more remarkable for their number than their architecture. With the exception of the Stone Church they are constructed of wood or plain brick in the simplest style. St. John's Church is the only one likely to attract the eye of a stranger. It is finely situated on the crest of Church Hill, overlooking the ever-beautiful river. The present edifice was built in 1808 on the site of what was known as Queen's Chapel, erected in 1732, and destroyed by fire December 24, 1806. The chapel was named in honor of Queen Caroline, who furnished the books for the altar and pulpit, the plate, and two solid mahogany chairs, which are still in use in St. John's. Within the chancel rail is a curious font of porphyry, taken by Colonel John Tufton Mason at the capture of Senegal from the French in 1758, and presented to the Episcopal Society in 1761. The peculiarly sweet-toned bell which calls the parishioners of St. John's together every Sabbath is, I believe, the same that formerly hung in the belfry of the old Queen's Chapel. If so, the bell has a history of its own. It was brought from Louisburg at the time of the reduction of that place in 1745, and given to the church by the officers of the New Hampshire troops.

The Old South Meeting-House is not to be passed without mention. It is among the most aged survivals of pre-revolutionary days. Neither its architecture nor its age, however, is its chief warrant for our notice. The absurd number of windows in this battered old structure is what strikes the passer-by. The church was erected by subscription, and these closely set large windows are due to Henry Sherburne, one of the wealthiest citizens of the period, who agreed to pay for whatever glass was used. If the building could have been composed entirely of glass it would have been done by the thrifty parishioners.

Portsmouth is rich in graveyards—they seem to be a New England specialty—ancient and modern. Among the old burial-places the one attached to St. John's Church is perhaps the most interesting. It has not been permitted to fall into ruin, like the old cemetery at the Point of Graves. When a headstone here topples over it is kindly lifted up and set on its pins again, and encouraged to do its duty. If it utterly refuses, and is not shamming decrepitude, it has its face sponged, and is allowed to rest and sun itself against the wall of the church with a row of other exempts. The trees are kept pruned, the grass trimmed, and here and there is a rosebush drooping with a weight of pensive pale roses, as becomes a rosebush in a churchyard.

The place has about it an indescribable soothing atmosphere of respectability and comfort. Here rest the remains of the principal and loftiest in rank in their generation of the citizens of Portsmouth prior to the Revolution—staunch, royalty-loving governors, counselors, and secretaries of the Province of New Hampshire, all snugly gathered under the motherly wing of the Church of England. It is almost impossible to walk anywhere without stepping on a governor. You grow haughty in spirit after a while, and scorn to tread on anything less than one of His Majesty's colonels or a secretary under the Crown. Here are the tombs of the Atkinsons, the Jaffreys, the Sherburnes, the Sheafes, the Marshes, the Mannings, the Gardners, and others of the quality. All around you underfoot are tumbled-in coffins, with here and there a rusty sword atop, and faded escutcheons, and crumbling armorial devices. You are moving in the very best society.

This, however, is not the earliest cemetery in Portsmouth. An hour's walk from the Episcopal yard will bring you to the spot, already mentioned, where the first house was built and the first grave made, at Odiorne's Point. The exact site of the Manor is not known, but it is supposed to be a few rods north of an old well of still-flowing water, at which the Tomsons and the Hiltons and their comrades slaked their thirst more than two hundred and sixty years ago. Odiorne's Point is owned by Mr. Eben L. Odiorne, a lineal descendant of the worthy who held the property in 1657. Not far from the old spring is the resting-place of the earliest pioneers.

"This first cemetery of the white man in New Hampshire," writes Mr. Brewster,* "occupies a space of perhaps one hundred feet by ninety, and is well walled in. The western side is now used as a burial-place for the family, but two thirds of it is filled with perhaps forty graves, indicated by rough head and foot stones. Who there rest no one now living knows. But the same care is taken of their quiet beds as if they were of the proprietor's own family. In 1631 Mason sent over about eighty emigrants many of whom died in a few years, and here they were probably buried. Here too, doubtless, rest the remains of several of those whose names stand conspicuous in our early state records."

Unguarded Gates

Wide open and unguarded stand our gates,
Named of the four winds, North, South, East, and West;
Portals that lead to an enchanted land
Of cities, forests, fields of living gold,

*Mr. Charles W. Brewster, for nearly fifty years the editor of the *Portsmouth Journal*, and the author of two volumes of local sketches to which the writer of these pages here acknowledges his indebtedness.

Vast prairies, lordly summits touched with snow,
Majestic rivers sweeping proudly past
The Arab's date-palm and the Norseman's pine—
A realm wherein are fruits of every zone,
Airs of all climes, for lo! throughout the year
The red rose blossoms somewhere—a rich land,
A later Eden planted in the wilds,
With not an inch of earth within its bound
But if a slave's foot press it sets him free.
Here, it is written, Toil shall have its wage,
And Honor honor, and the humblest man
Stand level with the highest in the law.
Of such a land have men in dungeons dreamed,
And with the vision brightening in their eyes
Gone smiling to the fagot and the sword.

Wide open and unguarded stand our gates,
And through them presses a wild motley throng—
Men from the Volga and the Tartar steppes,
Featureless figures of the Hoang-Ho,
Malayan, Scythian, Teuton, Kelt, and Slav,
Flying the Old World's poverty and scorn;
These bringing with them unknown gods and rites,
Those, tiger passions, here to stretch their claws.
In street and alley what strange tongues are loud,
Accents of menace alien to our air,
Voices that once the Tower of Babel knew!
O Liberty, white Goddess! is it well
To leave the gates unguarded? On thy breast
Fold Sorrow's children, soothe the hurts of fate,
Lift the down-trodden, but with hand of steel
Stay those who to thy sacred portals come
To waste the gifts of freedom. Have a care
Lest from thy brow the clustered stars be torn
And trampled in the dust. For so of old
The thronging Goth and Vandal trampled Rome,
And where the temples of the Caesars stood
The lean wolf unmolested made her lair.

HENRY AUGUSTUS SHUTE

Henry Augustus Shute (b. Exeter, New Hampshire, 1856; d. 1943) was
an active citizen in his hometown, which was the subject of his prose and
poetry. He served as a judge and for relaxation played in the town brass
band and worked in his garden.

The Real Diary of a Real Boy was published in Boston by Everett in
1902. Though written during Shute's mature years, the book purported
to be a childhood diary. The author's humorous accounts of pranks are
written in a style he deemed appropriate for a country schoolboy.

The following excerpt describes some typical boyhood exploits in Exeter more than a century ago.

FROM

The Real Diary of a Real Boy

Went to a sunday school concert in the evening. Keene and Cele sung now i lay me down to sleep. they was a lot of people sung together and Mister Gale beat time. Charlie Gerish played the violin and Miss Packerd sung. i was scart when Keene and Cele sung for i was afraid they would break down, but they dident, and people said they sung like night horks. i gess if they knowed how night horks sung they woodent say much. father felt pretty big and to hear him talk you wood think he did the singing. he give them ten cents apeace. i dident get none. you gest wait, old man till i get my cornet.

Went to a corcus last night. me and Beany were in the hall in the afternoon helping Bob Carter sprinkle the floor and put on the sordust. the floor was all shiny with wax and aufully slipery. so Bob got us to put on some water to take off the shiny wax. well write in front of the platform there is a low platform where they get up to put in their votes and then step down and Beany said, dont put any water there only jest dry sordust. so i dident. well that night we went erly to see the fun. Gim Luverin got up and said there was one man which was the oldest voter in town and he ought to vote the first, the name of this destinkuished sitizen was John Quincy Ann Pollard. then old mister Pollard got up and put in his vote and when he stepped down his heels flew up and he went down whak on the back of his head and 2 men lifted him up and lugged him to a seat, and then Ed Derborn, him that rings the town bell, stepped up pretty lively and went flat and swore terrible, and me and Beany nearly died we laffed so. well it kept on, people dident know what made them fall, and Gim Odlin sat write down in his new umbrella and then they sent me down stairs for a pail of wet sordust and when i was coming up i heard an auful whang, and when i got up in the hall they were lugging old mister Stickney off to die and they put water on his head and lugged him home in a hack. they say Bob Carter will lose his place. me and Beany dont know what to do. if we dont tell, Bob will lose his place and if we do we will get licked.

Mar. 12. Mister Stickney is all write today. gosh you bet me and Beany are glad.

Mar. 13, 186– brite and fair. Mr. Gravel has bought old Heads carrige shop. he is a dandy and wears shiny riding boots and a stove pipe hat and a velvet coat and goes with Dan Ranlet and George Perkins and Johny Gibson and the other dandies. i went down today and watched Fatty Walker stripe some wheels.

Mar. 14. clowdy. Elkins and Graves had an oxion to-night. Beany got ten cents for going round town ringing a bell and hollering oxion. i went with Beany and it was lots of fun. Beany wouldent treet. he says he is saving money for something. i know what it is it is a valintine for Lizzie Tole. it was mean of Beany not to treet becaus i did as much hollering as he did.

Mar. 15. The funniest thing happened to-day you ever saw. after brekfast me and father took a walk and then went and set down on the high school steps. father was telling me some of the things he and Gim Melcher used to do. father must have been a ripper when he was young. well ennyway while we was talking old Ike Shute came along through the school yard. Ike wears specks and always carries a little basket on his arm. he cant see very well, and father said to me, now you jest keep still and you will see some fun and when Ike came along father changed his voice so that it sounded awfully growly and said where in the devil are you going with that basket, and Ike was scart most to deth and said only a little way down here sir and father said, move on sir and move dam lively and i nearly died laffing to see Ike hiper. well after a while i see Ike coming back with old Swane and old Kize the policemen. i tell you i was scart but father only laffed and said you keep still and i will fix it all right. so when they came up he said to old Kize what is the trouble Filander and he said Mr. Shute here has been thretened by some drunken rascal, and father looked aufuly surprised and said that is an infernal shame, when did it happen Isak, and Ike said about fifteen minits ago and father said we have been here about as long as that and i dident see the scoundrel. how did he look Isak, and Ike said i coodent see him very well George but he was a big man and he had a awful deep voice and father said did he stagger enny and Ike said i coodent see wether he did or not but i cood tell he was drunk by his voice. so old Swain and old Kize went down behind the school house and off thru the carrige shop yard to see if they cood find him, and me and father walked home with Ike to protect him and father said now Isak if ennyone insults you again jest come to me and if i can catch him i will break every bone in his body, and father and Ike shook hands and Ike shook hands with me and then we went home and father began to laff and laffed all the way home and then he told mother and aunt Sarah and they said it was a shame to play such a trick upon him and father laffed all the more and said Ike hadent had so much exercise for a year and it wood do him good and give him something to think about. ennyway they said it was a shame to teech me such things, and father said he would rather i wood be tuf than be like Ike, and Aunt Sarah said i never wood be half as good as Ike for he never did a wrong thing in his life, and father laffed and said he dident dass to for his mother wood shet him in the closet. it was aufully funny, but i gess they was right. i shall never be half as good as Ike. i wonder if old Swane and old Kize have caught that man yet.

Mar. 16. Pewt dreened 18 marbles and 2 chinees out of me to-day. we was playing first in a hole. school today. sailed boats in the brook in J. Albert Clark's garden and got pretty wet.

Mar. 17. Scott Briggam has got some little flying squirrels. he is going to get me one for thirty-five cents. i am going to take it out of my cornet money.

Mar. 18. Father wont let me play marbles in ernest. it aint enny fun dreening a feller and then giving them back. i bet father didnt when he was a boy.

ALICE BROWN

Alice Brown (b. Hampton Falls, New Hampshire, 1856; d. Boston, 1948) attended Robinson Female Seminary in Exeter and later became a teacher, practically the only profession open to young women at that time. She grew to despise the classroom and turned to the only other available work, writing flagrantly commercial stories for such Boston magazines as *Youth's Companion*. Though introduced to Boston literary society, she did not achieve critical literary success for her local color stories until 1889, just as the genre was becoming unfashionable. A prolific writer, she continued to publish travel journals, short stories, and novels almost yearly until 1935. An intensely private individual, she ordered all her personal effects destroyed at her death.

Meadow-Grass: Tales of New England Life was published in Boston by Copeland and Day in 1895. *Jeremy Hamlin*, her last important novel, appeared in 1934, published by D. Appleton–Century Company in New York and London.

"Joint Owners in Spain," one of Brown's best-known short stories, is taken from *Meadow-Grass: Tales of New England Life*.

Alice Brown, date unknown, frontispiece of *Alice Brown* by Dorothea Walker, 1974. Courtesy of the Boston Athenaeum.

FROM

Meadow-Grass: Tales of New England Life

"Joint Owners in Spain"

The Old Ladies' Home, much to the sorrow of its inmates, "set back from the road." A long, box-bordered walk led from the great door down to the old turnpike, and thickly bowering lilac-bushes forced the eye to play an unsatisfied hide-and-seek with the view. The sequestered old ladies were quite unreconciled to their leaf-hung outlook; active life was presumably over for them, and all the more did they long to "see the passing" of the little world which had usurped their places. The house itself was very old, a stately, square structure, with pillars on either side of the door, and a fanlight above. It had remained unpainted now for many years, and had softened into a mellow lichen-gray, so harmonious and pleasing in the midst of summer's vital green, that the few art-ists who ever heard of Tiverton sought it out, to plant umbrella and easel in the garden, and sketch the stately relic; photogra-phers, also, made it one of their accustomed haunts. Of the artists the old ladies disapproved, without a dissenting voice. It seemed a "shaller" proceeding to sit out there in the hot sun for no result save a wash of unreal colors on a white ground, or a few hasty lines indicating no solid reality; but the photographers were their constant delight, and they rejoiced in forming themselves into groups upon the green, to be "took" and carried away with the house.

One royal winter's day, there was a directors' meeting in the great south room, the matron's parlor, a spot bearing the happy charm of perfect loyalty to the past, with its great fireplace, iron dogs and crane, its settle and entrancing corner cupboards. The hard-working president of the board was speaking hastily and from a full heart, conscious that another instant's discussion might bring the tears to her eyes:—

"May I be allowed to say—it's irrelevant, I know, but I should like the satisfaction of saying it—that this is enough to make one vow never to have anything to do with an institution of any sort, from this time forth for evermore?"

For the moment had apparently come when a chronic annoyance must be recognized as unendurable. They had borne with the trial, inmates and directors, quite as cheerfully as most ordinary people accept the inevitable; but suddenly the tension had become too great, and the universal patience snapped. Two of the old ladies, Mrs. Blair and Miss Dyer, who were settled in the Home for life, and who, before going there, had shown no special waywardness of temper, had proved utterly incapable of living in peace with any available human being; and as the Home had insufficient accommodations, neither could be isolated to fight her "black butterflies" alone. No inmate, though she were cousin to Hercules, could be given a room to herself; and the effect of this dual system on these two, possibly the most eccentric of the number, had proved disastrous in the extreme. Each had, in her own favorite fashion, "kicked over the traces," as the matron's son said in town-meeting (much to the joy of the village fathers), and to such purpose that, to continue the light-minded simile, very little harness was left to guide them withal. Mrs. Blair, being "high sperited," like all the Coxes from whom she sprung, had now so tyrannized over the last of her series of room-mates, so browbeaten and intimidated her, that the latter had actually taken to her bed with a slow fever of discouragement, announcing that "she'd ruther go to the poor-farm and done with it than resk her life there another night; and she'd like to know what had become of that hunderd dollars her nephew Thomas paid down in bills to get her into the Home, for she'd be thankful to them that laid it away so antic to hand it back afore another night went over her head, so't she could board somewheres decent till 'twas gone, and then starve if she'd got to!"

If Miss Sarah Ann Dyer, known also as a disturber of the public peace, presented a less aggressive front to her kind, she was yet, in her own way, a cross and a hindrance to their spiritual growth. She, poor woman, lived in a scarcely varying state of hurt feeling; her tiny world seemed to her one close federation, existing for the sole purpose of infringing on her personal rights; and though she would not take the initiative in battle, she lifted up her voice in aggrieved lamentation over the tragic incidents decreed for her alone. She had perhaps never directly reproached her own unhappy room-mate for selecting a comfortable chair, for wearing squeaking shoes, or singing "Hearken, ye sprightly," somewhat early in the morning, but she chanted those ills through all her waking hours in a high, yet husky tone, broken by frequent sobs. And therefore, as a result of these domestic whirlwinds and too stagnant pools, came the directors' meeting, and the helpless protest of the exasperated president. The two cases were discussed for an hour longer, in the dreary fashion pertaining to a question which has long been supposed to have but one side; and then it remained for Mrs. Mitchell, the new director, to cut the knot with the energy of one to whom a difficulty is fresh.

"Has it ever occurred to you to put them together?" asked she. "They are impossible people; so, naturally, you have selected the very mildest and most Christian women to endure their nagging. They can't live with the saints of the earth. Experience has proved that. Put them into one room, and let them fight it out together."

The motion was passed with something of that awe ever attending a Napoleonic decree, and passed, too, with the utmost good-breeding; for nobody mentioned the Kilkenny cats. The matron compressed her lips and lifted her brows, but said nothing; having exhausted her own resources, she was the more willing to take the superior attitude of good-natured scepticism.

The moving was speedily accomplished; and at ten o'clock, one morning, Mrs. Blair was ushered into the room where her forced colleague sat by the window, knitting. There the two were left alone. Miss Dyer looked up, and then heaved a tempestuous sigh over her work, in the manner of one not entirely surprised by its advent, but willing to suppress it, if such alleviation might be. She was a thin, colorless woman, and infinitely passive, save at those times when her nervous system conflicted with the scheme of the universe. Not so Mrs. Blair. She had black eyes, "like live coals," said her awed associates; and her skin was soft and white, albeit wrinkled. One could even believe she had reigned a beauty, as the tradition of the house declared. This morning, she held her head higher than ever, and disdained expression except that of an occasional nasal snort. She regarded the room with the air of an impartial though exacting critic; two little beds covered with rising-sun quilts, two little pine bureaus, two washstands. The sunshine lay upon the floor, and in that radiant pathway Miss Dyer sat.

"If I'd ha' thought I should ha' come to this," began Mrs. Blair, in the voice of one who speaks perforce after long sufferance, "I'd ha' died in my tracks afore I'd left my comfortable home down in Tiverton Holler. Story-'n'-a-half house, a good sullar, an' woods nigh-by full o' sarsaparilla an' goldthread! I've moved more times in this God-forsaken place than a Methodist preacher, fust one room an' then another; an' bad is the best. It was poor pickin's enough afore, but this is the crowner!"

Miss Dyer said nothing, but two large tears rolled down and dropped on her work. Mrs. Blair followed their course with gleaming eyes endowed with such uncomfortable activity that they seemed to pounce with every glance.

"What under the sun be you carryin' on like that for?" she asked, giving the handle of the water-pitcher an emphatic twitch to make it even with the world. "You 'ain't lost nobody, have ye, sence I moved in here?"

Miss Dyer put aside her knitting with ostentatious abnegation, and began rocking herself back and forth in her chair, which seemed not of itself to sway fast enough, and Mrs. Blair's voice rose again, ever higher and more metallic:—

"I dunno what you've got to complain of more'n the rest of us. Look at that dress you've got on—a good thick thibet, an' mine's a cheap, sleazy alpaca they palmed off on me because they knew my eyesight ain't what it was once. An' you're settin' right there in the sun, gittin' het through, an' it's cold as a barn over here by the door. My land! if it don't make me mad to see anybody without no more sperit than a wet rag! If you've lost anybody, why don't ye say so? An' if it's a mad fit, speak out an' say that! Give me anybody that's got a tongue in their head, *I* say!"

But Miss Dyer, with an unnecessary display of effort, was hitching her chair into the darkest corner of the room, the rockers hopelessly snarling her yarn at every move.

"I'm sure I wouldn't keep the sun off'n anybody," she said, tearfully. "It never come into my head to take it up, an' I don't claim no share of anything. I guess, if the truth was known, 'twould be seen I'd been used to a house lookin' south, an' the fore-room winders all of a glare o' light, day in an' day out, an' Madeira vines climbin' over 'em, an' a trellis by the front door; but that's all past an' gone, past an' gone! I never was one to take more 'n belonged to me; an' I don't care who says it, I never shall be. An' I'd hold to that, if 'twas the last word I had to speak!"

This negative sort of retort had an enfeebling effect upon Mrs. Blair.

"My land!" she exclaimed, helplessly. "Talk about my tongue! Vinegar's nothin' to cold molasses, if you've got to plough through it."

The other sighed, and leaned her head upon her hand in an attitude of extreme dejection. Mrs. Blair eyed her with the exasperation of one whose just challenge has been refused; she marched back and forth through the room, now smoothing a fold of the counterpane, with vicious care, and again pulling the braided rug to one side or the other, the while she sought new fuel for her rage. Without, the sun was lighting snowy knoll and hollow, and printing the fine-etched tracery of the trees against a crystal sky. The road was not usually much frequented in winter time, but just now it had been worn by the week's sledding into a shining track, and several sleighs went jingling up and down. Tiverton was seizing the opportunity of a perfect day and the best of "going," and was taking its way to market. The trivial happenings of this far-away world had thus far elicited no more than a passing glance from Mrs. Blair; she was too absorbed in domestic warfare even to peer down through the leafless lilac-boughs, in futile wonderment as to whose bells they might be, ringing merrily past. On one journey about the room, however, some chance arrested her gaze. She stopped, transfixed.

"Forever!" she cried. Her nervous, blue-veined hands clutched at her apron and held it; she was motionless for a moment. Yet the picture without would have been quite devoid of interest to the casual eye; it could have borne little significance save to one who knew the inner life history of the Tiverton Home, and thus might guess what slight events wrought all its joy and pain. A young man had set up his camera at the end of the walk, and thrown the cloth over his head, preparatory to taking the usual view of the house. Mrs. Blair recovered from her temporary inaction. She rushed to the window, and threw up the sash. Her husky voice broke strenuously upon the stillness:—

"Here! you keep right where you be! I'm goin' to be took! You wait till I come!"

She pulled down the window, and went in haste to the closet, in the excess of her eagerness stumbling recklessly forward into its depths.

"Where's my bandbox?" Her voice came piercingly from her temporary seclusion. "Where'd they put it? It ain't here in sight! My soul! where's my bunnit?"

These were apostrophes thrown off in extremity of feeling; they were not questions, and no listener, even with the most friendly disposition in the world, need have assumed the necessity of answering. So, wrapped in oblivion to all earthly considerations save that of her own inward gloom, the one person who might have responded merely swayed back and forth, in martyrized silence. But no such spiritual withdrawal could insure her safety. Mrs. Blair emerged from the closet, and darted across the room with the energy of one stung by a new despair. She seemed about to fall upon the neutral figure in the corner, but seized the chair-back instead, and shook it with such angry vigor that Miss Dyer cowered down in no simulated fright.

"Where's my green bandbox?" The words were emphasized by cumulative shakes. "Anybody that's took that away from me ought to be b'iled in ile! Hangin' 's too good for 'em, but le' me git my eye on 'em an' they shall swing for 't! Yes, they shall, higher 'n Gil'roy's kite!"

The victim put both trembling hands to her ears.

"I ain't deef!" she wailed.

"Deef? I don't care whether you're deef or dumb, or whether you're nummer 'n a beetle! It's my bandbox I'm arter. Isr'el in Egypt! you might grind some folks in a mortar an' you couldn't make 'em speak!"

It was of no use. Intimidation had been worse than hopeless; even bodily force would not avail. She cast one lurid glance at the supine figure, and gave up the quest in that direction as sheer waste of time. With new determination, she again essayed the closet, tossing shoes and rubbers behind her in an unsightly heap, quite heedless of the confusion of rights and lefts. At last, in a dark corner, behind a blue chest, she came upon her treasure. Too hurried now for reproaches, she drew it forth, and with trembling fingers untied the strings. Casting aside the cover, she produced a huge scoop bonnet of a long-past date, and setting it on her head, with the same fevered haste, tied over it the long figured veil destined always to make an inseparable part of her state array. She snatched her stella shawl from the drawer, threw it over her shoulders, and ran out of the room.

Miss Dyer was left quite bewildered by these erratic proceedings, but she had no mind to question them; so many stories were rife in the Home of the eccentricities embodied in the charitable phrase "Mis' Blair's way" that she would scarcely have been amazed had her terrible room-mate chosen to drive a coach and four up the chimney, or saddle the broom for a midnight revel. She drew a long breath of relief at the bliss of solitude, closed her eyes, and strove to regain the lost peace, which, as she vaguely remembered, had belonged to her once in a shadowy past.

Silence had come, but not to reign. Back flew Mrs. Blair, like a whirlwind. Her cheeks wore each a little hectic spot; her eyes were flaming. The figured veil, swept rudely to one side, was borne backwards on the wind of her coming, and her thin hair, even in those few seconds, had become wildly disarranged.

"He's gone!" she announced, passionately. "He kep' right on while I was findin' my bunnit. He come to take the house, an' he'd ha' took me an' been glad. An' when I got that plaguy front door open, he was jest drivin' away; an' I might ha' hollered till I was black in the face, an' then I couldn't ha' made him hear."

"I dunno what to say, nor what not to," remarked Miss Dyer, to her corner. "If I speak, I'm to blame; an' so I be if I keep still."

The other old lady had thrown herself into a chair, and was looking wrathfully before her.

"It's the same man that come from Sudleigh last August," she said, bitterly. "He took the house then, an' said he wanted another view when the leaves was off; an' that time I was laid up with my stiff ankle, an' didn't git into it, an' to-day my bunnit was hid, an' I lost it ag'in."

Her voice changed. To the listener, it took on an awful meaning.

"An' I should like to know whose fault it was. If them that owns the winder, an' set by it till they see him comin', had spoke up an' said, 'Mis' Blair, there's the photograph man. Don't you want to

be took?' it wouldn't ha' been too late! If anybody had answered a
civil question, an' said, 'Your bunnit-box sets there behind my
blue chist,' it wouldn't ha' been too late then! An' I ain't had my
likeness took sence I was twenty year old, an' went to Sudleigh Fair
in my changeable *visite* an' leghorn hat, an' Jonathan wore the
brocaded weskit he stood up in, the next week Thursday. It's
enough to make a minister swear!"

Miss Dyer rocked back and forth.

"Dear me!" she wailed. "Dear me suz!"

The dinner-bell rang, creating a blessed diversion. Mrs. Blair,
rendered absent-minded by her grief, went to the table still in her
bonnet and veil; and this dramatic entrance gave rise to such mor-
bid though unexpressed curiosity that every one forbore, for a
time, to wonder why Miss Dyer did not appear. Later, however,
when a tray was prepared and sent up to her (according to the pro-
gramme of her bad days), the general commotion reached an almost unruly point, stimulated as it was by the matron's son, who
found an opportunity to whisper one garrulous old lady that Miss
Dyer had received bodily injury at the hands of her roommate, and
that Mrs. Blair had put on her bonnet to be ready for the sheriff
when he should arrive. This report, judiciously started, ran like
prairie fire; and the house was all the afternoon in a pleasant state
of excitement. Possibly the matron will never know why so many
of the old ladies promenaded the corridors from dinner-time until
long after early candlelight, while a few kept faithful yet agitated
watch from the windows. For interest was divided; some preferred
to see the sheriff's advent, and others found zest in the possibility
of counting the groans of the prostrate victim.

When Mrs. Blair returned to the stage of action, she was much
refreshed by her abundant meal and the strong tea which three
times daily heartened her for battle. She laid aside her bonnet, and
carefully folded the veil. Then she looked about her, and, per-
sistently ignoring all the empty chairs, fixed an annihilating gaze
on one where the dinner-tray still remained.

"I s'pose there's no need o' my settin' down," she remarked,
bitingly. "It's all in the day's work. Some folks are waited on; some
ain't. Some have their victuals brought to 'em an' pushed under
their noses, an' some has to go to the table; when they're there,
they can take it or leave it. The quality can keep their waiters set-

tin' round day in an' day out, fillin' up every chair in the room. For my part, I should think they'd have an extension table moved in, an' a snowdrop cloth over it!"

Miss Dyer had become comparatively placid, but now she gave way to tears.

"Anybody can move that waiter that's a mind to," she said, tremulously. "I would myself, if I had the stren'th; but I 'ain't got it. I ain't a well woman, an' I 'ain't been this twenty year. If old Dr. Parks was alive this day, he'd say so. 'You 'ain't never had a chance,' he says to me. 'You've been pull-hauled one way or an-other sence you was born.' An' he never knew the wust on't, for the wust hadn't come."

"Humph!" It was a royal and explosive note. It represented scorn for which Mrs. Blair could find no adequate utterance. She selected the straightest chair in the room, ostentatiously turned its back to her enemy, and seated herself. Then, taking out her knit-ting, she strove to keep silence; but that was too heavy a task, and at last she broke forth, with renewed bitterness:—

"To think of all the wood I've burnt up in my kitchen stove an' air-tight, an' never thought nothin' of it! To think of all the wood there is now, growin' an' rottin' from Dan to Beersheba, an' I can't lay my fingers on it!"

"I dunno what you want o' wood. I'm sure this room's warm enough."

"You don't? Well, I'll tell ye. I want some two-inch boards, to nail up a partition in the middle o' this room, same as Josh Mar-den done to spite his wife. I don't want more'n my own, but I want it mine."

Miss Dyer groaned, and drew an uncertain hand across her forehead.

"You wouldn't have no gre't of an outlay for boards," she said, drearily. "'Twouldn't have to be knee-high to keep me out. I'm no hand to go where I ain't wanted; an' if I ever was, I guess I'm cured on't now."

Mrs. Blair dropped her knitting in her lap. For an instant, she sat there motionless, in a growing rigidity; but light was dawning in her eyes. Suddenly she came to her feet, and tossed her knitting on the bed.

"Where's that piece o' chalk you had when you marked out your tumbler-quilt?" The words rang like a martial order.

Miss Dyer drew it forth from the ancient-looking bag, known as a cavo, which was ever at her side.

"Here 'tis," she said, in her forlornest quaver. "I hope you won't do nothin' out o' the way with it. I should hate to git into trouble here. I ain't that kind."

Mrs. Blair was too excited to hear or heed her. She was briefly, flashingly, taking in the possibilities of the room, her bright black eyes darting here and there with fiery insistence. Suddenly she went to the closet, and, diving to the bottom of a baggy pocket in her "t'other dress," drew forth a ball of twine. She chalked it, still in delighted haste, and forced one end upon her bewildered roommate.

"You go out there to the middle square o' the front winder," she commanded, "an' hold your end o' the string down on the floor. I'll snap it."

Miss Dyer cast one despairing glance about her, and obeyed.

"Crazy!" she muttered. "Oh my land! she's crazy's a loon. I wisht Mis' Mitchell'd pitch her tent here a spell!"

But Mrs. Blair was following out her purpose in a manner exceedingly methodical. Drawing out one bed, so that it stood directly opposite her kneeling helper, she passed the cord about the leg of the bedstead and made it fast; then, returning to the middle of the room, she snapped the line triumphantly. A faint chalk-mark was left upon the floor.

"There!" she cried. "Leggo! Now, you gi' me the chalk, an' I'll go over it an' make it whiter."

She knelt and chalked with the utmost absorption, crawling along on her knees, quite heedless of the despised alpaca; and Miss Dyer, hovering in a corner, timorously watched her. Mrs. Blair staggered to her feet, entangled by her skirt, and pitching like a ship at sea.

"There!" she announced. "Now here's two rooms. The chalk-mark's the partition. You can have the mornin' sun, for I'd jest as soon live by a taller candle if I can have somethin' that's my own. I'll chalk a lane into the closet, an' we'll both keep a right o' way there. Now I'm to home, an' so be you. Don't you dast to speak a word to me unless you come an' knock here on my headboard—that's the front door—an' I won't to you. Well, if I ain't glad to be alone! I've hung my harp on a willer long enough!"

It was some time before the true meaning of the new arrangement penetrated Miss Dyer's slower intelligence; but presently she drew her chair nearer the window and thought a little, chuckling as she did so. She, too, was alone. The sensation was new and very pleasant. Mrs. Blair went back and forth through the closet-lane, putting her clothes away, with high good humor. Once or twice she sang a little—"Derby's Ram" and "Lord Lovel"—in a cracked voice. She was in love with solitude.

Just before tea, Mrs. Mitchell, in some trepidation, knocked at the door, to see the fruits of contention present and to come. She had expected to hear loud words; and the silence quite terrified her, emphasizing, as it did, her own guilty sense of personal responsibility. Miss Dyer gave one appealing look at Mrs. Blair, and then, with some indecision, went to open the door, for the latch was in her house.

"Well, here you are, comfortably settled!" began Mrs. Mitchell. She had the unmistakable tone of professional kindliness; yet it rang clear and true. "May I come in?"

"Set right down here," answered Miss Dyer, drawing forward a chair. "I'm real pleased to see ye."

"And how are you this morning?" This was addressed to the occupant of the other house, who, quite oblivious to any alien presence, stood busily rubbing the chalk-marks from her dress.

Mrs. Blair made no answer. She might have been stone deaf, and as dumb as the hearth-stone bricks. Mrs. Mitchell cast an alarmed glance at her entertainer.

"Isn't she well?" she said, softly.

"It's a real pretty day, ain't it?" responded Miss Dyer. "If 'twas summer time, I should think there'd be a sea turn afore night. I like a sea turn myself. It smells jest like Old Boar's Head."

"I have brought you down some fruit." Mrs. Mitchell was still anxiously observing the silent figure, now absorbed in an apparently futile search in a brocaded work-bag. "Mrs. Blair, do you ever cut up bananas and oranges together?"

No answer. The visitor rose, and unwittingly stepped across the dividing line.

"Mrs. Blair—" she began, but she got no further.

Her hostess turned upon her, in surprised welcome.

"Well, if it ain't Mis' Mitchell! I can't say I didn't expect you, for I see you goin' into Miss Dyer's house not more'n two minutes ago. Seems to me you make short calls. Now set right down here, where you can see out o' the winder. That square's cracked, but I guess the directors'll put in another."

Mrs. Mitchell was amazed, but entirely interested. It was many a long day since any person, official or private, had met with cordiality from this quarter.

"I hope you and our friend are going to enjoy your room together," she essayed, with a hollow cheerfulness.

"I expect to be as gay as a cricket," returned Mrs. Blair, innocently. "An' I do trust I've got good neighbors. I like to keep to myself, but if I've got a neighbor, I want her to be somebody you can depend upon."

"I'm sure Miss Dyer means to be very neighborly." The director turned, with a smile, to include that lady in the conversation. But the local deafness had engulfed her. She was sitting peacefully by the window, with the air of one retired within herself, to think her own very remote thoughts. The visitor mentally improvised a little theory, and it seemed to fit the occasion. They had quarrelled, she thought, and each was disturbed at any notice bestowed on the other.

"I have been wondering whether you would both like to go sleighing with me some afternoon?" she ventured, with the humility so prone to assail humankind in a frank and shrewish presence. "The roads are in wonderful condition, and I don't believe you'd take cold. Do you know, I found Grandmother Eaton's foot-warmers, the other day! I'll bring them along."

"Law! I'd go anywheres to git out o' here," said Mrs. Blair, ruthlessly. "I dunno when I've set behind a horse, either. I guess the last time was the day I rid up here for good, an' then I didn't feel much like lookin' at out-door. Well, I guess you *be* a new director, or you never'd ha' thought on't!"

"How do you feel about it, Miss Dyer?" asked the visitor. "Will you go—perhaps on Wednesday?"

The other householder moved uneasily. Her hands twitched at their knitting; a flush came over her cheeks, and she cast a childishly appealing glance at her neighbor across the chalkline. Her eyes were filling fast with tears. "Save me!" her look seemed to entreat. "Let me not lose this happy fortune!" Mrs. Blair interpreted the message, and rose to the occasion with the vigor of the intellectually great.

"Mis' Mitchell," she said, clearly, "I may be queer in my notions, but it makes me as nervous as a witch to have anybody hollerin' out o' my winders. I don't care whether it's company nor whether it's my own folks. If you want to speak to Miss Dyer, you come along here arter me—don't you hit the partition now!—right out o' my door an' into her'n. Here, I'll knock! Miss Dyer, be you to home?"

The little old lady came forward, fluttering and radiant in the excess of her relief.

"Yes, I guess I be," she said, "an' all alone, too! I see you go by the winder, an' I was in hopes you'd come in!"

Then the situation dawned upon Mrs. Mitchell with an effect vastly surprising to the two old pensioners. She turned from one to the other, including them both in a look of warm loving-kindness. It was truly an illumination. Hitherto, they had thought chiefly of her winter cloak and nodding ostrich plume; now, at last, they saw her face, and read some part of its message.

"You poor souls!" she cried. "Do you care so much as that? O you poor souls!"

Miss Dyer fingered her apron and looked at the floor, but her companion turned brusquely away, even though she trod upon the partition in her haste.

"Law! it's nothin' to make such a handle of," she said. "Folks don't want to be under each other's noses all the time. I dunno's anybody could stan' it, unless 'twas an emmet. They seem to git along swarmin' round together."

Mrs. Mitchell left the room abruptly.

"Wednesday or Thursday, then!" she called over her shoulder.

The next forenoon, Mrs. Blair made her neighbor a long visit. Both old ladies had their knitting, and they sat peacefully swaying back and forth, recalling times past, and occasionally alluding to their happy Wednesday.

"What I really come in for," said Mrs. Blair, finally, "was to ask if you don't think both our settin'-rooms need new paper."

The other gave one bewildered glance about her.

"Why, 'tain't been on more'n two weeks," she began; and then remembrance awoke in her, and she stopped. It was not the scene of their refuge and conflict that must be considered; it was the house of fancy built by each unto herself. Invention did not come easily to her as yet, and she spoke with some hesitation.

"I've had it in mind myself quite a spell, but somehow I 'ain't been able to fix on the right sort o' paper."

"What do you say to a kind of a straw color, all lit up with tulips?" inquired Mrs. Blair, triumphantly.

"Ain't that kind o' gay?"

"Gay? Well, you want it gay, don't ye? I dunno why folks seem to think they've got to live in a hearse because they expect to ride in one! What if we be gittin' on a little mite in years? We ain't underground yit, be we? I see a real good ninepenny paper once, all covered over with green brakes. I declare if 'twa'n't sweet pretty! Well, whether I paper or whether I don't, I've got some thoughts of a magenta sofy. I'm tired to death o' that old horsehair lounge that sets in my clock-room. Sometimes I wish the moths would tackle it, but I guess they've got more sense. I've al'ays said to myself I'd have a magenta sofy when I could git round to it, and I dunno's I shall be any nearer to it than I be now."

"Well, you *are* tasty," said Miss Dyer, in some awe. "I dunno how you come to think o' that!"

"Priest Rowe had one when I wa'n't more 'n twenty. Some o' his relations give it to him (he married into the quality), an' I remember as if 'twas yesterday what a tew there was over it. An' I said to myself then, if ever I was prospered I'd have a magenta sofy. I 'ain't got to it till now, but now I'll have it if I die for 't."

"Well, I guess you're in the right on't." Miss Dyer spoke absently, glancing from the window in growing trouble. "O Mis' Blair!" she continued, with a sudden burst of confidence, "you don't think there's a storm brewin', do you? If it snows Wednesday, I shall give up beat!"

Mrs. Blair, in her turn, peered at the smiling sky.

"I hope you ain't one o' them kind that thinks every fair day's a weather breeder," she said. "Law, no! I don't b'lieve it will storm; an' if it does, why, there's other Wednesdays comin'!"

CELIA THAXTER

Celia Thaxter (b. Portsmouth, New Hampshire, 1835; d. 1894) grew up
on the Isles of Shoals, where her family operated a hotel whose guests
included Hawthorne, Emerson, Lowell, Whittier, Samuel Clemens, and
Sarah Orne Jewett. Lowell and Whittier encouraged her literary efforts.
Dividing her time between the literary salons of Boston and the Isles of
Shoals, she became interested in Unitarianism and Indian mysticism, subjects that influenced her poetry.

Among the Isles of Shoals was published in Boston by J. R. Osgood in
1873, and *The Poems of Celia Thaxter* in 1891, by Houghton Mifflin
Company in Boston.

Celia Thaxter, circa 1880, from a lantern slide. Courtesy of Portsmouth, New Hampshire,
Library.

FROM

Among the Isles of Shoals

Within the lovely limits of summer it is beautiful to live almost anywhere; most beautiful where the ocean meets the land; and here particularly, where all the varying splendor of the sea encompasses the place, and the ceaseless changing of the tides brings continual refreshment into the life of every day. But summer is late and slow to come; and long after the mainland has begun to bloom and smile beneath the influence of spring, the bitter northwest winds still sweep the cold, green water about these rocks, and tear its surface into long and glittering waves from morning till night, and from night till morning, through many weeks. No leaf breaks the frozen soil, and no bud swells on the shaggy bushes that clothe the slopes. But if summer is a laggard in her coming, she makes up for it by the loveliness of her lingering into autumn; for when the pride of trees and flowers is despoiled by frost on shore, the little gardens here are glowing at their brightest, and day after day of mellow splendor drops like a benediction from the hand of God. In the early mornings in September the mists draw away from the depths of inland valleys, and rise into the lucid western sky,—tall columns and towers of cloud, solid, compact, superb; their pure, white, shining heads uplifted into the ether, solemn, stately, and still, till some wandering breeze disturbs their perfect outline, and they melt about the heavens in scattered fragments as the day goes on. Then there are mornings when "all in the blue, unclouded weather" the coast-line comes out so distinctly that houses, trees, bits of white beach, are clearly visible, and with a glass, moving forms of carriages and cattle are distinguishable nine miles away. In the transparent air the peaks of Mounts Madison, Washington, and Jefferson are seen distinctly at a distance of one hundred miles. In the early light even the green color of the trees is perceptible on the Rye shore. All through these quiet days the air is full of wandering thistle-down, the inland golden-rod waves its plumes, and close by the water's edge, in rocky clefts, its seaside sister blossoms in gorgeous color; the rose-haws redden, the iris unlocks its shining caskets, and casts its closely packed seeds about, gray berries cluster on the bayberry-bushes, the sweet life-everlasting sends out its wonderful delicious fragrance, and the pale asters spread their flowers in many-tinted sprays. Through October and into November the fair, mild weather lasts. At the first breath of October, the hillside at Appledore fires up with the living crimson of the huckleberry-bushes, as if a blazing torch had been applied to it; the slanting light at sunrise and sunset makes a wonderful glory across it. The sky deepens its blue; beneath it the brilliant sea glows into violet, and flashes into splendid purple where the "tide-rip," or eddying winds, make long streaks across its surface (poets are not wrong who talk of "purple seas,") the air is clear and sparkling, the lovely summer haze withdraws, all things take a crisp and tender outline, and the cry of the curlew and the plover is doubly sweet through the pure, cool air. Then sunsets burn in clear and tranquil skies, or flame in piled magnificence of clouds. Some night a long bar lies, like a smouldering brand, along the horizon, deep carmine where the sun has touched it; and out of that bar breaks a sudden gale before morning, and a fine fury and tumult begins to rage. Then comes the fitful weather,—wild winds and hurrying waves, low, scudding clouds, tremendous rains that shut out everything; and the rocks lie weltering between the sea and sky, with the brief fire of the leaves quenched and swept away on the hillside,—only rushing wind and streaming water everywhere, as if a second deluge were flooding the world.

After such a rain comes a gale from the southeast to sweep the sky clear,—a gale so furious that it blows the sails straight out of the boltropes, if any vessel is so unfortunate as to be caught in it with a rag of canvas aloft; and the coast is strewn with the wrecks of such craft as happen to be caught on the lee shore, for

> Anchors drag, and topmasts lap,

and nothing can hold against this terrible, blind fury. It is appalling to listen to the shriek of such a wind, even though one is safe upon a rock that cannot move; and more dreadful is it to see the destruction one cannot lift a finger to avert.

As the air grows colder, curious atmospheric effects become visible. At the first biting cold the distant mainland has the appearance of being taken off its feet, as it were,—the line shrunken and distorted, detached from the water at both ends: it is as if one looked under it and saw the sky beyond. Then, on bright mornings with a brisk wind, little wafts of mist rise between the quick, short waves, and melt away before noon. At some periods of intense cold these mists, which are never in banks like fog, rise in irregular, whirling columns reaching to the clouds,—shadowy phantoms, torn and wild, that stalk past like Ossian's ghosts, solemnly and noiselessly throughout the bitter day. When the sun drops down behind these weird processions, with a dark-red, lurid light, it is like a vast conflagration, wonderful and terrible to see. The columns, that strike and fall athwart the island, sweep against the windows with a sound like sand, and lie on the ground in ridges, like fine, sharp hail; yet the heavens are clear, the heavily rolling sea dark-green and white, and, between the breaking crests, the misty columns stream toward the sky.

Sometimes a totally different vapor, like cold, black smoke, rolls out from the land, and flows over the sea to an unknown distance, swallowing up the islands on its way. Its approach is hideous to witness. "It's all thick o' black vapor," some islander announces, coming in from out of doors; just as they say, "It's all thick o' white foam," when the sudden squall tears the sea into fringes of spray.

In December the colors seem to fade out of the world, and utter ungraciousness prevails. The great, cool, whispering, delicious sea, that encircled us with a thousand caresses the beautiful summer through, turns slowly our sullen and inveterate enemy; leaden it lies beneath a sky like tin, and rolls its "white, cold, heavy-plunging foam" against a shore of iron. Each island wears its chalk-white girdle of ice between the rising and falling tides (edged with black at low-water, where the lowest-growing seaweed is exposed), making the stern bare rocks above more forbidding by their contrast with its stark whiteness,—and the whiteness of salt-water ice is ghastly. Nothing stirs abroad, except perhaps

> A lonely sea-bird crosses,
> With one waft of wing,

your view, as you gaze from some spray-incrusted window; or you behold the weather-beaten schooners creeping along the blurred coast-line from Cape Elizabeth and the northern ports of Maine towards Cape Ann, laden with lumber or lime, and sometimes, rarely, with hay or provisions.

After winter has fairly set in, the lonely dwellers at the Isles of Shoals find life quite as much as they can manage, being so entirely thrown upon their own resources that it requires all the philosophy at their disposal to answer the demand. In the village, where several families make a little community, there should be various human interests outside each separate fireside; but of their mode of life I know little. Upon three of the islands live isolated families, cut off by the "always wind-obeying deep" from each other and from the mainland, sometimes for weeks together, when the gales are fiercest, with no letters nor intercourse with any living thing. Some sullen day in December the snow begins to fall, and the last touch of desolation is laid upon the scene; there is nothing any more but white snow and dark water, hemmed in by a murky horizon; and nothing moves or sounds within its circle but the sea harshly assailing the shore, and the chill wind that sweeps across. Toward night the wind begins to rise, the snow whirls and drifts, and clings wherever it can find a resting-place; and though so much is blown away, yet there is enough left to smother up the rock and make it almost impossible to move about on it. The drifts sometimes are very deep in the hollows; one winter, sixteen sheep were buried in a drift, in which they remained a week, and, strange to say, only one was dead when they were discovered. One goes to sleep in the muffled roar of the storm, and wakes to find it still raging with senseless fury; all day it continues; towards night the curtain of falling flakes withdraws, a faint light shows westward; slowly the clouds roll together, the lift grows bright with pale, clear blue over the land, the wind has hauled to the northwest, and the storm is at an end. When the clouds are swept away by the besom of the pitiless northwest, how the stars glitter in the frosty sky! What wondrous streamers of northern lights flare through the winter darkness! I have seen the sky at midnight crimson and emerald and orange and blue in palpitating sheets along the whole northern half of the heavens, or rosy to the zenith, or belted with a bar of solid yellow light from east to west, as if the world were a basket, and it the golden handle thereto. The weather becomes of the first importance to the dwellers on the rock; the changes of the sky and sea, the flitting of the coasters to and fro, the visits of the sea-fowl, sunrise and sunset, the changing moon, the northern lights, the constellations that wheel in splendor through the winter night,—all are noted with a love and careful scrutiny that is seldom given by people living in populous places. One grows accustomed to the aspect of the constellations, and they seem like the faces of old friends looking down out of the awful blackness; and when in summer the great Orion disappears, how it is missed out of the sky! I remember the delight with which we caught a glimpse of the planet Mercury, in March, 1868, following close at the heels of the sinking sun, redly shining in the reddened horizon,—a stranger mysterious and utterly unknown before.

For these things make our world: there are no lectures, operas, concerts, theatres, no music of any kind, except what the waves may whisper in rarely gentle moods; no galleries of wonders like the Natural History rooms, in which it is so fascinating to wander; no streets, shops, carriages, no postman, no neighbors, not a doorbell within the compass of the place! Never was life so exempt from interruptions. The eight or ten small schooners that carry on winter fishing, flying to and fro through foam and squall to set and haul in their trawls, at rare intervals bring a mail,—an accumulation of letters, magazines, and newspapers that it requires a long time to plod through. This is the greatest excitement of the long winters; and no one can truly appreciate the delight of letters till he has lived where he can hear from his friends only once in a month.

But the best balanced human mind is prone to lose its elasticity, and stagnate, in this isolation. One learns immediately the value of work to keep one's wits clear, cheerful, and steady; just as much real work of the body as it can bear without weariness being always beneficent, but here indispensable. And in this matter women have the advantage of men, who are condemned to fold their hands when their tasks are done. No woman need ever have a vacant minute,—there are so many pleasant, useful things which she may, and had better do. Blessed be the man who invented knitting! (I never heard that a woman invented this or any other art.) It is the most charming and picturesque of quiet occupations, leaving the knitter free to read aloud, or talk, or think, while steadily and surely beneath the flying fingers the comfortable stocking grows.

No one can dream what a charm there is in taking care of pets, singing-birds, plants, etc., with such advantages of solitude; how every leaf and bud and flower is pored over, and admired, and loved! A whole conservatory, flushed with azaleas, and brilliant with forests of camellias and every precious exotic that blooms, could not impart so much delight as I have known a single rose to give, unfolding in the bleak bitterness of a day in February, when this side of the planet seemed to have arrived at its culmination of hopelessness, with the Isles of Shoals the most hopeless speck upon its surface. One gets close to the heart of these things; they are almost as precious as Picciola to the prisoner, and yield a fresh and constant joy, such as the pleasure-seeking inhabitants of cities could not find in their whole round of shifting diversions. With a bright and cheerful interior, open fires, books, and pictures, windows full of thrifty blossoming plants and climbing vines, a family of singing-birds, plenty of work, and a clear head and quiet conscience, it would go hard if one could not be happy even in such loneliness. Books, of course, are inestimable. Nowhere does one follow a play of Shakespeare's with greater zest, for it brings the whole world, which you need, about you; doubly precious the deep thoughts wise men have given to help us,—doubly sweet the songs of all the poets; for nothing comes between to distract you.

FROM

The Poems of Celia Thaxter

Land-Locked

Black lie the hills; swiftly doth daylight flee;
    And, catching gleams of sunset's dying smile,
    Through the dusk land for many a changing mile
The river runneth softly to the sea.

O happy river, could I follow thee!
    O yearning heart, that never can be still!
    O wistful eyes, that watch the steadfast hill,
Longing for level line of solemn sea!

Have patience; here are flowers and songs of birds,
    Beauty and fragrance, wealth of sound and sight,

All summer's glory thine from morn till night,
And life too full of joy for uttered words.

Neither am I ungrateful; but I dream
   Deliciously how twilight falls to-night
   Over the glimmering water, how the light
Dies blissfully away, until I seem

To feel the wind, sea-scented, on my cheek,
   To catch the sound of dusky flapping sail
   And dip of oars, and voices on the gale
Afar off, calling low,—my name they speak!

O Earth! thy summer song of joy may soar
   Ringing to heaven in triumph. I but crave
   The sad, caressing murmur of the wave
That breaks in tender music on the shore.

Off Shore

Rock, little boat, beneath the quiet sky;
Only the stars behold us where we lie,—
Only the stars and yonder brightening moon.

On the wide sea to-night alone are we;
The sweet, bright summer day dies silently,
Its glowing sunset will have faded soon.

Rock softly, little boat, the while I mark
The far off gliding sails, distinct and dark,
Across the west pass steadily and slow.

But on the eastern waters sad, they change
And vanish, dream-like, gray, and cold, and strange,
And no one knoweth whither they may go.

We care not, we, drifting with wind and tide,
While glad waves darken upon either side,
Save where the moon sends silver sparkles down,

And yonder slender stream of changing light,
Now white, now crimson, tremulously bright,
Where dark the lighthouse stands, with fiery crown.

Thick falls the dew, soundless on sea and shore:
It shines on little boat and idle oar,
Wherever moonbeams touch with tranquil glow.

The waves are full of whispers wild and sweet;
They call to me,—incessantly they beat
Along the boat from stern to curvèd prow.

Comes the careering wind, blows back my hair,
All damp with dew, to kiss me unaware,
Murmuring "Thee I love," and passes on.

Sweet sounds on rocky shores the distant rote;
Oh could we float forever, little boat,
Under the blissful sky drifting alone!

The Sandpiper

Across the narrow beach we flit,
    One little sandpiper and I,
And fast I gather, bit by bit,
    The scattered driftwood bleached and dry.
The wild waves reach their hands for it,
    The wild wind raves, the tide runs high,
As up and down the beach we flit,—
    One little sandpiper and I.

Above our heads the sullen clouds
    Scud black and swift across the sky;
Like silent ghosts in misty shrouds
    Stand out the white lighthouses high.
Almost as far as eye can reach
    I see the close-reefed vessels fly,
As fast we flit along the beach,—
    One little sandpiper and I.

I watch him as he skims along,
    Uttering his sweet and mournful cry.
He starts not at my fitful song,
    Or flash of fluttering drapery.
He has no thought of any wrong;
    He scans me with a fearless eye.

Stanch friends are we, well tried and strong,
  The little sandpiper and I.

Comrade, where wilt thou be to-night
  When the loosed storm breaks furiously?
My driftwood fire will burn so bright!
  To what warm shelter canst thou fly?
I do not fear for thee, though wroth
  The tempest rushes through the sky:
For are we not God's children both,
  Thou, little sandpiper, and I?

The Spaniards' Graves

AT THE ISLES OF SHOALS

O sailors, did sweet eyes look after you
  The day you sailed away from sunny Spain?
Bright eyes that followed fading ship and crew,
  Melting in tender rain?

Did no one dream of that drear night to be,
  Wild with the wind, fierce with the stinging snow,
When on yon granite point that frets the sea,
  The ship met her death-blow?

Fifty long years ago these sailors died:
  (None know how many sleep beneath the waves)
Fourteen gray headstones, rising side by side,
  Point out their nameless graves,—

Lonely, unknown, deserted, but for me,
  And the wild birds that flit with mournful cry,
And sadder winds, and voices of the sea
  That moans perpetually.

Wives, mothers, maidens, wistfully, in vain
  Questioned the distance for the yearning sail,
That, leaning landward, should have stretched again
  White arms wide on the gale,

To bring back their beloved. Year by year,
   Weary they watched, till youth and beauty passed,
And lustrous eyes grew dim and age drew near,
   And hope was dead at last.

Still summer broods o'er that delicious land,
   Rich, fragrant, warm with skies of golden glow:
Live any yet of that forsaken band
   Who loved so long ago?

O Spanish women, over the far seas,
   Could I but show you where your dead repose!
Could I send tidings on this northern breeze
   That strong and steady blows!

Dear dark-eyed sisters, you remember yet
   These you have lost, but you can never know
One stands at their bleak graves whose eyes are wet
   With thinking of your woe!

SAM WALTER FOSS

Sam Walter Foss (b. Candia, New Hampshire, 1858; d. 1911) moved with his family to Portsmouth when he was fourteen. He graduated from Portsmouth High School in 1877 as the class poet. After attending Tilton Seminary and Boston University, Foss became proprietor and editor of the *Saturday Union* of Lynn, Massachusetts, and also worked as an editorial writer for the *Boston Globe*. In 1898 he became librarian of the Somerville Public Libraries. He combined his interest in libraries and journalism by writing a column on libraries for the *Christian Science Monitor*. He was elected president of the Massachusetts Literary Club in 1906. He continued to write mostly humorous light verse until his death.

Back Country Poems was published by Lee and Shepard of Boston in 1894; *Dreams in Homespun* by Lothrop, Lee and Shepard Co. of Boston in 1897; and *Whiffs from Wild Meadows* by Lee and Shepard of Boston in 1899.

"Deserted Farms," from Foss's last published volume, anticipates the theme of rural decline so pronounced in a number of Robert Frost's poems.

Deserted Farms

Yes, the farms is all deserted; there is no one here to see
But jest a few ol' women an' a few ol' men like me;
But we still cling, like ol' gray moss, a little totterin' band—
We cling like ol' gray moss aroun' the ruins of the land.

Ol' Christopher Columbus, in fourteen ninety-two,
He lifted up a bright green worl' from out the ocean blue;
But all thet New Worl' hereabouts—an' Pokumville ain't
   small,—
Our young men hez diskivered ain't worth livin' in at all.

There ain't no room atween the rocks to dig a livin' out;
Our soil is much too thin and poor to make a fortune sprout;
Our scrub-oaks bear no greenback leaves, an' in our tater-hills
We have to dig too long an' hard to scratch out dollar bills.

An' so our boys hez travelled off to where the millions go
To dig a golden harvesting without a spade or hoe;
An' down the railroad, through the gulch, be'end their father's
   sight,
They went an' left us ol' men to the shadders of the night.

But some hez foun' the rocks an' weeds still choke a barren land,
An' life is not all intervale, but some is dusty sand;
An' he who digs a harvest in the country or the town
Must hoe among the stubborn rocks an' keep the thistles down.

But 'tis better for the young man an' the ol' man side by side
To drive life's team together, an' so down the journey ride;
An' w'en the ol' man, tires out an' falls asleep some day,
The young man, he can take the reins an' ride upon his way.

But our farms is all deserted; there is no one here to see
But jest a few ol' women an' a few ol' men like me;
But we still cling, like ol' gray moss, a little totterin' band—
We cling like ol' gray moss aroun' the ruins of the land.

The Candidates at the Fair

The two opposing candidates went to the county fair.
One had cologne upon his clothes, one hayseed in his hair;
One travelled burdened with ten trunks that bore his twenty
    suits,
One bore the soil from fourteen towns upon his shineless boots.

The prim dude candidate was wise in economic lore,
And soaked them full of statesmanship till they could hold no
    more.
He cited economic laws in terms abstruse and deep,
And principles and precedents until they went to sleep.

He quoted from Calhoun and Clay and Jefferson at will;
From Adam Smith, Sir Thomas More, and from John Stuart
    Mill;
From Plato and from Aristotle, Guizot, and Herbert Spencer;
And all the while he talked and talked their ignorance grew
    denser.

And then the hayseed candidate stood up there at the fair,
While his unlimbered whiskers waved and flaunted through the
    air,
And told them how he raised his corn, and how he cut his hay,
And how through fifty working years he'd made his farming pay.

He told them how he'd drained his swamp, and how he'd built
    his fence,
And showed them what hard work can do when mixed with
    common-sense.
"And now send me to Congress, friends," said plain old Silas
    Brown,
"An' I'll make things you sell go up, an' things you buy come
    down.

"I hain't no learned prinserples; I'm plain ol' Stick-in-the-Mud,
A blunt, plain man like you an' you, an ignorant ol' cud;
An' I don't know no books an' things, like this wise chap from
    town;
But I'll make things you sell go up, an' things you buy come
    down.

"I ain't no statesman who can talk purtection or free trade;
My han's too stiff to hol' a pen, that's made to hol' a spade;
Them ten-foot eddicated words my tongue can't wallop roun';
But I'll make things you sell go up, an' things you buy come
    down.

"I can't talk on the currency, nor on the revenue,
An' on the laws an' statoots I'm as ignorant as you;
An' I jest simply promise you, sure's I am Silas Brown,
I'll make the things you sell go up, an' things you buy come
    down."

The fair-ground echoed wide with cheers and loud huzzas
    thereat;
For who can ask a better scheme of statesmanship than that?
And next week at the polls he beat his rival high and dry—
But things we sell continue low, and things we buy are high.

EDNA DEAN PROCTOR

Edna Dean Proctor (b. Henniker, New Hampshire, 1829; d. 1923) attended Mount Holyoke Seminary and later moved to New York. For thirty years she lived in Brooklyn and often spent her summers in Henniker. One of her relatives remarked, "No Persian ever turned more worshipfully to the sun than she to her beloved mountains."

She became attached to the cause of the abolition of slavery, and several of her poems on the topic brought her to national attention. She also wrote of her extensive travels in *A Russian Journey* (1872).

The Complete Poetical Works of Edna Dean Proctor was published in Boston by Houghton Mifflin Company in 1925.

Edna Dean Proctor, date unknown. Courtesy of Special Collections, Dimond Library, University of New Hampshire.

New Hampshire

"A goodly realm!" said Captain Smith,
Scanning the coast by the Isles of Shoals,
While the wind blew fair, as in Indian myth
Blows the breeze from the Land of Souls;
Blew from the marshes of Hampton spread
Level and green that summer day,
And over the brow of Great Boar's Head
From the pines that stretched to the west away;
And sunset died on the rippling sea,
Ere to the south, with the wind, sailed he.
But he told the story in London streets,
And again to court and Prince and King;
"A truce," men cried, "to Virginia's heats;
The North is the land of hope and spring!"
And in sixteen hundred and twenty-three,
For Dover meadows and Portsmouth river,
Bold and earnest they crossed the sea,
And the realm was theirs and ours forever!
Up from Piscataqua's brine and spray,
Slowly, slowly they made their way
Back to Merrimack's eager tide
Poured through its meadows rich and wide;
And to Sunapee's lake whose cloistered shores
Had heard but the dip of the Red Man's oars;
And westward turned for the warmer gales
And the wealth of Connecticut's intervales;
And to Winnipesaukee's tranquil sea,
Bosomed in hills and bright with isles,
Asleep in the shadow of Ossipee,
Or fair as Eden when sunlight smiles;—
Up and on to the mountains piled,
Peak o'er peak, in the northern air,
Home of streams and of winds that wild
Torrent and tempest valeward bear—
Where the great Stone-Face looms changeless, calm
As the Sphinx that couches on Egypt's sands,
And the fir and the sassafras yield their balm

Sweet as the odors of morning-lands—
Where the eagle floats in the summer noon,
While his comrade-clouds drift, silent, by,
And the waters fill with a mystic tune
The fane the cliffs have built to the sky!
And, beyond, to the woods where the huge moose browsed,
And the dun deer drank at the rill unroused
By hound or horn, and the partridge brood
Was alone in the leafy solitude;
And the lake where the beaver housed her young,
And the loon's shrill cry from the border rung—
The lake whence the Beauteous River flows,
Its fountains fed by Canadian snows.

What were the labors of Hercules
To the toils of heroes such as these?—
Guarding their homes from savage foes
Cruel as fiends in craft and scorn;
Felling the forest with mighty blows;
Planting the meadow plots with corn;
Hunting the hungry wolf to his lair;
Trapping the panther and prowling bear;
Rearing, in faith by sorrow tried,
The church and the schoolhouse, side by side;
Fighting the French on the long frontier,
From Louisburg, set in the sea's domains,
To proud Quebec and the woods that hear
Ohio glide to the sunset plains;
And when rest and comfort they yearned to see,
Risking their all to be nobly free!

Honor and love for the valiant dead!
With reverent breath let their names be read—
Hiltons, Pepperells, Sullivans, Weares,
Broad is the scroll the list that bears
Of men as ardent and brave and true
As ever land in its peril knew,
And women of pure and glowing lives
Meet to be heroes' mothers and wives!
For not alone for the golden maize,

And the fisher's spoils from the teeming bays,
And the treasures of forest and hill and mine,
They gave their barks to the stormy brine—
Liberty, Learning, righteous Law,
Shone in the vision they dimly saw
Of the Age to come and the Land to be;
And, looking to Heaven, fervently
They labored and longed, through the dawning gray,
For the blessed break of that larger day!

When the wail of Harvard in sore distress
Came to their ears through the wilderness—
Harvard, the hope of the colonies twain,
Planted with prayers by the lonely main—
It was loyal, struggling Portsmouth town
That sent this gracious message down:
"Wishing our gratitude to prove,
And the country and General Court to move
For the infant College beset with fears,
(Its loss an omen of ill would be!)
We promise to pay it, for seven years,
Sixty pounds sterling, an annual sum,
Trusting that fuller aid will come"—
And the Court and the country heard their plea,
And the sapling grew to the wide-boughed tree.
And when a century had fled,
And the war for Freedom thrilled with dread
Yet welcome summons every home—
By the firelit hearth, 'neath the starry dome,
They vowed that never their love should wane
For the holy cause they burned to gain,
Till right should rule, and the strife be done!
List to the generous deed of one:—
In the Revolution's darkest days
The Legislature at Exeter met;
Money and men they fain would raise,
And despair on every face was set
As news of the army's need was read;
Then, in the hush, John Langdon said:

"Three thousand dollars have I in gold;
For as much I will pledge the plate I hold;
Eighty casks of Tobago rum;
All is the country's. The time will come,
If we conquer, when amply the debt she'll pay;
If we fail, our property's worthless." A ray
Of hope cheered the gloom, while the Governor said:
"For a regiment now, with Stark at its head!"
And the boon we gained through the noble lender
Was the Bennington day and Burgoyne's surrender!

Conflict over and weary quest,
Hid in their hallowed graves they rest,
Nor the voice of love, nor the cannon's roar
Wins them to field or fireside more!
Did the glory go from the hills with them?
Nay! for the sons are true to the sires!
And the gems they have set in our diadem
Burn with as rare and brilliant fires;
And the woodland streams and the mountain airs
Sing of the fathers' fame with theirs!
One, in the shadow of lone Kearsarge
Nurtured for power, like the fabled charge
Of the gods, by Pelion's woody marge;—
So lofty his eloquence, stately his mien,
That, could he have walked the Olympian plain,
The worshiping, wondering crowds had seen
Jove descend o'er the feast to reign!
And one, with a brow as Balder's fair,
And his life the grandeur of love and peace;—
Easing the burdens the race must bear,
Toiling for good that all might share,
Till his white soul found its glad release!
And one—a tall Corinthian column,
Of the temple of justice prop and pride—
The judge unstained, the patriot tried,
Gone to the bar supernal, solemn,
Nor left his peer by Themis' side!
Ah! when the Old World counts her kings,

And from splendor of castle and palace brings
The dainty lords her monarchies mould,
We'll turn to the hills and say, "Behold
Webster, and Greeley, and Chase, for three
Princes of our Democracy!"

Land of the cliff, the stream, the pine,
Blessing and honor and peace be thine!
Still may thy giant mountains rise,
Lifting their snows to the blue of June,
And the south wind breathe its tenderest sighs
Over thy fields in the harvest moon!
And the river of rivers, Merrimack,
Whose current never shall faint or lack
While the lakes and the bounteous springs remain—
Welcome the myriad brooks and rills
Winding through meadows, leaping from hills,
To brim its banks for the waiting wheels
That thrill and fly to its dash and roar
Till the rocks are passed, and the sea-fog steals
Over its tide by Newbury's shore!—
For the river of rivers is Merrimack,
Whether it foams with the mountain rain,
Or toils in the mill-race, deep and black,
Or, conqueror, rolls to the ocean plain!
And still may the hill, the vale, the glen,
Give thee the might of heroic men,
And the grace of women pure and fair
As the Mayflower's bloom when the woods are bare;
And Truth and Freedom aye find in thee
Their surest warrant of victory;—
Land of fame and of high endeavor,
Strength and glory be thine forever!

Monadnock in October

Up rose Monadnock in the northern blue,
A mighty minster builded to the Lord!
The setting sun his crimson radiance threw

On crest, and steep, and wood, and valley sward,
Blending their myriad hues in rich accord,
Till, like the wall of heaven, it towered to view.
Along its slope, where russet ferns were strewn
And purple heaths, the scarlet maples flamed,
And reddening oaks and golden birches shone—
Resplendent oriels in the black pines framed,
The pines that climb to woo the winds alone.
And down its cloisters blew the evening breeze,
Through courts and aisles ablaze with autumn bloom,
Till shrine and portal thrilled to harmonies
Now soaring, dying now in glade and gloom.
And with the wind was heard the voice of streams—
Constant their Aves and Te Deums be—
Lone Ashuelot murmuring down the lea,
And brooks that haste where shy Contoocook gleams
Through groves and meadows, broadening to the sea.
Then holy twilight fell on earth and air,
Above the dome the stars hung faint and fair,
And the vast minster hushed its shrines in prayer;
While all the lesser heights kept watch and ward
About Monadnock builded to the Lord!

The Hills Are Home
OLD HOME WEEK, 1899

Forget New Hampshire? By her cliffs, her meads, her brooks
    afoam,
With love and pride where'er we bide, the Hills, the Hills are
    Home!
On Mississippi or by Nile, Ohio, Volga, Rhine,
We see our cloud-born Merrimack adown its valley shine;
And Contoocook—Singing Water—Monadnock's drifts have fed,
With lilt and rhyme and fall and chime flash o'er its pebbly bed;
And by Como's wave, yet fairer still, our Winnipesaukee spread.

Alp nor Sierra, nor the chains of India or Peru,
Can dwarf for us the white-robed heights our wondering
    childhood knew—

The awful Notch, and the great Stone-Face, and the Lake where
   the echoes fly,
And the sovereign dome of Washington throned in the eastern
   sky;—
For from Colorado's Snowy Range to the crest of the Pyrenees
New Hampshire's mountains grandest lift their peaks in the airy
   seas,
And the winds of half the world are theirs across the main and
   the leas.

Yet far beyond her hills and streams New Hampshire dear we
   hold;
A thousand tender memories our glowing hearts enfold;
For in dreams we see the early home by the elms or the maples
   tall,
The orchard-trees where the robins built, and the well by the
   garden wall;
The lilacs and the apple-blooms make paradise of May,
And up from the clover-meadows floats the breath of the new-
   mown hay;
And the Sabbath bells, as the light breeze swells, ring clear and
   die away.

And oh, the Lost Ones live again in love's immortal year!
We are children still by the hearth-fire's blaze while night steals
   cold and drear;
Our mother's fond caress we win, our father's smile of pride,
And "Now I lay me down to sleep" say, reverent, at their side.
Alas! alas! their graves are green, or white with a pall of snow,
But we see them yet by the evening hearth as in the long ago,
And the quiet churchyard where they rest is the holiest spot we
   know.

Forget New Hampshire? Let Kearsarge forget to greet the sun;
Connecticut forsake the sea; the Shoals their breakers shun;
But fervently, while life shall last, though wide our ways decline,
Back to the Mountain-Land our hearts will turn as to a shrine!
Forget New Hampshire? By her cliffs, her meads, her brooks
   afoam,
By all her hallowed memories—our lode-star while we roam—
Whatever skies above us rise, the Hills, the Hills are Home!

DENMAN THOMPSON

Denman Thompson (b. Girard, Pennsylvania, 1833; d. 1911) moved to Swanzey, New Hampshire, the birthplace of his mother, when a teenager. At seventeen he traveled to Boston, where he got his start in entertainment by working for a circus. After playing a variety of roles with the Royal Lyceum Company of Toronto, Ontario, he acted in London from 1862 to 1868. Returning to America, he commenced writing and acting in a dramatic sketch that eventually became the four-act play, *The Old Homestead*, which earned approximately three million dollars. He spent the rest of his life touring the play, portraying the simple rustic character Josh Whitcomb, and thus became a veritable "professional Yankee." He died in Swanzey, where the play is still performed annually on Old Home Day.

The Old Homestead was first produced at the Fourteenth Street Theatre in New York in 1887. The excerpt that follows, Act I, scene 1, is from a typescript in the Library of the Performing Arts at Lincoln Center in New York City.

Denman Thompson, circa 1908, illustration for "The Embodiment of a National Tradition," *Current Literature Magazine*, Vol. 45. Courtesy of Dimond Library, University of New Hampshire.

FROM

The Old Homestead

ACT I

SCENE: Farm at Swanzey.

MATILDA: Our visitors are having a good time. Well, I like to see it. Shows they're happy. Sent word to Joshua by Bennett's boy to come to the house. He's down in the meadow helping the hired man; wish he'd come. Suppose he wants to get all his hay raked up in case it should rain 'fore mornin'. What's that they're playing over there, Rickety Ann? Some new kind of a ballgame, ain't it?

RICKETY ANN: Guess 'tis, Aunt Tilda. Never seed one like it afore, cum pretty near breaking a window while ago too.

MATILDA: Did they? Well, now, that's dreadful careless. You tell them, Rickety Ann, that they must be careful.

RICKETY ANN: Yessum. Say, you folks, Aunt Tilda says if you break a window she'll make you pay for it.

FRANK: You don't say so!

RICKETY ANN: Yes, I do say so.

MATILDA: Why, Rickety Ann, I didn't say nothin' of the sort.

RICKETY ANN: Wal, if you didn't, you thinked it.

MATILDA: Never mind what I think, you do what I say.

RICKETY ANN: All right, Aunt Tilda, but I didn't mean nothin'.

MATILDA: All right then, bring in the wood and we'll finish getting supper.

RICKETY ANN: That new hired gal don't know nothin'. Put the ice in the well the other day to cool the water.

MATILDA: Rickety Ann!

RICKETY ANN: Yes'm, I'm comin'. What are you laughin' at, is they anythin' on me?

FRANK: Quite a wild flower, isn't she? A daisy, eh?

RICKETY ANN: Now what are you laughin' at me for?

FRANK: Oh, nothing in particular, but we must have *something* to laugh at.

RICKETY ANN: Think they're smart. I'll bet they don't know beans when the bag's ontied.

FRANK: Well, we are doing very well. Only been here two hours— tennis net up, trunks in our rooms, and by jove, I'm as hungry as a hunter.

ANNIE: So am I.

NELLIE: If supper isn't ready soon, I shall ask for something to eat.

ANNIE: Well, if I have to wait much longer I shall faint.

NELLIE: So shall I.

FRANK: Oh! Come over here and get a whiff of this.

ALL: What is it?

FRANK: Fried pork!

ALL: Oh! Doesn't it smell good.

FRANK: Yes, and I never could bear it at home.

ALL: Nor I!

RICKETY ANN: Look out for snakes!

JOSHUA: Hello! Hello! Hello! What's all this hollerin' about?

ALL: Snakes!

JOSHUA: Snakes? I don't see any snakes

FRANK: Well that sun flower over there said there were!

RICKETY ANN: Oh, I didn't nuther! I said look *out* for snakes!

FRANK: What did you say that for?

RICKETY ANN: Well, I got to have something to laugh at, hain't I?

JOSHUA: Want to know if you be Henry Hopkins' boy?

FRANK: Yes, Mr. Whitcomb.

JOSHUA: How de-do. Knows yer father fust rate. He and I used to go skewl together.

MATILDA: Looks a leetle mite like Henry used to, don't you think so, Joshua?

JOSHUA: Yes, a little mite. But his hair ain't red. I want to know if you are Henry's darter?

ANNIE: Yes, Mr. Whitcomb.

JOSHUA: Well it beats all natur' amazin' how these youngsters do grow!

MATILDA: She favors the Richardsons.

JOSHUA: So she does.

MATILDA: I can see it. Looks like her mother. Know'd your mother fust rate when she was a gal.

JOSHUA: So did I, too.

FRANK: Mr. Whitcomb.

JOSHUA: What is it?

FRANK: Allow me to introduce Miss Patterson.

JOSHUA: How do you do, miss. Glad ter see yer. How be you?

FRANK: She was on her way home from the White Mountains and I took the liberty of asking her to stop over a day or two.

JOSHUA: That's right! That's right! We'll stow her somewhere. Now I want to call you all to order on one pint!

ALL: What is it?

JOSHUA: Call me uncle and Matilda aunt, then we'll get acquainted quicker.

ALL: Why certainly!

JOSHUA: Gosh! You are all dressed up like a circus.

FRANK: These are lawn tennis suits.

JOSHUA: Little too slick to hay in! You'll hev ter get on yer old clothes tomorrow.

FRANK: But we're all going fishing in the morning.

JOSHUA: Gosh! I thought so, I see your net stuck up to dry over on the grass there. Now what do you expect to catch in a skoop like that?

FRANK: What you see over there is a lawn tennis net and this is a racquet.

JOSHUA: Want to know.

FRANK: A new one on you, isn't it?

JOSHUA: Shouldn't wonder a mite.

RICKETY ANN: Aunt Matilda, that new hired gal wants ter know if she'll peel the potatoes or bile them with their jackets on?

MATILDA: Lan' sakes alive. That gal will be the death of me.

JOSHUA: Bile the potatoes with their jackets on. It wouldn't surprise me if she biled them with their overcoats on, not a mite!

RICKETY ANN: Hush! Don't say a word, but if any of you has any gold watches you'd batter hide 'em, cause I jest seed the awfullest lookin' tramp runnin' round one of the hay stacks thet I ever sees in my life.

ANNIE: A tramp? Why, We'll all be robbed!

JOSHUA: Here! Here! They ain't no danger! Not a mite! What's the matter with ye? Want to scare everybody to death?

RICKETY ANN: Well, if he ain't a robber, I jest bet he's a wild man escaped out of a moragerie.

JOSHUA: Stop yer yawpin' and go and git me a towel and I'll wash up. And help your Aunt get supper ready. And tell Miss O'Flackerty to get the milkin' done afore dark too.

FRANK: How is the fishing around here, Uncle Joshua?

JOSHUA: Gosh, I don't know; hain't been fishin' sence I was a boy.

FRANK: How is that?

JOSHUA: Hain't had time.

FRANK: No?

JOSHUA: No, we hev to scratch up here like a hen with forty chickens to pay taxes and keep out o' the poor house; we don't hev much time to go fishin', I can tell yer. We hev to git up early and work late. Keep right at it from mornin' till night. No time to fish. How's yer father?

FRANK: Quite well, thanks.

JOSHUA: Got rich I hear.

FRANK: Yes, rated at over a million.

JOSHUA: Christopher Columbus! A million dollars?

FRANK: Quite a sum of money, isn't it?

JOSHUA: Gosh! I guess it is! Only think on't. He and I set on the same bench together in the district skewl.

FRANK: Yes, I've often heard him speak of it.

JOSHUA: You can see the old skewl house down there, jest over the tops o' them trees. Stands right across the road from that old barn with a load of hay in front of it.

FRANK: Yes, I see it.

JOSHUA: 'Twas a new building then, but age is beginnin' to tell on it. We're growing old together. Many's the time yer old dad and I got our jackets tanned, I can tell you.

FRANK: I suppose so.

JOSHUA: New York must be a pretty smart sort of a village I guess, ain't it?

FRANK: Well, I should say it is. Were you ever there?

JOSHUA: No sir! Never set foot in it. But I'm goin' there one of these days to look for my boy.

FRANK: Why, have you a son in New York?

JOSHUA: I don't know; I did have four or five months ago, ain't heard nothin' from him sence.

FRANK: He went there thinking to make his fortune, I suppose.

JOSHUA: Well, not exactly. Guess I might as well tell you first as last, cause you're sure to hear on't and I want you to hear on't right. Pull up a chair and sit down.

FRANK: Yes, thank you, I will.

JOSHUA: About a year ago now he was a cashier in the Cheshire Bank in Keene a few miles from here. Well, it seems one day a party of sharpers from Boston went up to Keene and went into the Bank, and when some of them was talking to Reub, one of the mean sneaks got into the vault and stole a lot of money.

FRANK: He did!

JOSHUA: Oh, yes. It all come out in the trial. Well, they pitched onto my boy and had him arrested right here before a lot of visitors I had from Boston, on suspicion of robbin' the bank! But they let him go again pretty quick I can tell you. When I think on't I get so mad I pretty near froth. Charged with stealin' something he didn't know no more about than the man in the moon.

FRANK: What a shame!

JOSHUA: I guess it was, and he felt it dreadful, too. I don't believe the poor boy ever had a good night's sleep sense. Always imagined people pinted at him and was downhearted and low spirited. So one day he packed up his trunk and started for New York. There. Now you know all about it.

FRANK: So you think of going there to look for him, do you?

JOSHUA: I certainly do.

FRANK: Why not go back with us?

JOSHUA: Gosh! I will if my new boots are done in time. Durned if I don't. Thank ye, thank ye. Now I am going to ask you something and I know you will laugh at me.

FRANK: Why should I?

JOSHUA: Cos it is so foolish. Say, do you believe in dreams? That's right—laugh. I don't blame you a mite.

FRANK: Why do you ask?

JOSHUA: Because I've had 'em about my boy lately, so natral it almost seems as though they must be true.

FRANK: That is the result of constantly thinking of him, nothing more, believe me.

JOSHUA: I hope not, I hope not.

RICKETY ANN: Say, Uncle, Aunt Tildy says to ask you if you won't come in and cut some dried beef for supper.

JOSHUA: Why sartin'. Won't you come in the house, young man?

FRANK: No thanks, I'll stop out here and look around if you have no objections.

JOSHUA: Oh no, make yerself ter home. I don't care what you do as long as you don't sit on my bee-hives, be careful about that.

RICKETY ANN: Say, who be you anyway? I didn't know you was comin'.

FRANK: No? Then there must be something wrong about it, isn't there?

RICKETY ANN: Oh, I don't know.

FRANK: Well, I'm Frank Hopkins and I'm from New York. Now who are you?

RICKETY ANN: Well—my name is Mary Ann Maynard but they call me Rickety Ann.

FRANK: What for?

RICKETY ANN: I don't know. Guess 'cos I hed the rickets when I was little.

FRANK: Indeed.

RICKETY ANN: Yep. Say, do you know what?

FRANK: No, what?

RICKETY ANN: Weel, I can climb a tree jest as good as a boy. Want to see me?

FRANK: No, no—I'll take your word for it.

RICKETY ANN: Say, do you know you are awful nice lookin'?

FRANK: Thanks.

RICKETY ANN: Yes, you be.

FRANK: Say, Rickety Ann, have you always lived here?

RICKETY ANN: No! I was borrowed out of the poor house jest to help Aunt Tildy when the visitors was here. But I guess I'll never go back there any more.

FRANK: No?

RICKETY ANN: No, 'cos Aunt Tildy says if I am a good gal, I kin stay here jes' as long as I'm a mind to and I'm goin' to try and be good. Wouldn't you?

FRANK: I certainly should.

RICKETY ANN: Say, you never lived in the poor house, did you?

FRANK: I should say not.

RICKETY ANN: Oh, you wouldn't like it a bit.

FRANK: No?

RICKETY ANN: No, 'cos you don't get half enough to eat, only on prize days.

FRANK: What do you get on prize days?

RICKETY ANN: Well, on prize days, the one that eats the most puddin' and milk gets a great big piece of pumpkin pie. The last time I eat the most puddin' and milk.

FRANK: And you got the pie, of course.

RICKETY ANN: No—eat too much puddin' and milk, couldn't eat no pie. Oh, here comes the cows. I must go and drive them in the barn yard. Co—Boss—Co—Boss.

FRANK: She eat so much puddin' and milk she couldn't eat no pie.

EXIT

THE GRANITE MONTHLY

The *Granite Monthly*, the literary magazine of the state of New Hampshire, was published from 1877 to 1930. The magazine contained short stories, serialized novels, poems, essays, and historical and biographical sketches, as well as obituaries of prominent citizens. The following obituary and poem are typical of the publication's literary fare.

"Gilman Tuttle"

Gilman Tuttle was born in Sanbornton, N. H., October 4th, 1818. As a boy, with nothing but his hands to rely on, he drifted to Lowell, Mass., and later to Boston, where, after establishing a business and, with characteristic generosity, admitting a younger brother to an interest in his growing fortunes, he became one of the heaviest contractors of the metropolis.

As a builder, his works praise him, and hundreds of the finest residences in Boston as well as business blocks without number in the "burned district" and elsewhere, attest the thoroughness of his handiwork.

Horticultural Hall, numerous imposing school edifices built for the city, a portion of the United States sub-treasury and Boston post office, breweries, and family hotels, give evidence of an enterprise and ability of which no man need be ashamed. The shrinkage of a large amount of real estate, in 1875, proved disastrous, and he left Boston with the wreck of his fortune and a brave heart to end his days away from the bustle and turmoil of the city, among his loved New Hampshire hills.

A man of simple tastes, honesty of purpose, unbounded hospitality, and charitable habits, his place as friend and neighbor will long remain unfilled.

As a husband and father his first thought was of his family and all that goes to make home what it should be, and nothing was neglected to promote the comfort of the stranger within his gates. While the community can ill afford to lose a public-spirited citizen who stands ready to further any work of public improvement to the extent of his means and hands. He was a member of the Masonic and Odd Fellows societies, the latter participating in the funeral exercises which were largely attended by sympathizing friends. Mr. Tuttle died in East Concord, N. H., May 27th, 1880, after a lingering illness of four months,—a sad sequel to an industrious and energetic career.

He leaves a widow and two daughters—Mrs. C. E. Staniels and Mrs. John E. Frye, both of East Concord. Two aged brothers—Gen. B. S. Tuttle and R. C. Tuttle, Esq., of Meredith Village—still survive him.

The Old Home Week Festal Day

The Reverend N. F. Carter

Blow fresh from the mountains, ye North winds, blow,
To temper the heat of the noontide glow;
Blow, winds of the South, from the orange grove's shade
Full laden with odors their blossoms have made;
Blow, winds of the East, for ye blow not in vain,
Though bringing so often the cloud and the rain;
Blow gently, O winds that come from the West;—
The wind that blows home is the wind that blows best.
No blast of the bugle, nor beating of drum,
  No thunder of cannon sends signals afar;
But heart calls to heart and the children will come,
  Led home by the light of some beckoning star;—
Led home for the welcome as hearty and warm
  As the loved ones of old still loyal can give,—
A welcome to homes giving shelter from storms,
  Giving joy, till we feel it is blessèd to live.

So the old-time children are with you again,
Now beautiful women and sturdy old men;
They call for a blessing with merriest shout,
Glad to enter your doors—for the latch-string is out.
They come for the joy of your presence awhile,
The hand-clasp, the greeting, and rosiest smile;
They come for renewal of friendships long past,
Live over their childhood too blissful to last.
O the sights and the songs of this dear old town,
  As beautiful now as in days long gone,
Its jubilant river still winding down
  Through the valley so lovely, and evermore on.
We listen with joy to the honey bees' hum,
  The anthem of birds in the evening gloam,—
Ever sweeter than sound of the trumpet or drum;—
  That music is sweetest that blesses the home.

Sweet music comes up from the ripple of rills;
So grandly still stand the sentinel hills;

The forests are waving their banners of green;
The meadows lie smiling in billowy sheen;
Forgetting all care and the troubles of life,
Forgetting the folly and evils of strife,
Let Love in its glory, revealing its power,
With heart-songs of joy make blessèd the hour.
The stories and games we remember so well,
  With the nuts and apples that vanished so fast,
And the long days of learning to cipher and spell,
  In the old red schoolhouse, now lost in the past.
The bonfires and skatings on meadows so glare,—
  The old-time athletics we happily took,—
The coastings down hill in the crisp winter air,
  The fishing for trout in the spring-swollen brook.

We remember the beechnuts and chestnuts so brown,
Which the winds of the autumn shook merrily down
For the children to gather with passionate greed,
In plentiful store for their winter of need;
And butternuts also, which splendidly crack
Under hammer of one understanding the knack;—
So royally toothsome the meat of them all,
The glad days are days when in plenty they fall.
Not the hurry and rush of the present then,
  So simple, so frugal, so restful the days,
How blessèd to live them over again,
  In the peace and contentment that merits our praise.
Oh, gladsome those days of the olden time,
  When fathers and mothers made happy the home,
Wrought wisely and well, with a faith sublime,
  Content with the home-life, nor caring to roam.

In finishing their work they have left us a name,
Not blazoned, indeed, on the scrolls of fame,
But remembered for virtues, if homely, as grand
As the picturesque mountains that girdle the land.
Heroic and patient when burdened and tried,
Enduring the hardship of pleasures denied;—
We honor them for duties so faithfully done,
And cherish their memories every one.

Are we, in the life we are living today,
    As faithful to trusts, with hearts tender and warm?
Do we bear as bravely the storms of the way,
    As cheerfully, gladly, life's duties perform?
In the full of life's pressure, the full of its strain,
    Whatever we do, and wherever we roam,
In the wail of the wind, in the thick of the rain,—
    Let us labor to make a glad Heaven of home.

THE CHANGING ORDER
Decline and Revolt

THE IMPETUS for idealization of the community in New Hampshire literature was a small-town, Anglo-Saxon, Protestant culture. At its core were old Yankee families whose folk memories extended back to the great migrations of the seventeenth century. These people found their central position in the culture increasingly threatened after the Civil War. The accelerated shift from agriculture to industry, the westward movement of population, and the growing influence of urban culture forced the natives into a defensive position. Furthermore, their once-homogeneous society disintegrated before waves of new immigrants.

Writers who felt obliged to grapple with these issues could not ignore the altered landscape for long. William Dean Howells and Winston Churchill described the declining vigor of the Yankee race, the weakening of its influence, and the growing corruption of its politics. Howells's novel *The Landlord at Lion's Head* deals with the dilemma of the rural Yankee and also heaps scorn on the patrician Brahmins of Beacon Hill who waste their lives in the snobbery of trivial social customs. The central character and chief survivor is a young man from the mountains who does not live by the old values but creates his own rules as he climbs to success at the expense of those convenient to his purpose. And in *Coniston*, Winston Churchill produced a *roman à clef* based on a New Hampshire political boss named Ruell Durkee. He carried this fictionalized version of political corruption a step further with *Mr. Crewe's Career*, a story based on his own unsuccessful campaign as a reform candidate for the Republican nomination for the governorship of New Hampshire.

Robert Frost likewise discovered themes for many poems in the predicament of farm families who bravely hung on to a way of life that the modern world seemed intent on making ever more irrelevant.

The movement known as "the revolt from the village" completed the demolition of the idealized community with an assault on those hometowns that, it was now asserted, were never citadels of the old values, but rather, whited sepulchers enshrining organized hypocrisy. The later work of Alice Brown suggested these altered attitudes, and *Peyton Place* by Grace Metalious made it all explicit.

WILLIAM DEAN HOWELLS

William Dean Howells (b. Martin's Ferry, Ohio, 1837; d. 1920) was the son of Swedenborgians. Prior to the Civil War he moved East and met Lowell, Emerson, Hawthorne, and other literary luminaries. He was rewarded for writing Lincoln's campaign biography by being appointed U.S. consul in Venice during the Civil War. After the war he had a sixteen year career as editor of the *Atlantic Monthly* and became the single most influential critic and advocate of realism in literature. He served as editor for such diverse talents as Samuel Clemens and Henry James. After leaving the *Atlantic* he concentrated on his own writing. Becoming disenchanted with the genteel literary society of Boston that he had done much to perpetuate, he moved to New York City before the turn of the century. For the last twenty years of his life he wrote a column for *Harper's*. Although his formal education was limited, he is remembered as the greatest influence on late nineteenth-century American literature. During much of his life he was a frequent summer resident of New Hampshire and later bought a home in Kittery, Maine.

In the following excerpt, the beginning of Howells's *Landlord at Lion's Head*, Howells presents the setting, contrasts the native Yankees with the tourists, and establishes Mrs. Durgin and baby Jeff as strong characters in contrast with the rest of their family.

The Landlord at Lion's Head was published in 1897 by Harper & Brothers in New York.

FROM

The Landlord at Lion's Head

I.

If you looked at the mountain from the west, the line of the summit was wandering and uncertain, like that of most mountain-tops; but seen from the east, the mass of granite showing above the dense forests of the lower slopes had the form of a sleeping lion. The flanks and haunches were vaguely distinguished from the mass; but the mighty head, resting with its tossed mane upon the vast paws stretched before it, was boldly sculptured against the sky. The likeness could not have been more perfect, when you had it in profile, if it had been a definite intention of art; and you could travel far north and far south before the illusion vanished. In winter the head was blotted by the snows; and sometimes the vagrant clouds caught upon it and deformed it, or hid it, at other seasons; but commonly, after the last snow went in the spring until the first snow came in the fall, the Lion's Head was a part of the landscape, as imperative and importunate as the Great Stone Face itself.

Long after other parts of the hill country were opened to summer sojourn, the region of Lion's Head remained almost primitively solitary and savage. A stony mountain road followed the bed of the torrent that brawled through the valley at its base, and at a certain point a still rougher lane climbed from the road along the side of the opposite height to a lonely farm-house pushed back on a narrow shelf of land, with a meagre acreage of field and pasture broken out of the woods that clothed all the neighboring steeps. The farm-house level commanded the best view of Lion's Head, and the visitors always mounted to it, whether they came on foot, or arrived on buckboards or in buggies, or drove up in the Concord stages from the farther and nearer hotels. The drivers of the coaches rested their horses there, and watered them from the spring that dripped into the green log at the barn; the passengers scattered about the door-yard to look at the Lion's Head, to wonder at it and mock at it, according to their several makes and moods. They could scarcely have felt that they ever had a welcome from the stalwart, handsome woman who sold them milk, if they

wanted it, and small cakes of maple sugar if they were very stren-
uous for something else. The ladies were not able to make much of
her, from the first; but some of them asked her if it were not rather
lonely there, and she said that when you heard the catamounts
scream at night, and the bears growl in the spring, it did seem
lonesome. When one of them declared that if she should hear a
catamount scream, or a bear growl, she should die, the woman answered, Well, she presumed we must all die some time. But the
ladies were not sure of a covert slant in her words, for they were
spoken with the same look she wore when she told them that the
milk was five cents a glass, and the black maple sugar three cents a
cake. She did not change when she owned upon their urgence that
the gaunt man whom they glimpsed around the corners of the
house was her husband, and the three lank boys with him were her
sons; that the children whose faces watched them through the
writhing window-panes were her two little girls; that the urchin
who stood shyly twisted, all but his white head and sunburnt face,
into her dress, and glanced at them with a mocking blue eye, was
her youngest, and that he was three years old. With like coldness
of voice and face, she assented to their conjecture that the space
walled off in the farther corner of the orchard was the family bur-
ial-ground; and she said, with no more feeling that the ladies could
see than she had shown concerning the other facts, that the graves
they saw were those of her husband's family and of the children
she had lost: there had been ten children, and she had lost four.
She did not visibly shrink from the pursuit of the sympathy which
expressed itself in curiosity as to the sicknesses they had died of;
the ladies left her with the belief that they had met a character, and
she remained with the conviction, briefly imparted to her husband, that they were tonguey.

The summer folks came more and more, every year, with little
variance in the impression on either side. When they told her that
her maple sugar would sell better if the cake had an image of
Lion's Head stamped on it, she answered that she got enough of
Lion's Head without wanting to see it on all the sugar she made.
But the next year the cakes bore a rude effigy of Lion's Head, and
she said that one of her boys had cut the stamp out with his knife;
she now charged five cents a cake for the sugar, but her manner
remained the same. It did not change when the excursionists drove

away, and the deep silence native to the place fell after their chatter. When a cock crew, or a cow lowed, or a horse neighed, or one of the boys shouted to the cattle, an echo retorted from the granite base of Lion's Head, and then she had all the noise she wanted, or, at any rate, all the noise there was, most of the time. Now and then a wagon passed on the stony road by the brook in the valley, and sent up its clatter to the farm-house on its high shelf, but there was scarcely another break from the silence, except when the coaching parties came. The continuous clash and rush of the brook was like a part of the silence, as the red of the farm-house and the barn was like a part of the green of the fields and woods all round them: the black-green of pines and spruces, the yellow-green of maples and birches, dense to the tops of the dreary hills, and breaking like a baffled sea around the Lion's Head.

The farmer stopped at his work, with a thin, inward-curving chest, but his wife stood straight at hers; and she had a massive beauty of figure, and a heavily moulded regularity of feature that impressed such as had eyes to see her grandeur among the summer folks. She was forty when they began to come, and an ashen gray was creeping over the reddish heaps of her hair, like the pallor that overlies the crimson of the autumnal oak. She showed her age earlier than most fair people, but since her marriage at eighteen she had lived long in the deaths of the children she had lost. They were born with the taint of their father's family, and they withered from their cradles. The youngest boy alone, of all her brood, seemed to have inherited her health and strength. The rest as they grew up began to cough, as she had heard her husband's brothers and sisters cough, and then she waited in hapless patience the fulfillment of their doom. The two little girls whose faces the ladies of the first coaching party saw at the farm-house windows had died away from them; two of the lank boys had escaped, and in the perpetual exile of California and Colorado had saved themselves alive. Their father talked of going too, but ten years later he still dragged himself spectrally about the labors of the farm, with the same cough at sixty which made his oldest son at twenty-nine look scarcely younger than himself.

WINSTON CHURCHILL

Winston Churchill (b. St. Louis, Missouri, 1871; d. 1947) was an upper-middle-class descendant of two socially prominent New England families, a fact that he did not consider unimportant. He graduated from the U.S. Naval Academy in 1890 but resigned his commission to pursue a career in journalism. After marrying a wealthy St. Louis woman, he wrote a series of popular historical novels. Spurred by a repugnance to the corrupt influence of the Boston and Maine Railroad, Churchill became involved in New Hampshire politics after moving to Cornish in 1898. After serving in the state legislature, he ran as a reform Republican candidate for governor in 1906, and lost. Believing the pen might serve where the ballot box did not, he wrote several novels about New Hampshire politics that did result in some political reforms. He continued to write about political and social problems until the First World War, after which he retired from literary and political pursuits.

"The Woodchuck Session," which follows, is the best known chapter in Churchill's novel *Coniston*. It demonstrates the means Jethro Bass uses to dominate the New Hampshire legislature. In order to obtain a quorum of his followers and thus ensure passage of a bill allowing a favored railroad to get a franchise, Bass gives free theater passes to all legislators who may vote in opposition and then holds a special session while those are at the play. The president of the opposing railroad is detained in his library. The term *woodchuck session* refers to special sessions called ostensibly to pass legislation on such minor matters as the control of woodchucks.

The excerpt from *The Dwelling Place of Light* establishes the setting of the novel. The excerpt from *Mr. Crewe's Career* describes a pillar of the community who has sold out to the railroad.

Coniston was published in 1906; *Mr. Crewe's Career* in 1908, and *The Dwelling-Place of Light* in 1917, all by Macmillan Company in New York.

FROM

Coniston

CHAPTER XV

The Woodchuck Session

Mr. Amos Cuthbert named it so—our old friend Amos who lives high up in the ether of Town's End ridge, and who now represents Coniston in the Legislature. He is the same silent, sallow person as when Jethro first took a mortgage on his farm, only his skin is beginning to resemble dried parchment, and he is a trifle more cantankerous. On the morning of that memorable day when "Uncle Tom's Cabin" came to the capital, Amos had entered the Throne Room and given vent to his feelings in regard to the gentleman in the back seat who had demanded an evening sitting on behalf of the farmers.

"Don't that beat all!" cried Amos. "Let them have their darned woodchuck session; there won't nobody go to it. For cussed, crisscross contrariness, give me a moss-back Democrat from a one-hoss, one-man town like Suffolk. I'm a-goin' to see the show."

"G-goin' to the show, be you, Amos?" said Jethro.

"Yes, I be," answered Amos, bitterly. "I hain't a-goin' nigh the house to-night." And with this declaration he departed.

"I wonder if he really is going?" queried Mr. Merrill, looking at the ceiling. And then he laughed.

"Why shouldn't he go?" asked William Wetherell.

Mr. Merrill's answer to this question was a wink, whereupon he, too, departed. And while Wetherell was pondering over the possible meaning of these words the Honorable Alva Hopkins entered, wreathed in smiles, and closed the door behind him.

"It's all fixed," he said, taking a seat near Jethro in the window.

"S-seen your gal—Alvy—seen your gal?"

Mr. Hopkins gave a glance at Wetherell.

"Will don't talk," said Jethro, and resumed his inspection through the lace curtains of what was going on in the street.

"Cassandry's got him to go," said Mr. Hopkins. "It's all fixed, as sure as Sunday. If it misses fire, then I'll never mention the governorship again. But if it don't miss fire," and the Honorable Alva leaned over and put his hand on Jethro's knee, "if it don't miss fire, I get the nomination. Is that right?"

"Y-you've guessed it, Alvy."

"That's all I want to know," declared the Honorable Alva; "when you say that much, you never go back on it. And you can go ahead and give the orders, Jethro. I have to see that the boys get the tickets. Cassandry's got a head on her shoulders, and she kind of wants to be governor, too." He got as far as the door, when he turned and bestowed upon Jethro a glance of undoubted tribute. "You've done a good many smart things," said he, "but I guess you never beat this, and never will."

"H-hain't done it yet, Alvy," answered Jethro, still looking out through the window curtains at the ever changing groups of gentlemen in the street. These groups had a never ceasing interest for Jethro Bass.

Mr. Wetherell didn't talk, but had he been the most incurable of gossips he felt that he could have done no damage to this mysterious affair, whatever it was. In a certain event, Mr. Hopkins was promised the governorship: so much was plain. And it was also evident that Miss Cassandra Hopkins was in some way to be instrumental. William Wetherell did not like to ask Jethro, but he thought a little of sounding Mr. Merrill, and then he came to the conclusion that it would be wiser for him not to know.

"Er—Will," said Jethro, presently, "you know Heth Sutton— Speaker Heth Sutton?"

"Yes."

"Er—wouldn't mind askin' him to step in and see me before the session—if he was comin' by—would you?"

"Certainly not."

"Er—if he was comin' by," said Jethro.

Mr. Wetherell found Mr. Speaker Sutton glued to a pillar in the rotunda below. He had some difficulty in breaking through the throng that pressed around him, and still more in attracting his attention, as Mr. Sutton took no manner of notice of the customary form of placing one's hand under his elbow and pressing gently up. Summoning up his courage, Mr. Wetherell tried the second method of seizing him by the buttonhole. He paused in his harangue, one hand uplifted, and turned and glanced at the storekeeper abstractedly.

"Mr. Bass asked me to tell you to drop into Number 7," said Wetherell, and added, remembering express instructions, "if you were going by."

Wetherell had not anticipated the magical effect this casual message would have on Mr. Sutton, nor had he thought that so large and dignified a body would move so rapidly. Before the astonished gentlemen who had penned him in could draw a breath, Mr. Sutton had reached the stairway and was mounting it with an agility that did him credit. Five minutes later Wetherell saw the Speaker descending again, the usually impressive quality of his face slightly modified by the twitching of a smile.

Thus the day passed, and the gentlemen of the Lovejoy and Duncan factions sat as tight as ever in their seats, and the Truro Franchise bill still slumbered undisturbed in Mr. Chauncey Weed's committee.

At supper there was a decided festal air about the dining room of the Pelican House, the little band of agricultural gentlemen who wished to have a session not being patrons of that exclusive hotel. Many of the Solons had sent home for their wives, that they might do the utmost justice to the Honorable Alva's hospitality. Even Jethro, as he ate his crackers and milk, had a new coat with bright brass buttons, and Cynthia, who wore a fresh gingham which Miss Sukey Kittredge of Coniston had helped to design, so far relented in deference to Jethro's taste as to tie a red bow at her throat.

The middle table under the chandelier was the immediate firmament of Miss Cassandra Hopkins. And there, beside the future governor, sat the president of the "Northwestern" Railroad, Mr. Lovejoy, as the chief of the revolving satellites. People began to say that Mr. Lovejoy was hooked at last, now that he had lost his head in such an unaccountable fashion as to pay his court in public; and it was very generally known that he was to make one of the Honorable Alva's immediate party at the performance of "Uncle Tom's Cabin."

Mr. Speaker Sutton, of course, would have to forego the pleasure of the theatre as a penalty of his high position. Mr. Merrill, who sat at Jethro's table next to Cynthia that evening, did a great deal of joking with the Honorable Heth about having to preside over a woodchuck session, which the Speaker, so Mr. Wetherell thought, took in astonishingly good part, and seemed very willing to make the great sacrifice which his duty required of him.

After supper Mr. Wetherell took a seat in the rotunda. As an observer of human nature, he had begun to find a fascination in watching the group of politicians there. First of all he encountered Mr. Amos Cuthbert, his little coal-black eyes burning brightly, and he was looking very irritable indeed.

"So you're going to the show, Amos?" remarked the storekeeper, with an attempt at cordiality.

To his bewilderment, Amos turned upon him fiercely.

"Who said I was going to the show?" he snapped.

"You yourself told me."

"You'd ought to know whether I'm a-goin' or not," said Amos, and walked away.

While Mr. Wetherell sat meditating upon this inexplicable retort, a retired, scholarly looking gentleman with a white beard, who wore spectacles, came out of the door leading from the barber shop and quietly took a seat beside him. The storekeeper's attention was next distracted by the sight of one who wandered slowly but ceaselessly from group to group, kicking up his heels behind, and halting always in the rear of the speakers. Needless to say that this was our friend Mr. Bijah Bixby, who was following out his celebrated tactics of "going along by when they were talkin' sly." Suddenly Mr. Bixby's eye alighted on Mr. Wetherell, who by a stretch of imagination conceived that it expressed both astonishment and approval, although he was wholly at a loss to understand these sentiments. Mr. Bixby winked—Mr. Wetherell was sure of that. But to his surprise, Bijah did not pause in his rounds to greet him.

Mr. Wetherell was beginning to be decidedly uneasy, and was about to go upstairs, when Mr. Merrill came down the rotunda whistling, with his hands in his pockets. He stopped whistling when he spied the storekeeper, and approached him in his usual hearty manner.

"Well, well, this is fortunate," said Mr. Merrill; "how are you, Duncan? I want you to know Mr. Wetherell. Wetherell writes that weekly letter for the *Guardian* you were speaking to me about last year. Will, this is Mr. Alexander Duncan, president of the 'Central.'"

"How do you do, Mr. Wetherell?" said the scholarly gentleman with the spectacles, putting out his hand. "I'm glad to meet you, very glad, indeed. I read your letters with the greatest pleasure."

Mr. Wetherell, as he took Mr. Duncan's hand, had a variety of emotions which may be imagined, and need not be set down in particular.

"Funny thing," Mr. Merrill continued, "I was looking for you, Duncan. It occurred to me that you would like to meet Mr. Wetherell. I was afraid you were in Boston."

"I have just got back," said Mr. Duncan.

"I wanted Wetherell to see your library. I was telling him about it."

"I should be delighted to show it to him," answered Mr. Duncan. That library, as is well known, was a special weakness of Mr. Duncan's.

Poor William Wetherell, who was quite overwhelmed by the fact that the great Mr. Duncan had actually read his letters and liked them, could scarcely utter a sensible word. Almost before he realized what had happened he was following Mr. Duncan out of the Pelican House, when the storekeeper was mystified once more by a nudge and another wink from Mr. Bixby, conveying unbounded admiration.

"Why don't you write a book, Mr. Wetherell?" inquired the railroad president, when they were crossing the park.

"I don't think I could do it," said Mr. Wetherell, modestly. Such incense was overpowering, and he immediately forgot Mr. Bixby.

"Yes, you can," said Mr. Duncan, "only you don't know it. Take your letters for a beginning. You can draw people well enough, when you try. There was your description of the lonely hill-farm on the spur—I shall always remember that: the gaunt farmer, toiling every minute between sun and sun; the thin, patient woman bending to a task that never changed or lightened; the children growing up and leaving one by one, some to the cities, some to the West, until the old people are left alone in the evening of life—to the sunsets and the storms. Of course you must write a book."

Mr. Duncan quoted other letters, and William Wetherell thrilled. Poor man! he had had little enough incense in his time, and none at all from the great. They came to the big square house with the cornice which Cynthia had seen the day before, and walked across the lawn through the open door. William Wetherell had a glimpse of a great drawing-room with high windows, out of which was wafted the sound of a piano and of youthful voices and laughter, and then he was in the library. The thought of one man owning all those books overpowered him. There they were, in stately rows, from the floor to the high ceiling, and a portable ladder with which to reach them.

Mr. Duncan, understanding perhaps something of the store-keeper's embarrassment, proceeded to take down his treasures: first editions from the shelves, and folios and missals from drawers in a great iron safe in one corner and laid them on the mahogany desk. It was the railroad president's hobby, and could he find an appreciative guest, he was happy. It need scarcely be said that he found William Wetherell appreciative, and possessed of a knowledge of Shakespeareana and other matters that astonished his host as well as pleased him. For Wetherell had found his tongue at last.

After a while Mr. Duncan drew out his watch and gave a start.

"By George!" he exclaimed, "it's after eight o'clock. I'll have to ask you to excuse me to-night, Mr. Wetherell. I'd like to show you the rest of them—can't you come around to-morrow afternoon?"

Mr. Wetherell, who had forgotten his own engagement and "Uncle Tom's Cabin," said he would be happy to come. And they went out together and began to walk toward the State House.

"It isn't often I find a man who knows anything at all about these things," continued Mr. Duncan, whose heart was quite won. "Why do you bury yourself in Coniston?"

"I went there from Boston for my health," said the storekeeper.

"Jethro Bass lives there, doesn't he?" said Mr. Duncan, with a laugh. "But I suppose you don't know anything about politics."

"I know nothing at all," said Mr. Wetherell, which was quite true. He had been in dreamland, but now the fact struck him again, with something of a shock, that this mild-mannered gentleman was one of those who had been paying certain legislators to remain in their seats. Wetherell thought of speaking to Mr. Duncan of his friendship with Jethro Bass, but the occasion passed.

"I wish to heaven I didn't have to know anything about politics," Mr. Duncan was saying; "they disgust me. There's a little matter on now, about an extension of the Truro Railroad to Harwich, which wouldn't interest you, but you can't conceive what a nuisance it has been to watch that House day and night, as I've had to. It's no joke to have that townsman of yours, Jethro Bass, opposed to you. I won't say anything against him, for he may be a friend of yours, and I have to use him sometimes myself." Mr. Duncan sighed. "It's all very sordid and annoying. Now this evening, for instance, when we might have enjoyed ourselves with those books, I've got to go to the House, just because some backwoods farmers want to talk about woodchucks. I suppose it's foolish," said Mr. Duncan; "but Bass has tricked us so often that I've got into the habit of being watchful. I should have been here twenty minutes ago."

By this time they had come to the entrance of the State House, and Wetherell followed Mr. Duncan in, to have a look at the woodchuck session himself. Several members hurried by and up the stairs, some of them in their Sunday black; and the lobby above seemed, even to the storekeeper's unpractised eye, a trifle active for a woodchuck session. Mr. Duncan muttered something, and quickened his gait a little on the steps that led to the gallery. This place was almost empty. They went down to the rail, and the railroad president cast his eye over the House.

"Good God!" he said sharply, "there's almost a quorum here." He ran his eye over the members. "There *is* a quorum here."

Mr. Duncan stood drumming nervously with his fingers on the rail, scanning the heads below. The members were scattered far and wide through the seats, like an army in open order, listening in silence to the droning voice of the clerk. Moths burned in the gas flames, and June-bugs hummed in at the high windows and tilted against the walls. Then Mr. Duncan's finger nails whitened as his thin hands clutched the rail, and a sense of a pending event was upon Wetherell. Slowly he realized that he was listening to the Speaker's deep voice.

"'The Committee on Corporations, to whom was referred House Bill Number 109, entitled, *An Act to extend the Truro Railroad to Harwich*, having considered the same, report the same with the following resolution: Resolved, that the bill ought to pass. Chauncey Weed, for the Committee.'"

The Truro Franchise! The lights danced, and even a sudden

weakness came upon the storekeeper. Jethro's trick! The Duncan and Lovejoy representatives in the theatre, the adherents of the bill here! Wetherell saw Mr. Duncan beside him, a tense figure leaning on the rail, calling to some one below. A man darted up the centre, another up the side aisle. Then Mr. Duncan flashed at William Wetherell from his blue eye such a look of anger as the storekeeper never forgot, and he, too, was gone. Tingling and perspiring, Wetherell leaned out over the railing as the Speaker rapped calmly for order. Hysteric laughter, mingled with hoarse cries, ran over the House, but the Honorable Heth Sutton did not even smile.

A dozen members were on their feet shouting to the chair. One was recognized, and that man Wetherell perceived with amazement to be Mr. Jameson of Wantage, adherent of Jethro's—he who had moved to adjourn for "Uncle Tom's Cabin"! A score of members crowded into the aisles, but the Speaker's voice again rose above the tumult.

"The doorkeepers will close the doors! Mr. Jameson of Wantage moves that the report of the Committee be accepted, and on this motion a roll-call is ordered."

The doorkeepers, who must have been inspired, had already slammed the doors in the faces of those seeking wildly to escape. The clerk already had the little, short-legged desk before him and was calling the roll with incredible rapidity. Bewildered and excited as Wetherell was, and knowing as little of parliamentary law as the gentleman who had proposed the woodchuck session, he began to form some sort of a notion of Jethro's generalship, and he saw that the innocent rural members who belonged to Duncan and Lovejoy's faction had tried to get away before the roll-call, destroy the quorum, and so adjourn the House. These, needless to say, were not parliamentarians, either. They had lacked a leader, they were stunned by the suddenness of the onslaught, and had not moved quickly enough. Like trapped animals, they wandered blindly about for a few moments, and then sank down anywhere. Each answered the roll-call sullenly, out of necessity, for every one of them was a marked man. Then Wetherell remembered the two members who had escaped, and Mr. Duncan, and fell to calculating how long it would take these to reach Foster's Opera House, break into the middle of an act, and get out enough partisans to come back and kill the bill. Mr. Wetherell began to wish he could witness the scene there, too, but something held him here, shaking with excitement, listening to each name that the clerk called.

Would the people at the theatre get back in time?

Despite William Wetherell's principles, whatever these may have been, he was so carried away that he found himself with his watch in his hand, counting off the minutes as the roll-call went on. Foster's Opera House was some six squares distant, and by a liberal estimate Mr. Duncan and his advance guard ought to get back within twenty minutes of the time he left. Wetherell was not aware that people were coming into the gallery behind him; he was not aware that one sat at his elbow until a familiar voice spoke directly into his ear.

"Er—Will—held Duncan pretty tight—didn't you? He's a hard one to fool, too. Never suspected a mite, did he? Look out for your watch!"

Mr. Bixby seized it or it would have fallen. If his life had depended on it, William Wetherell could not have spoken a word to Mr. Bixby then.

"You done well, Will, sure enough," that gentleman continued to whisper. "And Alvy's gal done well, too—you understand. I guess she's the only one that ever snarled up Al Lovejoy so that he didn't know where he was at. But it took a fine, delicate touch for her job and yours, Will. Godfrey, this is the quickest roll-call I ever seed! They've got halfway through Truro County. That fellow can talk faster than a side-show ticket-seller at a circus."

The clerk was, indeed, performing prodigies of pronunciation. When he reached Wells County, the last, Mr. Bixby so far lost his habitual *sangfroid* as to hammer on the rail with his fist.

"If there hain't a quorum, we're done for," he said. "How much time has gone away? Twenty minutes! Godfrey, some of 'em may break loose and git here in five minutes!"

"Break loose?" Wetherell exclaimed involuntarily.

Mr. Bixby screwed up his face.

"You understand. Accidents is liable to happen."

Mr. Wetherell didn't understand in the least, but just then the clerk reached the last name on the roll; an instant of absolute silence, save for the June-bugs, followed, while the assistant clerk ran over his figures deftly and handed them to Mr. Sutton, who leaned forward to receive them.

"One hundred and twelve gentlemen have voted in the affirmative and forty-eight in the negative, and the report of the Committee is accepted."

"Ten more'n a quorum!" ejaculated Mr. Bixby, in a voice of thanksgiving, as the turmoil below began again. It seemed as though every man in the opposition was on his feet and yelling at the chair: some to adjourn; some to indefinitely postpone; some demanding roll-calls; others swearing at these—for a division vote would have opened the doors. Others tried to get out, and then ran down the aisles and called fiercely on the Speaker to open the doors, and threatened him. But the Honorable Heth Sutton did not lose his head, and it may be doubted whether he ever appeared to better advantage than at that moment. He had a voice like one of the Clovelly bulls that fed in his own pastures in the valley, and by sheer bellowing he got silence, or something approaching it,— the protests dying down to a hum; had recognized another friend of the bill, and was putting another question.

"Mr. Gibbs of Wareham moves that the rules of the House be so far suspended that this bill be read a second and third time by its title, and be put upon its final passage at this time. And on this motion," thundered Mr. Sutton, above the tide of rising voices, "the yeas and nays are called for. *The doorkeepers will keep the doors shut.*"

"Abbey of Ashburton."

The nimble clerk had begun on the roll almost before the Speaker was through, and checked off the name. Bijah Bixby mopped his brow with a blue pocket-handkerchief.

"My God," he said, "what a risk Jethro's took! they can't git through another roll-call. Jest look at Heth! Ain't he carryin' it magnificent? Hain't as ruffled as I be. I've knowed him ever sence he wahn't no higher'n that desk. Never would have b'en in politics if it hadn't b'en for me. Funny thing, Will—you and I was so excited we never thought to look at the clock. Put up your watch. Godfrey, what's this?"

The noise of many feet was heard behind them. Men and women were crowding breathlessly into the gallery.

"Didn't take it long to git noised araound," said Mr. Bixby.

"Say, Will, they're bound to have got at 'em in the thea'tre. Don't see how they held 'em off, c-cussed if I do."

The seconds ticked into minutes, the air became stifling, for now the front of the gallery was packed. Now, if ever, the fate of the Truro Franchise hung in the balance, and, perhaps, the rule of Jethro Bass. And now, as in the distance, came a faint, indefinable stir, not yet to be identified by Wetherell's ears as a sound, but registered somewhere in his brain as a warning note. Bijah Bixby, as sensitive as he, straightened up to listen, and then the whispering was hushed. The members below raised their heads, and some clutched the seats in front of them and looked up at the high windows. Only the Speaker sat like a wax statue of himself, and glanced neither to the right nor to the left.

"Harkness of Truro," said the clerk.

"He's almost to Wells County again," whispered Bijah, excitedly. "I didn't callate he could do it. Will?"

"Yes?"

"Will—you hear somethin'?"

A distant shout floated with the night breeze in at the windows; a man on the floor got to his feet and stood straining: a commotion was going on at the back of the gallery, and a voice was heard crying out:—

"For the love of God, let me through!"

Then Wetherell turned to see the crowd at the back parting a little, to see a desperate man in a gorgeous white necktie fighting his way toward the rail. He wore no hat, his collar was wilted, and his normally ashen face had turned white. And, strangest of all, clutched tightly in his hand was a pink ribbon.

"It's Al Lovejoy," said Bijah, laconically.

Unmindful of the awe-stricken stares he got from those about him when his identity became known, Mr. Lovejoy gained the rail and shoved aside a man who was actually making way for him. Leaning far out, he scanned the house with inarticulate rage while the roll-call went monotonously on. Some of the members looked up at him and laughed; others began to make frantic signs, indicative of helplessness; still others telegraphed him obvious advice about reënforcements which, if anything, increased his fury. Mr. Bixby was now fanning himself with the blue handkerchief.

"I hear 'em!" he said, "I hear 'em, Will!"

And he did. The unmistakable hum of the voices of many men and the sound of feet on stone flagging shook the silent night without. The clerk read off the last name on the roll.

"Tompkins of Ulster."

His assistant lost no time now. A mistake would have been fatal, but he was an old hand. Unmindful of the rumble on the wooden stairs below, Mr. Sutton took the list with an admirable deliberation.

"One hundred and twelve gentlemen have voted in the affirmative, forty-eight in the negative, the rules of the House are suspended, and" (the clerk having twice mumbled the title of the bill) "the question is: Shall the bill pass? As many as are of opinion that the bill pass will say *Aye*, contrary minded *No*."

Feet were in the House corridor now, and voices rising there, and noises that must have been scuffling—yes, and beating of door panels. Almost every member was standing, and it seemed as if they were all shouting,—"personal privilege," "fraud," "trickery," "open the doors." Bijah was slowly squeezing the blood out of William Wetherell's arm.

"The doorkeepers has the keys in their pockets!" Mr. Bixby had to shout, for once.

Even then the Speaker did not flinch. By a seeming miracle he got a semblance of order, recognized his man, and his great voice rang through the hall and drowned all other sounds.

"And on this question a roll-call is ordered. *The doorkeepers will close the doors!*"

Then, as in reaction, the gallery trembled with a roar of laughter. But Mr. Sutton did not smile. The clerk scratched off the names with lightning rapidity, scarce waiting for the answers. Every man's color was known, and it was against the rules to be present and fail to vote. The noise in the corridors grew louder, some one dealt a smashing kick on a panel, and Wetherell ventured to ask Mr. Bixby if he thought the doors would hold.

"They can break in all they've a mind to now," he chuckled; "the Truro Franchise is safe."

"What do you mean?" Wetherell demanded excitedly.

"If a member hain't present when a question is put, he can't git into a roll-call," said Bijah.

The fact that the day was lost was evidently brought home to those below, for the strife subsided gradually, and finally ceased altogether. The whispers in the gallery died down, the spectators relaxed a little. Lovejoy alone remained tense, though he had seated himself on a bench, and the hot anger in which he had come was now cooled into a vindictiveness that set the hard lines of his face even harder. He still clutched the ribbon. The last part of that famous roll-call was conducted so quietly that a stranger entering the House would have suspected nothing unusual. It was finished in absolute silence.

"One hundred and twelve gentlemen have voted in the affirmative, forty-eight in the negative, and the bill passes. The House will attend to the title of the bill."

"An act to extend the Truro Railroad to Harwich," said the clerk, glibly.

"Such will be the title of the bill unless otherwise ordered by the House," said Mr. Speaker Sutton. "The doorkeepers will open the doors."

Somebody moved to adjourn, the motion was carried, and thus ended what has gone down to history as the Woodchuck Session. Pandemonium reigned. One hundred and forty belated members fought their way in at the four entrances, and mingled with them were lobbyists of all sorts and conditions, residents and visitors to the capital, men and women to whom the drama of "Uncle Tom's Cabin" was as nothing to that of the Truro Franchise Bill. It was a sight to look down upon. Fierce wrangles began in a score of places, isolated personal remarks rose above the din, but your New Englander rarely comes to blows; in other spots men with broad smiles seized others by the hands and shook them violently, while Mr. Speaker Sutton seemed in danger of suffocation by his friends. His enemies, for the moment, could get nowhere near him. On this scene Mr. Bijah Bixby gazed with pardonable pleasure.

"Guess there wahn't a mite of trouble about the river towns," he said, "I had 'em in my pocket. Will, let's amble round to the thea'tre. We ought to git in two acts."

William Wetherell went. There is no need to go into the psychology of the matter. It may have been numbness; it may have been temporary insanity caused by the excitement of the battle he had witnessed, for his brain was in a whirl; or Mr. Bixby may have hypnotized him. As they walked through the silent streets toward the Opera House, he listened perforce to Mr. Bixby's comments upon some of the innumerable details which Jethro had planned and quietly carried out while sitting in the window of the Throne Room. A great light dawned on William Wetherell, but too late.

Jethro's trusted lieutenants (of whom, needless to say, Mr. Bixby was one) had been commanded to notify such of their supporters whose fidelity and secrecy could be absolutely depended upon to attend the Woodchuck Session; and, further to guard against surprise, this order had not gone out until the last minute (hence Mr. Amos Cuthbert's conduct). The seats of these members at the theatre had been filled by accommodating townspeople and visitors. Forestalling a possible vote on the morrow to recall and reconsider, there remained some sixty members whose loyalty was unquestioned, but whose reputation for discretion was not of the best. So much for the parliamentary side of the affair, which was a revelation of generalship and organization to William Wetherell. By the time he had grasped it they were come in view of the lights of Foster's Opera House, and they perceived, among a sprinkling of idlers, a conspicuous and meditative gentleman leaning against a pillar. He was ludicrously tall and ludicrously thin, his hands were in his trousers pockets, and the skirts of his Sunday broadcloth coat hung down behind him awry. One long foot was crossed over the other and rested on the point of the toe, and his head was tilted to one side. He had, on the whole, the appearance of a rather mournful stork. Mr. Bixby approached him gravely, seized him by the lower shoulder, and tilted him down until it was possible to speak into his ear. The gentleman apparently did not resent this, although he seemed in imminent danger of being upset.

"How be you, Peleg? Er—you know Will?"

"No," said the gentleman.

Mr. Bixby seized Mr. Wetherell under the elbow, and addressed himself to the storekeeper's ear.

"Will, I want you to shake hands with Senator Peleg Hartington, of Brampton. This is Will Wetherell, Peleg,—from Coniston—you understand."

The senator took one hand from his pocket.

"How be *you?*" he said. Mr. Bixby was once more pulling down on his shoulder.

"H-haow was it here?" he demanded.

"Almighty funny," answered Senator Hartington, sadly, and waved at the lobby. "There wahn't standin' room in the place."

"Jethro Bass Republican Club come and packed the entrance," explained Mr. Bixby with a wink. "You understand, Will? Go on, Peleg."

"Sidewalk *and* street, too," continued Mr. Hartington, slowly. "First come along Ball of Towles, hollerin' like blazes. They crumpled him all up and lost him. Next come old man Duncan himself."

"Will kep' Duncan," Mr. Bixby interjected.

"That was wholly an accident," exclaimed Mr. Wetherell, angrily.

"Will wahn't born in the country," said Mr. Bixby.

Mr. Hartington bestowed on the storekeeper a mournful look, and continued:—

"Never seed Duncan sweatin' before. He didn't seem to grasp why the boys was there."

"Didn't seem to understand," put in Mr. Bixby, sympathetically.

"'For God's sake, gentlemen,' says he, 'let me in! The Truro Bill!' 'The Truro Bill hain't in the thea'tre, Mr. Duncan,' says Dan Everett. Cussed if I didn't come near laughin'. 'That's "Uncle Tom's Cabin," Mr. Duncan,' says Dan. 'You're a dam fool,' says Duncan. I didn't know he was profane. 'Make room for Mr. Duncan,' says Dan, 'he wants to see the show.' 'I'm a-goin' to see you in jail for this, Everett,' says Duncan. They let him push in about half a rod, and they swallowed *him*. He was makin' such a noise that they had to close the doors of the thea'tre—so's not to disturb the play-actors."

"You understand," said Mr. Bixby to Wetherell. Whereupon he gave another shake to Mr. Hartington, who had relapsed into a sort of funereal meditation.

"Well," resumed that personage, "there was some more come, hollerin' about the Truro Bill. Not many. Guess they'll all have to git their wimmen-folks to press their clothes to-morrow. Then Duncan wanted to git out again, but 'twan't ex'actly convenient. Callated he was suffocatin'—seemed to need air. Little mite limp when he broke loose, Duncan was."

The Honorable Peleg stopped again, as if he were overcome by the recollection of Mr. Duncan's plight.

"Er—er—Peleg!"

Mr. Hartington started.

"What'd they do?—what'd they do?"

"Do?"

"How'd they git notice to 'em?"

"Oh," said Mr. Hartington, "cussed if that *wahn't* funny. Let's see, where was I? After a while they went over t'other side of the street, talkin' sly, waitin' for the act to end. But goldarned if it ever did end."

For once Mr. Bixby didn't seem to understand.

"D-didn't end?"

"No," explained Mr. Hartington; "seems they hitched a kind of nigger minstrel show right on to it—banjos and thingumajigs in front of the curtain while they was changin' scenes, *and* they hitched the second act right on to that. Nobody come out of the thea'tre at all. Funny notion, wahn't it?"

Mr. Bixby's face took on a look of extreme cunning. He smiled broadly and poked Mr. Wetherell in an extremely sensitive portion of his ribs. On such occasions the nasal quality of Bijah's voice seemed to grow.

"You see?" he said.

"Know that little man, Gibbs, don't ye?" inquired Mr. Hartington.

"Airley Gibbs, hain't it? Runs a livery business daown to Rutgers, on Lovejoy's railroad," replied Mr. Bixby, promptly. "I know him. Knew old man Gibbs well's I do you. Mean cuss."

"This Airley's smart—wahn't quite smart enough, though. His bright idea come a little mite late. Hunted up old Christy, got the key to his law office right here in the Duncan Block, went up through the skylight, clumb down to the roof of Randall's store next door, shinned up the lightnin' rod on t'other side, and stuck his head plump into the Opery House window."

"I want to know!" ejaculated Mr. Bixby.

"Somethin' terrible pathetic was goin' on on the stage," resumed Mr. Hartington; "the folks didn't see him at first,—they was all cryin' and everythin' was still, but Airley wahn't affected. As quick as he got his breath he hollered right out loud's he could: 'The Truro Bill's up in the House, boys. We're skun if you don't git thar quick.' Then they tell me the lightnin' rod give way; anyhow, he came down on Randall's gravel roof considerable hard, I take it."

Mr. Hartington, apparently, had an aggravating way of falling into mournful revery and of forgetting his subject. Mr. Bixby was forced to jog him again.

"Yes, they did," he said, "they did. They come out like the thea'tre was afire. There was some delay in gettin' to the street, but not much—not much. All the Republican Clubs in the state couldn't have held 'em then, and the profanity they used wahn't especially edifyin'."

"Peleg's a deacon—you understand," said Mr. Bixby. "Say, Peleg, where was Al Lovejoy?"

"Lovejoy come along with the first of 'em. Must have hurried some—they tell me he was settin' way down in front alongside of Alvy Hopkins's gal, and when Airley hollered out she screeched *and* clutched on to Al, and Al said somethin' he hadn't ought to and tore off one of them pink gew-gaws she was covered with. He was the *maddest* man I ever see. Some of the club was crowded inside, behind the seats, standin' up to see the show. Al was so anxious to git through he hit Si Dudley in the mouth—injured him some, I guess. Pity, wahn't it?"

"Si hain't in politics, you understand," said Mr. Bixby. "Callate Si paid to git in there, didn't he, Peleg?"

"Callate he did," assented Senator Hartington.

A long and painful pause followed. There seemed, indeed, nothing more to be said. The sound of applause floated out of the Opera House doors, around which the remaining loiterers were clustered.

"Goin' in, be you, Peleg?" inquired Mr. Bixby.

Mr. Hartington shook his head.

"Will and me had a notion to see somethin' of the show," said Mr. Bixby, almost apologetically. "I kep' my ticket."

"Well," said Mr. Hartington, reflectively, "I guess you'll find some of the show left. That hain't b'en hurt much, so far as I can ascertain."

* * *

The next afternoon, when Mr. Isaac D. Worthington happened to be sitting alone in the office of the Truro Railroad at the capital, there came a knock at the door, and Mr. Bijah Bixby entered.

Now, incredible as it may seem, Mr. Worthington did not know Mr. Bixby—or rather, did not remember him. Mr. Worthington had not had at that time much of an experience in politics, and he did not possess a very good memory for faces.

Mr. Bixby, who had, as we know, a confidential and winning manner, seated himself in a chair very close to Mr. Worthington—somewhat to that gentleman's alarm.

"How be you?" said Bijah, "I-I've got a little bill here—you understand."

Mr. Worthington didn't understand, and he drew his chair away from Mr. Bixby's.

"I don't know anything about it, sir," answered the president of the Truro Railroad, indignantly; "this is neither the manner nor the place to present a bill. I don't want to see it."

Mr. Bixby moved his chair up again. "Callate you will want to see this bill, Mr. Worthington," he insisted, not at all abashed. "Jethro Bass sent it—you understand—it's *engrossed*."

Whereupon Mr. Bixby drew from his capacious pocket a roll, tied with white ribbon, and pressed it into Mr. Worthington's hands. It was the Truro Franchise Bill.

It is safe to say that Mr. Worthington understood.

FROM

Mr. Crewe's Career

CHAPTER I

The Honourable Hilary Vane Sits for His Portrait

I may as well begin this story with Mr. Hilary Vane, more frequently addressed as the Honourable Hilary Vane, although it was the gentleman's proud boast that he had never held an office in his life. He belonged to the Vanes of Camden Street,—a beautiful village in the hills near Ripton,—and was, in common with some other great men who had made a noise in New York and the nation, a graduate of Camden Wentworth Academy. But Mr. Vane, when he was at home, lived on a wide, maple-shaded street in the "city" of Ripton, cared for by an elderly housekeeper who had more edges than a new-fangled mowing machine. The house was a porticoed one which had belonged to the Austens for a hundred years or more, for Hilary Vane had married, towards middle age, Miss Sarah Austen. In two years he was a widower, and he never tried it again; he had the Austens' house, and that many-edged woman, Euphrasia Cotton, the Austens' housekeeper.

The house was of wood, and was painted white as regularly as leap year. From the street front to the vegetable garden in the extreme rear it was exceedingly long, and—perhaps for propriety's sake—Hilary Vane lived at one end of it and Euphrasia at the other. Hilary was sixty-five, Euphrasia seventy, which is not old for frugal people,—though it is just as well to add that there had never been a breath of scandal about either of them, in Ripton or elsewhere. For the Honourable Hilary's modest needs one room sufficed, and the front parlour had not been used since poor Sarah Austen's demise, thirty years before this story opens.

In those thirty years, by a sane and steady growth, Hilary Vane had achieved his present eminent position in the State. He was trustee for I know not how many people and institutions, a deacon in the first church, a lawyer of such ability that he sometimes was accorded the courtesy-title of "Judge." His only vice—if it could be called such—was in occasionally placing a piece, the size of a pea, of a particular kind of plug tobacco under his tongue,—and this was not known to many people. Euphrasia could not be called a wasteful person, and Hilary had accumulated no small portion of this world's goods, and placed them as propriety demanded, where they were not visible to the naked eye: and be it added in his favour that he gave as secretly to institutions and hospitals, the finances and methods of which were known to him.

As concrete evidence of the Honourable Hilary Vane's importance, when he travelled he had only to withdraw from his hip pocket a book in which many coloured cards were neatly inserted, an open-sesame which permitted him to sit without payment even in those wheeled palaces of luxury known as Pullman cars. Within the limits of the State he did not even have to open the book, but merely say, with a twinkle of his eyes to the conductor, "Good morning, John," and John would reply with a bow and a genial and usually witty remark, and point him out to a nobody who sat in the back of the car. So far had Mr. Hilary Vane's talents carried him.

The beginning of this eminence dated back to the days before the Empire, when there were many little principalities of railroads fighting among themselves. For we are come to a changed America. There was a time, in the days of the sixth Edward of England, when the great landowners found it more profitable to consolidate the farms, seize the common lands, and acquire riches hitherto undreamed of. Hence the rising of tailor Ket and others, and the levelling of fences and barriers, and the eating of many sheep. It may have been that Mr. Vane had come across this passage in English history, but he drew no parallels. His first position of trust had been as counsel for that principality known in the old days as the Central Railroad, of which a certain Mr. Duncan had been president, and Hilary Vane had fought the Central's battles with such telling effect that when it was merged into the one Imperial Railroad, its stockholders—to the admiration of financiers—were guaranteed ten per cent. It was, indeed, rumoured that Hilary drew the Act of Consolidation itself. At any rate, he was too valuable an opponent to neglect, and after a certain interval of time Mr. Vane became chief counsel in the State for the Imperial Railroad, on which dizzy height we now behold him. And he found, by degrees, that he had no longer time for private practice.

It is perhaps gratuitous to add that the Honourable Hilary Vane was a man of convictions. In politics he would have told you—with some vehemence, if you seemed to doubt—that he was a Republican. Treason to party he regarded with a deep-seated abhorrence, as an act for which a man should be justly outlawed. If he were in a mellow mood, with the right quantity of Honey Dew tobacco under his tongue, he would perhaps tell you why he was a Republican, if he thought you worthy of his confidence. He believed in the gold standard, for one thing; in the tariff (left unimpaired in its glory) for another, and with a wave of his hand would indicate the prosperity of the nation which surrounded him,—a prosperity too sacred to tamper with.

One article of his belief, and in reality the chief article, Mr. Vane would not mention to you. It was perhaps because he had never formulated the article for himself. It might be called a faith in the divine right of Imperial Railroads to rule, but it was left out of the verbal creed. This is far from implying hypocrisy to Mr. Vane. It was his foundation-rock and too sacred for light conversation. When he allowed himself to be bitter against various "young men with missions" who had sprung up in various States of the Union, so-called purifiers of politics, he would call them the unsuccessful with a grievance, and recommend to them the practice of charity, forbearance, and other Christian virtues. Thank God, his State was not troubled with such.

FROM

The Dwelling-Place of Light

CHAPTER I

In this modern industrial civilization of which we are sometimes wont to boast, a certain glacier-like process may be observed. The bewildered, the helpless—and there are many—are torn from the parent rock, crushed, rolled smooth, and left stranded in strange places. Thus was Edward Bumpus severed and rolled from the ancestral ledge, from the firm granite of seemingly stable and lasting things, into shifting shale; surrounded by fragments of cliffs from distant lands he had never seen. Thus, at five and fifty, he found himself gate-keeper of the leviathan Chippering Mill in the city of Hampton.

That the polyglot, smoky settlement sprawling on both sides of an historic river should be a part of his native New England seemed at times to be a hideous dream; nor could he comprehend what had happened to him, and to the world of order and standards and religious sanctions into which he had been born. His had been a life of relinquishments. For a long time he had clung to the institution he had been taught to believe was the rock of ages, the Congregational Church, finally to abandon it; even that assuming a form fantastic and unreal, as embodied in the edifice three blocks distant from Fillmore Street which he had attended for a brief time, some ten years before, after his arrival in Hampton. The building, indeed, was symbolic of a decadent and bewildered Puritanism in its pathetic attempt to keep abreast with the age, to compromise with anarchy, merely achieving a nondescript medley of rounded, knob-like towers covered with mulberry-stained shingles. And the minister was sensational and dramatic. He looked like an actor, he aroused in Edward Bumpus an inherent prejudice that condemned the stage. Half a block from this tabernacle stood a Roman Catholic Church, prosperous, brazen, serene, flaunting an eternal permanence amidst the chaos which had succeeded permanence!

There were, to be sure, other Protestant churches where Edward Bumpus and his wife might have gone. One in particular, which he passed on his way to the mill, with its terraced steeple and classic façade, preserved all the outward semblance of the old Order that once had seemed so enduring and secure. He hesitated to join the decorous and dwindling congregation,—the remains of a social stratum from which he had been pried loose; and—more irony—this street, called Warren, of arching elms and white-gabled houses, was now the abiding place of those prosperous Irish who had moved thither from the tenements and ruled the city.

On just such a street in the once thriving New England village of Dolton had Edward been born. In Dolton Bumpus was once a name of names, rooted there since the seventeenth century, and if you had cared to listen he would have told you, in a dialect precise but colloquial, the history of a family that by right of priority and service should have been destined to inherit the land, but whose descendants were preserved to see it delivered to the alien. The God of Cotton Mather and Jonathan Edwards had been tried in the balance and found wanting. Edward could never understand this; or why the Universe, so long static and immutable, had suddenly begun to move. He had always been prudent, but in spite of youthful "advantages," of an education, so called, from a sectarian college on a hill, he had never been taught that, while prudence may prosper in a static world, it is a futile virtue in a dynamic one. Experience even had been powerless to impress this upon him. For more than twenty years after leaving college he had clung to a clerkship in a Dolton mercantile establishment before he felt justified in marrying Hannah, the daughter of Elmer Wench, when the mercantile establishment amalgamated with a rival—and Edward's services were no longer required. During the succession of precarious places with decreasing salaries he had subsequently held, a terrified sense of economic pressure had gradually crept over him, presently growing strong enough, after two girls had arrived, to compel the abridgment of the family. . . . It would be painful to record in detail the cracking-off process, the slipping into shale, the rolling, the ending up in Hampton, where Edward had now for some dozen years been keeper of one of the gates in the frowning brick wall bordering the canal,—a position obtained for him by a compassionate but not too prudent childhood friend who had risen in life and knew the agent of the Chippering Mill, Mr. Claude Ditmar. Thus had virtue failed to hold its own.

One might have thought in all these years he had sat within the gates staring at the brick row of the company's boarding houses on the opposite bank of the canal that reflection might have brought a certain degree of enlightenment. It was not so. The fog of Edward's bewilderment never cleared, and the unformed question was ever clamouring for an answer—how had it happened? Job's cry. How had it happened to an honest and virtuous man, the days of whose forebears had been long in the land which the Lord their God had given them? Inherently American, though lacking the saving quality of push that had been the making of men like Ditmar, he never ceased to regard with resentment and distrust the hordes of foreigners trooping between the pillars, though he refrained from expressing these sentiments in public; a bent, broad shouldered, silent man of that unmistakable physiognomy which, in the seventeenth century, almost wholly deserted the old England for the new. The ancestral features were there, the lips—covered by a grizzled moustache—moulded for the precise formation that emphasizes such syllables as *el*, the hooked nose and sallow cheeks, the grizzled brows and grey eyes drawn down at the corners. But for all its ancestral strength of feature, it was a face from which will had been extracted, and lacked the fire and fanaticism, the indomitable hardness it should have proclaimed, and which have been so characteristically embodied in Mr. St. Gaudens's statue of the Puritan. His clothes were slightly shabby, but always neat.

Little as one might have guessed it, however, what may be called a certain transmuted enthusiasm was alive in him. He had a hobby almost amounting to an obsession, not uncommon amongst Americans who have slipped downward in the social scale. It was the Bumpus Family in America. He collected documents about his

ancestors and relations, he wrote letters with a fine, painful pen-
manship on a ruled block he bought at Hartshorne's drug store to
distant Bumpuses in Kansas and Illinois and Michigan, common
descendants of Ebenezer, the original immigrant, of Dolton. Many
of these western kinsmen answered: not so the magisterial Bumpus
who lived in Boston on the water side of Beacon, whom likewise
he had ventured to address,—to the indignation and disgust of his
elder daughter, Janet.

"Why are you so proud of Ebenezer?" she demanded once,
scornfully.

"Why? Aren't we descended from him?"

"How many generations?"

"Seven," said Edward, promptly, emphasizing the last syllable.

Janet was quick at figures. She made a mental calculation.

"Well, you've got one hundred and twenty-seven other ancestors
of Ebenezer's time, haven't you?"

Edward was a little surprised. He had never thought of this, but
his ardour for Ebenezer remained undampened. Genealogy—his
own—had become his religion, and instead of going to church he
spent his Sunday mornings poring over papers of various degrees
of discolouration, making careful notes on the ruled block.

This consciousness of his descent from good American stock
that had somehow been deprived of its heritage, while a grievance
to him, was also a comfort. It had a compensating side, in spite
of the lack of sympathy of his daughters and his wife. Hannah
Bumpus took the situation more grimly: she was a logical projec-
tion in a new environment of the religious fatalism of ancestors
whose God was a God of vengeance. She did not concern herself as
to what all this vengeance was about; life was a trap into which all
mortals walked sooner or later, and her particular trap had a
treadmill,—a round of household duties she kept whirling with an
energy that might have made their fortunes if she had been the
head of the family. It is bad to be a fatalist unless one has an in-
controvertible belief in one's destiny,—which Hannah had not.
But she kept the little flat with its worn furniture—which had
known so many journeys—as clean as a merchant ship of old
Salem, and when it was scoured and dusted to her satisfaction she
would sally forth to Bonnaccossi's grocery and provision store on
the corner to do her bargaining in competition with the Italian

housewives of the neighborhood. She was wont, indeed, to pause outside for a moment, her quick eye encompassing the coloured prints of red and yellow jellies cast in rounded moulds, decked with slices of orange, the gaudy boxes of cereals and buckwheat flour, the "Brookfield" eggs in packages. Significant, this modern package system, of an era of flats with little storage space. She took in at a glance the blue lettered placard announcing the current price of butterine, and walked around to the other side of the store, on Holmes Street, where the beef and bacon hung, where the sidewalk stands were filled, in the autumn, with cranberries, apples, cabbages, and spinach.

With little outer complaint she had adapted herself to the constantly lowering levels to which her husband had dropped, and if she hoped that in Fillmore Street they had reached bottom, she did not say so. Her unbetrayed regret was for the loss of what she would have called "respectability"; and the giving up, long ago, in the little city which had been their home, of the servant girl had been the first wrench. Until they came to Hampton they had always lived in *houses*, and her adaptation to a flat had been hard— a flat without a parlour. Hannah Bumpus regarded a parlour as necessary to a respectable family as a wedding ring to a virtuous woman. Janet and Lise would be growing up, there would be young men, and no place to see them save the sidewalks. The fear that haunted her came true, and she never was reconciled. The two girls went to the public schools, and afterwards, inevitably, to work, and it seemed to be a part of her punishment for the sins of her forefathers that she had no more control over them than if they had been boarders; while she looked on helplessly, they did what they pleased; Janet, whom she never understood, was almost as much a source of apprehension as Lise, who became part and parcel of all Hannah deemed reprehensible in this new America which she refused to recognize and acknowledge as her own country.

To send them through the public schools had been a struggle. Hannah used to lie awake nights wondering what would happen if Edward became sick. It worried her that they never saved any money: try as she would to cut the expenses down, there was a limit of decency; New England thrift, hitherto justly celebrated, was put to shame by that which the foreigners displayed, and which would have delighted the souls of gentlemen of the Manchester school. Every once in a while there rose up before her fabulous instances of this thrift, of Italians and Jews who, ignorant emigrants, had entered the mills only a few years before they, the Bumpuses, had come to Hampton, and were now independent property owners. Still rankling in Hannah's memory was a day when Lise had returned from school, dark and mutinous, with a tale of such a family. One of the younger children was a classmate.

"They live on Jordan Street in a *house*, and Laura has roller skates. I don't see why I can't."

This was one of the occasions on which Hannah had given vent to her indignation. Lise was fourteen. Her open rebellion was less annoying than Janet's silent reproach, but at least she had something to take hold of.

"Well, Lise," she said, shifting the saucepan to another part of the stove, "I guess if your father and I had put both you girls in the mills and crowded into one room and cooked in a corner, and lived on onions and macaroni, and put four boarders each in the other rooms, I guess we could have had a house, too. We can start in right now, if you're willing."

But Lise had only looked darker.

"I don't see why father can't make money—other men do."

"Isn't he working as hard as he can to send you to school, and give you a chance?"

ROBERT FROST

Robert Frost (b. San Francisco, 1874; d. 1963) suffered the loss of his father at an early age. His mother, a follower of Swedenborg, took her family back to New England before Robert was a teenager. Frost eked out an existence as a small farmer and teacher to support his family. He farmed for several years in Derry, New Hampshire and later taught at what is now Plymouth State College in Plymouth, New Hampshire. His first book of poems was published when he was almost forty. When fame and prizes did come (he won four Pulitzer Prizes), Frost remained the unofficial poet laureate of the United States until his death.

Frost's *Complete Poems* was published by Holt, Rinehart and Winston in New York in 1967.

Robert Frost, February, 1916, from a series of photographs of the poet in various poses taken in his parlor in Franconia, N.H. by Mr. Huntington of the *Boston Post*. Courtesy of Special Collections, Dimond Library, University of New Hampshire.

New Hampshire

I met a lady from the South who said
(You won't believe she said it, but she said it):
"None of my family ever worked, or had
A thing to sell." I don't suppose the work
Much matters. You may work for all of me.
I've seen the time I've had to work myself.
The having anything to sell is what
Is the disgrace in man or state or nation.

I met a traveler from Arkansas
Who boasted of his state as beautiful
For diamonds and apples. "Diamonds
And apples in commercial quantities?"
I asked him, on my guard. "Oh, yes," he answered,
Off his. The time was evening in the Pullman.
"I see the porter's made your bed," I told him.

I met a Californian who would
Talk California—a state so blessed,
He said, in climate, none had ever died there
A natural death, and Vigilance Committees
Had had to organize to stock the graveyards
And vindicate the state's humanity.
"Just the way Stefansson runs on," I murmured,
"About the British Arctic. That's what comes
Of being in the market with a climate."

I met a poet from another state,
A zealot full of fluid inspiration,
Who in the name of fluid inspiration,
But in the best style of bad salesmanship,
Angrily tried to make me write a protest
(In verse I think) against the Volstead Act.
He didn't even offer me a drink
Until I asked for one to steady *him*.
This is called having an idea to sell.

It never could have happened in New Hampshire.

The only person really soiled with trade
I ever stumbled on in old New Hampshire
Was someone who had just come back ashamed
From selling things in California.
He'd built a noble mansard roof with balls
On turrets like Constantinople, deep
In woods some ten miles from a railroad station,
As if to put forever out of mind
The hope of being, as we say, received.
I found him standing at the close of day
Inside the threshold of his open barn,
Like a lone actor on a gloomy stage—
And recognized him through the iron gray
In which his face was muffled to the eyes
As an old boyhood friend, and once indeed
A drover with me on the road to Brighton.
His farm was "grounds," and not a farm at all;
His house among the local sheds and shanties
Rose like a factor's at a trading station.
And he was rich, and I was still a rascal.
I couldn't keep from asking impolitely,
Where had he been and what had he been doing?
How did he get so? (Rich was understood.)
In dealing in "old rags" in San Francisco.
Oh, it was terrible as well could be.
We both of us turned over in our graves.
Just specimens is all New Hampshire has,
One each of everything as in a show-case
Which naturally she doesn't care to sell.

She had one President (pronounce him Purse,
And make the most of it for better or worse.
He's your one chance to score against the state).
She had one Daniel Webster. He was all
The Daniel Webster ever was or shall be.
She had the Dartmouth needed to produce him.

I call her old. She has one family
Whose claim is good to being settled here

Before the era of colonization,
And before that of exploration even.
John Smith remarked them as he coasted by
Dangling their legs and fishing off a wharf
At the Isles of Shoals, and satisfied himself
They weren't Red Indians, but veritable
Pre-primitives of the white race, dawn people,
Like those who furnished Adam's sons with wives;
However uninnocent they may have been
In being there so early in our history.
They'd been there then a hundred years or more.
Pity he didn't ask what they were up to
At that date with a wharf already built,
And take their name. They've since told me their name—
Today an honored one in Nottingham.
As for what they were up to more than fishing—
Suppose they weren't behaving Puritanly,
The hour had not yet struck for being good,
Mankind had not yet gone on the Sabbatical.
It became an explorer of the deep
Not to explore too deep in others' business.

Did you but know of him, New Hampshire has
One real reformer who would change the world
So it would be accepted by two classes,
Artists the minute they set up as artists,
Before, that is, they are themselves accepted,
And boys the minute they get out of college.
I can't help thinking those are tests to go by.

And she has one I don't know what to call him,
Who comes from Philadelphia every year
With a great flock of chickens of rare breeds
He wants to give the educational
Advantages of growing almost wild
Under the watchful eye of hawk and eagle—

Dorkings because they're spoken of by Chaucer,
Sussex because they're spoken of by Herrick.

She has a touch of gold. New Hampshire gold—
You may have heard of it. I had a farm
Offered me not long since up Berlin way
With a mine on it that was worked for gold;
But not gold in commercial quantities,
Just enough gold to make the engagement rings
And marriage rings of those who owned the farm.
What gold more innocent could one have asked for?
One of my children ranging after rocks
Lately brought home from Andover or Canaan
A specimen of beryl with a trace
Of radium. I know with radium
The trace would have to be the merest trace
To be below the threshold of commercial;
But trust New Hampshire not to have enough
Of radium or anything to sell.
A specimen of everything, I said.
She has one witch—old style. She lives in Colebrook.
(The only other witch I ever met
Was lately at a cut-glass dinner in Boston.
There were four candles and four people present.
The witch was young, and beautiful (new style),
And open-minded. She was free to question
Her gift for reading letters locked in boxes.
Why was it so much greater when the boxes
Were metal than it was when they were wooden?
It made the world seem so mysterious.
The S'ciety for Psychical Research
Was cognizant. Her husband was worth millions.
I think he owned some shares in Harvard College.)

New Hampshire *used* to have at Salem
A company we called the White Corpuscles,
Whose duty was at any hour of night
To rush in sheets and fools' caps where they smelled
A thing the least bit doubtfully perscented
And give someone the Skipper Ireson's Ride.

One each of everything as in a show-case.
More than enough land for a specimen
You'll say she has, but there there enters in
Something else to protect her from herself.
There quality makes up for quantity.
Not even New Hampshire farms are much for sale.
The farm I made my home on in the mountains
I had to take by force rather than buy.
I caught the owner outdoors by himself
Raking up after winter, and I said,
"I'm going to put you off this farm: I want it."
"Where are you going to put me? In the road?"
"I'm going to put you on the farm next to it."
"Why won't the farm next to it do for you?"
"I like this better." It was really better.

Apples? New Hampshire has them, but unsprayed,
With no suspicion in stem-end or blossom-end
Of vitriol or arsenate of lead,
And so not good for anything but cider.
Her unpruned grapes are flung like lariats
Far up the birches out of reach of man.

A state producing precious metals, stones,
And—writing; none of these except perhaps
The precious literature in quantity
Or quality to worry the producer
About disposing of it. Do you know,
Considering the market, there are more
Poems produced than any other thing?
No wonder poets sometimes have to *seem*
So much more business-like than business men.
Their wares are so much harder to get rid of.

She's one of the two best states in the Union.
Vermont's the other. And the two have been
Yoke-fellows in the sap-yoke from of old
In many Marches. And they lie like wedges,
Thick end to thin end and thin end to thick end,
And are a figure of the way the strong
Of mind and strong of arm should fit together,

One thick where one is thin and vice versa.
New Hampshire raises the Connecticut
In a trout hatchery near Canada,
But soon divides the river with Vermont.
Both are delightful states for their absurdly
Small towns—Lost Nation, Bungey, Muddy Boo,
Poplin, Still Corners (so called not because
The place is silent all day long, nor yet
Because it boasts a whisky still—because
It set out once to be a city and still
Is only corners, cross-roads in a wood).
And I remember one whose name appeared
Between the pictures on a movie screen
Election night once in Franconia,
When everything had gone Republican
And Democrats were sore in need of comfort:
Easton goes Democratic, Wilson 4
Hughes 2. And everybody to the saddest
Laughed the loud laugh, the big laugh at the little.
New York (five million) laughs at Manchester,
Manchester (sixty or seventy thousand) laughs
At Littleton (four thousand), Littleton
Laughs at Franconia (seven hundred), and
Franconia laughs, I fear,—did laugh that night—
At Easton. What has Easton left to laugh at,
And like the actress exclaim, "Oh, my God" at?
There's Bungey; and for Bungey there are towns,
Whole townships named but without population.

Anything I can say about New Hampshire
Will serve almost as well about Vermont,
Excepting that they differ in their mountains.
The Vermont mountains stretch extended straight;
New Hampshire mountains curl up in a coil.

I had been coming to New Hampshire mountains.
And here I am and what am I to say?
Here first my theme becomes embarrassing.
Emerson said, "The God who made New Hampshire
Taunted the lofty land with little men."

Another Massachusetts poet said,
"I go no more to summer in New Hampshire.
I've given up my summer place in Dublin."
But when I asked to know what ailed New Hampshire,
She said she couldn't stand the people in it,
The little men (it's Massachusetts speaking).
And when I asked to know what ailed the people,
She said, "Go read your own books and find out."
I may as well confess myself the author
Of several books against the world in general.
To take them as against a special state
Or even nation's to restrict my meaning.
I'm what is called a sensibilitist,
Or otherwise an environmentalist.
I refuse to adapt myself a mite
To any change from hot to cold, from wet
To dry, from poor to rich, or back again.
I make a virtue of my suffering
From nearly everything that goes on round me.
In other words, I know wherever I am,
Being the creature of literature I am,
I shall not lack for pain to keep me awake.
Kit Marlowe taught me how to say my prayers:
"Why, this is Hell, nor am I out of it."
Samoa, Russia, Ireland, I complain of,
No less than England, France, and Italy.
Because I wrote my novels in New Hampshire
Is no proof that I aimed them at New Hampshire.

When I left Massachusetts years ago
Between two days, the reason why I sought
New Hampshire, not Connecticut,
Rhode Island, New York, or Vermont was this:
Where I was living then, New Hampshire offered
The nearest boundary to escape across.
I hadn't an illusion in my hand-bag
About the people being better there
Than those I left behind. I thought they weren't.
I thought they couldn't be. And yet they were.
I'd sure had no such friends in Massachusetts

As Hall of Windham, Gay of Atkinson,
Bartlett of Raymond (now of Colorado),
Harris of Derry, and Lynch of Bethlehem.

The glorious bards of Massachusetts seem
To want to make New Hampshire people over.
They taunt the lofty land with little men.
I don't know what to say about the people.
For art's sake one could almost wish them worse
Rather than better. How are we to write
The Russian novel in America
As long as life goes so unterribly?
There is the pinch from which our only outcry
In literature to date is heard to come.
We get what little misery we can
Out of not having cause for misery.
It makes the guild of novel writers sick
To be expected to be Dostoievskis
On nothing worse than too much luck and comfort.
This is not sorrow, though; it's just the vapors,
And recognized as such in Russia itself
Under the new régime, and so forbidden.
If well it is with Russia, then feel free
To say so or be stood against the wall
And shot. It's Pollyanna now or death.
This, then, is the new freedom we hear tell of;
And very sensible. No state can build
A literature that shall at once be sound
And sad on a foundation of well-being.

To show the level of intelligence
Among us: it was just a Warren farmer
Whose horse had pulled him short up in the road
By me, a stranger. This is what he said,
From nothing but embarrassment and want
Of anything more sociable to say:
"You hear those hound-dogs sing on Moosilauke?
Well they remind me of the hue and cry
We've heard against the Mid-Victorians
And never rightly understood till Bryan
Retired from politics and joined the chorus.

The matter with the Mid-Victorians
Seems to have been a man named John L. Darwin."
"Go 'long," I said to him, he to his horse.

I knew a man who failing as a farmer
Burned down his farmhouse for the fire insurance,
And spent the proceeds on a telescope
To satisfy a life-long curiosity
About our place among the infinities.
And how was that for other-worldliness?

If I must choose which I would elevate—
The people or the already lofty mountains,
I'd elevate the already lofty mountains.
The only fault I find with old New Hampshire
Is that her mountains aren't quite high enough.
I was not always so; I've come to be so.
How, to my sorrow, how have I attained
A height from which to look down critical
On mountains? What has given me assurance
To say what height becomes New Hampshire mountains,
Or any mountains? Can it be some strength
I feel as of an earthquake in my back
To heave them higher to the morning star?
Can it be foreign travel in the Alps?
Or having seen and credited a moment
The solid molding of vast peaks of cloud
Behind the pitiful reality
Of Lincoln, Lafayette, and Liberty?
Or some such sense as says how high shall jet
The fountain in proportion to the basin?
No, none of these has raised me to my throne
Of intellectual dissatisfaction,
But the sad accident of having seen
Our actual mountains given in a map
Of early times as twice the height they are—
Ten thousand feet instead of only five—
Which shows how sad an accident may be.
Five thousand is no longer high enough.
Whereas I never had a good idea
About improving people in the world,

Here I am over-fertile in suggestion,
And cannot rest from planning day or night
How high I'd thrust the peaks in summer snow
To tap the upper sky and draw a flow
Of frosty night air on the vale below
Down from the stars to freeze the dew as starry.

The more the sensibilitist I am
The more I seem to want my mountains wild;
The way the wiry gang-boss liked the log-jam.
After he'd picked the lock and got it started,
He dodged a log that lifted like an arm
Against the sky to break his back for him,
Then came in dancing, skipping, with his life
Across the roar and chaos, and the words
We saw him say along the zigzag journey
Were doubtless as the words we heard him say
On coming nearer: "Wasn't she an i-deal
Son-of-a-bitch? You bet she was an i-deal."

For all her mountains fall a little short,
Her people not quite short enough for Art,
She's still New Hampshire, a most restful state.

Lately in converse with a New York alec
About the new school of the pseudo-phallic,
I found myself in a close corner where
I had to make an almost funny choice.
"Choose you which you will be—a prude, or puke,
Mewling and puking in the public arms."
"Me for the hills where I don't have to choose."
"But if you had to choose, which would you be?"
I wouldn't be a prude afraid of nature.
I know a man who took a double ax
And went alone against a grove of trees;
But his heart failing him, he dropped the ax
And ran for shelter quoting Matthew Arnold:
"Nature is cruel, man is sick of blood;
There's been enough shed without shedding mine.
Remember Birnam Wood! The wood's in flux!"
He had a special terror of the flux

That showed itself in dendrophobia.
The only decent tree had been to mill
And educated into boards, he said.
He knew too well for any earthly use
The line where man leaves off and nature starts,
And never over-stepped it save in dreams.
He stood on the safe side of the line talking;
Which is sheer Matthew Arnoldism,
The cult of one who owned himself "a foiled,
Circuitous wanderer," and "took dejectedly
His seat upon the intellectual throne."
Agreed in frowning on these improvised
Altars the woods are full of nowadays,
Again as in the days when Ahaz sinned
By worship under green trees in the open.
Scarcely a mile but that I come on one,
A black-cheeked stone and stick of rain-washed charcoal
Even to say the groves were God's first temples
Comes too near to Ahaz' sin for safety.
Nothing not built with hands of course is sacred.
But here is not a question of what's sacred;
Rather of what to face or run away from.
I'd hate to be a runaway from nature.
And neither would I choose to be a puke
Who cares not what he does in company,
And, when he can't do anything, falls back
On words, and tries his worst to make words speak
Louder than actions, and sometimes achieves it.
It seems a narrow choice the age insists on.
How about being a good Greek, for instance?
That course, they tell me, isn't offered this year.
"Come, but this isn't choosing—puke or prude?"
Well, if I have to choose one or the other,
I choose to be a plain New Hampshire farmer
With an income in cash of say a thousand
(From say a publisher in New York City).
It's restful to arrive at a decision,
And restful just to think about New Hampshire.
At present I am living in Vermont.

The Census-Taker

I came an errand one cloud-blowing evening
To a slab-built, black-paper-covered house
Of one room and one window and one door,
The only dwelling in a waste cut over
A hundred square miles round it in the mountains:
And that not dwelt in now by men or women.
(It never had been dwelt in, though, by women,
So what is this I make a sorrow of?)
I came as census-taker to the waste
To count the people in it and found none,
None in the hundred miles, none in the house,
Where I came last with some hope, but not much
After hours' overlooking from the cliffs
An emptiness flayed to the very stone.
I found no people that dared show themselves,
None not in hiding from the outward eye.
The time was autumn, but how anyone
Could tell the time of year when every tree
That could have dropped a leaf was down itself
And nothing but the stump of it was left
Now bringing out its rings in sugar of pitch;
And every tree up stood a rotting trunk
Without a single leaf to spend on autumn,
Or branch to whistle after what was spent.
Perhaps the wind the more without the help
Of breathing trees said something of the time
Of year or day the way it swung a door
Forever off the latch, as if rude men
Passed in and slammed it shut each one behind him
For the next one to open for himself.
I counted nine I had no right to count
(But this was dreamy unofficial counting)
Before I made the tenth across the threshold.
Where was my supper? Where was anyone's?
No lamp was lit. Nothing was on the table.
The stove was cold—the stove was off the chimney—
And down by one side where it lacked a leg.

The people that had loudly passed the door
Were people to the ear but not the eye.
They were not on the table with their elbows.
They were not sleeping in the shelves of bunks.
I saw no men there and no bones of men there.
I armed myself against such bones as might be
With the pitch-blackened stub of an ax-handle
I picked up off the straw-dust covered floor.
Not bones, but the ill-fitted window rattled.
The door was still because I held it shut
While I thought what to do that could be done—
About the house—about the people not there.
This house in one year fallen to decay
Filled me with no less sorrow than the houses
Fallen to ruin in ten thousand years
Where Asia wedges Africa from Europe.
Nothing was left to do that I could see
Unless to find that there was no one there
And declare to the cliffs too far for echo,
"The place is desert and let whoso lurks
In silence, if in this he is aggrieved,
Break silence now or be forever silent.
Let him say why it should not be declared so."
The melancholy of having to count souls
Where they grow fewer and fewer every year
Is extreme where they shrink to none at all.
It must be I want life to go on living.

ALICE BROWN

The following chapter from *Jeremy Hamlin* illustrates the less confident attitudes in Alice Brown's later work. There is a marked contrast between the simple townsfolk of Tiverton in her early short stories and the more sophisticated characters of *Jeremy Hamlin*.

Jeremy Hamlin

I

Old Jeremy Hamlin had been the one rich man of the straggling New England town of Bridebrook. He had now been dead six weeks, and on this afternoon of late February, his daughter Juliana sat by a front window of what was called the Old House and wondered whether she was at the point of "naught's had, all's spent." She was more than middle-aged, but her hunger for life had not been dulled by time or a habit of dutiful behavior. As to life, she was bewitched by it and had always been. You couldn't starve her out of her passionate fancies; and these were not often set to the tune of love between men and women. They were as likely to sprout up in desire for a ride over deserts she had found burning in print or a breathless night in a boat on an African river, hearing the sounds of menace and terror about her, or the finding of a bright splash of orchid in a New England swamp, or music, or the valiance of a little self-heal in the roadway, threatened all summer by hoofs and tires and, never once weakening, blooming on, a spot of purple to the last. It was life she was amazed by and her own manner of living it, and she wondered, with an intensity she commonly avoided, if it was because she was merely stupid that she had failed to fit herself into the uses of this lovely and terrible world. Since her father's death she had had a free mind, only at intervals troubled by what might have been the fantastic loyalties of the past, and she could not help seeing how monstrous a thing it looked to recognize loyalty as fantastic and whether the more enlightened mind of a wider world would call it so.

She was a vivid looking creature who was sometimes plain, and never of any race or time, strong, yet slender, with an implication of a skeleton perfectly hung: this in the way she moved. Her nose and forehead were noble and her eyes were brown. Her hair also was brown, with a patina of copper and here and there threads of prophetic gray. When she smiled, there might have been the smallest dimple in the cheek, not enough to play comedy with her face, but only the hint of a hidden childishness. Sometimes she threw

back her head and laughed, and those who saw her then stared
uneasily, feeling that things must be wilder and gayer than they
had ever had a chance to know. They were aggrieved over it and
half disliked her until she subdued herself again. She owed a great
deal to her clothes, women were accustomed to imply, in one way
or another, and artists would have upheld them in it. Take her in
brown velvet, with a deep-toned feather round her hat, and she
was the stuff for portraiture and picture galleries; but when you
found her in the kitchen with Ellen, the "help," she seemed, in
careful attention to spoon and bowl, the very moral of an absorbed domesticity and had no idea of looking beyond it. She was
"going on fifty-two," as it was computed when she came into a
more vivid local interest at the time of her father's death, and that
seemed not to concern her: for though she had a healthy shrinking
from the cruelties of time, she had never shirked them, and made a
brave humility her only refuge. People had different—and often
surprising—ways of admiring her. A traveling preacher, whose five
children were motherless, had even quoted Shakespeare on the
ground of her "infinite variety," and Naomi, her niece, hearing it,
had taken the savor out of it by saying she was simply the nicest
type of maiden aunt. Naomi evidently intended this for a merciful
warning: but the preacher had amorously countered by saying
there weren't any maiden aunts nowadays, there being no such
thing as age, and Naomi had told him he'd better read the Vic-
torians. He'd find Aunt Julie there. And Juliana, being invited to
mother what he called his little flock, declined with so sweet a
composure as to turn it almost into acceptance. It was perhaps the
next day that the preacher realized what he had got. But though
she was keen in the race for newness and bright aspects of the universe, she really did scant thinking about herself, either where she
belonged in the race of time or where Naomi, being young, must
of necessity place her, though she never omitted the sagacious rites
which Naomi darkly classified under "not letting yourself go."
Long or short, the journey to the grave seemed to them both to be
at least alleviated by a definite cult of physical well-being.

And now her self, however she might see it, was beset by a wave
of circumstance. Her father being dead, after these thirty years
or more since her mother's death, everything was different. Her

brother Charles was abroad with his motherless daughter, the young Naomi, and he had not come home, in his father's short illness or at his death, presumably, according to Juliana's belief, because World Peace demanded his presence at Geneva. She was glad he was not here. Things—discomforting things connected with daily living—had always taken too much out of Charles. He had never, like her, borne the tremendous weight of his father's personality in silence. He had flinched from it, writhed out from under it and then, after some tentative attempts, run wildly away, never to return. She had not blamed him. She understood him, though her father she could never understand, and scarcely tried to. Her own lot, like her mother's, she accepted as one of acquiescence. That was the way things were, and it was for women to take them so. With Charles it was different. Let him run away and stay away and good luck to him. Here she was in the Old House which had been one of her mother's legacies to her; but an eighth of a mile away, farther back and up a pine-wooded slope, was the amazing scene her father had created for himself: a wilderness of terraced and pergolaed buildings which cried from every roof and pillar that it was the fitting monument to a man who wanted more money than any other man and was mighty in getting it. Juliana, when she saw it growing up, those years ago, had an unwilling suspicion that the architect of the magnificent yet disconcerting structures had met her father on his own ground and cynically embodied for him the man's inchoate designs. "Do you want it thus and so?" the architect had inwardly inquired. Then he had proceeded with his bitter jest. "It shall be so—the mirror of your own desires. 'Jeremy Hamlin, His mark' for time to laugh at."

Juliana had always hated the residential building which was the center of it all, at first because she knew her mother, too, was hating it and had, perhaps for that very reason, left her this old Georgian house and the equally plain yet dignified one in Boston, in an unfashionable street. And what to do now? Should she continue a decent loyalty to her father's mode of life because he was her father, or could she escape from this multitudinous activity of wealth embodied in orchards, poultry runs, fox farms, greenhouses, rose gardens, and go wherever her feet would take her, into the wider world or some deeper seclusion where you could live at peace with simple people because you did not hire them?

She had no illusions about her father's arbitrary hand on her life. He had not compelled her to stay with him in his pillared splendor. It had simply been decent to stay. Her mother came into it, too, and the years she also had stayed, taking care of the old man— though he had not always been old—who went padding about the place on his great feet, a giant of a creature, clumsy, silent, but with the foresight of a wizard where money was concerned and, whatever he made or whatever he spent, giving no sign of excitement or pleasure. Had her mother been a sort of mother to him, trying to awaken a soul in that insensate clay, as she might in a child of her body born with special aptitudes and yet abnormal as to all the uses of the life of man? Must she, Juliana, feel herself bound to the same curative loyalty and wait upon his somberness until some silent ray, she knew not whence, might come to pierce it? Her life had been one long patience, yet a patience curiously shot through with those hidden diversions of her own, wilful escapades that might last an hour or a night, which cooled the blood of her fancy a very little and helped it run more equally into the channels of every day. She, too, like her brother, had her own ways of escape, though, unlike him, she always knew they were part of a temporary expediency. She must always come back.

And now her father had gone, still silent though a little troubled at the last, as if his clouded eyes were asking what it was all about, and here was she in the old parlor with its calm ivory paneling and accordant furniture, and she was amazedly at peace. And in upon her broke a caller, a large, heavily humorous gentleman who had seemed, with his cohorts of clerks and appraisers, to have been about the place daily for at least three weeks, chiefly in the Great House library poring over papers and not troubling her often down here. This was Seth Wheeler, of Wheeler and Son, and he was irritating her a little by what she read in him as a tolerant amusement over her father's business methods, his failure to put the telephone to its utmost usefulness, his persistence in sending a clerk to carry a message when he could have flashed it along the wires, his general lack of adaptability to the present age. And now as he was sitting before her, with his jowled banker face as typical as if he had made up for it, easily humorous as befitted a man who had always done business among his peers in the higher walks of life, she felt she liked him less than ever. Father was dead. Some

sobriety of silence was owed him now that he could not answer
back. Nobody should find him funny, as a man who had known
how to make millions upon millions of the wizard screw and other
appliances and also, mysteriously, in the market, and turn his hav-
ings into more land than he could walk over in a year and the ad-
juncts by which a gentleman of leisure can keep himself busy—
and yet who was in no sort of society and did not entertain. But
Mr. Wheeler began very well, gravely as if father were not an eccentric figure waiting to be put on a cartoon.

"I was relieved," he said, when they had shaken hands and disposed themselves each at a front window, "I was relieved to find
you'd moved out of the Great House. Wasn't that what your father
called it up there? Very wise of you to start in here."

She felt the heat in her face. The words were irreproachable, but
the amused tolerance was there.

"It is the Great House," she corrected him perversely. "Much
larger than this. Too large for me. Too much service. I sent them all
away, all but Jake and Ellen. They were the old 'help,' you know.
We packed up as soon as we could and moved in here."

"Very wise," said he. "Very practical. Were there—you'll excuse
me, won't you? but you know we're the administrators, and I shall
have to ask you a lot of questions—were there arrears, of wages
and so on? Have you done anything about that?"

"Oh, yes," said Juliana, innocent of making any implication
against her father's probity, "everything was in arrears. I'd no idea
their wages had got so behind. I didn't know you could. But I had
quite a big deposit in the First National and I could pay them out
of that. Yes, they're paid off and most of them gone. It was all
queer. They seemed grateful, somehow, as if they hadn't expected
it."

"Admirable!" said he, with a smile that seemed softer to her,
more affectionate even than any she could remember from their
past intercourse. It was also as if he were mysteriously sorry for
her. She was used to comparing human looks with the words of
the human tongue and wondering, like a child, which were the
trustier. Perhaps it went back to old habits of short story writing as
she had done it years ago: rather clumsily, as she thought now, remembering her absorption in it. Perhaps, that, too, was a part of
what she loved of earth and could not well express. There are

those, she thought, who are strangers in this world, enchanted by it or terrified, but to no end. Perhaps they have too much imagination to concur in the daily scheme and not enough for creating worlds of their own to live and dream in.

"Miss Juliana," said he, remembering he wanted to get away before dark, "do you know what the state of things really is? your father's business, his debts, his liabilities?"

She looked at him in an untroubled clarity.

"No," she said. "I haven't the least idea. He never talked about business. Yes, though, he did say, some weeks ago, that the factory was running at a loss, and he was going to shut down. He'd had to turn off a lot of men. He said there wasn't any building to speak of, and orders weren't coming in. That was when he told me steel had dropped. It had to, he said. But he couldn't keep on turning out his products and no market. I'd begun to be worried about him—his health, you know—and I thought things would start up again, and to tell the truth my mind was chiefly on him, how to get him to call in a doctor. Not to be careless."

She looked so troubled, in an uncomplaining way, that he thought how removed she'd always been from actual life and what a pity it was she hadn't any training in it to carry her through these coming years. And yet how could she have informed herself about the holes in old Hamlin's web of being when he wouldn't have admitted her to a glimpse of them, wouldn't have admitted even Wheeler and Son if he hadn't needed expert advice in affairs of such magnitude? He wanted to rally her a little, wanted to wake her up out of her decorum, say to her: "What have you been thinking about all this time while your father made his money and lost it and made it again? Why didn't you squander some of it yourself, live abroad a year or two, or even go the pace here at home, and have something to remember now when the evil days are come upon you?"

But she was a dignified person, as well as a silent one on her own grounds, and he couldn't do it. He tried another approach.

"Miss Julie," said he, in his attractive confidential manner which had drawn many a secret from unwilling lips, "have you the least idea of the sort of man your father really was?"

She took no offense. She was so clear-minded, he saw, that she wouldn't have been ready with suspicious demurral even if she had loved her father warmly. And he had his own suspicion that she never had, perhaps that she had loved no one. She was looking at him with the lifted brows of an untroubled anticipation.

"Why, no," she said, "I fancy not. Father and I weren't much alike. I suppose I took him for granted. We do, don't we?"

"Sometimes," said he, smiling at her, now consciously trying to beguile her into the free air of unreasoning confidence. "It makes for one thing anyway: pleasant family living. But I'm not sure whether it's the best preparation for taking up the sort of load you may have to shoulder."

"Me?" said Juliana, in a perfect though untroubled surprise. "Do you mean—now tell me what you mean."

He settled to it, frankly owning to himself he wished he were quicker at the uptake. But need she be so stupid? Old Hamlin ought to have been an easy proposition to a woman who could get herself into print. He'd never read any of her stories. He understood they were idyllic, that sort of thing, sentimental probably, with a pleasant ending. He put the outside of his mind on first editions himself and sometimes wondered what the devil he was a lawyer for anyway. But now he would expound.

"Jeremy Hamlin," he said, in the tone of one who was feeling out an obituary notice he might later be called on to deliver, and arranging his periods with all possible accuracy, "Jeremy Hamlin was a man of limited intelligence of an eccentric kind. He had a queer sort of insight. It gave him a disproportioned power. Possibly it's the sort of thing you inherited that made you write your little sketches. But it did just one thing for him. It showed him how to make money. Hand over fist. The manufacturing wasn't all. That just gave him something to start on. But the market—he was a wizard. That's why he could buy up all the farms round here, acres upon acres. What for? He didn't want the land. What's he done with it?"

"He started things," she said, defensively. She, too, had wondered why he had encumbered himself with all this earth and in-operative power, why he hired so many men to keep it in order, began so many activities he scarcely visited except to be sure they were still there. Mere bigness seemed to conquer him. He acquired a thing for its own sake, acquired it painfully, and having seen how big it was, set about increasing it by the bigness adjoining it.

"Wasn't there a theater?" he asked, chiefly to set her off on revelations of her own. "Didn't he build a theater and give a performance or two and then shut it up and let it go to pieces, so to speak? Wasn't that so?"

"It was an old barn," she told him, mildly, as if that explained it. "No, there was only one play given, and that was for a special occasion: the town celebration of its founding. We had no particular call for it after that."

He dismissed the theater. It was only a bit of picturesque evidence.

"That's it," he said. "Your father bought and tore down and built and never looked twice at anything he'd done. The money he poured into it all! But he had the money to pour. These are days when nobody's got any money. Did you know that?"

"I wish," she said irrelevantly, "my brother would come home."

And yet she was not sure she did wish it. The habit of wanting to save Charles all possible anxiety was an old one. This was simply an unthinking cry for help.

"Charles? Yes," said he, "I wish so, too. But I don't know. He's got a fine berth over there. I don't see what real good he could do here. Besides, everything's left to you. Though I assume Charles wouldn't feel any resentment over that. And nobody knows so much about the estate as we do. Our firm's been as near your father as any of 'em, when it comes to that. And the Boston house. That's yours. Good idea of your mother, leaving it to you. Sure you understand about that, are you?"

"I know it's mine," said Juliana, in a painstaking effort to make something he might consider sentimental sound reasonable enough to bear the light. "But you know Charles has been living in it. He's lived in it for years, he and Naomi. It was natural for me to be here with father. I had an idea I might make it over to Charles as soon as he came back. I don't know."

"No, no," said Mr. Wheeler decisively. "Get that right out of your head. Keep what you've got. You can't tell when you'll get anything more. But there's something else, something I venture to say you've never once considered. Your father had a unique position here, something you don't find nowadays. It was more like the old 'squires' of country towns. Men brought him their money to invest. They liked to have him keep it. He paid 'em a better rate of interest than they got out of any corporation, and they felt safer, too. They thought he was a kind of a god over money. Did you know that? And he did take their savings, and sometimes he bought stock with it and sometimes he didn't. But all with their consent. Mostly they'd let it lie. Rather, you see. They knew where it was, down here in old Hamlin's safe. That is, that's how it looked to them. And now he's gone, Juliana, and these are bad times and everything's got to see the light of day."

He thought she scarcely understood, but he saw she had a trembling lip.

"The place can be sold," she said. "The mill's shut down, you know, but can't that be sold, too? Charles would say the same. I know he would."

"No market for it," he said, feeling very sorry for her, but judging it best to get it over. "It's a bad time, you see. No market for real estate anywhere, and if there was, who'd want all this uncouth sort of grandeur? Uncouth, that's what I call it. Don't you call it uncouth?"

At present, she could call it nothing. Through these weeks of her father's illness she had not been tempted to ask herself whether she was feeling a deep affection for him or whether everything in her was swallowed up in pity. But surely when the work of his lifetime was being assailed, she could not call it uncouth.

Mr. Wheeler, by this time, was so absorbed in his little obituary game of constructing a character out of picturesque data, that he continued happily:

"Queerest phenomenon you could imagine! man has a trick with money, special aptitude, as it might be with chess or cards, but absolutely nothing to do with it when he gets it, except to buy things: land, trees, bricks, mortar. And you wouldn't be surprised if the bricks fell on him in the end and jammed him flat. If it was in a story, you know. But they didn't. He 'made a good end' on't. Isn't that in Shakespeare? you ought to know."

Juliana, while recognizing his friendly intentions, did feel that she must, in some fashion, stand up for her father, range herself by his side, or, if he really was crushed flat, in all decency somehow manage to be crushed with him. Possibly, she thought, she might divert the stream of oratorical attack to herself.

"I wonder," she said, "if I could keep on here in this house indefinitely. I haven't made up my mind what I can do—in the end."

And what was the end? she thought. If she could choose it, what would she like the end to be?

"Oh, yes, yes," he said. "Didn't I just say so? This house is yours, all right. Has been ever since your mother's death. It's the estate I'm talking about—your father's. It can't be settled for I don't know how long. We're going to have no end of trouble with all these people that'll want their money short off, and they won't see why they can't have it. But that's to be expected. My dear, I've bored you to death, but you've got to know how things are, now haven't you? It'll come out all right. Give us time. You stay put down here in this nice parlor, and we'll see what there's going to be left for you to live on—if there's anything—" but there he pulled himself up, and the last minutes were devoted to summoning his car and accepting the parting cup of tea he had previously refused, and he surprised Juliana by kissing her cheek and telling her she was a good faithful girl. And he went away. She felt he had done the best he could for her in a difficult place and was patiently touched by the unwanted kiss and the useless imputation of being a girl. He was really an old dear, she thought, her eyes running over with two tears only, and then she set herself to the task of thinking further into her own future and perhaps finding some new ground of understanding between her father and herself. It seemed necessary to know whether there was anything she had to adjust for his still living personality, left pathetically in her hands. For he had been, in a manner, attacked, set up before the bar of worldly judgment. She kept recalling phrases Mr. Wheeler had used, the sense of them, if not the form. Her father had made money and not known what to do with it. Mere bigness, that was what he had been in love with. Out of the dignity of death he appeared before her as one who had been insensate to the beauty of life. He had built a theater for a special occasion, but had not known how to make it contribute to pleasure or pain, the tragic meaning of things. She herself had had vague thoughts of what might be done with it, but she had been timid with him and had never mentioned them. He would have denied her nothing, but his responses would never have been the right ones for any of her possible doubts. Mr. Wheeler was not far wrong. Old Jeremy had lived behind a screen of bigness, huge figures he had himself built up. Possibly he had, like her, like all mortals in this fleeting drama of life, expected to reach some satisfaction, some island of content after he had piled bigness upon itself until it would, with another stone, have toppled over. It was like an island with queer monuments. And what was her own island? Not like his; but there was an island. That was what the rushing progress of being meant. And at that moment there was the sound of a step and the feeling of a person in the room, the aura that announces while the bodily presence is still unseen.

"Yes," said Juliana. "What is it, Ellen? Come round where I can see you."

GRACE METALIOUS

Grace Metalious (b. Manchester, New Hampshire, 1924; d. 1964) was raised in a working-class neighborhood in the largest mill town in New Hampshire. While bringing up three children she wrote magazine articles and the novels upon which her fame—and notoriety—rest. Although she shattered the pastoral image of small-town life, she has gone virtually unrecognized by the literary establishment.

Peyton Place was published by Julian Messner in New York in 1956.

In the following excerpt, from the beginning of the novel, Metalious establishes the setting and introduces some of the characters.

FROM
Peyton Place

I

Indian summer is like a woman. Ripe, hotly passionate, but fickle, she comes and goes as she pleases so that one is never sure whether she will come at all, nor for how long she will stay. In northern New England, Indian summer puts up a scarlet-tipped hand to hold winter back for a little while. She brings with her the time of the last warm spell, an unchartered season which lives until Winter moves in with its backbone of ice and accoutrements of leafless trees and hard frozen ground. Those grown old, who have had the youth bled from them by the jagged-edged winds of winter, know sorrowfully that Indian summer is a sham to be met with hard-eyed cynicism. But the young wait anxiously, scanning the chill autumn skies for a sign of her coming. And sometimes the old, against all the warnings of better judgment, wait with the young and hopeful, their tired, winter eyes turned heavenward to seek the first traces of a false softening.

One year, early in October, Indian summer came to a town called Peyton Place. Like a laughing, lovely woman Indian summer came and spread herself over the countryside and made everything hurtfully beautiful to the eye.

The sky was low, of a solidly unbroken blue. The maples and oaks and ashes, all dark red and brown and yellow, preened themselves in the unseasonably hot light, under the Indian summer sun. The conifers stood like disapproving old men on all the hills around Peyton Place and gave off a greenish yellow light. On the roads and sidewalks of the town there were fallen leaves which made such a gay crackling when stepped upon and sent up such a sweet scent when crushed that it was only the very old who walked over them and thought of death and decay.

The town lay still in the Indian summer sun. On Elm Street, the main thoroughfare, nothing moved. The shopkeepers, who had rolled protective canvas awnings down over their front windows, took the lack of trade philosophically and retired to the back rooms of their stores where they alternately dozed, glanced at the

Peyton Place Times and listened to the broadcast of a baseball game.

To the east on Elm Street, beyond the six blocks occupied by the business section of the town, rose the steeple of the Congregational church. The pointed structure pierced through the leaves of the surrounding trees and shone, dazzlingly white, against the blue sky. At the opposite end of the business district stood another steepled structure. This was St. Joseph's Catholic Church, and its spire far outshone that of the Congregationalists, for it was topped with a cross of gold.

Seth Buswell, the owner and editor of the *Peyton Place Times*, had once written, rather poetically, that the two churches bracketed and held the town like a pair of gigantic book ends, an observation which had set off a series of minor explosions in Peyton Place. There were few Catholics in town who cared to be associated in any partnership with the Protestants, while the Congregationalists had as little desire to be paired off with the Papists. If imaginary book ends were to exist in Peyton Place they would both have to be of the same religious denomination.

Seth had laughed at the arguments heard all over town that week, and in his next edition he reclassified the two churches as tall, protective mountains guarding the peaceful business valley. Both Catholics and Protestants scanned this second article carefully for a trace of sarcasm or facetiousness, but in the end everyone had taken the story at its face value and Seth laughed harder than before.

Dr. Matthew Swain, Seth's best friend and oldest crony, grunted, "Mountains, eh? More like a pair of goddamned volcanoes."

"Both of 'em breathin' brimstone and fire," Seth added, still laughing as he poured two more drinks.

But the doctor would not laugh with his friend. There were three things which he hated in this world, he said often and angrily: death, venereal disease and organized religion.

"In that order," the doctor always amended. "And the story, clean or otherwise, that can make me laugh at one of these has never been thought up."

But on this hot October afternoon Seth was not thinking of opposing religious factions or, for that matter, of anything in particular. He sat at his desk behind the plate glass window of his street floor office, sipping at a cold drink and listened desultorily to the baseball game.

In front of the courthouse, a large white stone building with a verdigris-colored dome, a few old men lounged on the wooden benches which seem to be part of every municipal building in America's small towns. The men leaned back against the warm sides of the courthouse, their tired eyes shaded by battered felt hats, and let the Indian summer sun warm their cold, old bones. They were as still as the trees for which the main street had been named.

Under the elms the black-tarred sidewalks, ruffled in many places by the pushing roots of the giant trees, were empty. The chime clock set into the red brick front of the Citizens' National Bank, across the street from the courthouse, struck once. It was two-thirty on a Friday afternoon.

2

Maple Street, which bisected Elm at a point halfway through the business section, was a wide, tree-shaded avenue which ran north and south from one end of town to the other. At the extreme southern end of the street, where the paving ended and gave way to an empty field, stood the Peyton Place schools. It was toward these buildings that Kenny Stearns, the town handyman, walked. The men in front of the courthouse opened drowsy eyes to watch him.

"There goes Kenny Stearns," said one man unnecessarily, for everyone had seen—and knew—Kenny.

"Sober as a judge, right now."

"That won't last long."

The men laughed.

"Good at his work though, Kenny is," said one old man named Clayton Frazier, who made a point of disagreeing with everybody, no matter what the issue.

"When he ain't too drunk to work."

"Never knew Kenny to lose a day's work on account of liquor," said Clayton Frazier. "Ain't nobody in Peyton Place can make things grow like Kenny. He's got one of them whatcha call green thumbs."

One man snickered. "Too bad Kenny don't have the same good luck with his wife as he has with plants. Mebbe Kenny'd be better off with a green pecker."

This observation was acknowledged with appreciative smiles and chuckles.

"Ginny Stearns is a tramp and a trollop," said Clayton Frazier, unsmilingly. "There ain't much a feller can do when he's married to a born whore."

"'Cept drink," said the man who had first spoken.

The subject of Kenny Stearns seemed to be exhausted, and for a moment no one spoke.

"Hotter'n July today," said one old man. "Damned if my back ain't itchin' with sweat."

"'Twon't last," said Clayton Frazier, tipping his hat back to look up at the sky. "I've seen it turn off cold and start in snowin' less than twelve hours after the sun had gone down on a day just like this one. This won't last."

"Ain't healthy either. A day like this is enough to make a man start thinkin' about summer underwear again."

"Healthy or not, you'd hear no complaints from me if the weather stayed just like this clear 'til next June."

"'Twon't last," said Clayton Frazier, and for once his words did not provoke a discussion.

"No," the men agreed. "'Twon't last."

They watched Kenny Stearns turn into Maple Street and walk out of sight.

The Peyton Place schools faced each other from opposite sides of the street. The grade school was a large wooden building, old, ugly and dangerous, but the high school was the pride of the town. It was made of brick, with windows so large that each one made up almost an entire wall, and it had a clinical, no-nonsense air of efficiency that gave it the look more of a small, well-run hospital than that of a school. The elementary school was Victorian architecture at its worst, made even more hideous by the iron fire escapes which zigzagged down both sides of the building, and by the pointed, open belfry which topped the structure. The grade school bell was rung by means of a thick, yellow rope which led down from the belfry and was threaded through the ceiling and floor of the building's second story. The rope came to an end and hung, a constant temptation to small hands, in the corner of the first floor hall. The school bell was Kenny Stearns' secret love. He kept it polished so that it gleamed like antique pewter in the October sun. As he approached the school buildings now, Kenny looked up at the belfry and nodded in satisfaction.

"The bells of heaven ain't got tongues no sweeter than yours," he said aloud.

Kenny often spoke aloud to his bell. He also talked to the school buildings and to the various plants and lawns in town for which he cared.

From the windows of both schools, open now to the warm afternoon, there came a soft murmuring and the smell of pencil shavings.

"Hadn't oughta keep school on a day like this," said Kenny.

He stood by the low hedge which separated the grade school from the first house on Maple Street. A warm, green smell, composed of the grass and hedges which he had cut that morning, rose around him.

"This ain't no kind of a day for schoolin'," said Kenny and shrugged impatiently, not at his inarticulateness but in puzzlement at a rare emotion in himself.

He wanted to throw himself face down on the ground and press his face and body against something green.

"*That's* the kind of day it is," he told the quiet buildings truculently. "No kind of a day for schoolin'."

He noticed that a small twig in the hedge had raised itself, growing above the others and marring the evenness of the uniformly flat hedge tops. He bent to snip off this precocious bit of green with his fingers, a sharp tenderness taking form within him. But suddenly a wildness came over him, and he grabbed a handful of the small, green leaves, crushing them until he felt their yielding wetness against his skin while passion tightened itself within him and his breath shook. A long time ago, before he had taught himself not to care, he had felt this same way toward his wife Ginny. There had been the same tenderness which would suddenly be overwhelmed by a longing to crush and conquer, to possess by sheer strength and force. Abruptly Kenny released the handful of broken leaves and wiped his hand against the side of his rough overall.

"Wish to Christ I had a drink," he said fervently and moved toward the double front doors of the grade school.

It was five minutes to three and time for him to take up his position by the bell rope.

"Wish to Christ I had a drink, and that's for sure," said Kenny and mounted the wooden front steps of the school.

Kenny's words, since they had been addressed to his bell and therefore uttered in loud, carrying tones, drifted easily through the windows of the classroom where Miss Elsie Thornton presided over the eighth grade. Several boys laughed out loud and a few girls grinned, but this amusement was short lived. Miss Thornton was a firm believer in the theory that if a child were given the inch, he would rapidly take the proverbial mile, so, although it was Friday afternoon and she was very tired, she restored quick order to her room.

"Is there anyone here who would like to spend the thirty minutes after dismissal with me?" she asked.

The boys and girls, ranging in age from twelve to fourteen, fell silent, but as soon as the first note sounded from Kenny's bell, they began to scrap and shuffle their feet. Miss Thornton rapped sharply on her desk with a ruler.

"You will be quiet until I dismiss you," she ordered. "Now. Are your desks cleared?"

"Yes, Miss Thornton." The answer came in a discordant chorus.

"You may stand."

Forty two pairs of feet clumped into position in the aisles between the desks. Miss Thornton waited until all backs were straight, all heads turned to the front and all feet quiet.

"Dismissed," she said, and as always, as soon as that word was out of her mouth, had the ridiculous feeling that she should duck and protect her head with her arms.

Within five seconds the classroom was empty and Miss Thornton relaxed with a sigh. Kenny's bell still sang joyously and the teacher reflected with humor that Kenny always rang the three o'clock dismissal bell with a special fervor, while at eight-thirty in the morning he made the same bell toll mournfully.

If I thought it would solve anything, said Miss Thornton to herself, making a determined effort to relax the area between her shoulder blades, I, too, would wish to Christ that I had a drink.

Smiling a little, she stood and moved to one of the windows to watch the children leave the schoolyard. Outside, the crowd had begun to separate into smaller groups and pairs, and Miss Thornton noticed only one child who walked alone. This was Allison MacKenzie, who broke away from the throng as soon as she reached the pavement and hurried down Maple Street by herself.

A peculiar child, mused Miss Thornton, looking at Allison's disappearing back. One given to moods of depression which seemed particularly odd in one so young. It was odd, too, that Allison hadn't one friend in the entire school, except for Selena Cross. They made a peculiar pair, those two, Selena with her dark, gypsyish beauty, her thirteen-year-old eyes as old as time, and Allison MacKenzie, still plump with residual babyhood, her eyes wide open, guileless and questioning, above that painfully sensitive mouth. Get yourself a shell, Allison, my dear, thought Miss Thornton. Find one without cracks or weaknesses so that you will be able to survive the slings and arrows of outrageous fortune. Good Lord, I *am* tired!

Rodney Harrington came barreling out of the school, not slowing his pace when he saw little Norman Page standing directly in his path.

Damned little bully, thought Miss Thornton savagely.

She despised Rodney Harrington, and it was a credit to her character and to her teaching that no one, least of all Rodney himself, suspected this fact. Rodney was an oversized fourteen-year-old with a mass of black, curly hair and a heavy-lipped mouth. Miss Thornton had heard a few of her more aware eighth grade girls refer to Rodney as "adorable," a sentiment with which she was not in accord. She would have gotten a great deal of pleasure out of giving him a sound thrashing. In Miss Thornton's vast mental file of school children, Rodney was classified as A Troublemaker.

He's too big for his age, she thought, and too sure of himself and of his father's money and position behind him. He'll get his comeuppance someday.

Miss Thornton bit the inside of her lip and spoke severely to herself. He is only a child. He may turn out all right.

But she knew Leslie Harrington, Rodney's father, and doubted her own words.

Little Norman Page was felled by the oncoming Rodney. He went flat on the ground and began to cry, remaining prone until Ted Carter came along to help him up.

Little Norman Page. Funny, thought Miss Thornton, but I've never heard an adult refer to Norman without that prefix. It has almost become part of his name.

Norman, the schoolteacher observed, seemed to be constructed entirely of angles. His cheekbones were prominent in his little face, and as he wiped at his wet eyes, his elbows stuck out in sharp, bony points.

Ted Carter was brushing at Norman's trousers. "You're O.K., Norman," his voice came through the schoolroom window. "Come on, you're O.K. Stop crying now and g'wan home. You're O.K."

Ted was thirteen years old, tall and broad for his age, with the stamp of adulthood already on his features. Of all the boys in Miss Thornton's eighth grade, Ted's voice was the only one which had "changed" completely so that when he spoke it was in a rich baritone that never cracked or went high unexpectedly.

"Why don't you pick on someone your own size?" Ted asked, turning toward Rodney Harrington.

"Ha, ha," said Rodney sulkily. "You, f'rinstance?"

Ted moved another step closer to Rodney. "Yeah, me," he said.

"Oh, beat it," said Rodney. "I wouldn't waste my time."

But, Miss Thornton noticed with satisfaction, it was Rodney who "beat it." He strolled cockily out of the schoolyard with an over-developed seventh grade girl named Betty Anderson at his heels.

"Why don'cha mind your own business," yelled Betty over her shoulder to Ted.

Little Norman Page snuffled. He took a clean white handkerchief from his back trouser pocket and blew his nose gently.

"Thank you, Ted," he said shyly. "Thank you very much."

"Oh, scram," said Ted Carter. "G'wan home before your old lady comes looking for you."

Norman's chin quivered anew. "Could I walk with you, Ted?" he asked. "Just until Rodney's out of sight? Please?"

"Rodney's got other things on his mind besides you right now," said Ted brutally. "He's forgotten that you're even alive."

Scooping his books up off the ground, Ted ran to catch up with Selena Cross, who was now halfway up Maple Street. He did not look around for Norman, who picked up his own books and moved slowly out of the schoolyard.

Miss Thornton felt suddenly too tired to move. She leaned her head against the window frame and stared absently at the empty yard outside. She knew the families of her school children, the kind of homes they lived in and the environments in which they were raised.

Why do I try? she wondered. What chance have any of these children to break out of the pattern in which they were born?

At times like this, when Miss Thornton was very tired, she felt that she fought a losing battle with ignorance and was overcome with a sense of futility and helplessness. What sense was there in nagging a boy into memorizing the dates of the rise and fall of the Roman Empire when the boy, grown, would milk cows for a living, as had his father and grandfather before him? What logic was there in pounding decimal fractions into the head of a girl who would eventually need to count only to number the months of each pregnancy?

Years before, when Miss Thornton had been graduated from Smith College, she had decided to remain in her native New England to teach.

"You won't have much opportunity to be radical up there," the dean had told her.

Elsie Thornton had smiled. "They are my people and I understand them. I'll know what to do."

The dean had smiled, too, from her heights of superior knowledge. "When you discover how to break the bone of the shell-backed New Englander, Elsie, you will become world famous. Anyone who does something for the first time in history becomes famous."

"I've lived in New England all my life," said Elsie Thornton, "and I have never heard anyone actually say, 'What was good enough for my father is good enough for me.' That is a decadent attitude and a terrible cliché, both of which have been unfairly saddled on the New Englander."

"Good luck, Elsie," said the dean sadly.

Kenny Stearns crossed Miss Thornton's line of vision, and abruptly her chain of thought broke.

Nonsense, she told herself briskly. I have a roomful of fine, intelligent children who come from families no different from other families. I'll feel better on Monday.

She went to the closet and took out her hat, which was seeing service for the seventh autumn in a row. Looking at the worn brown felt in her hand, she was reminded of Dr. Matthew Swain.

"I'd be able to tell a schoolteacher anywhere," he had told her.

"Really, Matt?" she had laughed at him. "Do we all, then, have the same look of frustration?"

"No," he had replied, "but all of you do look overworked, underpaid, poorly dressed and underfed. Why do you do it, Elsie? Why don't you go down to Boston or somewhere like that? With your intelligence and education you could get a good-paying job in business."

Miss Thornton had shrugged. "Oh, I don't know, Matt. I just love teaching, I guess."

But in her mind then, as now, was the hope which kept her at her job, just as it has kept teachers working for hundreds of years.

If I can teach something to one child, if I can awaken in only one child a sense of beauty, a joy in truth, an admission of ignorance and a thirst for knowledge, then I am fulfilled.

One child, thought Miss Thornton, adjusting her old brown felt, and her mind fastened with love on Allison MacKenzie.

3

Allison MacKenzie left the schoolyard quickly, not stopping to talk with anyone. She made her way up Maple Street and walked east on Elm, avoiding the Thrifty Corner Apparel Shoppe, which her mother owned and operated. Allison walked rapidly until she had left the stores and houses of Peyton Place behind her. She climbed the long, gently sloping hill behind Memorial Park and came, eventually, to a place where the paved road ended. Beyond the pavement, the land fell away in a sharp decline and was covered with rocks and bushes. The drop off was barred with a wide wooden board which rested at either end on a base resembling an outsized sawhorse. The crosspiece had red letters printed on it. ROAD'S END. These words had always satisfied something in Allison. She reflected that the board could have read, PAVEMENT ENDS or CAUTION—DROP OFF, and she was glad that someone had thought to label this place ROAD'S END.

Allison luxuriated in the fact that she had two whole days, plus what was left of this beautiful afternoon, in which to be free from the hatefulness that was school. In the time of this short vacation she would be free to walk up here to the end of the road, to be by herself and to think her own thoughts. For a little while she could find pleasure here and forget that her pleasures would be considered babyish and silly by older, more mature twelve-year-old girls.

The afternoon was beautiful with the lazy, blue beauty of Indian summer. Allison said the words "October afternoon" over and over to herself. They were like a narcotic, soothing her, filling her with peace. "October afternoon," she said, sighing, and sat down on the board that had ROAD'S END lettered on its side.

Now that she was quiet and unafraid, she could pretend that she was a child again, and not a twelve-year-old who would be entering high school in less than another year, and who should be interested now in clothes and boys and pale rose lipstick. The delights of childhood were all around her, and here on the hill she did not feel that she was peculiar and different from her contemporaries. But away from this place she was awkward, loveless, pitifully aware that she lacked the attraction and poise which she believed that every other girl her age possessed.

Very rarely, she felt a shred of this same secret, lonely happiness at school, when the class was reading a book or a story which pleased her. Then she would look up quickly from the printed page to find Miss Thornton looking at her, and their eyes would meet and hold and smile. She was careful not to let this happiness show, for she knew that the other girls in her class would laugh to let her know that this kind of joy was wrong, and that they would tag it with their favorite word of condemnation—babyish.

There would not be many more days of contentment for Allison, for now she was twelve and soon would have to begin spending her life with people like the girls at school. She would be surrounded by them, and have to try hard to be one of them. She was sure that they would never accept her. They would laugh at her, ridicule her, and she would find herself living in a world where she was the only odd and different member of the population.

If Allison MacKenzie had been asked to define the vague "they" to whom she referred in her mind, she would have answered, "Everybody except Miss Thornton and Selena Cross, and sometimes even Selena." For Selena was beautiful while Allison believed herself an unattractive girl, plump in the wrong places, flat in the wrong spots, too long in the legs and too round in the face. She knew that she was shy and all thumbs and had a headful of silly dreams. That was the way everybody saw her, except Miss Thornton, and that was only because Miss Thornton was so ugly and plain herself. Selena would smile and try to dismiss Allison's inadequacies with a wave of her hand. "You're O.K., kid," Selena would say, but Allison could not always believe her friend. Somewhere along the path of approaching maturity she had lost her sense of being loved and of belonging to a particular niche in the world. The measure of her misery was in the fact that she thought these things had never been hers to lose.

Allison looked across the emptiness beyond Road's End. From up here, she could see the town, spread out below her. . . .

THE RETURN

WITH THE INCREASING standardization and homogenization of contemporary life, the decline of characteristics that distinguish regional differences, and the sense that individuality is being lost in nationwide blandness, many writers have sought out an environment that retains something of the authentic and unique. This environment is characterized not only by beautiful landscape, but also by the qualities in people's lives that exemplify respect for the past, love of tradition, concern for others, and hope for the future. New Hampshire, by virtue of its location, has withstood the extremes of isolation and involvement; its society has experienced a rise, decline, and renascence. Three and a half centuries of history have left their effect.

The result is an exciting and rewarding location in which to write and to make a home, a place that is at once a refuge and an arena for an active life. For May Sarton, Thomas Williams, Noel Perrin, Donald Hall, and others who have at some time made a decision to live in New Hampshire, the place has left a mark upon their writing. The hunter who roams the hills in so many of Thomas Williams's novels, the angry young man who tries to save a bank of wildflowers from a bulldozer in May Sarton's *Kinds of Love*, or old Wesley Wells still tending the ancestral farm in Donald Hall's *String Too Short To Be Saved*—all in their own way share a love for New Hampshire expressive of their authors' feelings. Other places may have their attractions, but this is home.

And so, gifted writers have returned. There is in their work an honest but not uncritical appreciation of what they have found here. They do not idealize the community, but neither do they revolt from the village. Theirs is a felicitous amalgam of much that was best in the past. Like their literary predecessors two and a half centuries ago, New Hampshire has provided them with a new challenge. In a way, the cycle is complete.

THOMAS WILLIAMS

Thomas Williams (b. Duluth, Minnesota, 1926) received two degrees from the University of New Hampshire, where he has taught for more than twenty years. His fiction has been published for more than twenty-five. His numerous literary prizes include the National Book Award (1975).

Town Burning was published in New York in 1959 by Macmillan. A High New House was published by Dial Press in New York in 1963. The Hair of Harold Roux was published by Random House in New York in 1974. "The Buck in Trotevale's" is from A High New House.

The Buck in Trotevale's

I watch my son pursue an apple across the floor. He is seven months old. He grabs the shiny globe with both hands and puts it to his mouth: *squeak, squeak,* he gums it. There it goes, rolling bumpily beneath a chair, while he gravely watches. Onward! He'll corner the damned thing. Some day he'll get his teeth into such promising fruit. Meanwhile, he tries. And tries again—he won't give up. I am sure that I was never so determined. Although his eyes are mirror images of mine, I am uncomfortably aware of an alien deepness there, as if even now he were governed by a discipline I have never known. He works at his apple as he does at his world, singlemindedly, until it either accommodates him or shows itself to be impervious. Now the apple has escaped him again, and he watches it until it stops rolling, marks it well before arranging himself for the long crawl toward it. He rarely cries . . . and I wonder, knowing that they will always be mine, at the injustice of this stranger's inevitable wounds. . . .

When I was fourteen, coping with that world of benevolent rulers—coping with an instinctive directness much like my son's— Mr. Brown rented our furnished room. Now, I believe Mr. Brown to have been a kind of Yankee, although I didn't at first because he came from the South—from Massachusetts, where all those Massachusetts hunters come from, the ones who park in the middle of the road and shoot heifers for deer, not knowing the difference; proudly (it is said every year) bearing their pied trophies through Leah Town Square on the fenders of their Buicks, deer tags fluttering from bovine ears. I never saw this, myself, but at fourteen, New Hampshire boys are careful license-plate watchers. *Massachusetts.* I still hear some disapproval echoing in my older voice.

I didn't know Mr. Brown very well at first. He was very quiet, and had a talent for missing squeaky boards and squeaky stairs. I'd see him in the upstairs hall once in a while, between his room and the bathroom. He'd come home from work, wash, and change his clothes before walking downtown to the Welkum Diner for his supper. I can see him walking down Maple Street: tall, superbly balanced, each foot reaching the sidewalk as if searching carefully for purchase. His heels rose lightly before each step, and I believed that if the sidewalk had suddenly tipped right up on its side, Mr. Brown would have been ready for it. He was in his late sixties, I suppose—an almost too handsome man with his tanned face and thick white hair, his straight shoulders—and yet I like to think of him as being in his seventies. Seventy-seven makes me think of him: the two numerals spare and lean as the man, trim as are most men who grow old and active. He walked a lot. He even skied, and on winter Sundays we would see him on Pike Hill doing his graceful old-fashioned christies on the unbroken snow, each long ski under control, his ski clothes fresh and dry. In the summer he hired a high-school boy and a motorboat and water-skied on Lake Cascom. His age was a little more apparent when he wore bathing trunks, of course. His belly bulged out. But even then, seeing that taut little pot, you knew that it contained only enough innards to run the lean body. There was no surplus about Mr. Brown.

He hunted, too. His shotgun was a Purdey. He let me see it in its oak-and-leather case, luminous as if a fire burned beneath the French walnut stock, the metal covered with delicate English scrollwork. His deer rifle was almost too beautiful for my young eyes, and I have never seen another like it. It was made in Austria, between the wars, and had two barrels, over and under, like a shotgun, but with a high carved comb to the stock to bring Mr. Brown's cool eye up to an iron sight. I held this masterpiece, a prince among our common Winchesters and Marlins.

"I have it because, in its own way, it's almost as beautiful as a deer," he said. "I'm sure the deer couldn't care less, but I do."

But precious as it was, I would have chosen my father's Winchester. With that familiar weapon in my hand, my vision of myself as a Yankee boy, thin-lipped and taciturn, was complete. Such foreign beauties as the over-and-under could not seduce me from the common dream.

One conforms, of course, without knowing it—and not only to the common dream, for I was skillfully eased into my after-school job at Trotevale's without once questioning the justice of this sentence. Collusion it was, I know now, between my parents and *their* dream of Education. Mr. Brown was Trotevale's shoe clerk, and that was how I got to know him a little better.

Every day after school, and on the long Saturdays, I found myself a clerk among the socks and shirts, with a button on the cash register sacred to my hesitant finger. Hair combed, white shirt and bow tie, I hid down the long aisles of glass-fronted, varnished counters, pretending to be a customer.

I couldn't find anything. I couldn't tie a knot on a parcel, I counted change too many times before reluctantly giving it up to a customer. "Where are the handkerchiefs?" I would desperately ask a passing clerk. "Where are the boys' blue denim pants sizes three or four, and what does that mean—age, or inches?" All day I trotted back and forth between customer and source of information, and by the end of the first long Saturday I was amazed and a little frightened by the number of things there was to know, just to being a clerk. Having exhausted everyone else's patience (how could they remember how many times I'd asked the same question?), I had taken to asking Mr. Brown everything. He never chided me for my profound lack of interest; he had an extremely dependable fund of gentle patience.

"Don't you have a family?" I asked him once. "Why do you live in our furnished room? Are you going to live here forever?"

"No, I don't have a family," he said, no obvious opinion of families in his voice; "no mother, no father, no wife, no children. And most likely I won't stay here or any place else forever. And that's not such an uncommon way to be." He smiled that private smile of experience. "I'm what you might call an old bastard. Nobody claims me but myself."

I know now that this is not so terribly uncommon. There are many nomadic old bastards come to Leah and pass through, not all of them bums or lumberjacks with a quick eye for a bottle. Many are short-order cooks, those skinny food-haters: you can see their bones, their silver identification bracelets, tattoos and spatulas in any diner, their sunken faces framed by the exhaust fan. There are other kinds: awning-menders, embalmers, one-shot salesmen fleeing some private suburban nightmare—and clerks, like Mr. Brown. They stay a year or two and head around the circuit once again: Rhode Island, Massachusetts, New Hampshire, Maine, Vermont. Old men, mostly, pretty set in their ways, they almost have to be single. The jobs pay little, but there's always a job somewhere.

Trotevale's store is no longer on Leah's square. A couple of years

ago the Cascom Savings Bank, next door, took over both buildings, and now the two look like one. Built in 1854 of wood, mod-
ernized by a sheathing of red brick in 1907, they are now modern-
ized again, rather gaudily, in three-colored cathedral stone which
seems to be held together by chrome strips, like a modern auto-
mobile. You hardly notice the disappearance. Trotevale's sign
was black, framed by gilt paint, and the raised gilt letters said
TROTEVALE'S. That's all. Two counters ran down the middle of
the store, piled with sweaters, shirts, gloves, and other kinds of
"good" clothes. Work clothes were in the basement, piled on plain
tables. On the left side of the main floor shoe boxes filled the wall
from front to back, and Mr. Brown, if there were no customers, sat
composedly in one of the four wooden armchairs. On the right,
glass-fronted cases reached to the ceiling, and every ten feet or so a
pair of long-handled tweezers, long enough to reach the highest
five-dollar Dobbs, leaned against the cabinets. Ladies' undisplay-
ables were upstairs, along with the office and the tailor's room, on
a wide balcony that went all the way around, close below the
stamped-metal ceiling. The balustrade was carved orange cypress:
balls, flutes, grapes, Corinthian capitals and Roman arches. The
whole store was fine, consistent 1907, except for the surface of the
main floor, which had been covered with plastic tile in wide green
and white squares. Upon this miraculous surface the old mahogany counters, the cast-iron adjustable tie racks, the jigsawed
buttresses and varnished legs all seemed to float, as in a painting
by Dali, an inch or so above the floor. It was Trotevale's first con-
cession to those two-page magazine ads (before and after), and of
course it wasn't enough. All it did was knock the pins out from
under 1907.

Each day after school I'd go home, change my clothes and go to
Trotevale's for the two hours until closing time. On Saturday I
came in at eight-thirty in the morning. Eleven-and-a-half hours!
And those long, dusty afternoons were rarely broken by anything
amusing. I watched the second hand of the white-faced clock at
the back of the store, and sometimes it stopped dead for what
seemed like whole seconds. Long ones they were, too. Sometimes
I looked at myself, back, front and sides, in the tricky fitting-
mirrors, not caring at all for my profile. Better the front view, and I
could practice my frigid Yankee stare—that bright aggressive look

I found legitimate upon the faces of my friends—the one that declares equality and asks: *What kind of a damn fool are you?*

At other times, in that mirror, I could wish upon my face bones the crisp dignity of Mr. Brown's straight nose, the regal depth of those blue eyes. Old man that he was, I began to pay him the compliment of imitation. When he spoke—while showing me how to tie the string around a package without having to let go of one end to tie the knot, without asking the customer for the use of a finger—he emitted a low, rather kindly humming sound. "Mmmm," he would croon for "Yes," or for "Oh, is that so?" or for mere wordless sympathy. I believe he meant to let you know that he was listening, or that he understood exactly how you felt, and this nonword was the least interrupting of all assents. I don't know. Perhaps it led to a certain distance between himself and the person he communicated with, as meaningful words would not. But I'd hear it, deep in his chest somewhere, a kind of cellolike vibrato, as hard to locate as a partridge drumming in the deep woods.

I began doing this myself, and found that Mr. Brown's idiosyncrasies and his *presence*, in a way, were noted. "Listen!" my father said at supper, "he's doing *that*, like Mr. Brown!" Strangely, I was pleased, rather than embarrassed. But of course I stopped doing it. I developed, instead, a slow smile—one that took several seconds to mature, like Mr. Brown's. My mother's comment was less pleasing: "If I didn't know how old you were, I'd say you were filling your pants."

Bessie Sleeper was the secretary and bookkeeper for Old Man Trotevale, who had shingles and rarely came to the store. Bessie weighed two hundred pounds, but had tiny feet. In the back of the store an open-shaft service elevator ran from the basement to the office on the balcony, and this was known, not to Bessie, as Bessie's Hoist. It creaked as she stepped upon it and pulled the rope which started huge flywheels in the basement. *Clang* went the collapsible gate that somehow never caught your fingers in its disappearing parallelograms, and Bessie rose. She walked as if she carried a bucket of water in each hand, her face bitterly clenched with effort, her tiny blue eyes stabbing about for a place to sit her burden down. She was always very nice to me. She loved Mr. Brown.

Her feet were truly perfect, he said, and every week she bought a pair of shoes. I can see her, wedged into one of the old wooden armchairs, a spot of molten thrill somewhere deep, deep—certainly not showing—as Mr. Brown, cool in his white shirt and black arm garters, held her foot in his strong, dry hand. She wasn't the only woman in town who bought too many pairs of shoes.

If any one person, in the continuing absence of Old Man Trotevale, ran the store, it was Mr. Hummington, a busy little middle-aged man who wore rimless octagonal glasses the color of an old photograph. You could see his eyes way down in there in the mauve twilight, moving around. They didn't seem to have any whites. He had black hair that seemed to grow all on one side of his head, form a rigid slab across the top and end rootlessly above the opposite ear. I knew his secret: I saw him bend too far over one time, behind the overcoats, and as one expects something to follow when a cover flies open, I half expected his brains to fall out. He was always busy arranging things, changing things—the plastic floor was his project—marking prices and code upon labels: an expert, a dynamo. It was he who totaled up the cash register and told jokes in a high and businesslike voice. I remember him best in a series of gestures: he breaks a roll of pennies over his finger (it didn't hurt), spills them into a little rubber capsule, slaps the capsule into its carriage and snaps the handle which shoots it on a wire up to Bessie's balcony cash register.

"Was a clerk. Young feller. No longer with us." (Snicker.) "Put a mouse in the tube and sent it up to Bessie!" All this in a tone as smooth as steel, with a look half warning, half prediction. Should I have laughed? Perhaps I tried one of Mr. Brown's slow smiles.

There were other clerks: pale, retail creatures who fade quickly from memory. One was Randall Perkins, whose father owned the Leah Paper Mill. His father, having evidently assessed his son's talents, had arranged the job for him in the restful atmosphere of Trotevale's. A tall, vacant boy, I see him standing with a suit of long winter underwear in limp hands, the virile red wool, the functional flaps in interesting contrast to his ennui.

All this while there have been rumblings from above—a permanent, threatening overtone. In his little enclosure on the balcony my personal ogre was at work, his sewing machine ripping off machine-gun bursts. Oaths and maledictions! I dreaded Mr. Halperin, the tailor. He cursed in odd languages, he sat like a malignant toad and blamed me for the pants I brought him. His wet gray eyes glared across ridges of brown flesh. His head was large, bald, and thrust itself forward from shoulders hardly wider than his neck. His behind was as wide as a woman's, and hid his stool completely, as if the legs went up and stuck right into meat. He always wore a complete black suit, and on the top of his head a black skullcap which I thought to be a mask, like an eye patch, covering some horrible concavity.

"In Berlin I am a tailor! I do not make with such *dreck!*"

I was unused to such foreign behavior. My Yankee family, had it come to such screaming, would have found itself wading in fresh blood. Occasionally I came close to crying under Mr. Halperin's barrages, and I dreaded Mr. Hummington's purposeful approach, suit folded over his arm: "Take this up to the Jew."

"I can't stand it," I said to Mr. Brown. "He *yells* at me."

"Mr. Halperin is a very good tailor," Mr. Brown said.

"Why doesn't he tailor, then, and not yell at me?" To my shame, tears of injustice did come to my eyes.

"Now, now. He doesn't mean anything by it. Mr. Halperin's had a hard life and he's angry about it."

"I don't like him," I said. "I don't like him one little bit." With a bitter look toward the balcony, I retired to my hiding place behind the overcoat racks. Above, the machine rattled viciously.

I held it against Mr. Brown that he and the tailor were friendly. The tailor never screamed at Mr. Brown, nor was he sullen, as he was with Mr. Trotevale and Mr. Hummington. A strange pair they were on the cozy, elm-lined streets of Leah! One was far too handsome, the other far too ugly: both deformed, I'm sure, in Leah's eyes. They were watched and snickered after as they walked, one tall and too smoothly graceful; the other on thick legs, humping along to keep up.

One evening Mr. Brown came downstairs and stood in our living-room archway, wearing a long silk smoking jacket. My mother and father immediatley stood up, then sat down, embarrassed by their instinctive gesture of respect.

"I came to ask," Mr. Brown said formally, "if it would be all right if Mr. Halperin visited me in my room. We'll play chess, which is a very quiet game, although by nature Mr. Halperin is not always quiet." He smiled.

"Oh, fine! Perfectly all right! Sure!" came from my mother and father at the same time. I'm sure they had hardly heard a word. An exquisite orange-and-gold dragon climbed about Mr. Brown's chest and breathed scarlet fire over his breast pocket. We were all stunned by this animal.

And so, a few days later, Mr. Brown introduced the old tailor to my mother and father. Mr. Halperin bowed, called my mother something German, and shook hands too much. After the introducing was done there was a short, deep silence while everyone's eyes shifted here and there, and then Mr. Brown took the tailor upstairs.

I didn't consider myself especially sneaky. But there were two of me, and the separation was sometimes hard to mark. Blame could be shifted. And in that constant pursuit of personality I would have done away with one. The other I called Tabber, a sort of north-of-Boston Simon Templar, a creature of the erotic or violent night, a cool customer. The window of Mr. Brown's room opened onto the front-porch roof, and so did the window of mine.

Of course I expected to see, in that familiar room, nothing more horrifying than two old men playing chess. But Tabber, a dark blanket wrapped about his shoulders, eased himself along the shingles to his observation post beneath the whicking leaves of the black maple. He was not afraid of the dark. I was, occasionally. He was entirely fascinated by The Abomination. I was afraid of it. In my half-innocent mind the canon of sin was infinitely long: Demonology, Sex, The Elders of Zion, Werewolves, Toads with Jewels in Their Heads, Warts at a Touch, Step on a Crack and Break Your Mother's Back! I didn't want to believe any of it. Tabber depended upon his Winchester, I upon a skepticism that was too much a protest against the ghoulish residue of childhood.

We crouched there in the cool September night, deliciously illegal, hidden from the neighbors by the tree and from Mr. Brown and Mr. Halperin by the photonic qualities of the window screen. My mother had lent Mr. Brown her card table, and there sat the two men. I looked directly over Mr. Brown's square shoulder at the tailor's thick scowl. Two empty beer bottles stood on the dresser, and beside Mr. Brown's walnut chessboard were the two glass steins he had bought for the occasion. Both men smoked pipes, the tailor's a hornlike meerschaum that rested against the knot of his tie, Mr. Brown's a thin briar. Streamers of smoke passed slowly through the window screen and past my face without changing shape, like ghosts passing through a wall.

I watched them for a long time as they played. They hardly spoke. When the tailor drank he didn't take his pipe out of his mouth, just shoved it around to the side with his stein!

"Well?" the tailor said.

Mr. Brown didn't answer for a second or two, then the white head began to nod. I could tell by his ears that he smiled.

"Well done," he said. "Very well done. I didn't know it had happened to me until just now."

"Four moves," the tailor said.

Mr. Brown kept on nodding. "You are very good, Mr. Halperin."

"From you? A compliment." Somehow the tailor managed to look pleased while still scowling. "You are not bad, Mr. Brown."

"I know that, but I'm nowhere near as good as you."

"It is good that you say it!" The tailor may have tried to smile beneath the rolls of his cheeks. "I knew you would be good, of course," he said.

"You did!"

"Of course I did!"

For some unaccountable reason the tailor was becoming angry. His gray eyes glittered, his baggy lids quivered. Tabber may have reached for his Winchester, but I was glad that the capable back of Mr. Brown screened me, even as little as it did, from the sight of the tailor's anger.

My admiration for Mr. Brown increased, too, because he remained perfectly calm. I could almost hear his basal hum—his sympathetic, yet impersonal purr.

"Tell me why, Mr. Halperin," he said soothingly.

The tailor got up, jarring the card table and teetering the chessmen, and stamped around the room for a while. He began to breathe short, explosive little gasps, and finally he turned toward Mr. Brown. With an ominously quick hand he pulled out his wallet and extracted a photograph in a plastic cover.

"Look at this! Look at it! And tell me if there is no resemblance!"

Mr. Brown took the photograph. Over his shoulder I saw the

two men in the picture, one short and one tall. They wore bathing suits with funny tops, like summer underwear, and that was all I could see.

"It is my favorite picture. Why! Because next to me he is Adonis. Such a toad as me!" the tailor said proudly. "He was the same, like you. There are persons who are naturally beautiful, naturally graceful. It is my theory! They are good at everything."

Mr. Brown had been watching the tailor, not the picture, and he said, "Who was he, then?"

The tailor scowled worse than ever, ground his teeth and began to make a high, whining noise, as if he were in terrible pain. He put his hands over his ears and his head began to sway from side to side. "He was my brother. My brother Hy . . . " (My face ached from unconscious imitation, as if I too were bound to speak.) "My brother *Hyman!*" And tears poured, a solid faucet-stream of tears poured down his face. "I am sorry! So stupid! Forgive me!" he said in a voice that seemed to come bubbling up from under water.

Mr. Brown seemed completely unaffected. He gravely studied the photograph. The tailor wiped his face and blew his nose, emerging from this process unscathed, his face exactly as it had been before. Mr. Brown finally looked up.

"Yes, there is a resemblance," he said at last, and handed the picture back with a steady hand. I could see his other hand beneath the table, kneading his thigh.

Beneath my blanket, kneeling on the mossy shingles, I watched and recovered with the tailor. Tabber had returned to his simpler world of bang-you're-dead, and I was alone. I had never seen a man cry. I, myself, hadn't really *cried* for a long time—maybe a whole year. And why were the sloppy tears of this old man, whom I disliked, so catching? I was absolutely disgusted with myself, and with whatever undependable lever had pulled those tears out of me. I felt tricked, unfairly manipulated by the tailor. "God damn you," I whispered, "God damn you old bastard!" and wiped the traitorous tears into my blanket.

The tailor, completely recovered, began to set up the chessboard again, but Mr. Brown said that he was too tired. I retreated into the leaves until they left the room. When Mr. Brown came back, the tailor then walking lumpily beneath the street light on his way home, I came back to the window. Mr. Brown sat down in his easy chair, motionless for a moment, his face tight and unhappy. Then he raised his hands to the level of his eyes. They were shaking. I watched him for a while, but he just sat there, so I left him.

In the afternoons that followed Mr. Halperin's outbreak and on the long Saturdays, he became, as I watched, overly friendly toward Mr. Brown. The tall man was as precisely friendly as before, but the tailor would rush downstairs to talk excitedly, his hands dangerously wild among the racks and stacks of the main floor. He was making Mr. Brown a suit, and to the barely perceptible annoyance of Mr. Brown descended upon him even when he was waiting on a customer, looped a tape about his chest, the thick arms roughly pushing, the ugly face brushing Mr. Brown's ear. Then he whipped the tape off and brought it close to his eyes.

"Forty! Thirty-two!" He roared for everyone in the store to hear. "Magnificent! It is for such men suits should fit!" Humming, nodding, grunting, waving his yellow tape, he rushed back upstairs to his shop.

At times he came to argue, especially when Chief Atmon stopped by to talk to Mr. Brown about guns. The tailor did not like uniforms and our Chief of Police did little to reassure him. To Chief Atmon the tailor was a living joke, and the sight of him was enough to bring on a ponderous merriment. "Gay cock off in yawm," he would suggest to the infuriated tailor.

"If you are going to speak Yiddish, why don't you correct yourself?" the tailor said.

"I learned it in the army," Chief Atmon explained.

Mr. Brown would not join the Cascom River Fish and Game Club, but he did listen—he had little choice—to Atmon's hunting stories. Atmon was a big man, as big as anyone in Leah. His blue uniform fitted tightly as the bark of a tree around his great legs and torso. He was an excellent pistol shot, and it was always surprising to see the loud man so steady, so suddenly cool and precise as he fired on the Cascom River range, then bursting again in the vacuum of a crushing bang, breathing the fumes of his smokeless powder, looking for the hole he always found in the black.

When he hunted he cursed the animal he pursued. "There goes the son of a bitch! Kill the bastard!" he would yell as a deer slipped away through the alders. And when he killed: "I got the son of a bitch right in the boiler room! Right in the goddam boiler room!"

He was a successful hunter, hunted legally, and got his deer through study and marksmanship. The boys of Leah admired him for this, and we grinned painfully but sincerely as our clavicles unbent after one of his whacks on the back. The big man was fierce and loud, but friendly—there was no doubt about that. He even wanted Mr. Halperin to like him—you could see the little eyes up there in the open red face, searching nervously for signs of affection.

"A murderer," Mr. Halperin said, staring at Chief Atmon's departing back and at the huge Colt .44 that Atmon carried tight and black against his hip.

Mr. Brown considered this. "No. But maybe he could be."

"He hates the animals," Mr. Halperin said. "He kills out of hate. He carries proudly his pistol. He plays with it."

"Chief Atmon isn't a bad man, though," Mr. Brown said slowly. "Look how he loves his little beagle. . . ."

"Of course! He is a sentimental slob. The worst kind of murderer. I've seen such swine crying over their dogs while men died. And what is this beagle? A murder dog, meant to break the backs of rabbits!"

"No. A fine little dog, doing what he is meant to do. But Chief Atmon, now," Mr. Brown said thoughtfully, "he loves his little dog. You see, it doesn't run away from him. I suppose he believes the little dog loves him." He smiled. "Don't ever run away from him, Mr. Halperin."

"I have run away from worse than that punchinello," Mr. Halperin said.

"I neither like him nor dislike him," Mr. Brown said. "I don't hunt with him."

"Yes, you hunt, don't you," Mr. Halperin said disgustedly. "How can you? Do you gloat over the red blood you spill?"

"Do you think I do?"

"I cannot think of a reason for murder."

"If you think it is murder I can't begin to explain it to you," Mr. Brown said tolerantly.

"But why? But why?" The tailor waved his hands in Mr. Brown's face. "Look at it! Here is a beautiful deer, a fine animal; he eats only the little grasses, the little twigs from the trees. He hurts nobody. All he asks is to live, to grow tall and beautiful. You sneak to wound him, shoot big balls of lead through his living body. What did he do to you ? He has pain! He falls!" The tailor's eyes were full of tears.

"Mr. Halperin," Mr. Brown said calmly (but from my inconspicuous distance I remembered his shaking hands). "A buck is not a man. He is better equipped than a man. If you want to make a man out of him, the man you make will be an unpleasant one. He is murderous in the rut. He lets his does go first across any dangerous ground. He is completely disloyal, completely selfish. I don't make a man out of him, and I don't judge him. He is beautiful and correct for what he is. We've driven off most of his natural enemies, like the wolf, because we thought they threatened us. And now he has two major enemies left, Mr. Halperin. Neither is man. One is starvation, and none of his fine talents give him a chance against that horror. Another is the breeding of the defective among him, which will make him small, ugly and stupid and even wipe him out. Hunting man is the only enemy left that he is equipped to overcome. And if the slow and feeble among him are not killed, he will no longer be the most beautiful animal on earth."

Mr. Halperin looked away, his head bent, his hands held out, palms up. "I have heard such theories before, in Germany," he said.

"You're talking about people, Mr. Halperin. I'm talking about deer. . . ."

"So there's a difference?" the tailor said, and abruptly turned away.

I had never heard such beautiful theories, but in the town of Leah, where hunting is part of life, where school is for girls on the first of November and the paper mill is closed, we never thought too much about *killing* deer. You *got* a deer, and he was yours. From the wild flash and flag of him, the noise of his canny rush for escape, he changed. He became your own, to touch, to show, and finally to eat. I retreated to my coat-rack hideaway, gloating over Mr. Brown's victorious argument. I went to the fitting-mirrors and practiced him, ignoring my pointy profile.

Mr. Halperin didn't speak about hunting again, but if anything, his demonstrative affection for Mr. Brown increased. The swoops to measure him, the constant cornerings and contacts began to

tell. Once I saw Mr. Brown avoid him—saw him turn and go back
to the basement when he saw that Mr. Halperin was waiting for
him by the shoe-fitting chairs. The tailor would come up often and
put his hand on Mr. Brown's shoulder—a shoulder held rigid. Finally Mr. Brown turned to him, and said, in a clear, cold voice,
"Don't *lean* on me, Mr. Halperin."

The tailor jumped back, his hand still in the air at the height of
Mr. Brown's shoulder. "What? What?" he asked.

Mr. Brown ignored him, and continued to wait on Bessie, who
was stolidly buying her weekly pair of shoes—her weekly impersonal foot caress at the hands of Mr. Brown.

At the foot of the stairs the tailor turned around. His eyes were
wet again, and he smiled a twisty little smile. "So!" he said to me.
"So we know! When didn't it? Look! He waits on that fat pig who
has the soul of a garbage can, the mouth like a hemorrhoid!" He
shook his head. "Ah, he is so just like! So cold!"

When he had the time he still worked on Mr. Brown's suit, still
made the necessary measurements—but formally now, with prior
permission. Most of the time he sat in his little room, firing off
bursts of stitches, waiting to cuss me out.

. . . Until that morning in November. Leah Town Square was
sere, hardened by a morning frost; the tall elms were creaky in the
cold sunlight, and I was hardened and hopeless at the beginning of
another endless Saturday. I crossed the green but dying grass,
passed the empty benches that would soon be taken in. It was the
first day of hunting season and I must wear a necktie and white
shirt, hear the sporadic shots echoing down from the dark hills of
Leah. The deer, jumped by hunters, would be moving nervously
through the quiet spruce, leaping past the bright beeches into
darkness. And I must wait on people who didn't care enough—
who didn't care at all.

From a distance I had seen Bessie and Mr. Brown standing in
front of Trotevale's, but the frosty wind made my eyes water, and I
kept them down, not bothering to wonder why the two didn't go
straight inside on a cold morning. As I came nearer I saw that Bessie was in a state of unrest. Something jiggled that mass, made her
stamp her precious feet and open and shut her soundless mouth.
Mr. Brown stood next to her, and they both peered in through the
big window to the right of the front door. When I came up to them

it was a terrible and delicious shock to me, too: the big window was only half there. Slabs and splinters of glass glittered upon the sidewalk, wide sheets of it and millions of jagged darts of it had crushed Mr. Hummington's window display of two-dollar ties and ten-dollar hats.

"Something moving *around* in there!" Bessie whined. Through the unnatural hole we heard bumpings from the rear, thumps and breaking glass.

The rest of the clerks and Mr. Halperin had come by the time Mr. Hummington arrived at a run, his key foremost. "Late! Late!" he explained, as if his lateness were something so odd it must be proclaimed. Then he saw the broken window, and with military precision he stabbed the Yale lock with his key and overran it, nearly shattering the glass of the door with his forehead. We cautiously followed him inside—all except Bessie, who remained outside uttering complaining little squeaks.

The glass case that had contained men's jewelry—tie pins and cuff links of coated brass, little arrows meant to look as if they pierced your necktie, springlike instruments to skewer collars down, buckles to personalize bellies and their heaps of interchangeable letters in plastic mother-of-pearl—this case was smashed and trampled, and the shoddy brightwork spewed down the aisle. Stray neckties were everywhere, brightly coiling and dangling like tropical snakes in a zoo. The coat racks at the rear were all tipped over, and piles of blue and brown material lay heaped in rows, a plowed field sown with buttons.

We advanced, Mr. Hummington in the lead, silent except for the crunch of glass beneath our feet. No sound came from the dark areas at the rear of the store, and we all had the feeling of being watched.

"Got to call Mr. Trotevale," Mr. Hummington whispered.

"We ought to get out of here," Randall Perkins suggested. Though far in the rear, he had armed himself with or was merely carrying an empty tie rack. Bessie had moved through the door and scared us badly by screaming, "Are you all right?"

Mr. Hummington turned wrathfully, but before he could say anything the ominous presence we had all been conscious of, the author of this terrible derangement, rose before us; gathered itself before Mr. Hummington: a great buck with bone-white antlers, thick neck and deep, wild eyes. Mr. Hummington must have been close enough to feel the sharp explosions of wind from the buck's black nostrils.

With his hands slack at his sides, his mouth open, Mr. Hummington stared. All his famous energy had left him, drawn out at a look as awed sighs were drawn from us. The buck's brawny neck trembled with inhuman energy, his black eyes struck away what little nerve we had. In the sudden presence of his fierce strength we were all at once aware of our weakness. The coward's swift insight froze our shy bodies. I, for one, knew in my belly the force of those bony antlers, the power of those sharp hoofs. And the awesome dignity of the huge animal was not dispelled at all by the cheap neckties that flapped from his antlers, gaudy but unfunny: they might have been our own dangling guts.

After the long moment of fear, the deer rose on its hind legs to turn in the narrow aisle. Mr. Hummington fell solidly to the floor and scuttled, with swimming motions, back toward us on the slippery plastic. His head thumped against my shin, and he looked up, without his glasses, astounded at my unmoving presence. His eyes were metallic little beads deep under his forehead. None of the rest of us had run because the deer had—one smooth leap had taken him directly into the banister of the basement stairs. He took the heavy wood downstairs with him as easily as if it had been a spiderweb across a trail. From the basement we heard a clatter and a thump, then nothing. We had been hearing, but not caring about, Bessie's screams for help. She stood blocking the front door, importuning the town of Leah and the police. Eventually both came.

With the deer more or less safely in the basement, Mr. Hummington took charge. Bessie was led to the elevator and installed in her office on the balcony, Mr. Halperin was sent to his shop, and the rest of us were directed to begin cleaning up. The shoe department hadn't been damaged, and we didn't miss Mr. Brown. While we were sweeping up the jewelry he had been in the basement.

"He's back in the corner by the work shirts," Mr. Brown said. "I'm afraid he'll hurt himself."

"Hurt himself! *Hurt* himself!" Mr. Hummington said.

"He may break a leg if we scare him too badly."

"He may break his goddam neck! He damn well *will* break his goddam neck! I'll do it myself! Look at this place! Look at the hoof marks in my new floor! Look at the glass!" Mr. Hummington yelled.

Mr. Brown looked gravely down at him, a certain amount of contempt detectable in his calmness. Mr. Hummington turned away.

"What's Mr. Trotevale going to say? We can't get any new glass until Monday and he has the shingles again. We'll have to borrow a mattress box from the furniture store and put it over the hole and it'll look just goddam awful!" Some of this was private moan.

People had begun to gather on the sidewalk, and they stood two-deep, staring in, steaming the good window so that they had to keep wiping to see. They all seemed to be waving at us. The front door had been locked, but this didn't stop Chief Atmon, who jumped crushingly through the broken window, scattering hats and glass over the floor I'd just swept.

"Where is he?" Atmon yelled, his big hands held open and forward like a wrestler's.

"He's down in the basement and he's as big as a horse," Mr. Hummington said.

"Hah!"

"He's bigger'n you, Harold," Mr. Hummington said. "You're not going to wrestle him out of there."

Atmon looked questioningly at Mr. Brown.

"Three hundred pounds. Ten points," Mr. Brown said.

"Wow!" Atmon's hand dropped tentatively to the butt of his big revolver. On his face was an expression of fierce anticipation.

"Goddam, Harold! You shoot him and you'll ruin half the work clothes. Blood all over the place!" Mr. Hummington cried. "You can't do that! All those chinos! You can't do it!"

"I can drop him in his tracks. One shot. No splatter. Right in the goddam boiler room."

"No! No! You've got to lasso him. Tie him up!"

"I ain't no cowboy," Atmon said. "What about you, Brown!"

"You might tie him up, but by the time you do he'll have wrecked everything down there, and hurt himself," Mr. Brown said.

"Shoot him!" Atmon said. "Only thing *to* do."

"Why don't we just let him go?" Mr. Brown said.

An immediate, wondering silence. We all looked at Mr. Brown

as if at a stranger, and from that point on he lost force; he seemed to fade before our eyes, and the more he said, the less his opinion counted. Aside from considerations of retribution for the damage done to the store, and especially the damage done to our equilibrium, the idea was impossible. The deer would have to come back upstairs and leave the store at street level. Then he would have to find his way back to the woods, a matter of a half-mile in the best direction. Such gaunt majesty as his would be too alone, too terrible upon the quiet streets of Leah. He'd be sure to get into more trouble somewhere along the line.

"He got in here by himself," Mr. Brown said. "If he isn't driven crazy he might be able to find his way back where he belongs."

"He don't belong *here*," Mr. Hummington said.

"Belongs in my freezer-locker, that's where he belongs," Chief Atmon said.

"Listen," Mr. Brown said, "he isn't stupid. He's big and he's old, and you don't get that way by being stupid."

"So who says he was?" Atmon said.

"He just doesn't belong here. You can't shoot him here. It's too strange for him. Out in the woods he'd make us all look like fools."

"So who says he wouldn't? Only he ain't out in the woods, by God!" Atmon said, grinning. "He ain't *out* in the woods."

"Why'd he have to come to town, anyway?" Mr. Hummington asked plaintively.

"I'll tell you why," Mr. Brown said. "Because so many brave hunters were out with jack lights last night. I never heard so many shots in the middle of a night. It's a wonder everybody in this town hasn't got his deer all tagged and hung up already. Somebody stampeded this buck. It's not his fault he ran into town."

"So whose fault is it? It ain't mine, but I got to get him out of here," Atmon said.

"How about the game warden?" Mr. Hummington asked hopefully.

"He's out with his thermometer testing to find them deer was jacked last night," Atmon said. "Who could find him?"

Chief Atmon had been edging impatiently toward the basement stairs; Mr. Hummington, who wanted a promise of no bloodshed, was backing away in front. Mr. Brown walked back to his shoe department, turned and stood motionless, watching.

And at that moment, without having to look behind him, Mr. Hummington *knew*. With barely a creak of stairs the buck appeared, whole and majestic. Quick as a squirrel on a tree, Mr. Hummington scrambled around in back of the Chief of Police. Tall and proud, the buck stood over us all, his head high, the magnificent rack of antlers gleaming. He looked from one side of the store to the other, seeming to calculate a mighty leap that would easily clear our heads. His muzzle was dark, yet a silvery fringe of white hairs showed his age. His neck was as thick as a man's waist—a trunk of rigid muscle to carry the great antlers. He held our eyes again—held them absolutely—an invincible magnetism in that wild beauty.

Atmon himself was struck silent for a long time. Then he had his Colt in his hand, and we all heard three cold clicks as he pulled back the long hammer.

"MURDERER!"

For a moment I thought this tearing sound was the expected shot, and then in the shocked silence after this astounding word we saw the tailor on the balcony, his squat legs spread, his stubby hands gripping the rail. His face was black with blood, his eyes burned down upon the startled Chief of Police.

"MURDERER! MURDERER! Mr. Brown! Do you see what he is doing? *What are you doing about it?*"

Like the buck itself, Mr. Brown did not move during this outburst. He stood quietly by his wall of shoe boxes, his eyes curiously still, as if he were blind, or in hiding.

The tailor watched him for a second, and then began to stamp his feet, to shriek in German, the words torn by great sobs and sneezes as he hit his disintegrated face with his fists.

The deer took this moment to make his try for freedom, catching us all with our eyes upon the bawling tailor. Chief Atmon's reaction was swift, and had been predicted. He fired, stunning us all, breaking the buck's long back in mid-air as he made his first arcing leap toward the front of the store. He came down upon rigid forelegs, his hindquarters useless, and slid to the feet of Mr. Brown.

"Got him!" Chief Atmon yelled triumphantly. It had been a tremendous, a classic shot from a handgun, yet we were silent, still. The buck still lived. Propped upon his forelegs, his rack still held high, he looked straight at Chief Atmon, waiting. Mr. Brown watched too. "I got him! I got him! I got him!"

"Not quite in the boiler room," Mr. Brown said quietly.

"God damn you! I got him, so shut your lousy mouth!" Chief Atmon screamed. A long sigh from the rest of us, and Chief Atmon whirled around. He seemed to look right at me. *This is what I am good at,* his eyes implored. *And wasn't that a beautiful shot?*

The deer's calm eyes were black and deep. His nostrils flared at each even breath. His rump lay broken behind him, the long, silky-haired legs splayed across the shiny plastic squares. Atmon came up, his revolver cocked.

"Get the hell out of the way. I'm going to finish him off." Mr. Brown moved away, carefully, quietly. The deer glanced at him once and then turned to watch Chief Atmon and the black gun that was pointed at his neck. He didn't try to move, but held his head as high as the good forelegs could hold it, waiting, breathing steadily, his ears erect and still as if he meant to hear, as well as see, the final explosion. . . . Which came. Chief Atmon was right: there was very little blood from either wound. The big slug broke the buck's neck and killed him. With a little sigh he dropped his head. An antler rang against the wall and he was very little quieter than he had been alive. His eyes were open, still luminous—but not so deep: those dark wells had silted up.

In the terrible vacuum of Chief Atmon's victory we watched Mr. Brown pace down the squares toward the cloak rack. Each foot precise upon a square, he hit no cracks. His handsome face was as unchangeable as if it were made of wax—the stern, expressionless mourning of waxwork nobility upon a tumbrel. He would look at none of us: whether it was disdain, or the wily ploy of a camouflaged animal who knows his eyes will shine, I didn't know. At the cloak rack he unhurriedly put on his coat and hat, then as proudly, or as carefully casual in the face of danger, he turned around and walked out.

The tailor's long wail of mourning grew above us, its waves and intensifications strangely formal and rhythmical, as if it were a rite of sorrow perfected by legions of the bereaved; as if no one death but the deaths of generations must have called forth such terrible music from the ugly man's throat.

And Bessie, too, her heavy face no longer under the protection of her habit of determination, made the answer to that high litany. She stood at the rail and wept.

Later in the morning, when Mr. Hummington's energy had restored the order of our existence, I found myself with a pair of pants in my hand, making the usual climb to the tailor's shop.

The bursts of his sewing machine were as abrupt as always, and this time he heard my step upon the stairs and turned toward me, dropping a stiff lapel upon his table.

"He is gone?" he asked, gray eyes popping miserably from the brown lids. And without waiting for my reply he asked again, "He is gone?"

"He didn't even say good-by," I said, echoing in the words of Mr. Hummington a disapproval I didn't feel.

"Good-by?" the tailor yelled, bringing his fist down upon the rubber bulb of his chalk marker. "Good-by?"

A cloud of blue dust rose above the scarred table. Blue chalk hung between us like a mist, and the tailor's eyes began to fill with rage and tears. I backed toward the stairs, feeling for the carved railing, a solid thing to follow back.

"Did you want him to say good-by? Are you still foolish? Do you cry because of this?" the tailor demanded, bringing his fist down on the table so hard the lapel jumped.

I *hadn't* cried. In spite of the tears I'd seen, I hadn't caught them, and I considered this a terrible insult—an unforgivable insult; considered this and suddenly burst out bawling, enraged by the underhanded trick.

"God damn you son of a bitch!" I yelled.

"Ah! That's better," the tailor said calmly, as if my tears had released and strengthened him. "Do you think I don't know you, my funny little one? It is *his* nature to try to escape. He does not know how *we* survive, eh? Never mind! *We* are the slobs who make the world." He motioned with his hand. "Now give me the pants you got in your hand and go back to work. Go on!"

I left him, seeing that shrewd and twisted smile as I fled to my hiding place behind the overcoats, to my private ceremony; the tearful funeral of that thin-lipped version of myself as Tabber, as a

Yankee boy of ice and few swift words. I heard again the tailor's long wail as it had grown over the deer's death and Mr. Brown's escape, and now I found the doleful music apt, as if it were part of a ritual some memory of my flesh found anything but alien and strange.

. . . Not so long ago, though Trotevale's and the things of Trotevale's are scattered to the rag bags and the antique shops of Leah.

My son fixes me to here and now, the only place and time there is: he has cornered his apple by the stairs, and found that he can break the skin by smashing it against the edge of the bottom step. He sits quietly, his little tongue busy on the split, his eyes darkly watchful. He reminds me of an animal—a young raccoon in some quiet corner of the deep woods—self-sufficient, aware. "You little bastard," I say admiringly, with perhaps too much affection in my voice, those easy tears precariously dammed behind my eyes. "You little bastard. . . ." Gently, because he is soft and young. And with fear, for I do not really know what I should hope for him.

NOEL PERRIN

Noel Perrin (b. New York City, 1927) graduated from Williams College and the University of North Carolina. Since 1959 he has been a professor at Dartmouth College in Hanover, New Hampshire. A regular contributor to the *New Yorker*, he has written on subjects as diverse as sugar making and medieval Japanese history.

The Amateur Sugar Maker was published by the University Press of New England in Hanover, New Hampshire in 1972. "Ah, New Hampshire" was published by St. Martin's Press in Perrin's book of essays *A Passport Secretly Green*.

"Ah, New Hampshire"

Old Mrs. Halks, who lives about half a mile from where I do in central New Hampshire, has a saying about the fatal attraction of the soil hereabouts. "The land kind o' reaches up and grabs ye," she says, "and 'twon't let go."

When I look around the township two of whose twelve hundred residents we are, I am forced to agree. Since the Halkses and the Spencers arrived in 1729, the land doesn't seem to have let go of anything. The two-room clapboard house erected by Henry Spencer in 1734, for example, stands by the Center Brook yet; these days it's the village library. An old barn they say Henry and his sons put up around 1740 is both standing and still in service. It's part of a three-barn complex used by my neighbor Alf Martineau to house his cows, his hay, and his dried citrus pulp. (He imports about forty tons a year from Florida for the cows.) I have a feeling that if you looked in the long grass beside the door, you could still find one of Henry Spencer's old hand-forged scythes, a bit rusty, perhaps, but protected and preserved and firmly held in its place by a chunk of our local granite. I know you'll find Henry Spencer himself, kept down by a larger piece of that same granite, over in the Center graveyard.

What really strikes me as remarkable, though, is the way the land can take a moving object and bring it to a halt. I'm not talking about the row of old Plymouths gradually growing into the soil behind Martineau's barn. I'm talking about the bright new trailers that swing carelessly down Route Eight, reach our neighborhood, and suddenly get trapped onto cement-block foundations. The township is full of these marooned wanderers. I would guess we have at least thirty-five, beached like whales along the township roads. A tenth of our population lives in them. Another tenth has plans.

It is said that other parts of the country are rich in trailers, too. Mr. Martineau, who not only imports feed from Florida, but who has been down there himself, reports that the whole state is dotted with trailer parks and that every day you can see great pink-and-chromium houses roll in behind cars with Ohio license plates and hook up for the winter. But these are mere fleeting visitors. Come

April they are due back in Ohio, and they trundle northward with mobility unimpaired—the modern gypsies of the Middle West. I think it is mainly here in New England that young trailers which have scarcely traveled fifty miles from the factory pluck off their wheels and settle down to become permanent parts of the landscape. It is an odd experience to watch them do it.

Still, I have to whether I like it or not. Between here and the Halks place, which I pass every day on my way to work, there are three of these monstrous settlers, in varying states of permanence. One, which arrived only last fall, is right across the road from the old house. It belongs to young Stephen Halks, who came home from a Long Island airplane factory last year with his new wife. The young couple haven't even had time to strip the tires off their house, but they have got the weight of it resting on concrete blocks, and they've built a picket fence all the way around, either to keep the baby in or (more likely) to make sure the whole caboodle doesn't run away with some passing Buick from Massachusetts. Next summer, Mrs. Halks says, they're going to get a proper granite base under her for sure.

The second trailer, a bright orange one with streamlined fittings, is only just around the corner from where I live. It belongs to a bachelor farmer named Roy Chipman. His previous dwelling, a quite beautiful Dutch colonial house built by a Spencer in the 1820's, burned three years ago, and Roy bought the trailer as a substitute. For a full year no one was sure whether he meant to stay up here in New Hampshire or move south, because all he did was roll his new house in about twenty feet from the town road and hook up a makeshift pump to the well. That fall when it got cold he stuck a rusty kerosene barrel on the back. (Roy doesn't hold with bottled gas.) But in the spring of 1958 he apparently came to some sort of decision. He laid a fieldstone foundation that ought to last two hundred years, and got his brother to help him mount the trailer on it. In odd moments during the summer he stretched an orange-and-green canvas awning all along the front, and he built a surprisingly trim toolshed onto the end that was designed to be hitched to cars. Just beyond that he's got his vegetable patch. What future improvements he intends, I don't know. Roy confides neither in Mrs. Halks nor in me.

I come now to the showpiece of our road, the real proof of what a New Englander can do with a trailer when he puts his mind on it. I'm speaking of the mobile home in which live the Boals, father, mother, and two children. The Boal mobile home is a securer part of our landscape than Mount Monadnock. Mr. Boal brought her in nearly ten years ago, and he's been anchoring her down and tying her closer to the soil ever since. Where Roy has that little toolshed, Boal has got a two-car garage attached, complete with a poured concrete floor. The four big doors are painted a glinty cobalt blue to match the exterior of the trailer. Running clear over the entire structure and extending out six inches on each side he has a second roof of asphalt shingles, built to last. She'll never weather out. He has a granite walk going up to her from the road, and an extra outer wall at the end opposite the garage, and a cobalt-blue trellis all along the back. He's even added a copper gutter with a downspout. All you can see of the actual trailer any more is the shimmering cobalt-blue and chromium front, which I am sure Mrs. Boal simonizes spring and fall. Anything securer from the ravages of time I have never met, except once in a cemetery in Scotland. There about every third tomb had in front of it a bowl of flowers, placed there sometime in the nineteenth century. All the flowers were identical, and all were made out of painted porcelain and wire, since flowers made of leaves and petals are known to fade. Over each porcelain bouquet was a large glass bell jar to keep the rain off. Over each bell jar was a wire cage to keep it from getting broken. You could just dimly make out the flowers, far inside.

I, alas, won't be here to see it, because I am made of frail flesh and blood, and I am beginning to weather already. But I know what New Hampshire is going to look like next century. Mount Monadnock will be an inch or so down. If we have war or really determined quarrying, it may be many feet lower. Most of the remaining clapboard houses will be gone, since what the termites miss fire will get. But chromium is incorruptible. Scattered over our valleys, winking in the sunlight, will be ten thousand thousand bright-hued, hideous lumps, each an immortal trailer, each looking as aboriginal and as immovable as the dolmens at Stonehenge. Ah, progress! Ah, New Hampshire!

DONALD HALL

Donald Hall (b. New Haven, Connecticut, 1928) graduated from Phillips Exeter (New Hampshire), Harvard, and Stanford. He has divided his efforts between college teaching and writing poetry, for which he has received numerous awards. He has taught at the University of Michigan and now lives on his ancestral farm in New Hampshire.

"Names of Horses" from *Kicking the Leaves* was published originally in *The New Yorker* in 1977. "The Black Faced Sheep" from *Kicking the Leaves* was published by Harper and Row in 1976.

Donald Hall. Courtesy of Special Collections, Dimond Library, University of New Hampshire.

Names of Horses

All winter your brute shoulders strained against collars, padding
and steerhide over the ash hames, to haul
sledges of cordwood for drying through spring and summer,
for the Glenwood stove next winter, and for the simmering
    range.

In April you pulled cartloads of manure to spread on the fields,
dark manure of Holsteins, and knobs of your own clustered with
    oats.
All summer you mowed the grass in meadow and hayfield, the
    mowing machine
clacketing beside you, while the sun walked high in the morning;

and after noon's heat, you pulled a clawed rake through the same
    acres,
gathering stacks, and dragged the wagon from stack to stack,
and the built hayrack back, uphill to the chaffy barn,
three loads of hay a day from standing grass in the morning.

Sundays you trotted the two miles to church with the light load
of a leather quartertop buggy, and grazed in the sound of hymns.
Generation on generation, your neck rubbed the windowsill
of the stall, smoothing the wood as the sea smooths glass.

When you were old and lame, when your shoulders hurt bending
    to graze,
one October the man, who fed you and kept you, and harnessed
    you every morning,
led you through corn stubble to sandy ground above Eagle Pond,
and dug a hole beside you where you stood shuddering in your
    skin,

and lay the shotgun's muzzle in the boneless hollow behind your
    ear,
and fired the slug into your brain, and felled you into your grave,
shoveling sand to cover you, setting goldenrod upright above
    you,
where by next summer a dent in the ground made your
    monument.

For a hundred and fifty years, in the pasture of dead horses,

roots of pine trees pushed through the pale curves of your ribs,
yellow blossoms flourished above you in autumn, and in winter
frost heaved your bones in the ground—old toilers, soil makers:

O Roger, Mackerel, Riley, Ned, Nellie, Chester, Lady Ghost.

The Black Faced Sheep

Ruminant pillows! Gregarious soft boulders!

If one of you found a gap in a stone wall,
the rest of you—rams, ewes, bucks, wethers, lambs;
mothers and daughters, old grandfather-father,
cousins and aunts, small bleating sons—
followed onward, stupid
as sheep, wherever
your leader's sheep-brain wandered to.

My grandfather spent all day searching the valley
and edges of Ragged Mountain,
calling "Ke-*day!*" as if he brought you salt,
"Ke-*day! Ke-day!*"

* * *

When a bobcat gutted a lamb at the Keneston place
in the spring of eighteen-thirteen
a hundred and fifty frightened black faced sheep
lay in a stupor and died.

* * *

When the shirt wore out, and darns in the woolen
shirt needed darning,
a woman in a white collar
cut the shirt into strips and braided it,
as she braided her hair every morning.
In a hundred years
the knees of her great-granddaughter
crawled on a rug made from the wool of sheep
whose bones were mud,
like the bones of the woman, who stares
from an oval in the parlor.

* * *

I forked the brambly hay down to you
in nineteen-fifty. I delved my hands deep
in the winter grass of your hair.

When the shearer cut to your nakedness in April
and you dropped black eyes in shame,
hiding in barnyard corners, unable to hide,
I brought grain to raise your spirits,
and ten thousand years
wound us through pasture and hayfield together,
threads of us woven
together, three hundred generations
from Africa's hills to New Hampshire's.

*   *   *

You were not shrewd like the pig.
You were not strong like the horse.
You were not brave like the rooster.
Yet none of the others looked like a lump of granite
that grew hair,
and none of the others
carried white fleece as soft as dandelion seed
around a black face,
and none of them sang such a flat and sociable song.

*   *   *

In November a bearded man, wearing a lambskin apron,
slaughtered an old sheep for mutton
and hung the carcass in north shade
and cut from the frozen sides all winter, to stew in a pot
on the fire that never went out.

*   *   *

Now the black faced sheep have wandered and will not return,
though I search the valleys
and call "Ke-*day*" as if I brought them salt.

Now the railroad draws
a line of rust through the valley. Birch, pine, and maple
lean from cellarholes
and cover the dead pastures of Ragged Mountain
except where machines make snow
and cables pull money up hill, to slide back down.

*   *   *

At South Danbury Church twelve of us sit—
cousins and aunts, sons—
where the great-grandfathers of the forty-acre farms
filled every pew.
I look out the window at summer places,
at Boston lawyers' houses
with swimming pools cunningly added to cowsheds,
and we read an old poem aloud, about Israel's sheep
—and I remember faces and wandering hearts,
dear lumps of wool—and we read

that the rich farmer, though he names his farm for himself,
takes nothing into his grave;
that even if people praise us, because we are successful,
we will go under the ground
to meet our ancestors collected there in the darkness;
that we are all of us sheep, and death is our shepherd,
and we die as the animals die.

MAY SARTON

May Sarton (b. Wondelgem, Belgium, 1912) emigrated to the United States in 1916 and became a citizen eight years later. Her father was a distinguished historian of science. She has written several novels, volumes of poetry and journals and has received numerous awards for literary achievement, including an honorary degree from the University of New Hampshire in 1976.

Plant Dreaming Deep was published in 1968 and *Collected Poems* in 1974, by W. W. Norton and Company in New York.

May Sarton, photograph by Jill Krementz. Courtesy of W. W. Norton and Company, Inc., New York.

As Does New Hampshire

Could poetry or love by the same lucky chance
Make summer air vibrate with such a brilliance?
A landscape which says little—
Grave green hills diminishing to blue
Against the foreground of a long blond meadow,
While from the near pine elegantly falls
The nuthatch's neat syllable—
A landscape which says little,
But says this simple phrase so well
That it takes on forever the dimension
(Space, sound, silence, light and shade)
Of which a summer's happiness is made.
Only most daring love would care to mention
So much, so simply, and so charge each word
As does New Hampshire "mountain," "meadow," "bird."

A Recognition
(for Perley Cole)

I wouldn't know how rare they come these days,
But I know Perley's rare. I know enough
To stop fooling around with words, and praise
This man who swings a scythe in subtle ways,
And brings green order, carved out of the rough.
I wouldn't know how rare, but I discover
They used to tell an awkward learning boy,
"Keep the heel down, son, careful of the swing!"
I guess at perils, and peril makes me sing.
So let the world go, but hold fast to joy,
And praise the craftsman till Hell freezes over!

I watched him that first morning when the dew
Still slightly bent tall, toughened grasses;
Sat up in bed to watch him coming through
Holding the scythe so lightly and so true
In slow sweeps and in lovely passes,
The swing far out, far out—but not too far,
The pause to wipe and whet the shining blade.

I felt affinities: farmer and poet
Share a good deal, although they may not know it.
It looked as easy as when the world was made,
And God could pull a bird out or a star.

For there was Perley in his own sweet way
Pulling some order out of ragged land,
Cutting the tough, chaotic growth away
So peace could saunter down a summer day,
For here comes Cole with genius in his hand!
I saw in him a likeness to that flame,
Brancusi, in his Paris studio,
Who pruned down, lifted from chaotic night
Those naked, shining images of flight—
The old man's gentle malice and bravado,
Boasting hard times: "It was my game!"

"*C'était mon jeu!*"—to wrest joy out of pain,
The endless skillful struggle to uncloud
The clouded vision, to reduce and prune,
And bring back from the furnace, fired again,
A world of magic, joy alone allowed.
Now Perley says, "God damn it!"—and much worse.
Hearing him, I get back some reverence.
Could you, they ask, call such a man your friend?
Yes (damn it!), and yes world without end!
Brancusi's game and his make the same sense,
And not unlike a prayer is Perley's curse.

So let the rest go, and heel down, my boy,
And praise the artist till Hell freezes over,
For he is rare, he with his scythe (no toy),
He with his perils, with his skill and joy,
Who comes to prune, to make clear, to uncover,
The old man, full of wisdom, in his prime.
There in the field, watching him as he passes,
I recognize that violent, gentle blood,
Impatient patience. I would, if I could,
Call him my kin, there scything down the grasses,
Call him my good luck in a dirty time.

Death of the Maple

Now for two winters we have lived together,
This rugged towering maple tree and I.
Through the rude buffets of New England weather
That stripped off leaves and tore some branches down
We shared this world and lived in amity.
We even once withstood a hurricane.
But I had always known it had to die,
Decaying, dangerous, on the way out,
Although it made a great arc in the sky
And stood there, splendid, like a dying shout.

Today in my raw youth I gave the order
To bring this courage down in all its pride,
Told men and their machines to go and murder
What I have loved and lived two years beside.
Two men with a small buzz saw maimed and killed—
The tree fought hard. It did not want to go.
And when it went, a hundred years were stilled.
And when it went, I did not want to know.

Great heart, you will be burned. Have I presumed
In my raw youth that we are all consumed,
And to die well, all die to feed some fire?
My winter blaze be your brave funeral pyre!

We Have Seen the Wind
New England Hurricane, 1938

We have seen the wind and we need not be warned.
It is no plunderer of roses. It is nothing sweet.
We have seen the torturer of trees, O we have learned
How it bends them, how it wrenches at their rooted feet,
Till the earth cracks like a cake round their torn feet.

We saw the strong trees struggle and their plumes go down,
The poplar bend and whip back till it split to fall,
The elm tear up at the root and topple like a crown,
The pine crack at the base—we had to watch them all.
The ash, the lovely cedar. We had to watch them fall.

They went so softly under the loud flails of air,
Before that fury they went down like feathers,
With all the hundred springs that flowered in their hair,
And all the years, endured in all the weathers—
To fall as if they were nothing, as if they were feathers.

Do not speak to us of the wind. We know now. We know.
We do not need any more of destruction than all these—
These that were proud and great and still so swift to go.
Do not speak to us any more of the carnage of the trees,
Lest the heart remember other dead than these—

Lest the heart split like a tree from root to crown
And, bearing all its springs, like a feather go down.

Plant Dreaming Deep
(after Du Bellay)

Happy the man who can long roaming reap,
Like old Ulysses when he shaped his course
Homeward at last toward the native source,
Seasoned and stretched to plant his dreaming deep.
When shall I see the chimney smoke once more
Of my own village; in a fervent hour
When maples blaze or lilac is in flower,
Push open wide again my plain white door?

Here is a little province, poor and kind—
Warmer than marble is the weathered wood;
Dearer than holy Ganges, the wild brook;
And sweeter than all Greece to this one mind
A ragged pasture, open green, white steeple,
And these whom I have come to call my people.

APPENDIX

SOME EARLY NEW HAMPSHIRE PRESSES[1]

1790s: Robert and Daniel Fowle (Portsmouth)
H. Ranlet (Exeter)
John Melcher (Portsmouth)
Robert Gerrish (Portsmouth)
David Carlisle, Jr. (Walpole)
I. Thomas (with Carlisle) (Walpole)
Samuel Bragg, Jr. (Dover)
Thomas Odiorne (Exeter)
Eliphalet Ladd (Dover)
Stearns and Winslow (Exeter)
C. Peirce (Portsmouth)
Moses Davis (Hanover)

1800–1850:   J. and J. W. Prentiss (Keene)
Roby, Kimball, and Merrill (Concord)
W. Treadwell (Portsmouth)
C. W. Brewster (Portsmouth)
Williams (Exeter)
Moore (Concord)
John Mann (Dover)
S. Whidden (Portsmouth)
G. P. Lyon (Concord)
Morrill Sillsby (Concord)
James Derby (Exeter)
I. Long (Hopkinton)
I. Hill (Concord)
A. McFarland (Concord)
David Newhall (Walpole)

[1] Source: Clarence S. Brigham, *History and Bibliography of American Newspapers*, vol. 1 *1690–1820*, (Worcester, Mass.: American Antiquarian Society, 1947).

NUMBER OF NEWSPAPERS IN 1820

New Hampshire	68
Massachusetts	175
Maine	40
Vermont	54

INDEX

"An Account of the Battle of Bennington" by Gen. John Stark, 45, 79

Adams, Henry, 11n

Adams, John, 2

"Ah, New Hampshire" by Noel Perrin, 322

Aldrich, Thomas Bailey, 134–35; author of *An Old Town by the Sea*, 7n, 10, 135; author of *The Story of a Bad Boy*, 6, 7, 133, 135; biography of, 154; idealization of small-town life, 10; selection from *An Old Town by the Sea*, 163; selection from *The Story of a Bad Boy*, 155; "Unguarded Gates," 167

"The Ambitious Guest" by Nathaniel Hawthorne, 91, 111

American Revolution, 3; impact on life of Matthew Patten, 23; new spirit in New Hampshire literature, 43

Among the Isles of Shoals by Celia Thaxter, 136, 189

"As Does New Hampshire" by May Sarton, 331

"At Sudleigh Fair" by Alice Brown, 136

Ball, Dr. Benjamin, 92; biography of, 127; selection from *Three Days on the White Mountains*, 128

Belknap, Rev. Jeremy, 3, 90; author of *The History of New Hampshire*, 3, 43, 44; biography of, 46; description of a happy society, 133; exponent of classical republicanism, 14; selection from *The History of New Hampshire*, 47

"The Black Cottage" by Robert Frost, 16

"The Black Faced Sheep" by Donald Hall, 327

Boston and Maine Railroad, 13

Brown, Alice, 133, 135, 138, 225, 271; author of "At Sudleigh Fair," 136; author of "Farmer Eli's Vacation," 136; author of *Jeremy Hamlin*, 17, 271; author of "Joint Owners in Spain," 136; author of *Meadow Grass: Tales of New England Life*, 9, 19, 133, 135; biography of, 173; comments on rural life, 8; idealizes small community, 7; "Joint Owners in Spain," selection from *Meadow Grass: Tales of New England Life*, 174; later work and

the "revolt from the village," 17; selection from *Jeremy Hamlin*, 272

"The Buck in Trotevale's" by Thomas Williams, 299

"The Candidates at the Fair" by Sam Walter Foss, 200

Cather, Willa, 16

"The Census-Taker" by Robert Frost, 15, 269

Chapin, Bela, editor of *The Poets of New Hampshire* (1883), 5

Chocorua, Indian chief, 6

Churchill, Winston, 13–14, 138, 224; author of *Coniston*, 13–14, 225; author of *The Dwelling-Place of Light*, 14; author of *Mr. Crewe's Career*, 13–14, 225; biography of, 230; selection from *Coniston*, 231; selection from *The Dwelling-Place of Light*, 251; selection from *Mr. Crewe's Career*, 248

Coniston by Winston Churchill, 13–14, 225, 231

Connecticut River Valley, 3

Cornish, N.H., home of Winston Churchill, 14

Crawford, Ethan Allen, 90–91

Crawford, Lucy Howe, 8, 90–91; biography of, 93; selection from *The History of the White Mountains*, 94

"Death of the Maple" by May Sarton, 333

"Deserted Farms" by Sam Walter Foss, 200

A Discourse Delivered at Easton, on the 17th of October, 1779 [*Thanksgiving Sermon*] by Rev. Israel Evans, 44, 75

Durkee, Ruell, New Hampshire politician, 13, 225

The Dwelling-Place of Light by Winston Churchill, 14, 251

Evans, Rev. Israel: author of *Thanksgiving Sermon*, 44; biography of, 74; selection from *A Discourse Delivered at Easton, on the 17th of October, 1779* (sometimes referred to as *Thanksgiving Sermon*), 75

"Farmer Eli's Vacation" by Alice Brown, 136

A Farmer's Diary by Matthew Patten, 2, 23, 24, 36

Female Quixotism: Exhibited in the Romantic Opinions and Extravagant Adventures of Dorcasina Sheldon by Tabitha Gilman Tenney, 4, 45, 86

First World War: changes which followed, 16; sense of disillusionment, 17

Fitch, Rev. Jabez, 23–24; biography of, 29; selection from *The Work of the Lord in the Earthquake*, 30; sermon in Portsmouth on the earthquake of 1727, 2, 22

Foss, Sam Walter: biography of, 199; "The Candidates at the Fair," 200; "Deserted Farms," 200; idealization of small-town life, 10

Freeman, Mary E. Wilkins, 135

Frost, Robert, 225; biography of, 257; "The Census-Taker," 269; "New Hampshire," 258; quote from "The Black Cottage," 16; quote from "The Census-Taker," 15; quotes from "New Hampshire," 1, 15; quote from "An Old Man's Winter Night," 15; sense of decline of rural New England, 14–16

"Gilman Tuttle" from *The Granite Monthly*, 220

The Granite Monthly: A New Hampshire Magazine Devoted to History, Biography, and State Progress, 7, 137–39, 219; idealization of small-town life, 9–10; selections from, 220, 221

"The Great Carbuncle" by Nathaniel Hawthorne, 91

"The Great Stone Face" by Nathaniel Hawthorne, 91

The Hair of Harold Roux by Thomas Williams, 18n

Hale, Sarah Buell: author of *Northwood: A Tale of New England*, 5, 14, 134; biography of, 140; comments on rural life, 8; idealization of small-town life, 7, 10; selection from *Northwood: A Tale of New England*, 141

Hall, Donald, 18, 296; affirmative response to New Hampshire, 19; author of *String Too Short To Be Saved*, 297; "The Black Faced Sheep," 327; biography of, 325; "Names of Horses," 326

Hampton Falls, N.H., 135

Hawthorne, Nathaniel, 90, 91; "The Ambitious Guest," 111; author of "The Ambitious Guest," 91; author of "The Great Carbuncle," 91; author of "The Great Stone Face," 91; author of "Roger Malvin's Burial," 25; biography of, 104; comments on the White Mountains, 6; selection from "Sketches from Memory," 105

"The Hills Are Home" by Edna Dean Proctor, 209

The History of New Hampshire by Rev. Jeremy Belknap, 3, 43, 44, 47

The History of the Wars of New England with the Eastern Indians by Samuel Penhallow, 2, 21, 22, 26

The History of the White Mountains by Lucy Howe Crawford, 90–91, 94

Howells, William Dean, 224; author of *The Landlord at Lion's Head*, 11–13, 224; author of *Mrs. Farrell*, 11–13; biography of, 226; selection from *The Landlord at Lion's Head*, 227

Jeremy Hamlin by Alice Brown, 17, 271, 272

Jewett, Sarah Orne, 135

"Joint Owners in Spain" from *Meadow-Grass: Tales of New England Life* by Alice Brown, 136, 174

Journal of a Solitude by May Sarton, 20

Kinds of Love by May Sarton, 20, 297

King, Thomas Starr, 92; author of *The White Hills: Their Legends, Landscape, and Poetry*, 6n; biography of, 119; selection from *The White Hills*, 120

"Land-Locked" by Celia Thaxter, 136, 194

The Landlord at Lion's Head by William Dean Howells, 11–13, 224, 227

Leavitt, Franklin (Frank), 90, 92; biography of, 131; "Through Crawford Notch by Rail," 132; "The Willey Slide," 132

Lewis, Sinclair, author of *Main Street*, 16

Longfellow, Henry W., 137

Lowell, Mass., textile strike of 1912, 14

Maine, homogeneity of, 2

Manchester, N.H., 19; industrial city, 11; probable setting for Winston Churchill's *Dwelling-Place of Light*, 14

Massachusetts, New Hampshire an early extension of, 2

Masters, Edgar Lee, author of *Spoon River Anthology*, 16

Mather, Cotton, views on Indians, 22

Meadow-Grass: Tales of New England

Life by Alice Brown, 9, 19, 133, 135, 174

Merrimack River, mill towns located near, 14; Merrimack River Valley, 3

Metalious, Grace: author of *Peyton Place*, 17–18, 225; biography of, 283; selection from *Peyton Place*, 284

"Monadnock in October" by Edna Dean Proctor, 208

Mount Washington: Dr. Ball attempts ascent, 128; Rev. J. Belknap attempts to climb, 3

Mr. Crewe's Career by Winston Churchill, 13–14, 225, 248

Mrs. Farrell by William Dean Howells, 11–13

"Names of Horses" by Donald Hall, 326

New England, New Hampshire as a microcosm of, 1

New Hampshire: authors find it a congenial atmosphere, 296; changes in economic and social structure, 11; Committee of Safety, 24; Declaration of Independence, 62; early literature evolves from direct experiences of writers, 21; earthquake of 1727, 22; epic phase of history, 3; growing urbanism, 19; eighteenth-century literature about, 3; literature idealizes the community, 6, 134; new literary subjects after the American Revolution, 5; people trust in God's benevolence, 22; unifying images of, 2; variety of, 1

"New Hampshire" by Edna Dean Proctor, 204

"New Hampshire" by Robert Frost, 1, 15, 258

Northwood: A Tale of New England by Sarah Buell Hale, 5, 14, 134, 141

Nytan, character in *The Oriental Philanthropist* by Henry Sherburne, 4

"Obituary of Gilman Tuttle" from *The Granite Monthly*, 220

"Off Shore" by Celia Thaxter, 195

The Old Homestead by Denman Thompson, 212

"The Old Home Week Festal Day" from *The Granite Monthly*, 221

"An Old Man's Winter Night" by Robert Frost, 15

An Old Town by the Sea by Thomas Bailey Aldrich, 7n, 10, 135, 163

The Oriental Philanthropist; or, The True Republican by Henry Sherburne, 4, 45, 83

Page, Thomas Nelson, 135

Patten, Matthew, Bedford, N.H., farmer and diarist, 2–3, 23–24; biography of, 35; selection from his diary, 36

Penhallow, Samuel, Portsmouth magistrate and chronicler of Indian Wars, 2–3, 19, 21–22, 23, 24; biography of, 25; selection from *Penhallow's Indian Wars*, 26; views on Indians, 22

Perrin, Noel, 18, 296; affirmative response to rural environment, 19; "Ah, New Hampshire," 322; biography of, 321

Peyton Place by Grace Metalious, 17–18, 225, 284

"The Piscataqua" by Benjamin Shillaber, 5

"Plant Dreaming Deep" by May Sarton, 20, 334

Portsmouth, N.H., 134; changes when the railroad arrived, 11; scene of T. B. Aldrich's boyhood and setting of *The Story of a Bad Boy*, 7; subject to Indian attacks, 21

Proctor, Edna Dean, 137; biography of, 203; "The Hills Are Home," 209; idealization of small-town life, 10; "Monadnock in October," 208; "New Hampshire," 204

Queen Anne's War (1701–1713), 2, 21

The Real Diary of a Real Boy by Henry Augustus Shute, 135, 170

"A Recognition" by May Sarton, 331

"Roger Malvin's Burial" by Nathaniel Hawthorne, 25

"Revolt from the village," term used by Carl Van Doren, 16

Rogers' Rangers, 138

Roosevelt, Theodore, 14

"The Sandpiper" by Celia Thaxter, 136–37, 196

Sarton, May, 18, 296; affirmative response to New Hampshire, 19–20; "As Does New Hampshire," 331; author of *Journal of a Solitude*, 20; author of *Kinds of Love*, 20, 297; author of *Plant Dreaming Deep*, 20; biography of, 330; "Death of the Maple," 333; ideas representative of authors returning to New Hampshire, 20; "Plant Dreaming Deep," 334; "A Recognition," 331; "We Have Seen the Wind," 333

Second World War, brings shift in emphasis of literature, 18

Sherburne, Henry, 3; author of *The Orien-*

tal Philanthropist; or, The True Republican, 4, 45; biography of, 82; selection from The Oriental Philanthropist; or, The True Republican, 83

Shillaber, Benjamin, author of "The Piscataqua," 5

Shute, Henry Augustus: author of The Real Diary of a Real Boy, 135; biography of, 169; comments on small-town life, 8; idealization of small-town life, 7, 10; selection from The Real Diary of a Real Boy, 170

"Sketches from Memory" by Nathaniel Hawthorne, 105

"The Spaniards' Graves" by Celia Thaxter, 197

Stark, General John, 45, 138; "An Account of the Battle of Bennington," 79; biography of, 78

The Story of a Bad Boy by Thomas Bailey Aldrich, 6, 7, 133, 135, 155

String Too Short To Be Saved by Donald Hall, 297

Tenney, Tabitha Gilman: author of Female Quixotism: Exhibited in the Romantic Opinions and Extravagant Adventures of Dorcasina Sheldon, 4, 45; biography of, 85; eighteenth-century characteristics of her work, 3; selection from Female Quixotism, 86

Thanksgiving Sermon by Rev. Israel Evans, 44, 75

Thaxter, Celia, 136–38; author of Among the Isles of Shoals, 136; biography of, 188; comments on life on the Isles of Shoals, 8; "Land-Locked," 136, 194; "Off Shore," 195; "The Sandpiper," 136–37, 196; selection from Among the Isles of Shoals, 189; "The Spaniards' Graves," 197

Thompson, Denman: biography of, 211; idealization of small-town life, 10; selection from The Old Homestead, 212

Three Days on the White Mountains by Dr. Benjamin Ball, 92, 128

"Through Crawford Notch by Rail" by Franklin Leavitt, 132

Town Burning by Thomas Williams, 18

"Unguarded Gates" by Thomas Bailey Aldrich, 167

Van Doren, Carl, the "revolt from the village," 16

Vaudreuil, Marquis de, governor of New France, 21

Vermont, homogeneity of, 2

Webster, Daniel, 138

"We Have Seen the Wind" by May Sarton, 333

The White Hills: Their Legends, Landscape, and Poetry by Thomas Starr King, 6n, 92, 120

White Mountains, 8, 90–92, 138; inspire awe in writers, 6

Whittier, John G., 137

Willey family, victims of landslide in White Mountains, 6

"The Willey Slide" by Franklin Leavitt, 132

Williams, Raymond, comments on "knowable communities," 7

Williams, Thomas, 296–97; author of Town Burning and The Hair of Harold Roux, 18; biography of, 298; "The Buck in Trotevale's," 299

The Work of the Lord in the Earthquake by Rev. Jabez Fitch, 2, 22, 23, 30

LIBRARY OF CONGRESS CATALOGING IN PUBLICATION DATA
Main entry under title:

New Hampshire literature.

Includes bibliographical references and index.
1. American literature—New Hampshire—History and criticism.   I. Gilmore, Robert C., 1922–
PS548.N4N48   810'.8'09742   81-51608
ISBN 0-87451-210-7
ISBN 0-87451-211-5 (pbk.)